Dear Reader,

When I first wandered into the fictional town of Los
Piños, Texas, several years ago, little did I know how
long I'd be staying. It's been eleven books and still
counting since the men and women of the Adams
clan first appeared in *A Christmas Blessing*, the first
story in the AND BABY MAKES THREE miniseries.

Way back then, it was my intention to write about
three strong-willed, tough-minded brothers. Men who
were true to their heritage. Men who were honorable.
Men who believed in family. In each story, there was
to be a child who played a significant role in turning
their lives upside down.

And, of course, at the head of that family there was
an indomitable force—Harlan Adams. Harlan is the
kind of father who wants the best for his children—
and who'll resort to just about anything legal to get it
for them. One by one—with Luke, then Jordan, and
then Cody—he's put them all to the test, made them
fight for what they wanted, challenged them to be a
better than even match for the women in their lives.

A lot of sparks fly in Los Piños—between parent and
child, between hero and heroine. But there's a lot of
love, too. The kind that lasts a lifetime, the kind that
inspires.

For those of you who weren't there at the beginning,
I invite you to take this journey back with me. For
those of you who were, I hope remembering will
make you smile—and maybe shed a tear or two.

With all good wishes for you and your family,

Sherryl Woods

SHERRYL WOODS

can't be far from the sea without getting downright claustrophobic. She's lived by the ocean on both coasts and now divides her time between Key Biscayne, Florida, and her childhood summer home in Colonial Beach, Virginia, where she's also opened a bookstore. Between April and December, she spends every weekend chatting with customers about her favorite topic—books. She spends the rest of her time doing her other favorite thing—writing books about falling in love and living happily ever after. The author of over sixty romance and mystery novels, Sherryl loves to hear from readers and can be reached at P.O. Box 490326, Key Biscayne, FL 33149. Or stop by her store—Potomac Sunrise, 308 Washington Avenue, Colonial Beach, VA 22443—and visit.

And Baby Makes Three

FIRST TRIMESTER

SHERRYL WOODS

Published by Silhouette Books

America's Publisher of Contemporary Romance

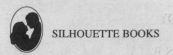 SILHOUETTE BOOKS

ISBN 0-373-20160-5

by Request

AND BABY MAKES THREE: FIRST TRIMESTER

Copyright © 1999 by Harlequin Books S.A.

The publisher acknowledges the copyright holders of the individual works as follows:

A CHRISTMAS BLESSING
Copyright © 1995 by Sherryl Woods

NATURAL BORN DADDY
Copyright © 1996 by Sherryl Woods

THE COWBOY AND HIS BABY
Copyright © 1996 by Sherryl Woods

Printed in U.S.A.

CONTENTS

AND BABY MAKES THREE

is the incredibly popular miniseries by Sherryl Woods.
The romances and adventures of the Adams family of Texas
have won the hearts of readers everywhere. And here's a
special opportunity to see how it all began!

Come trace the roots of this family legacy—
which is now on to the third generation!

THE ADAMS FAMILY TREE

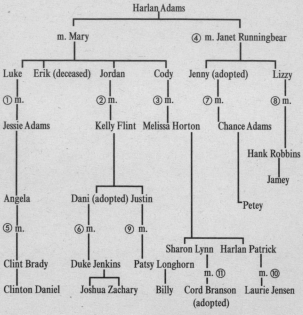

① *A Christmas Blessing*
② *Natural Born Daddy*
③ *The Cowboy and His Baby*
④ *The Rancher and His Unexpected Daughter*
⑤ *The Littlest Angel*
⑥ *Natural Born Trouble*
⑦ *Unexpected Mommy*
⑧ *The Cowgirl and the Unexpected Wedding*
⑨ *Natural Born Lawman*
⑩ *The Cowboy and His Wayward Bride*
⑪ *The Unclaimed Baby*

A Christmas Blessing

For Kristi, my goddaughter, and Frankie, and their firstborn son, Austin James—I wish you love and all the many blessings of the season.

Chapter One

Getting Consuela Martinez out of his kitchen was proving to be a much more difficult task than Luke Adams had ever envisioned. His housekeeper had found at least a dozen excuses for lingering, despite the fact that her brother was leaning on his car's horn and causing enough ruckus to deafen them all.

"Go, *amiga,*" Luke pleaded. "Enjoy your holidays with your family. *Feliz Navidad!*"

Consuela ignored the instructions and the good wishes. "The freezer is filled with food," she reminded him, opening the door to show him for the fourth time. Though there were literally dozens of precooked, neatly labeled packages, a worried frown puckered her brow. "It will be enough?"

"More than enough," he assured her.

"But not if you have guests," she concluded, removing her coat. "I should stay. The holidays are no time for a good housekeeper to be away."

"I won't be having any guests," Luke said tightly, picking the coat right back up and practically forcing her into it. "And if I do, I am perfectly capable of whipping up a batch of chips and dip."

"Chips and dip," she muttered derisively.

She added a string of Spanish Luke felt disinclined to translate. He caught the general drift; it wasn't complimentary. After all this time, though, Consuela should know that he wasn't the type to host a lot of extravagant, foolish parties. Leave that sort of thing to his brother Jordan or his parents. His brother thrived on kissing up to his business associates and his parents seemed to think that filling the house with strangers meant they were well loved and well respected.

"Consuela, go!" he ordered, barely curbing his impatience. "*Vaya con Dios.* I'll be fine. I am thirty-two years old. I've been out of my playpen for a long time."

One of the dangers of hiring an ex-nanny as a housekeeper, he'd discovered, was the tendency she had to forget that her prior charge had grown up. Yet he could no more have fired Consuela than he could have his own mother. In truth, for all of her hovering and bossiness, she was the single most important constant in his life. Which was a pretty pitiful comment on the state of his family, he decided ruefully.

Consuela's unflinching, brown-eyed gaze pinned him. Hands on ample hips, she squared off against him. "You will go to your parents' on Christmas, *sí?* The holidays are a time for families to be together. You have stayed away too long."

"Yes," he lied. He had no intention of going anywhere, especially not to his parents' house where everyone would be mourning, not celebrating, thanks to him.

"They will have enough help for all of the parties that are planned?"

Luke bit back a groan. "Consuela, you know perfectly well they will," he said patiently. "The place is crawling with your very own nieces and nephews. My parents haven't had to cook, clean or sneeze without assistance since you took over the running of that household forty years ago before they'd even met. When you came over here to work for me, you handpicked your cousin to replace you. Maritza is very good, yes?"

"*Sí,*" she conceded.

"This trip to see your family in Mexico is my present to you. It's long overdue. You said yourself not sixty seconds ago that the holidays are meant for families. You have not seen your own for several years. Your mother is almost ninety. You cry every time a letter comes from her."

"After all these years, I get homesick, that's true. I am a very emotional person, not like some people," she said pointedly.

Luke ignored the jibe. "Well, this is your chance

to see for yourself how your mother is doing. Now stop dawdling and go before you miss your plane and before your brother busts our eardrums with that horn of his.''

Consuela still appeared torn between duty to him and a longing to see her mother. Finally she heaved a sigh of resignation and buttoned her coat. ''I will go,'' she said grudgingly. ''But I will worry the whole time. You are alone too much, *niño*.''

It had been a long time since anyone had thought of Luke Adams as a little boy. Unfortunately, Consuela would probably never get the image out of her head, despite the fact that he was over six feet tall, operated a thriving ranch and had built himself a house twice the size of the very lavish one he'd grown up in.

''Ever since—'' she began.

''Enough,'' Luke said in a low, warning tone that silenced her more quickly than any shout would have.

Tears of sympathy sprang to her eyes, and she wrapped her plump arms around him in a fierce hug that had Luke wincing. For a sixty-year-old woman she was astonishingly strong. He didn't want her weeping for him, though. He didn't want her pity. And he most definitely didn't want her dredging up memories of Erik, the brother who'd died barely seven months ago, the brother whose death he'd caused.

''Go,'' he said more gently. ''I will see you in the new year.''

She reached up and patted his cheek, a gesture she dared only rarely. *"Te amo, niño."*

Luke's harsh demeanor softened at once. "I love you, too, Consuela."

The truth of it was that she was about the only human being on the face of the earth to whom he could say that without reservation. Even before Erik's death had split the family apart, Luke had had his share of difficulties with his father's attempted ironclad grip on his sons. His mother had always been too much in love with her husband to bother much with the four boys she had borne him. And Luke had battled regularly with his younger brothers, each of them more rebellious than the other. Erik had been a year younger, only thirty-one when he'd died. Jordan was thirty, Cody twenty-seven. Consuela had been the steadying influence on all of them, adults and children.

"Te amo, mi amiga," Luke said, returning her fierce hug.

Consuela was still calling instructions as she crossed the porch and climbed into her brother's car. For all he knew she was still shouting them as the car sped off down the lane to the highway, kicking up a trail of dust in its wake.

Alone at last, he thought with relief when Consuela was finally gone from view. Blessed silence for two whole weeks. His cattle were pastured on land far from the main house and were being tended by his foreman and a crew of volunteers from among the hands. The ranch's business affairs were tied up through the beginning of the new year. He had no obligations at all.

He opened a cupboard, withdrew an unopened bottle of Jack Daniel's whiskey from the supply he'd ordered, ostensibly to take along as gifts to all the holiday parties to which he'd been invited. He pulled down a nice, tall glass, filled it with ice and headed for his den and the big leather chair behind his desk.

Uncapping the bottle, he poured a shot, doubled it, then shrugged and filled the glass to the rim. No point in pretending he didn't intend to get blind, stinking drunk. No point in pretending he didn't intend to stay that way until the whole damned holiday season had passed by in a blur.

Just as he lifted the glass to his lips, he caught sight of the wedding photo on the corner of his desk, the one he'd turned away so that he wouldn't have to see Erik's smile or the radiance on Erik's wife's face. He'd destroyed two lives that day, three if he counted his own worthless existence. Erik was dead and buried, but Jessie's life had been devastated as surely as if she had been in that accident with him.

A familiar knot formed in his stomach, a familiar pain encircled his heart. He lifted his glass in a mockery of a toast. "To you, little brother."

The unaccustomed liquor burned going down, but in the space of a heartbeat it sent a warm glow shimmering through him. If one sip was good, two were better, and the whole damned bottle promised oblivion.

He drank greedily, waiting to forget, waiting for relief from the unceasing anguish, from the unending guilt.

The phone rang, stopped, then rang again. The old grandfather clock in the hall chimed out each passing hour as dusk fell, then darkness.

But even sitting there all alone in the dark with a belly full of the best whiskey money could buy, Luke couldn't shut off the memories. With a curse, he threw the bottle across the room, listened with satisfaction as it shattered against the cold, stone fireplace.

Finally, worn out, he fell into a troubled sleep. It wasn't his brother's face he saw as he passed out, though. It was Jessie's—the woman who should have been his.

The sky was dark as pitch and the roads were icing over. Jessie Adams squinted through the car's foggy windshield and wondered why she'd ever had the bright idea of driving clear across Texas for the holidays, instead of letting her father-in-law send his pilot for her. She wasn't even sure how Harlan and Mary Adams had persuaded her that she still belonged with them now that Erik was gone.

She'd always felt like an outsider in that big white Colonial house that looked totally incongruous sitting in the middle of a sprawling West Texas ranch. Someone in the family, long before Harlan's time, had fled the South during the Civil War. According to the oft-told legend, the minute they'd accumulated enough cash, they'd built an exact replica of the mansion they'd left behind in ashes. And like the old home, they'd called it White Pines, though she couldn't recall ever seeing a single pine within a thirty-mile radius.

The bottom line was the Adamses were rich as could be and had ancestry they could trace back to the *Mayflower,* while Jessie didn't even know who her real parents had been. Her adoptive parents had sworn they didn't know and had seemed so hurt by her wanting to find out that she'd reluctantly dropped any notion of searching for answers.

By the time they'd died, she'd pushed her need to know aside. She had met Erik, by then. Marrying him and adjusting to his large, boisterous family had been more than enough to handle. Mary Adams was sweet as could be, if a little superior at times, but Erik's father and his three brothers were overwhelming. Harlan Adams was a stern and domineering parent, sure of himself about everything. He was very much aware of himself as head of what he considered to be a powerful dynasty. As for Erik's brothers, she'd never met a friendlier, more flirtatious crew, and she had worked in her share of bars to make ends meet while she'd been in college.

Except for Luke. The oldest, he was a brooder. Dark and silent, Luke had been capable of tremendous kindness, but rarely did he laugh and tease as his brothers did. The expression in the depths of his

eyes was bleak, as if he was bearing in silence some
terrible hurt deep in his soul. There had been odd
moments when she'd felt drawn to him, when she'd
felt she understood better than anyone his seeming
loneliness in the midst of a family gathering, when
she had longed to put a smile on his rugged, handsome face.

That compelling sense of an unspoken connection had been ripped to shreds on the day Luke had
come to tell her that her husband was in the hospital
and unlikely to make it. In a short burst riddled with
agonized guilt, he'd added that he was responsible
for the overturning of the tractor that had injured
Erik. He'd made no apologies, offered no excuses.
He'd simply stated the facts, seen to it that she got
to the hospital, made sure the rest of the family was
there to support her, then walked away. He'd
avoided her from that moment on. Avoided everyone in the family ever since, from what Harlan and
Mary had told her. He seemed to be intent on punishing himself, they complained sadly.

If Luke hadn't been steering clear of White
Pines, Jessie wasn't at all sure she would have been
able to accept the invitation to come for the holidays. Seeing Luke's torment, knowing it mirrored
her own terrible mix of grief and guilt was simply
too painful. She hated him for costing her the one
person to whom she'd really mattered.

Searching for serenity, she had fled the ranch a
month after Erik's death, settled in a new place on
the opposite side of the state, gotten a boring job

that paid the bills and prepared to await the birth of her child. Erik's baby. Her only link to the husband she had adored, but hadn't always understood.

She stopped the dark thoughts before they could spoil her festive holiday mood. There was no point at all in looking back. She had her future—she rested a hand on her stomach—and she had her baby, though goodness knows she hadn't planned on being a single parent. Sometimes the prospect terrified her.

She found a station playing Christmas carols, turned up the volume and sang along, as she began the last hundred and fifty miles or so of the once familiar journey back to White Pines. Her back was aching like the dickens and she'd forgotten how difficult driving could be when her protruding belly forced her to put the seat back just far enough to make reaching the gas and brake pedals a strain.

"No problem," she told herself sternly. A hundred miles or more in this part of the world was nothing. She had snow tires on, a terrific heater, blankets in the trunk for an emergency and a batch of homemade fruitcakes in the back that would keep her from starving if she happened to get stranded.

The persistent ache in her back turned into a more emphatic pain that had her gasping.

"What the dickens?" she muttered as she hit the brake, slowed and paused to take a few deep breaths. Fortunately there was little traffic to worry about on the unexpectedly bitter cold night. She stayed on the side of the road for a full five minutes to make sure there wouldn't be another spasm on the heels of the first.

Satisfied that it had been nothing more than a pinched nerve or a strained muscle, she put the car back in gear and drove on.

It was fifteen minutes before the next pain hit, but it was a doozy. It brought tears to her eyes. Again, pulling to the side of the road, she scowled down at her belly.

"This is not the time," she informed the impertinent baby. "You will not be born in a car in the middle of nowhere with no doctor in sight, do you understand me? That's the deal, so get used to it and settle down. You're not due for weeks yet. Four weeks to be exact, so let's have no more of these pains, okay?"

Apparently the lecture worked. Jessie didn't feel so much as a twinge for another twenty miles. She was about to congratulate herself on skirting disaster, when a contraction gripped her so fiercely she thought she'd lose control of the car.

"Oh, sweet heaven," she muttered in a tone that was part prayer, part curse. There was little doubt in her mind now that she was going into labor. Denying it seemed pointless, to say nothing of dangerous. She had to take a minute here and think of a plan.

On the side of the road again, she turned on the car's overhead light, took out her map and searched for some sign of a hospital. If there was one within

fifty miles, she couldn't spot it. She hadn't passed
a house for miles, either, and she was still far from
Harlan and Mary's, probably a hundred miles at
least. She could make that in a couple of hours or
less, if the roads were clear, but they weren't. She
was driving at a safe crawl. It could take her hours
to get to White Pines at that pace.

There was someplace she could go that would be
closer, someplace only five miles or so ahead, unless she'd lost her bearings. It was the last place on
earth she'd ever intended to wind up, the very last
place she would want her baby to be born: Luke's
ranch.

Consuela would be there, she consoled herself as
she resigned herself to dropping by unannounced to
deliver a baby. Luke probably didn't want to see
her any more than she wanted to see him. And what
man wanted any part of a woman's labor, unless
she happened to be his wife? Luke probably
wouldn't be able to turn her over to Consuela fast
enough. With all those vacant rooms, they probably
wouldn't even bump into each other in the halls.

Jessie couldn't see that she had any choice. The
snow had turned to blizzard conditions. The world
around her was turning into a snow-covered wonderland, as dangerous as it was beautiful. The tires
were beginning to skid and spin on the road. The
contractions were maybe ten minutes apart. She'd
be lucky to make it these few miles to Luke's. Forget going any farther.

The decision made with gut-deep reluctance, she

accomplished the drive by sheer force of will. When she finally spotted the carved gate announcing the ranch, she skidded to a halt and wept with relief. She still had a mile of frozen, rutted lane to the house, but that would be a breeze compared to the five she'd just traveled.

A hard contraction, the worst yet, gripped her and had her screaming out loud. She clung to the steering wheel, panting as she'd seen on TV, until it passed. Sweat streamed down her face.

"Come on, sweet thing," she pleaded with the baby. "Only a few more minutes. Don't you dare show up until I get to the house."

She couldn't help wondering when that would be. There was no beckoning light in the distance, no looming shape of the house. Surely, though, it couldn't be much farther.

She drove on, making progress by inches, it seemed. At last she spotted the house, dark as coal against the blinding whiteness around it. Not a light on anywhere. No bright holiday decorations blinking tiny splashes of color onto the snow.

"Luke Adams, you had better be home," she muttered as she hauled herself out from behind the wheel at last.

Standing on shaky legs, she began the endless trek through the deepening snow, cursing and clutching her stomach as she bent over with yet another ragged pain. The wind-whipped snow stung her cheeks and mingled with tears. The already deepening drifts made walking treacherous and slow.

"A little farther," she encouraged herself. Three steps. Four. One foot onto the wide sweep of a porch. Then the other. She had made it! She paused and sucked in a deep breath, then looked around her.

The desolate air about the place had only intensified as she'd drawn closer. There was no wreath of evergreens on the front door, no welcoming light shining on the porch or from any of the rooms that she could detect. For the first time, she allowed a panicky thought. What if she had made it this far, only to find herself still alone? What if Luke had packed his bags and flown away for the holidays?

"Please, God, let someone be here," she prayed as she hit the doorbell again and again, listening to the chime echo through the house. She pounded on the glass, shouted, then punched the doorbell again.

She heard a distant crash, a loud oath, then another crash. Apparently Luke was home, she thought dryly, as she began another insistent round of doorbell ringing.

"For cripe's sakes, hold your horses, dammit!"

A light switch was thrown and the porch was illuminated in a warm yellow glow. Finally, just as another contraction ripped through Jessie, the door was flung open.

She was briefly aware of the thunderstruck expression on Luke's face and his disheveled state, only marginally aware of the overpowering scent of alcohol.

And then, after a murmured greeting she doubted made a lick of sense, she collapsed into the arms of the man who'd killed her husband.

Chapter Two

"What in blazes...?"

Luke folded his arms around the bundled-up form who'd just pitched forward. Blinking hard in an attempt to get his eyes to focus, he zeroed in on a face that had once been burned into his brain, a face he'd cursed himself for cherishing when he had no right at all. He'd seen that precious face only minutes ago in the sweetest dream he'd ever had. For an instant he wondered if he was still dreaming.

No, he could feel her shape, crushed against his chest. He drank in the sight of her. Her long, black hair was tucked up in a stocking cap. Her cheeks, normally pale as cream, had been tinted a too-bright pink by the cold. Her blue eyes were shadowed with what might have been pain, but there was no mistaking his sister-in-law.

"Jessie," he whispered, worriedly taking in the lines of strain on her forehead, the trickle of sweat that was likely to turn to ice if he didn't get her out of the freezing night in a hurry.

When in hell had it turned so bitter? he wondered, shivering himself. There hadn't been a snowflake in sight when he'd sent Consuela off. Now he couldn't see a patch of uncovered ground anywhere. Couldn't see much of anything beyond the porch, for that matter.

More important than any of that, what was his sister-in-law doing here of all places? Was she ill? Feverish? She would have had to be practically delusional or desperate to turn up on his doorstep.

He scooped her up, rocking back on his heels with the unexpected weight of her, startled that the little slip of a thing he'd remembered was bulging out of her coat. She moaned and clutched at her belly, shuddering against him.

She's going to have a baby, he realized at last, finally catching on to what would have been obvious to anyone who was not in an alcohol-altered state of mind. No one in the family had told him that. Not that he'd done more than exchange pleasantries with any of them in months. And Jessie would have been the last person they would have mentioned. Everyone walked on eggshells around him when it came to anything having to do with his late brother. If only they had known, if only they had realized that his guilt was compounded because he'd fallen for Erik's wife, they would never have spoken to him at all.

"You're going to have a baby," he announced in an awestruck tone.

Bright blue eyes, dulled by pain, snapped open. "You always were quick, Lucas," Jessie said tartly. "Do you suppose you could get me to a bed and find Consuela before I deliver right here in the foyer?"

"You're going to have a baby *now?*" he demanded incredulously, as the immediacy of the problem sank in. He would have dropped her if she hadn't been clinging to his neck with the grip of a championship arm wrestler.

"That would be my best guess," she agreed.

Luke was so stunned—so damned drunk—he couldn't seem to come to any rational decision. If Jessie had realized his condition, she would have headed for the barn and relied on one of the horses for help. He had a mare-who was probably more adept at deliveries than he was at this precise moment. His old goat, Chester, was pretty savvy, too. Jessie would have been in better hands with them, than she likely was with him.

"Lucas?" Her voice was low and sweet as honey. "Could you please…"

He sighed just listening to her. The sweetest little voice in all of Texas.

"Get me into a bed!"

The shout accomplished what nothing else had. He began to move. He staggered ever so slightly, but he got her into the closest bedroom, his, and settled her in the middle of sheets still rumpled from the previous night. And several nights before that, as near as he could recall. He'd ordered Consuela to stay the hell out of his bedroom after he'd found little packets of some sweet-smelling stuff in his sock drawer.

He stood gazing down at Jessie, rhapsodizing to himself about her presence in his bed, marveling at the size of that belly, awestruck by the fact that she was going to have a baby here and now.

"Luke," she said in a raspy voice that was edged with tension. "I'm going to need a little help here."

"Help?" he repeated blankly.

"My clothes."

"Oh." He blinked rapidly as he watched her trying to struggle out of her coat. Awkwardly, she shrugged it off one shoulder, then the other. When she started to fumble with the buttons on her blouse, his throat worked and his pulse zoomed into the stratosphere.

"Lucas!"

The shout got his attention. "Oh, yeah. Right," he said and tried to help with the buttons.

For a man who'd undressed any number of women in his time, he was suddenly all thumbs. In fact, getting Jessie out of her clothes—the simple cotton blouse, the oddly made jeans, the lacy bra and panties—was an act of torture no man should have to endure. Trying to be helpful, she wriggled and squirmed in a way that brought his fingers into contact with warm, smooth skin far too frequently. Trying to look everywhere except at her wasn't helping him with the task either. Every glimpse of bare flesh made his knees go weak.

The second she was stripped bare, he muffled a groan, averted his gaze and hunted down one of his shirts. He did it for his own salvation, not because she seemed aware of anything except the demands her baby was making on her body. Surely there was a special place in hell for a man whose thoughts were on sex when a woman was about to have a baby right before his eyes.

She looked tiny—except for that impressively swollen belly—and frightened as a doe caught in a hunter's sights. He felt a powerful need to comfort her, if only he could string an entire sentence together without giving away his inebriated state. If she knew precisely how drunk he was, she wouldn't be scared. She'd be flat-out terrified, and rightfully so. He wasn't so serene himself.

"Where's Consuela?" she asked, then let out a scream that shook the rafters. She latched on to his hand so hard he was sure that at least three bones cracked. That grip did serve a purpose, though. It snapped him back to reality. Pain had a way of making a man focus on the essentials.

The baby clearly wasn't going to wait for him to sober up. It wasn't going to wait for a doctor, even if one could make it to the ranch on the icy roads, which Luke doubted.

"Consuela's in Mexico by now," he confessed

without thinking. "She left earlier today." When panic immediately darkened her eyes, he instinctively patted her hand. "It's going to be okay, darlin'. Don't you worry about a thing."

"I'm…not…worried," she said between gasps. "Shouldn't you boil water or something?"

Water? Water was good, he decided. He had no idea what he'd do with it, but if it got him out of this bedroom for five seconds so he could try to gather his scattered thoughts, it had to be good. Coffee would be even better. Gallons of it.

"You'll be okay for a minute?" He grabbed a key chain made of braided leather off his dresser and gave it to her. "Hang on to this if another pain hits while I'm gone, okay? Bite into it or something." It had worked for cowboys being operated on under primitive conditions, or so he'd read. Of course, they'd also been liberally dosed with alcohol at the time.

Jessie's blue eyes regarded the leather doubtfully, but she nodded gamely. "Hurry, Luke. I don't know much about labor, but I don't think there's a lot of time left."

"I'll be back before you know it," he promised. Stone-cold sober, if he could manage it.

He fumbled the first pot he grabbed, spilled water everywhere, then finally got it onto the stove with the gas flame turned to high. With a couple of false starts, he got the coffee going as well, strong enough to wake the dead, which was pretty much how he felt.

For a moment he clung to the counter and tried to steady himself. It was going to be okay, he vowed. He'd delivered foals and calves. How much different could delivering a baby be? Of course, mares and cows had a pretty good notion of what they were doing. They didn't need a lot of assistance from him unless they got into trouble.

Jessie, on the other hand, seemed even more bemused by this state of affairs than he was. She'd obviously been counting on a doctor, a team of comforting nurses, a nice, sterile delivery room and plenty of high-tech equipment. A shot of some kind of painkiller, too, more than likely. What she was getting was a drunken amateur in an isolated ranch house. It hardly seemed fair after all she'd already been through. After all he'd put her through, he amended.

An agonized scream cut through the air and sent panic slicing through him. He tore down the hall to the bedroom. He found her panting, her face scrunched up with pain, sweat beading up on her brow and pouring down her cheeks. Damned if he didn't think she looked beautiful, anyway. The door to that place in hell gaped wider.

"You okay?" he asked, then shook himself. "Sorry. Dumb question. Of course, you're not okay."

He grabbed a clean washcloth from the linen closet, dashed into the bathroom to soak it with cool water, then wiped her brow. He might not be exactly sober yet, but his brain was beginning to function and his limbs were following orders. For the first time, he honestly believed they could get through this without calamity striking.

"You're doing fine," he soothed. "This is one hell of a pickle, but nothing we can't manage."

"Did…you…call…a doctor?" she asked.

A doctor? Why hadn't he acted on that thought back when he'd had it himself? Maybe because he'd figured it would be futile. More likely, because his brain cells had shut down hours ago just the way he'd wanted them to.

"Next thing on my list," he assured her.

She eyed him doubtfully. "You…have…a list?"

"Of course I have a list," he said, injecting a confident note into his voice. "The water's boiling. The coffee's on."

"Coffee?"

"For me. You don't want me falling asleep in the middle of all the fun, do you?"

"I doubt there's much chance of that," she said, sighing as the pain visibly eased.

Her gaze traveled over him from head to toe, examining him so intently that it was all Luke could do not to squirm. Under other circumstances, that examination would have made his pulse buck so hard he wouldn't have recovered for days. As it was, he looked away as fast as he could. Obviously, this was some sort of penance dreamed up for his sins. He was going to be stranded with Jessie, forced to deliver his brother's baby, and then he was going to have to watch the two of them walk out of his life. Unless, of course…

"Luke, can I ask you a question?"

He was relieved by the interruption. There was only heartache in the direction his thoughts were taking. "Seeing how we're going to be getting pretty intimate here in a bit, I suppose you can ask me anything you like."

"Are you drunk?"

He had hoped she hadn't noticed. "Darlin', I don't think you want to know the answer to that."

This time he doubted Jessie's groan of anguish had anything to do with her labor pains.

"Luke?"

"Yes, Jessie."

"Maybe you'd better bring me a very big glass of whatever it was you were drinking."

He grinned at the wistful note in her voice. "Darlin', when this baby turns up, you and I are going to drink one hell of a toast. Until then, I think maybe we'd both better stay as far away from that bottle as we can. Besides, as best I can recall, I smashed it against the fireplace."

She regarded him with pleading blue eyes. "Luke, please? I'm not sure I can do this without help. There's bound to be another bottle of something around here."

He thought of the cabinet filled with whiskey, considered getting a couple of shots to help both of them, then dismissed the temptation as a very bad idea. "You've got all the help you could possibly need. I'm right here with you. Besides, alcohol's not good for the baby. Haven't you read all those headlines warning about that very thing?''

''I don't think the baby's going to be inside me long enough to get so much as a sip,'' she said.

As if to prove her point, her body was seized with another contraction. Going with sheer instinct, Luke reached out and placed his hand over her taut belly. The skin was smooth and tight as a drum as he massaged it gently until the muscles relaxed.

He checked his watch, talked to her, and waited for the next contraction. It came three minutes later.

He wiped her brow. ''Hang in there, darlin'. I'll be right back.''

She leveled a blue-eyed glare on him. ''Don't you dare leave me,'' she commanded in a tone that could have stopped the D-Day invasion.

''I'm not going far. I just want some nice, sterile water in here when the baby makes its appearance. And we could use a blanket.'' And something to cut the umbilical cord, he thought as his brain finally began to kick in without prodding.

He'd never moved with more speed in his life. He tested the phone and discovered the lines were down. No surprise in this weather. He sterilized a basin, filled it with water, then cleaned the sharpest knife he could find with alcohol. He deliberately gave a wide berth to the cabinet with the whiskey. He was back in the bedroom before the next pain hit.

"See there. I didn't abandon you. Did you take natural childbirth classes?"

Jessie nodded. "Started two weeks ago. We'd barely gotten to the breathing part."

"Then we're in great shape," he said with confidence. "You're going to come through this like a champ." The truth was he was filled with admiration for her. He'd always known she had more strength and courage than most women he'd known, but tonight she was proving it in spades.

"Did you call a doctor?" she asked again.

"I tried. I couldn't get through. Don't let it worry you, though. You're doing just fine. Nature's doing all the work. The doctor would just be window dressing."

Jessie shot him a baleful look.

"Okay," he admitted. "It would be nice to have an expert on hand, but this baby's coming no matter who's coaching it into the world, so we might just as well count our blessings that you got to my house. What were you doing out all alone on a night like this anyway?"

"Going to your parents' house," she said. "They invited me for the holidays."

Luke couldn't believe that they'd allowed her to drive this close to the delivery of their first grandchild. "Why the hell didn't Daddy fly you over?"

"He offered. I'm not crazy about flying in such a little plane, though. I told him the doctor had forbidden it."

Luke suspected that was only half the story. He

grinned at her. "You sure that was it? Or did that streak of independence in you get you to say no, before you'd even given the matter serious thought?"

A tired smile came and went in a heartbeat. "Maybe."

He hitched a chair up beside the bed and tucked her hand in his. He would not, *would not* allow himself to think about how sweet it was to be sitting here with her like this, despite the fact that only circumstance had forced them together.

"Can't say that I blame you," he said. "If you don't kick up a fuss with Daddy every now and then, next thing you know he's running your life."

"Harlan just wants what's best for his family," she said.

Luke smiled at her prompt defense of her father-in-law. One thing about Jessie, she'd always been fair to a fault. She'd even told anyone who'd listen that she didn't blame him for Erik's death, even with the facts staring her straight in the face. It didn't matter. He'd blamed himself enough for both of them.

"Dad's also dead certain that he's the only one who knows what's best," he added. "Sometimes, though, he misses the mark by a mile."

Her gaze honed in on him. "You're talking about Erik, aren't you? You're thinking about how your father talked him into staying in ranching. If Harlan had let him go, maybe he'd still be alive."

And if Luke had been on that tractor, instead of

his brother, Erik would be here right now, he thought. He'd known Erik couldn't manage the thing on the rough terrain, but he'd sent him out there, anyway. He'd told him to grow up and do the job or get out of ranching if he couldn't hack it. Guilt cut through him at the memory of that last bitter dispute.

He glanced at Jessie. The mention of Erik threw a barrier up between them as impenetrable as a brick wall. For once, Luke was glad when the next contraction came. And the next. And the one after that. So fast now, that there was no time to think, no time to do anything except help Jessie's baby into the world.

"Push, darlin'," Luke coaxed.

Jessie screamed. Luke cursed.

"Push, dammit!"

"You don't like how I'm doing it, you take over," she snapped right back at him.

Luke laughed. "That's my Jessie. Sass me all you like, if it helps, but push! Come on, darlin'. I'm afraid this part here is entirely up to you. If I could do it for you, I would."

"Luke?"

There was a plaintive, fearful note in her voice that brought his gaze up to meet hers. "What?"

"What if something goes wrong?"

"Nothing is going to go wrong," he promised. "Everything's moved along right on schedule so far, hasn't it?"

"Luke, I'm having this baby in a ranch house.

Doesn't that suggest that the schedule has been busted to hell?''

"Your schedule maybe. Obviously the baby has a mind of its own. No wonder, given the way you take charge of your life. You're strong and brave and your baby's going to be just exactly like you,'' he said reassuringly.

"I think I've changed my mind,'' she said with a note of determination in her voice. "I'm not ready for this. I'm not ready to be a mother. I can't cope with a baby on my own.''

Luke laughed. "Too late now. Looks to me like that horse is out of the barn.''

Moments later, a sense of awe spread through him at the first glimpse of the baby's head, covered with dark, wet hair.

"My God, Jessie, I can see the baby. Just a little more work, darlin', and you'll have a fine, healthy baby in your arms. That's it. Harder. Push harder.''

"I can't,'' she wailed.

"You can,'' Luke insisted. "Here we go, darlin'.'' He slid his hands under the baby's tiny shoulders. "One more.'' Jessie bore down like a trooper and the baby slipped into his hands.

"Luke,'' Jessie whispered at once. "Is the baby okay? I don't hear anything.''

The baby let out a healthy yowl. Luke beamed at both of them. "I think that's your answer,'' he said.

He surveyed the squalling baby he was holding. "Let's see now. Ten tiny fingers. Ten itsy-bitsy toes. And the prettiest, sassiest blue eyes you ever did see. Just like her mama's."

"Her?" Jessie repeated. She struggled to prop herself up to get a look. "It's a girl?"

"A beautiful little angel," he affirmed as he cleaned the baby up, wrapped her in a huge blanket and laid her in Jessie's arms.

Even though her eyes were shadowed by exhaustion, even though her voice was raspy from screaming, the sight of her daughter brought the kind of smile to Jessie's face that Luke had doubted he would ever see again.

She looked up at him, her eyes filled with gratitude and warmth, and his heart flipped over. A world of forbidden possibilities taunted him.

"She is beautiful, isn't she?" Jessie said, her gaze locked on the tiny bundle in her arms.

"Just about the most gorgeous baby I've ever seen," he agreed, thinking how desperately he wished he could claim her as his own. His and Jessie's. He forced the thought aside. "Do you have a name picked out?"

"I thought I did," she said. "But I've changed my mind."

"Oh? Why is that?"

"Because she rushed things and decided to come at Christmas," she explained. "I'm going to call her Angela. That way I'll always remember that she was my Christmas miracle." She turned a misty-eyed gaze on Luke. "Thank you, Lucas."

If he lived a hundred years, Luke knew he would trade everything for this one moment out of time.

Later the guilt and recriminations would come back with a vengeance. Jessie would remember who he was and what he had done to ruin her life. The blame, no matter how hard she denied it, would be there between them.

But right now, for this one brief, shining moment, they were united, a part of something incredibly special that he could hold in his heart all the rest of his lonely days. They had shared a miracle.

Chapter Three

Jessie felt as if she'd run a couple of marathons back-to-back, but not even that bone-weary exhaustion could take away the incredible sense of joy that spread through her at the sight of her daughter sleeping so peacefully in her arms. Her seemingly healthy baby girl. Her little angel with the lousy sense of timing.

For perhaps the dozenth time since dawn had stolen into the room, bathing it in a soft light, she examined fingers and toes with a sense of amazement that anyone so small could be so perfect. Her gaze honed in on that tiny bow of a mouth, already forming the instinctive, faint smacking sounds of hunger even as she slept. Any minute now she would wake up and demand to be fed.

"Luke, she's hungry," Jessie announced with a mixture of awe and pride that quickly turned to worry. Not once during all the hours of labor or since had she given a single thought to what happened next. "What'll we do?"

Given their past history, it was amazing how quickly she'd come to rely on Luke, how easily she'd pushed aside all of her anger and grief just to make it through this crisis. And, despite his less than alert state on her arrival, despite all the reasons he had for never wanting to see her again, he hadn't let her down yet.

Of course, judging from the way he was sprawled in the easy chair in a corner of the bedroom with his eyes closed, the last bit of adrenaline that had gotten him through the delivery had finally worn off.

Faint, gray light filtered through the frosted window and cast him in shadows. She studied him surreptitiously and saw the toll the past months—or some mighty hard drinking—had taken on him.

The lines that time and weather had carved in his tanned, rugged face seemed deeper than ever. His jaw was shadowed by a day or more's growth of beard. His dark brown hair, which he'd always worn defiantly long, swept the edge of his collar. He looked far more like a dangerous rebel than the successful Texas rancher he was.

If he looked physically unkempt, his clothes were worse. His plaid flannel shirt was clean but rumpled, as if he'd grabbed it from a basket on his way to the door. It was unevenly buttoned and untucked, leaving a mat of dark chest hair intriguingly visible. The jeans he'd hauled on were dusty and snug and unbuttoned at the waist.

Jessie grinned as her gaze dropped to his feet. He had on one blue sock. The other foot was bare. She found the sight oddly touching. Clearly he'd never given a thought to himself all during the night. He'd concentrated on her and seeing to it that Angela made it safely into the world. She would never forget what he'd done for her.

"Luke?" she repeated softly.

The whisper accomplished what her intense scrutiny had not. His dark brown eyes snapped open. "Hmm?" He blinked. "Everything okay?"

"The baby's hungry. What'll we do?"

"Feed her?" he suggested with a spark of amusement.

"Thanks so much." She couldn't keep the faint sarcasm from her voice, but she smiled as she realized how often during the night she'd caught a rare teasing note in Luke's manner. In all the time she'd lived with Erik she'd never seen that side of Luke. He'd been brusque more often than not, curt to the point of rudeness. His attitude might have intimidated her, if she hadn't seen the occasional flashes of something lost and lonely in his eyes. In the past few hours, she'd seen another side of him altogether—strong, protective, unflappable. The perfect person to have around in a crisis. The kind of man on whom a woman could rely.

"Anytime," he teased despite her nasty tone.

Once again he'd surprised her, causing her to wonder if the quiet humor had always been there, if it had simply been overshadowed by his brothers' high spirits.

Still, Jessie was in no mood for levity, as welcome a change as it was. "Luke, I'm serious. She's going to start howling any second now. I can tell. And this diaper you cut from one of your old flannel shirts is sopping. We can't keep cutting up your clothes every time she's wet."

"I have shirts I haven't even taken out of their boxes yet," he said, making light of her concern for his wardrobe. "If I lose a few, it's for a good cause. Besides, I think she looks festive in red plaid."

As he spoke, he approached the bed warily, as if suddenly uncertain if he had a right to draw so close. He touched the baby's head with his fingertips in a caress so gentle that Jessie's breath snagged in her throat.

"As for her being hungry, last I heard, there was nothing better than a mama's own milk for a little one," he said, his gaze fixed on the baby.

"I wasn't planning on nursing her," Jessie protested. "It won't work with the job I have. She'll have to be with a sitter all day. I need bottles, formula." She moaned. There were rare times—and this was one of them—when she wondered how she would cope. She'd counted on Erik to be there for her and the baby. Now every decision, every bit of the responsibility, was on her shoulders.

"Well, given that she decided not to wait for you to get to a hospital or to arrange for a fancy set of bottles," Luke said, still sounding infinitely patient with her, "I'd say Angela is just going to have to settle for what's on hand for the time being. Don't you suppose you can switch her to a bottle easily enough?"

"How should I know?" she snapped unreasonably.

Luke's gaze caught hers. "You okay?"

"Just peachy."

His expression softened. "Aw, Jessie, don't start panicking now. The worst is over."

"But I don't know what to do," she countered, unexpectedly battling tears. "I have three more classes to take just to learn how to breathe right for the delivery, and a whole stack of baby books to read, and I was going to fix up a nursery." She sobbed, "I...I even...bought the wallpaper."

Her sobs seemed to alarm him, but Luke stayed right where he was. Her presence here might be a burden, her tears a nuisance, but he didn't bolt, as many men might have. Once more that unflappable response calmed Jessie.

"Seems to me you can forget the classes," he observed dryly, teasing a smile from her. "As for the wallpaper, you'll get to it when you can. I doubt Angela will have much to say about the decor, as long as her bed's warm and dry. And babies were being born and fed long before anybody thought to write parenting books. If you're not up to nursing her yet, it seems to me I heard babies can have a little sugar water.''

''How would you know a thing like that?''

''I was trapped once in a doctor's office with only some magazines on parenting to read.''

His gaze landed on her breasts, then shifted away immediately. Jessie felt her breasts swell where his gaze had touched. Her nipples hardened. The effect could have been achieved because of the natural changes in her body over the past twenty-four hours, but she didn't think that was it. Luke had always had that effect on her. A single look had been capable of making her weak in the knees. She had despised that responsiveness in herself. She was no prouder of it now.

''I have a hunch that left to your own devices, the two of you can figure it out,'' he said. ''I'll leave you alone. I've got chores to do, anyway.''

He headed for the door as if he couldn't get away from the two of them fast enough. Jessie glanced up at him then and saw that, while his cheeks were an embarrassed red, there was an expression in his eyes that was harder to read. Wistfulness, maybe? Sorrow? Regret?

''You'll holler if you need me?'' he said as he edged through the doorway. Despite the offer of help, he sounded as if he hoped he'd never have to make good on it.

''You'd better believe it,'' she said.

A slow, unexpected grin spread across his face. "And I guess we both know what a powerful set of lungs you've got. I'm surprised the folks on every other ranch in the county haven't shown up by now to see what all the fuss was about."

"A gentleman wouldn't mention that," she teased.

"Probably not," he agreed. Then, in the space of a heartbeat, his expression turned dark and forbidding. "It would be a mistake to think that I'm a gentleman, Jessie. A big mistake."

The warning startled her, coming as it did on the heels of hours of gentle kindness. She couldn't guess why Luke was suddenly so determined to put them back on the old, uneasy footing, especially since they were likely to be stranded together for some time if the snow kept up through the day as it seemed set on doing.

Maybe it was for the best, though. She didn't want to forget what had happened to Erik. And she certainly didn't want to be disloyal to her husband by starting to trust the man who rightly or wrongly held himself responsible for Erik's death. That would be the worst form of betrayal, worse in some ways perhaps than the secret, unbidden responses of her body. Luke had delivered her baby. She might be grateful for that, but it didn't put the past to rest.

"Well, Angela, I guess we're just going to have to make the best of this," she murmured.

Even as she spoke, she wasn't entirely certain

whether she was referring to her first fumbling attempt at breast-feeding or to the hours, maybe even days she was likely to spend in Luke's deliberately ill-tempered company. Days, she knew, she was likely to spend worrying over how great the temptation was to forgive him for what he'd done.

An hour later, the chores done, Luke stood in the doorway of his bedroom, a boulder-size lump lodged in his throat as he watched Jessie sleeping. The apparently well-fed and contented baby was nestled in her arms, her tiny bottom now covered in bright blue plaid. Erik's baby, he reminded himself sharply, when longing would have him claiming her—claiming both of them—for his own.

Sweet Jesus, how was he supposed to get through the next few days until the storm ended, the phone lines were up and the roads were cleared enough for him to get word to his family to hightail it over here and take Jessie off his hands? He'd gotten through the night only because he'd been in a daze and because there were so many things to be done that he hadn't had time to think or feel. Now that his head was clear and the crisis was past, he was swamped with feelings he had no right having.

He forced himself to back away from the door and head for his office. He supposed he could barricade himself inside and give Jessie the run of the house. He doubted she would need explanations for his desire to stay out of her path. Now that her baby

was safely delivered, she would no doubt be overjoyed to see the last of him.

Last night had been about need and urgency.
They had faced a genuine crisis together and sur-
vived. In the calm light of today, though, that urgency was past. He could retreat behind his cloak
of guilt. Jessie would never have to know what
sweet torment the past few hours had been.

He actually managed to convince himself that
hiding out was possible as morning turned into afternoon without a sound from his bedroom. He
napped on the sofa in his office off and on, swearing to himself that he was simply too tired to climb
the stairs to one of the guest suites. The pitiful truth
of it was that he wanted to be within earshot of the
faintest cry from either Jessie or the baby. A part
of him yearned to be the one they depended on.

Shortly before dusk, he headed back to the barn
to feed the horses and Chester. The wind was still
howling, creating drifts of snow that made the walk
laborious. Still, he couldn't help relishing the cold.
It wiped away the last traces of fog from his head.
He vowed then and there that no matter how bad
things got, he would never, ever try to down an
entire bottle of whiskey on his own again. The brief
oblivion wasn't worth the hangover. And he hoped
like hell he never again had to perform anything as
important as delivering a baby with his brain
clouded as it had been the night before.

He lingered over the afternoon chores as long as
he could justify. He even sat for a while, doling out

pieces of apple to the goat, muttering under his breath about the insanity of his feelings for a woman so far beyond his reach. Chester seemed to understand, which was more than he could say for himself.

When he realized he was about to start polishing his already well-kept saddle for the second time in a single day, he forced himself back to the house and the emotional dangers inside. Chester, sensing his indecisiveness, actually butted him gently toward the door.

The back door was barely closed behind him when he heard the baby's cries. He stopped in his tracks and waited for Jessie's murmured attempts to soothe her daughter. Instead, the howls only escalated.

Shrugging off his coat and tossing it in the general direction of the hook on the wall, Luke cautiously headed for the bedroom. He found Jessie still sound asleep, while Angela kicked and screamed beside her. Luke grinned. The kid had unquestionably inherited Jessie's powerful set of lungs. Definitely opera singer caliber.

Taking pity on her worn-out mama, he scooped the baby into his arms and carried her into the kitchen. Once there, he was at a loss.

He held the tiny bundle aloft and stared into wide, innocent eyes that shimmered with tears. "So, kid, it looks like it's just you and me for the time being. Your mama's tuckered out. Can't say I blame her. Getting you into the world was a lot of hard work.''

The flood of tears dried up. Angela's gaze remained fixed on his face so attentively that Luke was encouraged to go on. ''Seems to me that both of us have a lot to learn,'' he said, keeping his voice low and even, in a tone he hoped might lull her back to sleep. ''For instance, I don't know if you were screaming your head off in there because you're hungry or because you're soaking wet or because you're just in need of a little attention.''

He patted her bottom as he spoke. It was dry. She blew a bubble, which didn't answer the question but indicated Luke was definitely on the right track.

''I'm guessing attention,'' he said. ''I'm also guessing that won't last. Any minute now that pretty little face of yours is going to turn red and you're going to be bellowing to be fed. Seems a shame to wake your mama up, though. How about we try to improvise?''

Angela waved her fist in what he took for an approving gesture.

''Okay, then. A little sugar water ought to do it.'' Cradling her in one arm, he ran some water into a pan, added a little sugar and turned on the burner to warm it. Unfortunately, getting it from the saucepan into the baby required a little more ingenuity.

Luke considered the possibilities. A medicine dropper might work. He'd nourished a few abandoned animals that way as a kid, as well as an entire litter of kittens when the mother'd been killed. One glance into Angela's darkening expression told him he was going to have to do better than that and fast.

"Chester," he muttered in a sudden burst of inspiration. When the old goat had wandered into the path of a mean-spirited bull, Luke had wound up nursing him with a baby bottle for months while he recovered. Where the hell had he put the bottle?

Angela whimpered a protest at the delay.

"Shhh, sweetheart. Everything's going to be just dandy," he promised as he yanked open every single cupboard door in the kitchen. Consuela had the whole place so organized that a single old baby bottle should have stood out like a sore thumb. If it was there, though, he couldn't find it, which meant it was probably out in the barn. He couldn't very well take the baby out there looking for it.

"Damn!" he muttered under his breath.

Huge tears spilled down the baby's cheeks. Obviously she sensed that his plan was falling apart. Any second now she was clearly going to make her impatience known with angry, ear-splitting screams.

"Hey," Luke soothed. "Have I let you down yet?"

Spying Consuela's rubber gloves beside the sink, he had another flash of inspiration. He snatched them up, put another pot of water on to boil, then tossed the gloves in to sterilize them. He found a sewing kit in a drawer, extracted a needle and tossed that in as well.

So far, so good, he reassured himself. The problem came when he judged everything to be sterile. He couldn't poke a hole in one of the glove's fingers and then fill it with warm water while still holding the baby. He grabbed a roasting pan that looked to be about the right size, padded it with a couple of clean dish towels and settled the baby onto the makeshift bed. Judging from the shade of red that her face turned, she was not happy about being abandoned.

"It's only for a minute," he promised her as he completed the preparations by tying a bit of string tightly around the top of the glove. He eyed the water-filled thumb of the glove with skepticism, waiting for the contents to gush out, but it appeared the hole he'd made was just right. He held it triumphantly where Angela could see it. "There! Now didn't I tell you we could manage this? We're a hell of a team, angel."

He picked her up, then sank onto one of the hard kitchen chairs and offered her the improvised bottle. Her mouth clamped on it eagerly and within seconds she was sucking noisily. Luke regarded her with pride.

"You are brilliant," he applauded. "Absolutely the smartest baby ever born."

"You're pretty smart yourself," a sleepy—and damnably sexy—voice commented.

Luke's heart slammed against his ribs. He refused to look up, refused to permit himself so much as a single glance at the tousled hair or bare legs or full, swollen breasts he'd dreamed about too many times to count.

Unfortunately Jessie pulled out a chair smack in his line of vision. She was still wearing his shirt, which came barely to mid-thigh. Her shapely legs were in full view. How many times had he envisioned those legs clamped around him as he made love to her? Enough to condemn his spirit to eternal hell, no doubt about it.

"Feeling rested?" he inquired huskily, keeping his eyes determinedly on the baby he held.

"Some. When did the baby wake up?"

"About a half hour ago. She was hungry."

"So I see."

He could feel a dull, red flush climbing into his cheeks. "I didn't want to wake you. I figured we could manage. It gave me a chance to test that theory I read. Seems to be working. She likes it."

"I'm impressed."

He stood so suddenly that the makeshift bottle slid from Angela's mouth. She protested loudly. Luke shoved both baby and water into Jessie's arms.

"I have work to do." There was no mistaking the sudden expression of dismay in Jessie's eyes, the flicker of hurt at his harsh tone. He managed to grit out a few more words before fleeing. "Help yourself to whatever you need. I'll be in my office."

"Luke, you don't have to run off," she said quietly.

Something in her tone drew his gaze back to her face. The longing he read there shook him more than anything that had happened so far. "Yes, I do," he said tightly.

"Please, I'd like the company."

"No." He practically shouted the word as he bolted.

Her expression stayed with him. Had it truly been longing, he wondered to himself when he was safely away from the kitchen, a locked oak door between him and temptation. Surely he'd been mistaken. No sooner had he reached that conclusion than he cursed himself for a fool. Of course, Jessie was yearning for something right now, but not for him.

No, he told himself sternly, that look had been meant for her husband. It was only natural at a time like this that she would be thinking of Erik, missing him, wishing that he were the one beside her as she fed their first precious baby. Luke was nothing more than a poor substitute.

There was only one way he could think of to keep from making another dangerous mistake like that one. He had to stay inside this room with the door securely locked...and temptation on the other side of it.

Chapter Four

Unfortunately, temptation didn't seem inclined to stay out of Luke's path. Only one person could be tapping on his office door not an hour after he'd stalked off in a huff and left her all alone with her baby in the kitchen. Since that display of temper obviously hadn't scared her off, he wondered if she'd have sense enough to take the hint and go away if he didn't answer. He waited, still and silent, listening for some whisper of movement that would indicate she'd retreated as he desperately wanted her to do.

"Luke?" Jessie called softly. "Are you asleep?"

Apparently she didn't have a grain of sense, Luke decided with a sigh. "No, I'm awake. Come on in."

She opened the door and stood at the threshold, shifting uneasily under the glare he had to force himself to direct her way. Despite his irritation, he couldn't seem to take his eyes off her.

She'd wound her long hair up into some sort of knot on top of her head, but it threatened to spill down her back at any second. Luke stared at it in fascination, wondering what she'd do if he helped it along, if he tangled his fingers in those silky strands and tugged her close. An image of their bodies entwined flashed in his head with such vivid intensity it left him momentarily speechless—and racked with guilt.

"Are you hungry?" she asked quietly, ignoring the lack of welcome. "I've fixed enough supper for both of us. I hope you don't mind."

Luke thought of all the reasons he should reject the gesture. If not that, then tell her to bring the food to him in his office. Sharing a meal seemed like a lousy idea. He had no business sitting down across from her, making small talk, acting as if they were a couple or even as if they were friends. Every contact reminded him of the feelings he'd had for her while she'd been married to his brother. Every moment they were in the same room reminded him that those feelings hadn't died. He owed it to her— to both of them—to keep his distance.

Just when he planned to refuse her invitation to supper, he caught the hesitancy in her eyes, the anxious frown and realized that Jessie was every bit as uncertain about their present circumstances as he was. There apparently wasn't a lot of protocol for being stranded with the man responsible for a husband's death, especially when those feelings were all tangled up with feeling beholden to him for delivering her baby.

"Give me a minute," he said with a sigh of resignation.

He watched as she nodded, then closed the door. He shut his eyes and prayed for strength. The truth of it was it would take him an hour, maybe even days to be ready for the kind of time he was being forced to spend with his brother's widow. He had only seconds, not enough time to plan, far too much time to panic, to think of all the dangers represented by having Jessie in his home.

As soon as he'd gathered some semblance of composure, he got to his feet, gave himself a stern lecture about eating whatever she'd fixed in total, uncompromising silence, and then racing hell-bent for leather back to the safety of his den. That decided, he set out to find her.

When he reached the kitchen, where she'd chosen to serve the dinner on the huge oak table in front of a brick fireplace that Consuela had persuaded him to build, the first words out of his mouth were, "I don't want you waiting on me while you're here."

It was hardly a gracious comment, but he had to lay down a few rules or it would be far too easy to fall into a comfortable pattern that would feed all the emotions that had been simmering in him for years now.

She leveled her calm, blue-eyed gaze on him. "We both have to eat. It's no more trouble to fix for two people than it is for one," she said as she dished up a heaping spoonful of mashed potatoes. She passed the bowl to him.

Luke didn't have an argument for that that wouldn't sound even more ungracious than he'd already been, so he kept his mouth clamped shut and his attention focused on the food. The potatoes were creamy with milk and butter. The gravy was smooth and flavored with beef stock, just the way he liked it. The chicken fried steak was melt-in-the-mouth tender. The green beans had been cooked with salt pork.

"When did you have time to do all this?" he asked. He studied her worriedly, looking for signs of exhaustion. She looked radiant. "You're not even supposed to be on your feet yet, are you?"

"There wasn't much to do. Consuela saw to most of it. I've never seen so many little prepackaged, home-cooked meals. She must have been stocking your freezer for a month. How long is she going to be gone, anyway? Or has she abandoned you for good, because of your foul temper?"

"I wouldn't blame her if she had, but no." Luke allowed himself a brief, rueful grin. "She figured company might be dropping by during the holidays, but I doubt she imagined it happening quite this way."

"Neither did you, I suspect." Jessie's penetrating gaze cut right through him. "You'd holed up in here for the duration, hadn't you? You were planning to spend the holidays with your buddy Jack Daniel's." She gestured toward the cabinets. "I saw your supply."

Luke winced at the direct hit. "I've only touched one bottle and I smashed it halfway through," he said defensively.

"Too bad you didn't do it sooner," she observed.

"If I'd known you—and especially Angela—were coming, I would have."

"Now that we are here, what happens next?"

He regarded her cautiously. "What's your real question, Jessie? You might as well spit it out."

Her glance went back to the cabinet. "Are you planning to finish off the rest?"

"Not unless I'm driven to it," he said pointedly.

This time Jessie winced. "Believe me, I know what an imposition this is. We'll be out of your hair as soon as the roads are passable." She glanced toward the windows, where the steadily falling snow was visible. "When do you suppose that will be?"

Luke shrugged. "Don't know. I haven't heard a weather report."

"Are the phones still out?"

"Haven't tried 'em since last night."

"Don't you have a cellular phone? That ought to be working."

To be perfectly honest, Luke hadn't given his cellular phone a thought. He still wasn't used to carrying the damned thing around with him. Keeping track of it was a nuisance. It was probably outside on the seat of his pickup. "I'll check next time I have to go to the barn."

"I could get it. I need to get the rest of my clothes from my car."

Luke cursed himself for not thinking of that. Of course, she'd had luggage with her if she'd been intending a stay at White Pines for the holidays.

"I'll get 'em," he said, pushing away from the table, leaving most of his food uneaten. The excuse was just what he needed to escape this pleasure-pain of sitting across from her in a mockery of a normal relationship between a man and a woman.

"Finish your supper first."

"I'm not hungry," he lied. "I'll get something later. Besides, I'm sure you're anxious to call the folks with the good news. They'll be thrilled to know that you and Erik have a daughter. Doubt they'll be quite so thrilled to hear where you had it though. Dad will want to fly in a specialist to check you and the baby out. He'll probably have a med-evac copter in here before the night's out."

Though he couldn't quite keep the bitterness out of his tone, Jessie grinned at his assessment. "He probably will, won't he? But not even Harlan Adams can defy nature. Nobody's going to be taking off or landing in this blizzard."

"They will if Daddy pays them enough," Luke retorted dryly.

"Well, I won't have it," Jessie retorted with a familiar touch of defiance. "Nobody needs to risk a life on my account. The baby and I are perfectly fine here with you and I intend to tell Harlan exactly that."

Luke had to admire the show of gumption. Obviously, though, Jessie hadn't had to stand up to his father when he got a notion into his head. To save her the fight she couldn't win, he found himself saying, "Maybe it would be best not to make that call, then."

Jessie actually looked as if she was considering it. "But they'll be worried sick about me not showing up last night," she said eventually. "I have to let them know I'm okay."

So, reason had prevailed after all. Luke was more disappointed than he cared to admit.

"Darlin', they've seen the weather," he said, beginning a token and quite probably futile argument, one he had no business making in the first place. Perversity kept him talking, though. "Their phone lines are probably down, too. They'll understand that you probably had to stop along the way and can't get through to let them know."

"Not five seconds ago you were telling me I didn't know your daddy. Now who's kidding himself? Harlan probably has a search party organized. The Texas Rangers are probably out on full alert, sweeping the highways for signs of my car."

There was no denying the truth of that. Luke stood. "Then I suppose we'd better head them off at the pass. I'll get the phone."

He grabbed his heavy sheepskin jacket from the peg by the back door, realizing as he did that Jessie must have hung it there. As he recalled, he'd merely tossed it in that general direction when he'd heard the baby crying earlier. As he pulled it on, he could almost feel her touch. He imagined there was even the faint, lingering scent of her caught up in the fabric.

Outside, the swirling snow and bitter cold cleared his head and wiped away the dangerous sense of cozy familiarity he'd begun to feel sitting at that old oak table with Jessie across from him. He took his time getting Jessie's belongings from her car, then lingered a little longer in the cab of his truck.

As he'd suspected, the cellular phone was on the passenger seat. All he had to do was pick it up and dial home. There wasn't a doubt in his mind that his father would find some way to get Jessie out of his hair before dawn. He would be alone again and safe.

Christmas was only three days away, New Year's a week after that. Surely he could get through so few days without resorting to his original plan of facing them stinking drunk. And heaven knew, Jessie would be better off with his family where the celebrations would be in high gear despite the weather, despite his family's private mourning, where there would be dozens of people to fuss over Angela.

Feeling downright noble about the sacrifice he was making, he actually managed to pick up the phone. But when it came to dialing it, he couldn't bring himself to do it. He thought of the incredible, once-in-a-lifetime miracle he and Jessie had shared. He remembered how it had felt to hold Angela in his arms, to have those trusting, innocent eyes focused on him. Jessie and Angela's unexpected presence had been a gift from a benevolent God, who apparently didn't think his soul was beyond repair.

Would it be so wrong to steal a few more hours, maybe even a day or two with Jessie and Angela? Who could possibly be hurt by it?

Not Erik. He was way past being hurt by anything, not even the knowledge that his brother coveted his widow.

Not Jessie, because Luke would never in a million years act on the feelings she stirred in him.

Not the baby. There was no way he would ever allow anything or anyone to harm that precious child. His paternal instincts, which he'd not even been aware he possessed, had kicked in with the kind of vengeance that made a man reassess his entire existence.

So the only person who might be harmed by his deception would be himself. He stood to lose big time by pretending for even the briefest of moments that Jessie and Angela were a part of his life. Emotions he'd squelched with savage determination were already sneaking past his defenses. The mere fact that he was considering hiding the cellular phone was proof of that.

And yet, he couldn't bring himself to let them go just yet. He'd fallen for Angela as hard as he'd fallen for her mother. Looking into those big blue eyes, he'd felt a connection as strong and powerful as anything he'd ever felt before in his life. He couldn't sever it, not until he understood it.

Likewise, he couldn't watch Jessie disappear until he had finally processed this terrible hold she had on him. From the moment he'd set eyes on her, he'd been riveted. If a bolt of lightning had struck him at that instant, he doubted he would have noticed.

Over time he'd grown to admire her sharp wit, bask in her sensitivity, but in that first instant there had been only a gut-deep attraction unlike anything he'd ever experienced before or since. She had the same effect on him now. He was a man of reason. Surely he could analyze their relationship with cold, calculating logic and finally put it to rest.

He gripped the phone a little tighter and glanced around at the drifts of snow that were growing deeper with each passing minute. A quick toss and no one would find the sucker before spring.

Just as he was about to act on his impulse, that reason of which he was so proud kicked in. What if there was a genuine emergency? The cellular phone might be their only link to the outside world. Instead of burying it in snow, he tucked it into the truck's glove compartment, behind the assortment of maps and grain receipts and who-knew-what-else had been jammed in there without thought. Then he turned the lock securely and glanced guiltily back at the house, wondering if Jessie would guess that he was deliberately keeping her stranded, wondering what her reaction would be if she did know.

Even through the swirling snow, he could see the smoke rising from the chimney, the lights beckoning from the windows. An unexpected sense of peace stole over him. Suddenly, for the first time since he'd built it simply to make a statement to his father—a declaration of independence from Harlan Adams and his need to maintain a tight-fisted control over his sons—the huge, far-too-big monster of a house seemed like a home.

Jessie couldn't imagine what was taking Luke so long. Surely Luke hadn't lost his way in the storm. Though the snowfall was still steady, it was nowhere near as fierce and blinding as it had been.

And he knew every acre of his land as intimately as he might a woman. His voice low and seductive, he'd boasted often enough of every rise and dip, every verdant pasture. He'd done it just to rile his father with his independence, but that didn't lessen the depth of his pride or his sensual appreciation for the land. No, Luke wasn't lost, which meant he was dallying intentionally.

While he was taking his sweet time about getting back, she was tiring quickly. The last burst of adrenaline had long since worn off. She had already cleaned up the remains of the supper they'd barely touched, washed the dishes and put them away. For the past five minutes she'd been standing at the backdoor, peering into the contrasting world of impenetrable black and brilliant white.

She thought she could see Luke's shadow in the truck and wondered for a moment if he had a bottle stashed there. That array she'd found in his cupboard had worried her. She had never known him to take more than a social drink or two before, had never seen him as on-his-butt drunk as he'd been the night before when she'd arrived.

When at last he climbed out of the truck and headed for the house, she watched his progress with a critical eye. He didn't seem to be staggering, no more so than anyone would be in the deep snow. Shivering at the blast of frigid air, she nonetheless planted herself squarely in the middle of the open doorway, so he couldn't pass by without her getting a whiff of his breath.

"Everything okay?" she called as he neared.

"Fine. Get back inside before you freeze."

Jessie didn't budge. "You took so long I got worried."

He brushed past her, bringing the fresh scent of snow and the tingle of icy air into the house with him. There was no telltale trace of liquor mingling with the crisp winter aromas. She sighed with relief as she closed the door tightly against the night.

"Couldn't find the phone," he announced as he

plunked her bags in the middle of the floor. "I'm always forgetting it someplace or another. It'll turn up."

Jessie regarded him suspiciously. His tone seemed a little too hearty. "What about a CB? You must have one and I know your folks do."

"Mine's on the fritz. Haven't seen any reason to get it fixed since I got the phone."

He was deliberately avoiding her gaze. "Luke?" she began quizzically.

He glanced her way for the briefest of seconds. "What?"

Jessie debated calling him on what she suspected were a series of lies, then chastised herself for being far too suspicious. What possible motive would he have for lying? There wasn't a doubt in her mind that he wanted her gone just as badly as she wanted to go. Getting him to the dinner table hadn't been easy. Getting him to stay there had been impossible. He'd seized the first excuse he could to escape. Obviously he wasn't anxious to close the gap that had formed between them when Erik had died on this very ranch.

Last night's emergency and Luke's gentle, caring response to it had been an aberration brought on by extraordinary circumstances. Now they were back to the status quo. She couldn't help the vague feeling of disappointment that stole through her.

Finally she shook her head. "Nothing. I'll take my things to the bedroom." She glanced at him.

"Or would you rather I take them to one of the guest suites upstairs?"

Luke seemed unduly angered by the question. "I can take them and you'll stay in the room you're in now."

"But there's no reason for me to put you out of your own room, when there are bedrooms galore upstairs." Left unspoken was the fact that every time she thought about having delivered her baby not simply in Luke's house, but in his bed, an odd sensation stirred in the pit of her stomach. It was a sensation that wouldn't bear too close a scrutiny.

Luke's jaw took on the stubborn set that was a family trait. Erik had been equally bullheaded, his chin perpetually at the same defiant tilt. Yet Erik had been easily swayed, easily reasoned with. Luke, to the contrary, was no pushover.

"Jessie, you'll stay downstairs for as long as you're here," he insisted. "You won't have to climb stairs."

"But I'll be in your way," she protested.

His gaze settled on her. "You won't be in my way," he said with soft emphasis. "This is the way I want it."

She retreated from the argument she clearly had no way of winning. It was his house. She'd stay where he wanted her. "I'll be going to my room, then."

Before she could reach for her bags, Luke shot her a warning look, then picked them up and preceded her down the hall. Inside the room with its dark wood and masculine decor, he deposited the suitcases, then whirled to leave, practically colliding with her in his haste. Jessie's hands immediately went out to steady herself, landing on his chest. Luke jerked as if he'd been brushed by a branding iron. Their gazes clashed, then caught.

"Sorry," she murmured, pulling her hands away.

"Are you okay?"

"You just startled me when you turned around so fast. I stumbled a bit, that's all."

Luke shook his head ruefully. "I'm not used to having to watch out for other people underfoot. It's one of the habits that comes from living alone. Well, not alone exactly. Consuela's here, but she's used to dodging me. To hear her tell it, I've got all the grace of a bull in a china shop. Did I tell you she went to visit her family in Mexico?"

Listening to him, Jessie couldn't stop the smile that tugged at the corners of her mouth. "Lucas, you're babbling," she teased. "Are you nervous for some reason?"

"Nervous?" he repeated the word as if he were testing it. "What would I have to be nervous about?"

"That's what I was wondering. It's not as if we're strangers." Jessie blushed despite herself. "Especially after last night."

A dull red flush crept up Luke's neck. "Maybe it would be best if we didn't talk too much about last night."

"But what you did for me…" She tried to think of the right words to express her gratitude.

"I did what anybody would have under the circumstances."

"That's not true. Luke, if you hadn't been here, if you hadn't been who you are…"

"Who I am? You mean Erik's brother," he said on an odd, flat note.

"No," she said emphatically. "I mean the kind of man you are, completely unflappable, gentle, competent." She trembled when she thought of the tragedy his presence and his calm, quick actions had averted. "My God, Luke, you delivered my daughter, and if you were even half as terrified as I was, you never let on to me."

"Try three or four times as terrified," he corrected. "I just talked a good game."

Jessie reached up and rested her hand against his stubbled cheek, felt a faint shudder whisper through him, saw his eyes darken. "Don't joke," she chided. "I'm serious. I'm trying to thank you properly for what you did, for bringing my baby safely into the world. I'll never forget it."

"There's no need for thanks," he said, brushing aside her gratitude.

"There is," she insisted, trying to think of an adequate way of showing him how grateful she was. The perfect gesture suddenly came to her and she blurted it out impulsively, not pausing to think of the implications. "In fact, I would be honored if you would consider being Angela's godfather. I know that's what Erik would have wanted, too.''

Luke's eyes turned cold and he broke away from her touch. ''You're wrong, if you think that,'' he said flatly. ''I'm the last man in the world Erik would want anywhere near you or your daughter.''

Too late, Jessie realized she couldn't have shattered the quiet moment any more effectively if she'd tossed a live hand grenade into the room. By mentioning Erik, by reminding Luke of his brother, she had destroyed their fragile accord.

''Luke, that's not true…'' she began, but she was talking to herself. Luke had fled from the room as if he'd just been caught committing a crime and a posse of lawmen were after him, guns already blazing.

Troubled, Jessie stared after him. Not until she heard her daughter whimper did she move. Picking Angela up from her makeshift bed, a blanket-lined drawer, she paced the floor with her until she quieted.

''You know something, angel? Your Uncle Luke is a very complicated, perplexing man.''

No one knew more clearly than she did how dangerous those two traits could be in a man, especially for a woman who enjoyed nothing more than solving puzzles.

Chapter Five

There was a huge stack of unpaid bills on Luke's desk. Normally he hated sitting there with a calculator, checking the totals against his own records, writing the checks, meticulously balancing the books. The process bored him. The mistakes irritated him. If he'd wanted to do this much math, he'd have been a damned accountant.

Tonight, though, the tedium of the assignment drew him. In fact, he hadn't been able to leave that bedroom fast enough to get to his office and shut the door behind him. Only a vague sense of the absurdity of the action kept him from bolting it.

At any rate, as long as he had to concentrate on numbers written out in black and white, numbers that either added up or didn't, he wouldn't have to think about the woman in his bedroom who made no sense to him at all.

What had possessed Jessie to suggest that he be godfather to Angela? Couldn't she see how inappropriate that was? Couldn't she guess how deeply hurt the rest of the family would be over her choice? Hell, they probably wouldn't even show up for the baptism. They'd be certain she'd placed the baby's very soul in jeopardy by selecting her father's killer as the baby's godparent.

Okay, she was grateful for his help in delivering the baby. He could understand that. He didn't think thanks were necessary, but if Jessie did, she could have found a dozen ways of thanking him that wouldn't turn the entire family inside out. A framed snapshot of the baby would have sufficed. A dutiful note would have covered it.

Instead, with all the impulsiveness and generosity he'd always admired in her, she had made a grand gesture that would have ripped the family apart. They would have chosen sides. In the end, more than likely Jordan and Cody would have backed Jessie's choice. His parents would have been appalled. Even he cared enough for the family's feelings to want to avoid deliberately causing them any more anguish.

Fortunately, his head at least had been clear. He'd said no before she could get too carried away with her planning.

He raked his hand through his hair and muttered an oath under his breath. A tiny part of him regretted the necessity for declining her offer. Being godparent to the baby he'd helped deliver would have bound him to Jessie and Angela. It would have kept him on the fringes of their lives. It would have placed him where no one would have questioned his involvement, where he could watch out for them.

Where he could torture himself, he added bleakly. Saying no had been the right decision, the only decision.

Determinedly, he picked up the first invoice from the pile on his desk and went to work. Sometime between the first bill and the second, he fell soundly asleep. The next thing he knew it was morning and the very woman who'd been tormenting him in his dreams was hovering around in his office as if she belonged there.

''What the hell are you doing?'' he asked crankily, rubbing his aching shoulders as he eyed Jessie warily. For a woman who'd just had a baby less than forty-eight hours before, she was damned energetic. Normally he'd consider that an admirable trait, but at the moment it seemed a nuisance to have her bustling around as if he weren't even there. ''Jessie, whatever you're up to, give it a rest.''

''I'm getting some light in here. It's dark as pitch.'' She drew back the draperies with a flick of her wrist, revealing the blinding glare of sunlight on snow.

''Beautiful, isn't it?'' she asked cheerfully. ''I'll

be back in a minute with your breakfast. You really shouldn't sleep at your desk, Lucas. It's bad for your back.''

Given the fact that every muscle between his neck and his butt ached like the very dickens, Luke couldn't argue with her. If she hadn't taken off, though, he would have had a few things to say about her intrusion into his domain. He figured they could wait until she returned. If she brought strong, black coffee with her, he might even moderate his protest to a dull roar.

He stood up cautiously, testing to see if any of his parts actually worked. His legs held him upright, which was better than he deserved. He stretched carefully, slowly working the kinks loose. By the time he heard Jessie's returning footsteps, he was feeling almost civilized. That didn't mean he intended to tolerate her sudden burst of uninvited activity.

Unfortunately for his resolve, the aroma of coffee preceded her into the room. Oblivious to whatever order there might be to his desk, she brushed piles of papers aside and deposited a tray laden with pancakes, eggs, bacon and a pot of coffee. Luke glanced at the new disarray, considered bellowing in outrage, then took another whiff of that coffee and poured himself a cup instead. He sipped it gratefully as he sank back into his leather chair.

Maybe the bustling wasn't so bad, after all. Only trouble now was, she didn't go away. In fact, she seemed to be waiting for something. She hovered at the edge of his desk, her gaze fixed on him as if trying to determine how to broach whatever was on her mind.

"Coffee's good," he said, watching her uneasily. "Thanks."

"You're welcome."

"Don't worry about the dishes. I'll bring them back to the kitchen and wash up when I'm done," he said, hoping she'd take the hint and leave.

She actually grinned at that. "Trying to get rid of me?" she inquired.

Almost as if to taunt him, she pulled up a chair and sat down. What astonished him was the fact that even though she was wearing her oversize maternity clothes, she managed to look as sexy as if she'd been wearing something slinky. His imagination was perfectly capable of envisioning every curve under her shapeless top. As if it might make a difference, he turned his attention to the food she'd brought. He poured syrup on the pancakes and cut into the eggs.

"I told you yesterday that I didn't want you waiting on me," he reminded her even as he took his first bite of pancakes. They were light as air. He knew for a fact that Consuela hadn't left these, which meant Jessie had been cooking. "You need to rest. Taking care of a new baby is tiring. I want you concentrating on Angela."

"Angela's fine. She's been fed. Now she's sleeping. That's what newborns do."

He snapped a piece of crisp bacon into crumbs

and prayed for patience. "So, rest while you have the chance. Read a book. The library next door is filled with them."

"Maybe later."

He could see he was getting nowhere. Maybe if he divided up the chores and took the lion's share himself, she'd restrict herself to doing only what she'd been assigned.

"Okay, here's the deal," he said. "I'll fix breakfast and lunch. You can deal with supper, since Consuela already has those dishes prepared and ready to pop into the oven. I'll clean up. Agreed?"

"That hardly sounds fair," she said. "I'll cook all the meals. You clean up."

"No," Luke insisted, his voice tight. "We'll do it my way. And since you've already done breakfast today, I'll handle dinner. You're done for the day. Go take a nap."

"I wonder why I never noticed before what a bully you are," she commented, her expression thoughtful.

The observation didn't seem to trouble her a bit, but he found it insulting. "I am not a bully. I'm just trying to divvy things up fairly."

"You have an odd notion of fair," she observed. "Oh, well, never mind. I won't argue for the moment. Maybe you should consider the pancakes a bribe," she suggested.

Luke's gaze narrowed. "A bribe? For what?"

"So you'll do what I want, of course."

"Which is?"

She opened her mouth, seemed to reconsider, then closed it again. "No, I think we'll wait and talk about it later. I think you could use a little more buttering up." She stood and headed for the door.

Luke stared after her in astonishment. "Jessie!"

His bellow clearly caught her by surprise. She halted in the doorway and looked back. The glance she shot him couldn't have been more innocent if she'd been a newborn baby.

"Yes?" she said.

"What kind of game are you playing here?"

"No game," she insisted.

"You want something, though. What is it?"

"It can wait. Enjoy your breakfast."

"Tell me now," he ordered.

She smiled. "I don't think so."

She closed the door with quiet emphasis before he could even form another question. Suddenly, despite himself, he found himself laughing.

"Well, I'll be damned," he said aloud. "Maybe I underestimated you, after all, Jessie Adams. Seems to me you have gumption to spare, more than enough to take on the Adams men."

On the other side of the door, Jessie heard the laughter and the comment. "You ain't seen nothing yet, Luke Adams," she murmured sweetly.

Unlocking the puzzle that Luke represented had become a challenge she couldn't resist. And drawing Erik's family back together seemed like the best Christmas gift she could possibly give to all of them. She'd come to that conclusion during a long and restless night.

Erik wouldn't have wanted his death to split them apart. He wouldn't have wanted the unspoken accusations, the guilt and blame to stand between Luke and his parents. Whatever had happened on Luke's ranch that day, Erik would never have blamed the big brother he'd idolized. He would have forgiven him. As much as Erik had craved his independence, he had loved his family more. If he hadn't, he might have fought harder to break free from Harlan's influence.

If, if, if...so many turning points, so many choices made, a few of them deeply regretted.

If she had accepted Harlan's offer to fly to his ranch, then the storm and her unexpected labor wouldn't have forced Jessie into accepting Luke's help and his hospitality. If that wasn't a sign from God, she didn't know what was. Obviously, He had given her a mission here and the most readily accessible place to start was with Luke. After all, Christmas was a time for miracles.

With the snow plows uncertain, she figured she had a few days at least to utilize her powers of persuasion. By the time the roads were cleared, she was determined that she and Angela wouldn't be going on to Harlan and Mary's alone to celebrate the new year and a new beginning. Their son would be with her.

By late that afternoon, Jessie's plans and her temper were frayed. She hadn't seen more than the flash of Luke's shadow the entire day. He'd managed to sneak lunch onto the table and disappear before she could blink. She'd passed his office, just in time to see him vanish into the library. She'd bundled up and trailed him to the barn, only to see him riding away on horseback. A gimpy old goat had been gamely trying to follow him.

Shivering, she had trudged back inside only to hear Angela screaming at the top of her lungs. Nothing she'd done had settled the baby down. Angela was dry and fed. For the past twenty minutes, Jessie had been rocking her in front of the fire in the kitchen. Angela's great, hiccupping sobs continued unabated.

"A few more minutes of this and you'll have me in tears, too," Jessie murmured in distress. "Come on, sweetheart. You're tired. Go off to sleep, like mommy's little angel."

Blessed silence greeted the suggestion. Five seconds later, Angela screamed even louder than before. Obviously she'd only taken time off to rev up her engine.

Jessie could feel the first, faint beginnings of panic. Already uncertain about her mothering skills, her inability to soothe her baby seemed to confirm just how unprepared and inept she was.

Because the rocking seemed to be making both of them more jittery than serene, she stood and began to pace as she racked her brain for some new technique to try.

She tried crooning a lullaby, singing an old rock song at full volume, rubbing her back. She was at her wit's end when she heard the back door slam.

Luke hesitated just inside the threshold. "What's all this racket?" he demanded, but there was a teasing note in his voice and a spark of amusement in his eyes. "I could hear both of you all the way out at the barn. Chester took off for parts unknown. The horses are trying to hide their heads under the hay."

"Very funny," Jessie snapped just as Luke reached for the baby. She relinquished her all too readily.

"Come here, angel," he murmured consolingly. "You were just missing Uncle Luke, weren't you?"

Jessie's traitorous daughter gulped back a sob, then cooed happily. Held in the crook of Luke's arm, she looked tiny, but thoroughly contented. Jessie wanted to warn her that a man's arms weren't a guarantee of protection, but maybe that was a lesson it was too soon to teach. If the feel of Luke's strength could silence the baby's cries for now, Jessie had no complaints. She felt the oddest, most compelling yearning to have his arms around her as well. With her hormones bouncing around in the wake of the baby's birth, she seemed to be more insecure than ever.

Luke glanced her way. "Stop hovering. We're doing fine. I'm going to start supper and Angela's going to help, aren't you, munchkin?"

Jessie sank gratefully onto a kitchen chair and

watched Luke's efficient movements as he pulled packages from the freezer with one hand, all the while carrying on a nonsensical conversation with the baby. Jessie sighed with envy as she watched him.

"How do you do that?" she asked.

He shrugged. "Maybe it's like a horse. If it knows you're afraid, it'll buck you off sure thing. If you handle it with confidence, it'll go along with you."

Jessie sorted through the metaphor and came to the conclusion he thought she was scared to death of her own daughter. "In other words, I'm lousy at this."

He shot a glance over his shoulder at her. "Did I say that? I thought I was saying that she senses you're not sure of yourself."

"Well, I'm not."

"You will be."

"How did you get to be so good with babies?"

"Three younger brothers, I suppose. All three of them had very different temperaments. Jordan was the charmer from day one. He could wheedle anything out of anybody. He gurgled and smiled and cooed. Even Daddy wasn't immune to him. It's no wonder he's been such an incredible business success."

"And Cody?"

"He's the flirt. There hasn't been a woman born he couldn't win over. Daddy couldn't handle him worth a lick. Come to think of it, Mama could never handle him either, but he could always make her think she'd won. He wrapped Consuela around his little finger and, believe me, she's no patsy.''

''What about Erik? What was he like?'' Jessie asked cautiously, keeping her gaze on Luke's face. His expression didn't change, but he did hesitate. For a moment she almost regretted bringing him up.

''Erik was the diplomat,'' he said eventually. ''He was the master of compromise. If Mama gave him two chores, he'd make her settle for one. If Daddy ordered him to be home at midnight, Erik would compromise for twelve-thirty. He never, ever accepted their first offer. If he'd been in the foreign service, it was a skill that would have served him well. As it was, he compromised himself into waiting for the life he really wanted by offering to prove himself first as a rancher.''

There was a note of sorrow in his voice that resonated deep inside Jessie. ''He wanted so badly to be a teacher in junior high, the age when kids are testing themselves, and he would have been good at it, too,'' she said. ''He just wanted to please your father.''

''He should have known that nothing would impress Daddy except success,'' Luke said bitterly. ''If Erik had stuck to his guns and gone on to be a teacher, if he'd won recognition for that, it would have pleased Daddy more than seeing him trying to be a rancher and failing.''

Jessie felt a surge of anger on Erik's behalf. ''Don't belittle your brother for trying. At least he admitted that he was staying at the ranch in an attempt to gain your father's approval. You won't even admit that's what you're doing.'' She waved her hand to encompass the kitchen, the whole house. ''Isn't that what all of this is for, to impress your father, to prove you could start from scratch, without a dime of his money and have a bigger, more impressive ranch?''

As if she sensed the sudden tension, Angela whimpered. Luke soothed her with a stroke of his finger across her cheek and a murmured, ''Shh, angel. Everything's okay. Your mama and I are just having a slight difference of opinion.''

His angry gaze settled on Jessie. ''I bought this ranch because ranching is what I do. I built this house because I needed a home.''

''How many bedrooms, Luke? Five? Seven? More than there are over at White Pines, I'll bet. And how many rooms do you really live in? Two, maybe three, if you don't count the kitchen as Consuela's domain?''

''What's your point?''

''That you're every bit as desperate for approval from Harlan as Erik ever was. You're just determined to do it by besting him at his own game.''

''Or maybe I was just planning ahead for the time when I have a family to share this ranch with me,'' he said quietly, his gaze pinned on her. ''Maybe I was thinking about coming in from the cold and finding the woman I loved in front of the fire, holding my baby.''

The softly spoken remark, the seductive, danger-ous look in his eyes held Jessie mesmerized. His voice caressed her.

"Maybe I was imagining what it would be like when this was no longer just a house, but a home, filled with warmth and laughter and happiness. Or didn't you ever stop to think that I might have dreams?"

"So why don't you do something to turn it into a home?" she taunted before she could stop herself.

The look he shot her was unreadable, but there was something in the coiled intensity of his body language that sent a thrill shimmering straight through her.

"Perhaps I have," he said, his challenging gaze never leaving hers.

Then, while Jessie's breath was still lodged in her throat, he pressed a kiss to the baby's cheek, handed her back to her mother and sauntered from the room with the confidence of a man who'd just emerged triumphant from a showdown at the OK Corral.

That was the last she saw of him until after the supper she'd been forced to eat alone. She'd spent most of the evening the same way, alone in the kitchen, pondering what Luke had said—and what he hadn't. With the radio tuned to Christmas carols, her mood was a mix of nostalgia and wistfulness and confusion.

She hadn't especially wanted to spend the holi-days with Erik's family, hadn't been much in the

mood for celebrating at all in fact, but now that
Christmas was only two days away, she couldn't
help thinking of the way it had been the year before.
She wondered if she would ever recapture those
feelings.

The whole family and dozens of friends had been
crowded around a gigantic tree, its branches loaded
with perfectly matched gold ornaments and tiny
white lights, chosen by a decorator. Mary had
played carols on the baby grand piano, while the
rest of them sang along, their voices more exuberant than on key.

Jessie remembered thinking of all the quiet
Christmases as she'd been growing up, all the times
she'd longed for a boisterous houseful of people.
With her hand tucked in Erik's, she'd been so certain that for the first time she finally understood the
joy of the season. Her heart had been filled to overflowing. In agreeing to go to White Pines this year,
perhaps she'd been hoping to reclaim that feeling
for herself and eventually for her baby.

It seemed unlikely, though, that it would have
been the same. Erik had stolen her right to be there
from her, wiped it away in an instant of carelessness
that she'd never really doubted for a moment was
as much his fault as Luke's. Sometimes, when it
was dark and she was scared, she blamed Luke,
because it hurt too much to blame her husband.

Everything Luke had said earlier was true. Erik
had hated working on the ranch, whether his father's or his brother's. He'd had other dreams, but

his father had been too strong and Erik too weak to fight. He'd preferred working for Luke, who tolerated his flaws more readily than his father did. He'd accepted his fate by rushing through chores, by doing things haphazardly, probably in a subconscious bid to screw up so badly that his father or Luke would finally fire him.

Well, he'd screwed up royally, all right, but he'd died in the process, costing both of them the future they'd envisioned, costing Angela a father and her the extended family she'd grown to love. Sometimes Jessie was so filled with rage and bitterness over Erik's unthinking selfishness that she was convinced she hated him, that she'd never loved him at all.

At other times, like now, she regretted to her very core all the lost Christmases, all the lost moments in the middle of the night when they would have shared their hopes and dreams, all the children they'd planned on having.

"Jessie?" Luke said, interrupting her sad thoughts as he stood in the kitchen doorway, his hands shoved in the pockets of his jeans. "Are you okay?"

"Just thinking about last year and how much things have changed," she admitted.

Luke's eyes filled with dismay. "I'm sorry. I know facing a Christmas without Erik is the last thing you expected," he said, regarding her worriedly. "Why don't you come on in the living room? I've started a fire in there."

Without argument Jessie stood and followed him. She was frankly surprised by the unexpected invitation, but she had no desire to spend the rest of the evening alone with her thoughts, even if being with Luke stirred feelings in her that she didn't fully understand.

When Luke stood by the fireplace, Jessie crossed over to stand beside him. He looked so sad, so filled with guilt, an agonizing of guilt that had begun some seven months ago for both of them. Instinctively she reached for him, placing her hand on his arm. The muscle was rigid.

She tried to make things right. "I don't blame you for the way things are, Luke. I wanted to. I wanted to lash out at someone and you were the easiest target. You were there. You could have stopped him." She sighed. "The truth is, though, that Erik was always trying to prove himself, taking chances. You couldn't have kept him off that tractor if you'd tried."

He shrugged off her touch. "Maybe not, but I blame myself just the same. Look what I've cost you."

Jessie wanted to explain that it wasn't Erik she missed so much as the feeling of family that had surrounded them all that night as they sang carols. To say that aloud, though, would be a betrayal of her husband, an admission that their life together hadn't been perfect. She owed Erik better than that. He had given her the one thing she'd never had—

the feeling of belonging to a family with history and roots.

"Regrets are wasted, Lucas. We should be concentrating on the here and now. It's almost Christmas, the season of hope and renewal," she said.

She glanced around the living room, which looked as it would at any other time of the year—expensive and sterile. It desperately needed a woman's touch. Even more desperately, it needed to be filled with love.

"You'd never even know it was the holidays in here," she chided him. "There's not so much as a single card on display. I'll bet you haven't even opened them."

"Haven't even been out to the mailbox in days," he admitted.

She lifted her gaze to his. "How can you bear it?" Before he could answer, she shook her head. "Never mind. That was what the cabinet full of liquor was all about, wasn't it?"

"Sure," he said angrily. "It was about forgetting for a few blessed days, forgetting Christmas, forgetting Erik, forgetting the guilt that has eaten away at me every single day since my brother died right in front of my eyes."

Jessie flinched under the barrage of heated words. "Sounds like you've been indulging in more than whiskey. You sound like a man who's been wallowing in self-pity."

"Self-loathing," Luke said.

"Has it made you feel better?" she chided before

she could stop herself. She'd been there, done that. It hadn't helped. "Has anything been served by you sitting around here being miserable?"

He didn't seem to have an answer for that. He just stared at her, his expression vaguely startled by her outburst.

"Don't you think I feel guilty sometimes, too?" she demanded. "Don't you think I want to curl up in a ball and bemoan the fact that I lost a husband after only two years of marriage? Well, I do."

She was on a roll now, releasing months of pent-up anger and frustration. She scowled at him. "But I for one do not intend to ruin the rest of my life indulging in a lot of wasted emotions. I cried for Erik. I grieved for him. But a part of him lives on in Angela. I think that's something worth celebrating. Maybe you're content to spend the holidays all shut up in this bleak atmosphere, but I'm not."

Oblivious to his startled expression, oblivious to everything except the sudden determination to take charge of her life again, starting here and now, she declared, "The minute I get up tomorrow morning, I am going to make this damned house festive, if I have to make decorations from popcorn and scraps of paper."

She shot him a challenging look. She had had it with his veiled innuendoes and sour mood. "As for you, you can do what you damned well please."

Chapter Six

Sitting right where he was, staring after Jessie long after she'd gone, Luke realized he hadn't given a thought to Christmas beyond being grateful that he wouldn't be spending it with his family, enduring their arguments and silences, their grief. Consuela had dutifully purchased his gifts to everyone, wrapped them and sent them over to White Pines. He'd merely paid the bills.

Now, though, he would have had to be denser than stone to miss Jessie's declaration that the atmosphere around his house was awfully bleak for the season. That parting shot before she'd gone off to her room had been a challenge if ever he'd heard one. Just thinking about it was likely to keep him up half the night, wondering how he could give them both a holiday they would never forget. There was no question in his mind that with Jessie and Angela in the house, it would be wrong, if not impossible, to ignore the holiday—the baby's first.

A week ago he hadn't expected to feel much like celebrating, but for the past forty-eight hours his mood had been lighter than it had been in months. Part of that was due to Angela's untimely, but triumphant, arrival. She was truly a Christmas blessing. A far greater measure of his happiness was due, though, to this stolen time with Jessie and his sense that she truly didn't blame him for Erik's accident.

He finally admitted at some point in the middle of the night that instead of getting her out of his system, he was allowing her to become more firmly entrenched in his heart. He could readily see now that his initial attraction to Jessie had been pure chemistry, tinged with the magical allure of the forbidden. In some ways, his conscience insisted, she was even more out of reach to him now.

But he knew in his gut that the attraction went beyond her being unavailable to him. Traits he'd only suspected before were clear to him now. He was coming to know her strengths and her weaknesses in a whole new way and nothing he'd discovered disappointed him.

In addition to being beautiful and warmhearted, she was also quick-tempered. In addition to being strong and brave, she was also willful and stubborn. She had a quick wit and a ready laugh, but she could also be a bit of a nag when she believed in her cause. In his view the positives outweighed the negatives. The contrariness only made her more interesting.

Those discoveries solidified his long-held belief that she and Erik had been mismatched from the start. As much as he had adored his younger brother, he'd also recognized that Erik was weak, too weak to stand up to their father, too weak to provide much of a challenge to a woman like Jessie.

He'd wondered more than once what had drawn them together in the first place. Observing them in years past with a sort of detached fascination, he had had no problem guessing why Erik had chosen a woman with Jessie's strengths. Less clear was why she had fallen in love with his brother. The past couple of days had given him some insight into that.

He was beginning to realize that far from being the gold digger she had appeared to some distrusting family members at first glance, Jessie had simply craved being part of a family with history and roots. On the surface, anyway, his family was storybook caliber with its strong men, boisterous affection, deep-rooted ties to the Texas land and abiding sense of loyalty. Erik had been her passport to all of that.

He couldn't help wondering, though, why she had chosen to move across the state after Erik's death, when she could have stayed at White Pines, claimed her rightful place in the family she'd obviously grown to love, and been doted on.

As he understood it, his parents had begged her to stay, especially after they'd learned she was pregnant. Even though it had meant giving up something desperately important to her, Jessie had insisted on going.

Whatever her reasons, he admired her for standing up to them. He also knew she hadn't taken a dime when she'd left. It was yet more testament to her character, proof that she had married Erik for love, not for money.

Lingering in the barn, Luke was leaning against a stall door, still contemplating Jessie, when Chester butted him from behind. The old goat was obviously tired of being ignored. Luke turned on him with mock indignation.

"Hey, what was that all about? Goats who get pushy don't get treats."

Chester didn't get the message. He nudged Luke's coat pocket trying to get at the sections of apple he knew were there. Luke dug them out and fed them to him.

"So, what do you think, Chester? What can I do to make this holiday special?"

Since the goat didn't seem to have any sage advice, Luke headed back toward the house. He was almost there when inspiration struck. He might not be able to deliver a load of gifts or even an album of Christmas carols, but he could certainly come up with a tree.

He detoured to the woodpile for an ax, then headed into the stand of pine trees on the ridge behind the house. He'd planted most of them up there himself, full-grown pines that had cost a fortune. He supposed he'd done it just because his parents had no similar trees, despite the name of their home. The gesture had been some sort of perverse link to his past.

He surveyed the cluster of trees critically, dismissing several as too scrawny, a few more as misshapen, though they'd all seemed perfect to him when he'd chosen them from the nursery. Finally his gaze landed on a tree that was tall and full and fragrant.

He worked up a sweat and an appetite chopping it down, then dragging it through the snow all the way back to the house. Propped up against the back porch railing, the tree seemed ever-so-slightly larger than it had on the ridge. He eyed it uneasily and decided he might have been just a little optimistic about fitting it into the house. Still, there was no denying that it was impressive. It made a statement, one he hoped that Jessie couldn't mistake.

After stomping the snow off his boots and dusting it from his clothes, he snuck inside to make sure that Jessie was still in bed. During the night as he'd been sitting awake in the living room staring into the fire, he'd heard her pacing the floor with the baby. Hopefully, she was catching up on lost sleep this morning.

He tiptoed down the hall as silently as a man his size could manage, then edged the bedroom door open a crack. Down for the count, he decided, after watching the soft rise and fall of her chest for several seconds more than was entirely necessary.

Angela, however, was another story. In her makeshift bed, a drawer they had lined with blankets, she was cooing to herself and waving her arms as if to let him know she was ready for an adventure. Luke couldn't resist the invitation. There was something about holding that tiny bundle of brand new life in his arms that filled him with a sense of hope.

Swearing to himself that he was only picking the baby up to keep her from waking Jessie, he carried her, bed and all, into the kitchen. Those serious eyes of hers remained fixed on him trustingly all the way down the hall. He was certain they were filled with anticipation, indicating she was ready to try anything. He figured she was destined to break a good many hearts with what seemed to him her already-evident daredevil nature.

"Now, then, sweet pea, can you be very quiet while I bring the tree in? Just wait till you see it. It's your very first Christmas tree and, if I do say so myself, it's just about the prettiest one I've ever seen."

Angela seemed willing to be temporarily abandoned. Luke was on the porch and back in a flash, lugging the tree through the kitchen and into the living room. He found the perfect spot for it in the nook formed by a huge bay window. As soon as he'd put it down, he went back into the kitchen for the baby. This time he plucked her out of her bed and carried her in his arms, admiring the simple red plaid sleeper Jessie had apparently stitched up from another one of his old shirts.

"So, what do you think?" he asked as he stood before the tree, admiring the sweep of its branches against the ten-foot-high ceiling. Placing it in a stand, assuming he even had one that would fit its thick trunk, definitely would require a little trimming at the top.

Angela seemed fascinated. He echoed her approval. "Pretty awesome, huh? Wait till you see it with lights and decorations. You won't be able to take your eyes off it."

The only problem was the lights, the decorations and the tree stand were all stored upstairs. He had a hunch she wouldn't tolerate being put back in that drawer again. "Now that is a quandary," he said to Angela. "But we can solve it, can't we? I'll just settle you right here on the floor so you can see, put some pillows around you in case you happen to be precocious enough to roll over. I think that's a little advanced even for someone of your brilliance, but there's no point in taking chances."

Angela's face scrunched up the instant he deposited her among the pillows. He propped her up so she had a better view of the tree, an arrangement which seemed to improve her disposition. "Now don't let me down, angel," he cajoled. "No crying, okay? I promise I'll be back before you can say Santa Claus."

He darted worried glances over his shoulder all

the way out of the room. The baby seemed to have settled into her nest without a fuss. He doubted her contentment would last, though.

Thankfully, Consuela was the most organized human being he'd ever met. The Christmas decorations were tidily stacked and labeled in a storage closet, where he'd insisted they remain this year. She'd succeeded in sneaking a fat, pine-scented candle and a table decoration into the dining room, but that was all she'd dared after his firm instructions.

Luke managed to get all the boxes into his arms at once, then juggled them awkwardly as he made his way back downstairs. The boxes began to wobble dangerously halfway down. The top one tumbled off, then the one after that. There was no mistaking the tinkling sound of glass breaking. Mixed with his muttered oaths and Angela's first faint whimpers, it was apparently more than enough to wake Jessie.

He'd just turned the corner to the living room when she came staggering out of the bedroom, sleepily swiping at her eyes. "What's going on? Where's Angela?"

Luke stepped in front of her and blocked her view of the living room. "Everything's under control. Why don't you go back to bed? You must be exhausted after being up half the night."

"I'm awake now. What broke?"

"Nothing important."

"What's all that stuff you're carrying?"

"For someone who's half-asleep, you ask a lot of questions. Did you get a job I don't know about as a reporter?"

Ignoring the question, she blinked and took a step closer. Her heavy-lidded gaze studied the boxes. When the contents finally registered, her face lit up with astonishment. "Christmas decorations?"

Luke sighed. So much for his surprise. "Christmas decorations," he confirmed, then shifted out of her way so she could see past him.

"I thought Angela should have a tree for her first Christmas," he admitted sheepishly. "You made it pretty clear last night how you felt about the lack of holiday spirit around here. I decided you were right."

Jessie's eyes widened. "Luke, it's..."

"Awesome?" he suggested, after trying to study the tree objectively. Despite the impressive size of the room, the tree took up a significant portion of it.

"Huge," Jessie declared.

"I know. It didn't look nearly as big outside."

Before he realized what she intended, Jessie turned and threw her arms around his neck. "Thank you," she said, kissing him soundly.

Her lips were warm and pliant against his, impossibly seductive. The impulsive gesture almost caused him to drop the remaining boxes. "Jessie!" he protested softly, though there was some doubt in his mind if he was warning her away to save the decorations or his sanity.

She regarded him uncertainly for the space of a heartbeat, but apparently she chose to believe he was worried about the ornaments. She claimed several of the boxes and carried them into the living room. Then she took a thorough survey of the tree and pronounced it the most incredible tree she had ever seen. The glint of excitement in her eyes was enough to make Luke's knees go weak. If she ever directed a look half so ecstatic at him, he could die a happy man.

"Don't do a thing until I get back," she demanded as she headed from the room.

"Where are you going?"

"To get dressed and to make hot chocolate."

He thought she looked exquisite in her robe, a pale pink concoction that was all impractical satin and lace. As for the hot chocolate, he was plenty warm enough as it was. "Not on my account," he said.

"On mine," she said, visibly shivering. "I'm freezing in this robe."

The innocent comment lured him to look for evidence. He found it not in the expected goose bumps, but in the press of hard nipples against the robe's slinky fabric. "I'll turn the heat up," he countered eventually. Anything to keep her in that softly caressing robe.

Apparently she caught the choked note in his voice or the direction of his gaze, because her expression faltered a bit. A delectable shade of pink tinted her cheeks. "It'll only take a minute," she insisted. "Besides, we can't possibly decorate a tree without hot chocolate. I'm pretty sure there's a law to that effect."

Luke found himself grinning at the nonsense. "Well, we are nothing if not law abiding around here. I'll test the lights while you're gone."

"But don't start stringing them on the tree, okay? I want to help."

"You mean you want to give orders."

She grinned back at him and his heart flipped over. "Maybe," she admitted. "But you wouldn't want to end up with blank spaces and have to do it all over again, would you?"

He shot her a look that was part dare, part skepticism. "Who says I'd do it over?"

"It is Angela's first tree," she reminded him in that sweet, coaxing tone she used so effectively. "You want it to be perfect, don't you?"

He laughed. "So that's how it's going to be, is it? One teeny little mistake and you're going to accuse me of traumatizing the baby's entire perception of Christmas?"

He glanced down at Angela and saw that she'd fallen fast asleep amid her nest of pillows. "Look," he said triumphantly. "She's not even interested."

Jessie waved off the claim. "She won't sleep forever. Test the lights, but that's all, Lucas."

"Yes, ma'am."

When she'd gone, Luke tried to recall the last time he'd taken orders from anyone. Not once that he could think of since moving out of his father's house. More important, this was absolutely the only time he'd ever taken orders and actually enjoyed it.

Something had changed overnight, Jessie decided as she searched through her luggage for the festive red maternity sweater she'd bought for the holidays. She'd fallen in love with the scattered seed pearl trim around the neckline. Except for its roominess, it made a stylish ensemble with a pair of equally bright stirrup pants and dressy flats.

Suddenly she was overwhelmed by the Christmas spirit. It wasn't just the sight of that incredible tree. It was Luke's thoughtfulness in getting it for her. There was no mistaking that the tree and his shift in mood were his gifts to her.

She thought she'd seen something else in his eyes, as well, something she didn't dare examine too closely for fear she would confirm the attraction that had scared her away from White Pines.

Twenty minutes after she'd left him, she was back with a tray filled with mugs of steaming hot chocolate topped with marshmallows, and a plate of Christmas cookies she'd found in a tin, plus slices of her own homemade fruitcake. It made an odd sort of breakfast, but who cared? It fit the occasion. She also brought along the radio, which she immediately tuned to a station playing carols.

''Now?'' Luke asked dryly, when she had everything set up to her satisfaction.

Jessie surveyed the ambience and nodded. ''Ready. Did you check the lights?''

"All the strands are working," he confirmed. "More than we could possibly need even for this monster. I suspect half of them were used outside last year." He regarded her with a teasing glint in his eyes. "I assume you have a blueprint of some kind for their placement."

"Very funny."

He held out the first strand. "It's all yours."

Jessie's enthusiasm faltered slightly as her gaze traveled up the towering tree. "You have to do the first strand. I can't reach the top."

"I brought in a ladder."

She shot him a baleful look. "Never mind. Heights make me dizzy." So did Luke, but that was another story entirely. She was finding the powerful nature of her reactions to him increasingly worrisome.

"Are you sure you can trust me to do it right?" he teased.

"Of course," she said blithely. "I'll be directing you."

To his credit, he actually took direction fairly well. He seemed to lose patience only when she made him shift an entire strand one level of branches higher. "It'll be dark there, if you don't," she insisted.

"There are going to be a thousand lights on this tree at the rate we're going," he argued. "Nobody's even going to see the branches."

She turned her sweetest gaze on him. "The baby will like the lights."

The argument worked like a charm. Luke sighed and moved the strand.

"I'd better check the fuses before we turn this thing on," he complained. "It'll probably blow the power for miles around."

"Stop fussing. It's going to be spectacular. Let's do the ornaments next."

"Where did you intend to hang them? There's no space left."

She hid a grin at the grumbling. "Lucas, I could do this by myself."

He actually chuckled at that. "But you'd miss half the fun."

Jessie narrowed her gaze. "Which is?"

"Bossing me around."

"You have a point," she said agreeably. "But admit it, you're getting into the holiday spirit."

The teasing spark in his eyes turned suddenly serious. There was an unexpected warmth in his expression that made Jessie's pulse skitter wildly.

"I suppose I am," he said so quietly that she could practically hear the beating of her heart. "Can I tell you something?"

Jessie swallowed hard. "Anything."

"It's the first Christmas tree I've ever decorated."

She stared at him incredulously. "You're kidding."

He shook his head. "Mother always hired some decorator, who'd arrive with a new batch of the most stylish ornaments in the current holiday color scheme. We were never even allowed to be under-foot. By January second, it was all neatly cleared away, never to be duplicated.''

''That's terrible,'' Jessie said. ''I just assumed...''

''That we had some warm family tradition, like something out of a fairytale,'' he concluded. ''You were there. You saw the fuss Mother made over choosing the design for the tree.''

''I thought maybe it was something she'd started to do after you were all older and the family started doing more formal entertaining during the holidays.''

''Nope. Not even when we came home from school with little handmade decorations. Those went on Consuela's tree. I think she still has them all. Mother paid a fortune for the perfect tree. She wasn't about to have the design marred by tacky ornaments made by her children.''

Jessie's heart ached for the four boys who'd been deprived of the kind of tradition she'd always clung to. When she looked his way again, Luke's thoughtful gaze was on her as if he was waiting for her reaction to having one of her myths about his family shattered.

''Where are those decorations now?'' she asked, clearly surprising him.

''In Consuela's suite, I suppose. Why?''

''Can you find them?''

He gave her an odd look. ''Jessie, there's no need

to get all sentimental about a bunch of construction paper and plaster of paris decorations.''

''I want them on this tree,'' she insisted.

Luke shook his head at what he obviously considered a fanciful demand. ''I'll take a look later.''

''Promise?''

''I promise.'' He played along and solemnly crossed his heart. ''What about you, Jessie? What was it like at your house?''

''Quiet,'' she said, thinking back to those days that had been a mix of happy traditions and inexplicable loneliness. ''There were just the three of us. By the time I was adopted, my parents were already turning forty. There were no grandparents. I always thought how wonderful it would be if only there were aunts and uncles and cousins, but both of my parents had been only children.''

''Is that why you were coming back to White Pines this year? Did you want to maintain the ties so your baby would eventually have the large family you'd missed?''

''That was part of it. That and wanting her to know she's an Adams. I don't have that sense of the past that you have. I suppose it can be a blessing and a curse—Erik certainly saw it that way—but I envy it more than I can tell you.''

''Why didn't you ever search for your biological parents?''

She recalled how badly she'd once wanted to do exactly that. ''I thought about it right after I learned

I was adopted,'' she admitted. "But my parents were so distressed by the idea that I put it aside.''

He paused in hanging the decorations and studied her from atop the ladder. "Is it still important to you?''

Jessie felt his gaze on her and looked up at him from her spot on the floor amid the rapidly emptying boxes. "I think it is," she said quietly. "It's as though there's a piece of me missing and I'll never be whole until I find it. It's funny. I thought Erik and your family could fill that space, but I was wrong. It's still there.''

Luke climbed down from the ladder, then hunkered down in front of her and rested his hands on her knees. His gaze was even with hers and filled with compassion. "Then do it, Jessie. Find that missing part. I'll help in any way I can.''

Something deep inside her blossomed under the warmth of his gaze. And for the first time she could ever recall, it seemed there was no empty place after all.

Chapter Seven

Though it tested her patience terribly, Jessie agreed with Luke's idea that they not turn on the tree lights until evening. The decision to wait left her brimming with an inexplicable sense of anticipation, almost as if she were a child again. She could recall year after year when she'd huddled in her bed, pretending to sleep, listening for the sound of reindeer on the roof, the soft thud of Santa landing on the hearth after a slide down the chimney. She wanted those kinds of memories for her daughter, those and more.

She wanted Angela to grow up with memories of Christmas Eves gathered around a piano singing carols, of midnight church services, and of the chaos of Christmas morning with dozens of cousins and aunts and uncles. She couldn't give her those things, but Erik's family could. And as difficult as it might be at times to be around Luke without touching him, without openly loving him, she would see to it that the connection with the Adamses was never severed.

She glanced up to find Luke's gaze on her. She smiled, her eyes misty. "We'll make it sort of a Christmas Eve ceremony," she said, wondering at the magic that shimmered through her at the hint they were starting a tradition of their own. The memory of it was something she could hold tight, something no one could criticize or take away from her.

And yet, judging from the intent way Luke studied her, there must have been a note of sadness in her voice she hadn't realized was there.

"Are you sorry you're not spending Christmas Eve at my parents' house?" he asked.

There was an odd undercurrent to the question that Jessie couldn't interpret. Was he regretting not acting more aggressively to get her out of his hair? Or was the question exactly what it seemed? Was he worrying about her feelings?

"It's not the Christmas I was anticipating," she admitted, and saw the immediate and surprising flare of disappointment in his eyes. She hurried to reassure him. "It's better, Luke. No one could have done more to make this holiday special. You made sure I had a healthy baby. And how could I possibly regret the first Christmas with my daughter, wherever it is?''

Luke glanced at the baby she held cradled in her arms. Angela had just been fed and was already falling asleep again, her expression contented.

''She is what this season is all about, isn't she?'' he said. ''They say we don't always do so well with our own lives, but we can try harder to see that our children experience all of the magic of the holidays, that they get everything they deserve out of life.''

His bleak tone puzzled her. ''Luke, you sound as if your life is over and hasn't turned out the way you expected. That's crazy. There's still lots of time for you to fulfill all your dreams.''

His inscrutable gaze met hers. Something deep in his eyes reached out and touched her. It was that odd sense of connection she'd felt so often in the past, as if their souls understood things they'd never spoken of.

''I'm not so sure about that,'' he said quietly. ''I think maybe I missed out on the one thing that makes life worth living.''

''Which is?'' she asked, her voice oddly choked.

''Love.''

Something in the way he was looking at her turned Jessie's blood hot. Her pulse thumped unsteadily. There was no mistaking the desire in his hooded eyes, the longing threading through his voice.

Nor was there any way to deny the stubborn set of his jaw that said he would never act on whatever feelings he might have for her. Fueled by guilt or conscience, he had declared her off limits.

Which was as it should be, Jessie told herself staunchly. Yet she couldn't explain the warring of regret and relief that his silent decision stirred in her. Stranded here with him, she didn't dare explore any of her feelings too closely, but she had been reminded sharply of all of them. Most especially she had remembered how a simple glance could warm her, how easily the soft caress of Luke's voice could send a tremor of pure bliss rippling through her.

At White Pines, with Erik alive, those responses had been forbidden. She had felt the deep sting of betrayal every time she hadn't been able to control her reaction to her husband's brother. Now it seemed the denials had gone for naught. Luke had reawakened her senses without even trying. He, thank goodness, appeared far more capable of pretending, though, that he hadn't. The charade of casual distance between them would be maintained to protect them both from making a terrible mistake.

"I think I'll put Angela down for a while," she said, practically dashing from the room that vibrated with unspoken longings.

Only after she had the baby safely tucked into her makeshift bed again, only after she was curled up in a blanket herself did she give free rein to the wild fantasies that Luke set off in her. Dangerous, forbidden fantasies. Fantasies that hadn't died, after all, not even after her attempt to put time and distance between herself and this complex man who'd found a spot in her heart with his unspoken compassion and strength of character.

"Oh, Lucas," she whispered miserably. "How could I have done it? How could I have gone and fallen in love with you?"

There was no point in denying that love was what she was feeling. She had fought it practically from the moment she'd first set eyes on him. She had run from it, leaving him and White Pines behind. But three nights ago, when Luke had been there for her, when he had safely delivered her baby and treated her with such tenderness and compassion, the powerful feelings had come back with a vengeance.

That didn't mean she couldn't go on denying them with every breath left in her. She owed that to Erik.

More than that, she knew as well as Luke obviously did, the kind of terrible price they would pay, the loss of respect from the rest of the family if he ever admitted what she was beginning to suspect…that he was in love with her as well.

Luke was slowly but surely going out of his mind. There wasn't a doubt about it. Another few days of the kind of torment that Jessie's presence was putting him through and he'd be round the bend. His body was so hard, so often, that he wondered why he hadn't exploded.

All it took was a whispered remark, an innocent glance, a casual caress and he reacted as if he were being seduced, which was clearly the farthest thing from Jessie's mind. There were times it seemed she could barely stand to be in the same room with him. She'd bolted so often, even a blind man would have gotten the message.

He couldn't understand why she, of all the women in the world, had this mesmerizing effect on him. Maybe guilt had made all of his senses sharper, he consoled himself. Maybe he wouldn't be up to speed and ready to rock and roll, if there weren't such an element of danger involved. He was practically hoarse from telling himself that Jessie was not available to him ever, and his body still wasn't listening!

It had been tough enough with Erik alive. His sense of honor had forbidden him from acting on his impulse to sweep Jessie into his arms and carry her off to his own ranch. Erik and Jessie had made a legal and religious commitment to love each other till eternity. Luke had witnessed their vows himself, had respected those vows, in deed, if not always in thought. He'd been tormented day in and day out by the longings he could control only by staying as far from Jessie as possible. With her right here in the home in which he'd envisioned her so often, his control was stretched beyond endurance. He was fighting temptation minute by minute. Each tiny victory was an agony.

A lesser man might not have fought so valiantly. After all, Erik's death had removed any legal barriers to Luke's pursuit of Jessie. But he knew in his heart it hadn't diminished the moral commitment the couple had made before God and their family and friends. Maybe if Luke told himself that often enough, he could keep his hands off her for a few more days.

But not if she impulsively threw her arms around his neck again, not if he felt the soft press of her breasts against his chest, or the tantalizing brush of her lips against his. A man could handle only so much temptation without succumbing—and hating himself for it forever after.

The safe thing to do, the smart, prudent thing would be to retrieve that blasted cellular phone from his truck and call his parents.

And he would do just that, he promised himself. He would do it first thing Christmas morning. Tomorrow, Jessie would be out of his home, out of his life. She would be back where she belonged—at White Pines—and back in her rightful role as Erik's widow, mother of Harlan and Mary's first grandchild.

Tonight, though, he would have Jessie and Angela to himself for their own private holiday celebration. Just thinking about sitting with Jessie in a darkened room, the only lights those on the twinkling tree they'd had such fun decorating, made his pulse race. They would share a glass of wine, listen to carols, then at midnight they would toast Christmas together.

And tomorrow he would let her—let both of them—go.

That was the plan. If he had thought it would help him stick to it, he would have written it down and posted it on the refrigerator. Instead, he knew he was going to have to draw on his increasingly tattered sense of honor. He stood in his office for a good fifteen minutes, his gaze fixed on Erik and Jessie's wedding picture just to remind himself of the stakes. He figured his resolve was about as solid as it possibly could be.

He tried to pretend that there was nothing special about the evening by choosing to wear one of his many plaid shirts, the colors muted by too many washings, and a comfortable, well-worn pair of jeans. Consuela would have ripped him to shreds for his choice. His mother would have declared herself disgraced. He considered it one small attempt to keep the atmosphere casual.

There were more. He set the kitchen table with everyday dishes and skirted the temptation of candles with careful deliberation. He would have used paper plates and plastic knives and forks if he'd had them just to make his point.

Still, there was no denying the festive atmosphere as he heated the cornish game hens with wild rice, fresh rolls and pecan pie that Consuela had left for his holiday meal. The wine was one of his best, carefully selected from the limited, but priceless, assortment in his wine cellar. The kitchen was filled with delicious aromas by the time Jessie put in an appearance.

She'd dressed in an emerald green sweater that

had the look of softest cashmere. It hung loosely to just below her hips, suggesting hidden curves. Her slacks were a matching shade of wool. She'd brushed her coal black hair and left it to wave softly down her back.

"Something smells wonderful," she said peering into the oven. The movement sent her hair cascading over her shoulder. She shot him an astonished look. "Cornish game hens? Pecan pie?"

"Consuela," he confessed tightly as he fought the desire to run his fingers through her hair.

Her gaze narrowed speculatively. "She must have suspected you'd be having a special guest here for the holidays."

Was that jealousy in her voice? Luke wondered. Dear heaven, he hoped not. Jealousy might imply that his feelings were returned and he knew without any doubt that all it would take to weaken his resolve was a hint that Jessie felt as he did.

"Not suspected," he denied. "Hoped, maybe. Consuela is a hopeless romantic and my bachelor status is a constant source of dismay to her. She stays up nights watching old videos of Hepburn and Tracy, Fred Astaire and Ginger Rogers. I think she's worn out her tape of *An Affair to Remember.* She wakes me out of a sound sleep with her sniffling."

Jessie smiled. "A woman after my own heart. Maybe we should watch an old movie tonight. Does she have *It's A Wonderful Life* or *Miracle on 34th Street?*"

"I'm sure she does, but I refuse to watch them if you're going to start bawling."

"Can't stand to see a woman cry, huh?"

Certainly not this one woman in particular, he thought to himself. He would shift oceans, move continents if that's what it took to keep Jessie happy. His brother had broken her heart.

As soon as the disloyal thought formed, Luke banished it. Jessie had loved Erik. Their marriage had been solid. It wasn't for him to judge whether Erik's decisions had disappointed her. He dragged himself back to the present and caught Jessie studying him curiously.

"Nope, I never could stand to see a woman cry," he said, deliberately keeping his tone light. "I'm fresh out of hankies, too."

Jessie grinned. "No problem. I saw boxes of tissues stashed in the bathroom closet."

Luke heaved an exaggerated sigh of resignation. "I'll find the tapes right after dinner."

Dinner was sheer torture. Jessie found the candles Luke had avoided and lit them. The kitchen shimmered with candlelight and the glow from the fireplace. It was the kind of romantic lighting that turned a woman's complexion delectably soft and alluring, the kind of lighting that stirred the imagination. Luke's was working overtime. He could barely squeeze a bite of food past the lump lodged in his throat.

"You're awfully quiet," Jessie observed.

"Just enjoying the meal," he claimed.

She eyed his full plate skeptically. "Really?"

He was saved from stammering out some sort of explanation by the sound of whimpers from the bedroom. "Angela's awake," he announced unnecessarily and bolted before Jessie could even react.

With the baby safely tucked against his chest, it was easier somehow to keep his emotions in check. Right now he figured Angela was as critical to his survival as a bulletproof vest was to a cop working the violent streets.

"She's probably hungry," Jessie said when the two of them were settled back at the table.

The innocent observation had Luke's gaze suddenly riveted on Jessie's chest. So much for keeping his attention focused elsewhere.

"She's not making a fuss yet," he replied in a choked voice, clinging to the baby a trifle desperately. "Enjoy your dinner."

Jessie seemed about to protest, but finally nodded and picked up her fork. Luke kept his gaze firmly fixed on the baby.

"How are you doing, sweet pea? Ready for your very first Christmas? It's almost time for the big show, the lighting of the tree."

"It's amazing the effect you have on her," Jessie commented. "It must be your voice. It soothes her."

Luke grinned. "Can't tell you the number of women I've put to sleep by talking too much."

Blue eyes observed him steadily as if trying to assess whether he was only teasing or boasting. Apparently she decided he was joking. To his amazement, he could see a hint of satisfaction in her eyes.

"I doubt that," she countered dryly. "I suspect it's the kind of voice that keeps grown-up women very much awake."

"You included?" The words slipped out before he could stop them. His heart skidded to a standstill as he watched the color rise in her cheeks. Those telltale patches were answer enough. So he hadn't totally misread those occasional sparks of interest in her eyes. Nevertheless, a few sparks weren't enough to overcome a mountain of doubts.

Jessie seemed to struggle to find her voice. When she finally did, she said dryly, "Now that's the famous Luke Adams ego that's legendary around these parts."

"That's not an answer," he taunted, enjoying the deepening color in her cheeks.

"It's as close to one as you're likely to get," she taunted right back.

Luke chuckled. "Never mind. I already have my answer."

Jessie's gaze clashed with his, hers uncertain and very, very vulnerable. Luke finally relented. "You're immune to me. You've seen me at my worst."

"Bad enough to terrify the angels," she confirmed, her voice laced with unmistakable gratitude for the reprieve he'd granted.

She stood up with a brisk movement and reached for the baby, making her claim on the armor he'd clung to so desperately. "I'll feed her now," she said.

"You haven't had dessert," Luke protested, not relinquishing the baby. At this rate they'd be engaged in a tug-of-war over the child.

"We'll have it in front of the tree," Jessie said determinedly and held out her arms.

Reluctantly, he placed Angela in her mother's arms and watched them disappear down the hallway to the bedroom. Only when the door shut softly behind them did he breathe a heartfelt sigh of relief.

The reprieve, however, didn't last nearly long enough for him to regain his equilibrium. The clean-up kept him occupied briefly. Fixing coffee and pie to take into the living room took only moments longer.

In the living room, he plugged in the tree and turned on the radio, once again tuning it to a station playing carols. The room shimmered with a thousand twinkling colored lights. Luke was certain he had never seen a more beautiful tree, never felt so clearly the meaning of Christmas.

As he anticipated Jessie's return, he fingered the carved wooden figures in the crèche he'd placed beneath the tree, lingering over the baby Jesus. His thoughts were on another baby, one he wished with all of his jaded heart was his own.

He was standing, still and silent, when he sensed Jessie's approach. He heard her soft, indrawn breath. The faint scent of her perfume whispered through the air, something fresh and light and indescribably sexy.

"Oh, Luke, it's absolutely spectacular," she murmured. "The whole room feels as if it's alive with color."

He glanced down and saw reflected sparks of light shimmering in her eyes. Her lush mouth was curved in the sweetest smile he'd ever seen. Angela was nestled in her arms, spawning inevitable comparisons to the most finely drawn works of Madonna and child. In motherhood, even more than before, Jessie was both mysterious and beautiful, so very beautiful that it made his heart ache.

Nothing in heaven or hell could have prevented what happened next. Luke felt his control slipping, his resolve vanishing on a tide of desperate longing. He lowered his head slowly, pausing for the briefest of instants to gauge Jessie's reaction before gently touching his mouth to hers.

The kiss was like brushing up against fire, hot and dangerous and alluring. He lingered no longer than a heartbeat, but it was enough to send heat shimmering through him, to stir desire into a relentless, demanding need. The temptation to tarry longer, the need to savor, washed over him in great, huge, pulsing waves.

This one last time, though, the determination to cling to honor was powerful enough to save him, to save them both. He drew back reluctantly, examining Jessie's dazed eyes and flushed cheeks for signs of horror or panic. He saw—or thought he saw—only a hunger that matched his own and, to his deep regret, the grit to resist, the impulse to run.

"Merry Christmas," he said softly before she could flee.

She hesitated, her eyes shadowed with worry. "Merry Christmas," she said finally, apparently accepting the truce he was offering in their emotional balancing act.

Luke hid a sigh of relief. She hadn't run yet and he had just the thing to see that she didn't. "I found Consuela's tapes. What'll it be?"

Jessie blinked away what might have been tears, then said, "*Miracle on 34th Street,* I think."

"Good choice," he said too exuberantly. He slid the tape into the VCR and flipped on the TV while Jessie settled herself and the baby on the sofa.

Luke warned himself to sit in a chair on the opposite side of the room, warned himself to keep distance between them. He actually took a step in that direction, before reversing and sinking onto the far side of the sofa.

Jessie shot him a startled look, then seemed to measure the space between them. Apparently it was enough to reassure her, because slowly, visibly she began to relax, her gaze fixed on the TV screen where the holiday classic was unfolding.

They could have been watching *Dr. Zhivago* for all Luke saw. He couldn't seem to drag his gaze or his thoughts away from Jessie. Each breath he drew was ragged with desire. Each moment that passed was sheer torment as his head struggled between right and wrong.

And yet, despite the agony of doing what he knew deep in his gut was right, he thought he had never been happier or more content. The night held promise tantalizingly out of reach, but it shimmered with possibilities just the same. A few stolen hours, he vowed. No more. He would soak up the scent of her, the sight of her so that every fiber of his being could hold the memory forever.

Her laughter, as light as a spring breeze, rippled over him leaving him aroused and aching. Tears spilled down her cheeks unchecked, luring his touch. His fingers trembled as he reached to wipe away the sentimental traces of dampness. At his touch, her gaze flew to his, startled...hopeful.

That hint of temptation in her eyes was warning enough. If Jessie was losing her resolve tonight, then being strong, being stoic was going to be up to him.

He withdrew his hand and thought it was the hardest thing he had ever done. Only one thing he could imagine would ever be harder—letting her go. And tomorrow, just a few brief hours from now, he would be put to the test.

Chapter Eight

Christmas morning dawned sunny and clear. The snow shimmered like diamonds scattered across white velvet. Sparkling icicles clung to the eaves. The world outside was like a wonderland, all of its flaws covered over with a blanket of purest white.

For once Jessie had apparently gotten up before Luke. She hadn't heard him stirring when she fed Angela at 6:00 a.m. Nor was there any sign of him in the kitchen when she went for a cup of coffee before showering and getting dressed. Usually starting the coffeepot was the first thing he did in the morning. Today it hadn't even been plugged in. Jessie checked to make sure the electric coffee machine was filled with freshly ground beans and water, then plugged it in and switched it on.

After tying the belt on her robe a little more securely, she sat down at the kitchen table to wait for the coffee to brew. Her thoughts promptly turned to the night before. Every single second of their holiday celebration was indelibly burned on her memory: the delicious dinner, the sentimental old movie, the shared laughter, the twinkling lights of the tree, the kiss.

Ah, yes, the kiss, she thought, smiling despite herself. She wasn't sure which one of them had been more shocked by its intensity. Even though Luke had initiated it, he had seemed almost as startled as she had been by the immediate flaring of heat and hunger it had set off. Though his mouth against hers had been gentle and coaxing, the kiss had been more passionately persuasive than an all-out seduction. Fire had leapt through her veins. Desire had flooded through her belly. If he had pursued his advantage, there was no telling how far things might have gone.

Well, they couldn't have gone too far, she reassured herself. She had just had a baby, after all. Still, there was no talking away the fact that she'd displayed the resistance of mush. And once again Luke had proven the kind of man he was, strong and honorable.

His restraint, as frustrating as it had been at the time, only deepened her respect for him. She added it to the list of all of his admirable traits and wished with all her heart that she had met him first, before Erik, before any possibility of a relationship had become so tangled with past history and old loyalties, so twisted with guilt and blame.

Almost as soon as she acknowledged the wish, guilt spread through her. How could she regret loving Erik? How could she possibly regret having Angela? Life had blessed her with a husband who had loved her with all his heart, no matter his other flaws. She had been doubly blessed with a daughter because of that love. What kind of selfish monster would wish any of that away?

"Dear God, what am I thinking?" she whispered on a ragged moan, burying her head on her arms.

There was only one answer. She had to find some way to get away from Luke, to put her tattered restraint back together. She had to get to White Pines before she made a terrible mistake, before the whole family was ripped apart again by what would amount to a rivalry for her affections.

Despite their occasional differences, she knew how deep the ties among Erik's family members ran. They would consider themselves the protectors of Erik's interests. Luke would be viewed as a traitor, a man with no respect for his brother's memory. They would hold her actions against him, blaming him alone for their love when the truth was that she was the one who was increasingly powerless to resist it. She wouldn't allow that to happen.

An image came to her then, an image of Luke returning from his pickup, his expression filled with guilt as he'd sworn he couldn't find his cellular phone. More than likely she'd been in denial that night, longing for something that could never be, or she would have known what that expression on his face had meant.

Anger, quite possibly misdirected, surged through her. It gave her the will to act, to do what she knew in her heart must be done. She stood and grabbed Luke's heavy jacket, poked her bare feet into boots several sizes too large, snatched up his thick gloves, and stomped outside.

She was promptly felled by the first drift of snow. She stepped off the porch and into heavy, damp snow up to her hips. She dragged herself forward by sheer will, determined to get to the truck, determined to discover if Luke had deliberately kept her stranded here.

Her progress could have been measured in inches. Her bare skin between the tops of the boots and the bottom of the coat was stinging from the cold. Still, she trudged on until she finally reached the pickup and tugged at the door. The lock was frozen shut.

Crying out in frustration, Jessie tried to unlock it by scraping at the ice, then covering the lock with her gloved hands in a futile attempt to melt the thin, but effective coating of ice. She tried blowing on it, hoping her breath would be warm enough to help. When that didn't work, she slammed her fist against it, hoping to crack it.

Again and again, she jiggled the handle, trying to pry the door open. Eventually, when she could barely feel her feet, when her whole body was shuddering violently from the cold, the lock gave and the door came free. She jumped inside and slammed the door, relieved to be out of the biting wind.

Remembering that Erik had always left the keys above the visor, no matter how she'd argued with him about it, she checked to see if Luke had done the same. No keys. She doubted Luke was any more security conscious than his brother had been. She checked under the floor mat, then felt beneath the front seat.

That's where she eventually found them, tucked away almost beyond her reach. Her fingers awkward from the gloves and the cold, she finally managed to turn on the engine. It might take forever for the truck to warm up, but she intended to spend as long as it took to thoroughly check the pickup for that cellular phone.

It didn't take nearly as long as she might have wished. To her astonishment and instantaneous fury, she found it on the first try, right in the glove compartment. Luke hadn't even bothered to lock it, though it was obvious to her that he had made a passing attempt to hide the phone under some papers. Clutching the phone in her hand, she sank back against the seat and simply stared at it.

"Luke," she whispered, "what were you thinking?"

She was so caught up in trying to explain her brother-in-law's uncharacteristic behavior that she didn't hear the crunching of ice or the muttered oaths until Luke was practically on top of her. Suddenly the passenger door was flung open—the damned lock didn't even stick under his assault—and Luke jumped into the seat beside her.

Jessie shot him an accusing look. His gaze went from her face to the cellular phone and back again. He muttered a harsh oath under his breath.

"It was here all along, wasn't it?" she asked in a lethal tone.

He didn't even have the decency to lie. He just nodded.

"Why, Luke?" Her voice broke as she asked. Unexpected tears gathered in her eyes, threatening to spill over. She felt betrayed somehow, though she couldn't have explained why. Maybe it was because she had expected so much more of Luke. The hurt cut deeper and promised worse scars than anything Erik had ever done.

Luke shoved his hand through his hair and stared off into the distance. He didn't speak for so long that Jessie thought he didn't intend to answer, but eventually he turned to face her, his expression haggard.

"I couldn't make the call," he said simply. "I just couldn't make it."

"Do you hate your family so much?" she demanded. "How could you let them worry about me? How could you leave them wondering if there'd been an accident? My heaven, they must be out of their minds by now."

He shot her a look filled with irony. "Do you really think that was what it was about?"

"What else?" she demanded, her voice rising until she didn't recognize it. "What else could have made you do something so cruel?"

Before she could even guess what he was about, he reached out and clutched the fabric of the coat that was several sizes too large for her. He dragged her roughly to him. This time when he claimed her mouth, there was nothing sweetly tentative about it. The kiss was bruising, demanding. It was the kiss of a desperate man, a man who had kept his emotions on a tight leash for far too long.

Jessie recognized the passionate claiming even before she felt the raging heat. Even as a protest formed in her head, exhilaration soared in her heart. Furious with herself for the weakness, she gave herself up to the magic of that kiss. His cheeks were stubbled, his skin cold, except where his mouth moved against hers. There, there was only the most tempting heat and she couldn't deny herself the pleasure of it.

As if he sensed that she wasn't fighting him, as if he realized that she was fully participating in this conflagration of sensation, Luke's rough touch became a softer caress. Demand gave way to the gentler persuasion. Out-of-control hunger turned to a far sweeter coaxing.

Jessie was captivated, her body aswirl with a riot of new feelings, more powerful than anything she'd ever felt with Erik. Not even her carefully cultivated battle against disloyalty could keep her from giving her all to this one devastating kiss.

This man, though, this timing…she couldn't help thinking how wrong it was, when she could think at all. A spark of pure magic scampered down her spine, chased by a shiver of doubt. She suspected they could thank bulky coats and thick gloves for checking their actions, more than they could credit either of them with good sense.

Eventually Luke cupped her face in his gloved hands. With his eyes closed and his forehead barely touching hers, he sighed heavily.

"Oh, Jessie, I never meant for this to happen," he said on a ragged, desperate note.

"But it has," she said, not sure whether that was cause for regret or joy. Only time would tell. "Now what?"

Luke released her and sank back against the passenger seat, his gaze fixed on the ceiling. "You take that phone and you go inside and call the folks. Daddy will find some way to pick you up before the day is out."

Somehow shocked at his matter-of-fact dismissal, Jessie stared at him. "You want me to go?" she whispered, devastated. "Now?"

"Especially now." His gaze determinedly evaded hers.

"But why? It's all out in the open at last. The way you feel. The way I feel. It was all there in that kiss. Don't tell me you can still deny it. There's no turning back now, Lucas. We have to deal with it."

If he was shocked by her feelings for him, he

didn't show it. Instead, the look he turned on her was every bit as cold as the world outside that truck. "We are dealing with it. You're going and I'm staying. That's the way it has to be, the way it was meant to be."

Jessie shivered, chilled as much by his tone as the howling wind. "You can't mean that."

"I've never meant anything more," he insisted, his expression as steady and determined as she'd ever seen it. "Go to White Pines. It's where you belong."

A great, gnawing sensation started in the pit of Jessie's stomach. She sensed that if she did as he asked, if she left him here alone and went to be with his family, taking her place there as his brother's lonely, tragic widow, that would indeed be the end of it. Whatever might have been between them would die. Harlan, Mary, Jordan and Cody would be united in their opposition. The family and all of its complicated antagonisms and hurts would be like an insurmountable wall.

Well, she wouldn't have it. Maybe what she thought she felt for Luke was wrong. Maybe what he felt for her was some sort of terrible sin. Maybe they were both betraying Erik.

In a perfect world, her marriage would have fulfilled all of her dreams. It would have lasted a lifetime. And no man would ever have come along who was Erik's equal. She would have dutifully mourned until the end of time.

But her marriage hadn't worked. Erik had died.

And Luke Adams was twice the man Erik had been. That wasn't her fault. It wasn't Erik's. In his own way, Erik had tried to make her happy. He had never realized that she couldn't be happy as long as he was so obviously miserable with the choices he alone had made for his life.

Nor, though, was the fault Luke's. Their feelings simply were there. He had done nothing to exploit them.

And she couldn't believe a benevolent God would have conspired to force her here to have her baby, if something more hadn't been meant to come of it. If there was one thing Jessie believed in with all her heart, it was fate. Surely God had brought them together not just to forgive, not just to rid themselves of guilt, but to love.

"I will only go to White Pines if you will come with me," she announced, her chin set stubbornly.

Luke stared at her, an expression of incredulity spreading across his handsome face. His mouth formed a tight line. Disbelief sparked in his eyes. "No way."

"Then Angela and I are staying."

"No way," he repeated more firmly, reaching for the cellular phone that had started them inevitably down this path and now lay forgotten in her lap.

Jessie's hand closed around it first and before Luke could react, she opened the car door and threw it with all her might. Landing silently, it disappeared slowly, inevitably in a soft drift of snow.

Luke's shocked gaze followed its path, then returned to her face. His jaw worked. Jessie waited for an explosion of outrage, but instead his lips curved into an unexpected smile. Amusement sparkled in his eyes. He seemed to be choking back laughter.

"The situation is not amusing, Lucas."

"It's not the situation, it's you. I can't believe you did that," he said at last.

She glared at him, not entirely sure what to make of this new mood. "Well, believe it."

"We might not find it till spring."

"So what?"

"You were the one who mentioned how cruel it was to leave my parents wondering and worrying about you."

Jessie's determination faltered ever so slightly. Apparently she was every bit as thoughtless as he was. "The phone lines are bound to be up soon. We'll call then."

He regarded her quizzically. "And if there's an emergency?"

"What kind of emergency?" She couldn't seem to keep a faint tremor out of her voice.

"The house burning down. The baby getting sick."

Jessie felt the color drain out of her face. "Oh, my God," she murmured, clambering out of the pickup. She tumbled into the snow, then struggled back to her feet. Before she could steady herself, Luke was beside her.

"You okay?"

"We have to get that phone."

He gave her an inscrutable look. "I'll get it. You go on inside. Despite the charming winter attire you appropriated from me, you're not really dressed for this weather."

She eyed him distrustfully. "You'll bring it inside?"

"Hey, I'm not the one who tried to bury it. I knew exactly where it was in case we really needed it."

She scowled at him. "Don't start trying to make yourself into a saint now, Lucas. It's too late."

He turned back and, to her astonishment, he winked at her. "It always was, darlin'."

Luke retrieved the cellular phone and barely resisted the urge to roll in the snow in an attempt to cool off his overheated body. The effect Jessie had on him was downright shameful. His blood pounded hotly through his veins just getting a glimpse of her. The kiss they had just shared could have set off a wildfire that would consume whole acres of prairie grass.

Damn, why had she been so willing? Why hadn't she smacked him, put him in his place, blistered him with scathing accusations? The instant he had hauled her into his arms, he'd half-expected the solid whack of her palm across his cheek. When it hadn't come, he'd dared to deepen the kiss, dared to pretend for just a heartbeat that he had a right to taste her, a right to feel those cool, silky lips heat beneath his, a right to feel her body shuddering with need against his.

The truth of it was, though, that he had no rights at all where Jessie was concerned. Even though she seemed to feel that that kiss had opened up a whole new world for the two of them, he knew better. He knew it had paved the way to hell, destroying good and noble intentions in its path.

He stuck the phone in his pocket and continued on to the barn, where he fed Chester and the horses. Chester nudged his hand away from his pocket, searching for his treat. Instead, there was only the phone.

"Sorry, old guy. I left the house in a hurry. I forgot your apple. I'll bring two when I come back later."

The old goat turned a sympathetic look on him, as if he understood the turmoil that had caused Luke to fail him.

"Good grief, even the animals are starting to pity me," he muttered in disgust and made his way back to the house, where he found Jessie singing happily as she worked at the stove.

The table had been set with the good china. Orange juice had been poured into crystal goblets. The good silver gleamed at each place. Luke eyed it all warily.

"It's awful fancy for breakfast, don't you think?"

"We're celebrating," she said airily.

He wasn't sure he liked the sound of that. It

hinted that she wasn't letting go of the momentary craziness that had gripped the two of them in the pickup. "Celebrating what?"

She cast an innocent look in his direction. "Christmas, of course," she said sweetly.

"Oh."

She grinned. "Disappointed, Lucas?"

"Of course not." He glanced around a little desperately. "Where's Angela?"

"Sleeping."

"Are you sure? Maybe I should go check on her. She doesn't usually sleep this late."

Jessie actually laughed at that. "Surely a grown man doesn't have to rely on a three-day-old baby to protect him from me, does he?"

Luke felt color climb up the back of his neck and settle in his cheeks. "I just thought she ought to be here," he muttered. "It is her first Christmas morning."

"She'll be awake soon enough. Sit down. The biscuits are almost ready." '

He stared at her incredulously as she bent over to open the oven door. The view that gave him of her fanny made him weak.

"When did you have time to bake biscuits?" he inquired, his voice all too husky.

"You were in that barn a long time," she said. She glanced over her shoulder. "Cooling off?"

Luke stared at her. What had happened to the sweet, virtuous woman who'd arrived here only a few days earlier? What did she know about her ability to drive him to distraction? *Get real, Lucas,* he told himself sternly. *She was as responsible for the heat of that kiss as you were.*

"Jessie," he warned, his voice low.

"Yes, Lucas?"

She sounded sweetly compliant. He didn't trust that tone for a second. "Don't get into a game, unless you understand the rules," he advised her.

"Who made up these rules? Some man, I suspect."

"Oh, I think they pretty much go back to Adam and Eve," he countered. He fixed his gaze on her until her cheeks turned pink. "I figure that gives 'em some credibility. People have been living by 'em for centuries now."

Jessie shook her head. Judging from her expression, she seemed to be feeling sorry for him.

"You are pitiful, Lucas," she said, confirming his guess.

He stared at her, a knot forming in his stomach. "Pitiful?"

"You don't know what to do about how you feel, so you start out hiding behind an itsy-bitsy baby and now you want to put God and the Bible between us."

"Right's right," he insisted stubbornly.

"And what was meant to be was meant to be," she countered, looking perfectly confident in making the claim.

Obviously she wasn't worried about the two of them being stricken dead by a bolt of lightning.

Luke couldn't understand it. How could she be so calm, so sure of herself, when he'd never felt more off balance, more uncertain in all of his life?

"Whatever that means," he grumbled.

"It means, Lucas, that you might as well stop fighting so hard and accept the inevitable."

He studied her worriedly. "Which is?"

"Angela and I are in your life to stay."

He swallowed hard. "Well, of course you are," he said too heartily. "You're my sister-in-law. Angela's my niece."

Ignoring his comment, Jessie dished up scrambled eggs, bacon and golden biscuits. Only after she'd seated herself across from him did she meet his gaze.

"Give it up, Lucas. It's a battle you can't win."

Determination swept through him. "Try me," he said tightly.

To his annoyance, Jessie actually laughed at that. "Oh, Lucas, I intend to."

Chapter Nine

With Jessie's challenge ringing in his ears, Luke retreated to the barn. He figured it was the only safe place for him to be and still be within shouting distance of the house in case of a crisis. Inside, even in his office with the door shut, he couldn't escape Jessie's unrealistic expectations for their future. As brief as her presence had been, she had pervaded every room, leaving him with no place to hide from her or his unrelenting thoughts about her.

What she wanted from him, though, was impossible. How could they possibly have a relationship without bringing the wrath of the entire family she admired so much down on them? Couldn't she see that they were as doomed in their way as Romeo and Juliet had been? Or had she considered and then dismissed the problems? Could he possibly be that important to her?

He hunkered down on a bale of hay and distractedly tossed apple sections to Chester. The goat seemed to accept the unexpected largesse as his due. When Luke grew distracted and forgot to offer another chunk of apple, Chester butted him gently until he remembered. He scratched the goat behind his ears and wished that all relationships were this uncomplicated.

Dealing with goats and horses and cattle was a hell of a lot less troubling than dealing with a woman, Luke concluded when Chester finally tired of the game and wandered off. Food, attention, a little exercise, a few animal or human companions and their lives were happy. Women, to the contrary, sooner or later always developed expectations.

To avoid dealing with Jessie's fantasies, he considered saddling up one of the horses and riding off to check on the cattle. He manufactured a dozen excuses why such a trip was vital to the ranch's operations, even though he had a perfectly capable foreman in charge, a man who could probably account for every single head of longhorn cattle on the ranch without Luke's help.

Unfortunately, he could see through every excuse. He had no doubts at all that Jessie would be even quicker to see them for what they were: cowardly reasons to bolt from all the emotions he couldn't bear to face. While being someplace else—*anyplace else*—held a great deal of appeal at the moment, Luke wasn't a coward. Which meant, like it or not, staying and seeing this through.

Finally, tired of having only Chester and the horses for company when the most beautiful, if unavailable, woman in the world was inside, Luke heaved himself up and headed back to the house. Maybe Jessie had come to her senses while he was gone. Maybe his body had become resigned to celibacy.

And maybe pigs could fly, he thought despondently.

He found her sitting in front of the fireplace in the kitchen mending one of his shirts. As an inexplicable rage tore through him, he yanked the shirt out of her hands.

"What the hell are you doing?" he demanded.

Jessie didn't even blink at his behavior. "There was a whole basket of mending sitting in the laundry room waiting to be done," she said calmly as if that were explanation enough to offer a man who'd clearly lost his mind.

"Consuela's the housekeeper around here, not you."

"Is there some reason I shouldn't help her out?"

"It's her job," he insisted stubbornly.

Jessie merely shook her head, gave him that exasperating look that was filled with pity, and reached for another shirt. "It's my way of thanking her for all the meals she fixed before she left."

"She fixed them for me," Luke said, clinging to his stance despite the fact that even he could see he was being unreasonable. There was a quick and obvious remedy for what ailed him but he refused to pull Jessie into his arms, which was clearly where his body wanted her, where his long-denied hormones craved her to be.

One delicate eyebrow arched quizzically at his possessive claim on the meals Consuela had fixed. "Does that mean I'm no longer allowed to eat them?" Jessie inquired. "You planning to starve me into leaving?"

"Of course not," he snapped in frustration. "Just forget it. I'm going to my office."

"On Christmas?"

"If you can sew on Christmas, I can work."

"I'm not sure I see the connection," she commented mildly. She shrugged. "Whatever works for you."

Luke clenched his fists so tightly, his knuckles turned white. Why had he never noticed that Jessie was the most exasperating, the most infuriating woman on the face of the earth? She was so damned calm and...reasonable. He didn't miss the irony that he considered two such usually positive traits to be irritating.

To emphasize his displeasure, he plunked the cellular phone on the table in front of her. "Call my parents," he ordered tightly, then stalked away.

With any luck at all, Jessie would be tired by now of his attitude, he thought with only a faint hint of regret. After all, how long could a woman maintain this charade of complacency in the face of such galling behavior? She'd be packed and gone by the time he emerged from his office. His life could return to normal.

He glanced over his shoulder just as he headed through the doorway. She was humming to herself and, if he wasn't mistaken, there was a full-fledged smile on her face. He had the sinking realization that she wasn't going anywhere.

Jessie wasn't entirely sure why she was being so stubborn. One devastating, spine-tingling kiss hardly constituted a declaration of love.

Still, with every single bit of intuition she possessed, she believed that Luke was in love with her. That kiss was a symptom of stronger emotions. She was certain of it. She simply had to wait him out. Sooner or later, he would see that she wasn't afraid of the consequences if she stayed. He would see, in fact, that she welcomed them. Eventually he would realize that together they could even conquer all of the opposition they were likely to arouse.

The unexpected ringing of the cellular phone startled her so badly, she pricked her finger with the needle she'd been using to stitch buttons back onto Luke's shirts. Should she answer it? Or take it to Luke in his office? Of course, by the time she carried it through the house, whoever was calling would probably give up thanks to her indecisiveness.

It was guilt over her own failure to call Harlan

and Mary that finally convinced her to answer on the fifth ring.

"Hello," she said tentatively.

"Who the hell is this?" Harlan Adams's unmistakable voice boomed over the line.

An odd mix of pleasure and dismay spread through her. "It's Jessie, Harlan. Merry Christmas!"

"Jessie?" he repeated incredulously. "You're okay. What the devil are you doing over at Lucas's? Why haven't you called? My God, woman, Mary's been out of her mind with worry."

Jessie decided that rather than responding to the questions and the barely disguised accusations Harlan had thrown out at her, she'd better go on the offensive immediately.

"I went into labor on the way to your house," she explained. "I was scared to death I'd deliver the baby in a snow drift. Luke's ranch was the only place nearby. You have a beautiful granddaughter, Harlan. I've named her Angela."

As she'd expected, the announcement took the wind out of his sails. "You've had the baby? A girl?"

"That's right."

"Mary," he called. "Mary! Get on the other line. Jessie's at Luke's and she's had the baby!"

Jessie heard the echoing sound of footsteps on White Pines's hardwood floors, then the clatter of a juggled, then dropped, phone. Finally, Mary's breathless voice came over the line. "You had the baby?"

"A girl," Jessie confirmed. "Angela. She is so beautiful, Mary. I can't wait for you to see her."

"But why are you at Luke's? Why not a hospital?"

"Angela was too impatient to get here. With the blizzard and everything, I figured this was my best bet."

"But the doctor did get there in time?" Mary asked worriedly.

Jessie hauled in a deep breath before blurting, "Actually, Luke delivered her. He was incredible. Calm as could be. You would have been so proud of him. I don't know what I would have done without him."

The explanation drew no response. Jessie could hear Mary crying. Eventually, Harlan spoke up.

"I don't get it, girl. That was three days ago. Why haven't you called before now?"

"The phone lines are down and Luke had misplaced the cellular phone. He hunted all over for it. It finally turned up this morning, buried under some papers." It was a stretch of the truth, but Jessie had no intention of filling them in on her own battle with Luke over this very phone.

"No wonder we couldn't reach him," Harlan grumbled. "That boy would lose his head if it weren't tacked onto his neck."

Jessie sighed. She'd never noticed that Luke was particularly absentminded, not about anything that mattered. The observation was just another of Harlan's inconsequential put-downs, uttered without thought to their accumulated cutting nature. She'd practically bitten her lower lip raw listening to him do the same thing to Erik. If she had thought it would help, she would have told him to stop, but she had known the order had to come from Erik.

"Well, it doesn't matter now," Harlan said. "Now that we know where to find you, I'll have my pilot pick you up in an hour. There's a landing strip not far from Luke's. He should be able to get you there."

"No," Jessie said at once.

"Beg pardon?" Harlan said, sounding shocked by her unexpected display of defiance.

"Jessie, darling, you must be anxious to be away from there," Mary protested. "We know how difficult it was for you to see Luke after what happened to Erik. Please, let Harlan send for you. We want you here with us and we can't wait to see the baby. You should be with family now."

"Luke is family," she reminded them.

"Yes, but…well, under the circumstances, you must be under a terrible strain there."

"No," Jessie insisted. She took a deep breath and prepared to manufacture an excuse that not even strong-willed Harlan Adams could debate. "The baby has no business being dragged around in weather like this, not for a few more days anyway. By then the roads will be clear and I can drive the rest of the way."

"Oh, dear," Mary promptly murmured. "She is okay, isn't she?"

"She's just fine, but she's a newborn and it's freezing outside. I'll feel better about bundling her up and taking her out in a few days, I'm sure."

"Well, of course, you must do what you think is best for the baby," Mary conceded eventually, but there was no mistaking her disappointment.

"Nonsense," Harlan said, heading down the single track his mind had chosen with dogged determination. "I'll send a doctor along in the plane to check her out. The baby ought to be seen by a professional as soon as possible, anyway. I'm sure Luke did his best, but he's not a physician. Don't worry about a thing, Jessica. I'll have Doc Winchell at Luke's before nightfall. Then you can all come back together. We'll have you here in time for the party Mary has planned. It'll be a celebration to end all celebrations."

"But, Harlan, it's Christmas," Jessie argued. "You can't expect the doctor or the pilot to disrupt their plans with their families to make a trip like that."

"Of course I can," Harlan countered with the assurance of a man used to having his commands obeyed. "You just be ready. I'll call back when they're on their way. Put Lucas on."

Defeated, Jessie sighed. "I'll see if I can find him."

She took the phone she deeply regretted answering down the hall to Luke's office. She tapped on the door, then opened it. He was leaning back in his leather chair, staring out the window. There was something so lonely, so lost in his expression that her heart ached. If only he would let her into his life, then neither of them would be alone again.

"Luke, your parents are on the line," she said and held out the phone.

He searched her face for a moment, his expression unreadable. Finally, he took the phone and spoke to his father.

"She's fine, Daddy. The baby's fine. I'm sure it's not the way Jessie would have preferred to deliver her baby, but there were no complications. She came through like a real trooper. She was back on her feet in no time. And the baby's a little angel."

He closed his eyes and rubbed his temples. "No, Daddy, I'm sure Jessie hasn't been overdoing it. She knows her own strength." His expression hardened and his gaze cut to Jessie again. "No, she didn't mention that you were sending Doc Winchell. I'm sure she'll be relieved. Right. We'll be expecting him."

Most of Harlan's side of the conversation had been muffled, but Jessie heard him asking then if Luke intended to come to White Pines with her.

"No," Luke said brusquely. "I told Mother before that I have things to do here." His expression remained perfectly blank as he listened to whatever his father said next. Finally he said, "Yes, Merry Christmas to all of you, too. Give my best to Jordan and Cody."

He hung up the phone and turned back to the window. "Shouldn't you be packing?" he inquired quietly.

Tears welled up in Jessie's eyes. She hadn't expected him to be so stubborn. For some reason, she had thought when the time came, he would realize that he belonged at White Pines for the holidays every bit as much as she did. More so, in fact.

"I'm not leaving you here," she insisted.

He turned to confront her. "You don't have a choice. Harlan's taken it out of your hands. I told you that was exactly what would happen if you called him. It's for the best, anyway. It's time you were going."

"I didn't call. They called here." Jessie lost patience with the whole blasted macho clan of Adams men. "Oh, forget it. You can't bully me, any more than your father can. If I want to stay here, I'll stay here."

He regarded her evenly. "Even if I tell you that I want you to go?"

"Even then," she said, her chin tilted high.

"Why would you insist on staying someplace you aren't wanted?"

"Because I don't believe you don't want me here. I think you want me here too much," she retorted.

"You're dreaming, if you believe that," he said coldly.

Jessie's resolve almost wavered in the face of his stubborn, harsh refusal to admit his real feelings. "I guess that's the difference between us, then. I believe in you. I believe in *us*. You don't.''

''That's a significant difference, wouldn't you say?''

''It's only significant if you want it to be.''

''I do.''

A tear spilled over and tracked down her cheek. ''Damn you, Luke Adams.''

''You're too late, Jessie,'' he told her grimly. ''I was damned a long time ago.''

For all of her natural optimism, for all of her faith in what a future for the two of them could hold, Jessie couldn't stand up to that kind of bleak resignation.

''Angela and I will be gone before you know it,'' she said, fighting to hold back her tears as she finally admitted that she was defeated.

In the doorway she paused and looked back. ''One of these days you're going to regret forcing us out of your life, Luke. You're going to wake up and discover that you've turned into a bitter, lonely old man.''

That said, she straightened her spine and walked away from the man she'd come to love with all her heart.

Regrets? Luke was filled with them. They were chasing through his brain like pinballs bouncing erratically from one bumper to the next.

Was he doing the right thing? Of course, he was, he told himself firmly. He had to let Jessie go. He had to let her walk out of his life, taking the baby who'd stolen a little piece of his jaded heart with her. They weren't his to claim. They were Erik's and they were going home, where they belonged. They were going to a place where he no longer fit in.

He would have stayed right where he was, hidden away in his office, but Jessie was apparently determined to make him pay for forcing her out of his life. She appeared in the doorway of his office, bundled up, her long hair tucked into a knit cap, her cheeks rosy, either from anger or from a trek outdoors. He suspected the former.

"We're leaving," she announced unnecessarily.

Luke had seen Doc Winchell arrive in a fancy four-wheel-drive car a half hour earlier cutting a path through the fresh snow. He'd been expecting to see it driving away any minute now heading back to the airport. He'd been listening for the sound of the backdoor slamming shut behind them, then the roar of the car's engine. The silence had taunted him. Now, though, it seemed they were finally ready to go, and he was going to be forced to endure another goodbye.

"Have a safe trip," he said, refusing to meet her condemning gaze.

"Aren't you going to come and say goodbye to Angela?"

"No," he said curtly and felt his heart break.

"Lucas, please."

She didn't know what she was asking, that had

to be it, he decided as he finally got to his feet and followed her into the kitchen.

Doc Winchell, who'd been the family physician ever since Luke could recall, beamed at him. "Lucas, you did a fine job bringing this little one into the world. Couldn't have done better myself. We'll get her weighed and checked out from head to toe tomorrow, but she looks perfectly healthy to me."

Luke kept his gaze deliberately averted from the bundled-up baby. "She really is okay, then?"

"Perfect," the doctor confirmed.

"Being out in this weather won't hurt her?"

"The truck's heater works. She's wrapped up warmly. She'll be fine."

"What about flying?"

"It shouldn't be a problem and I'll be right there to keep an eye on her."

Luke nodded, his hands shoved in his pockets to keep from reaching out to hold the baby one last time. "Take good care of her, Doc. She's my first delivery." He grinned despite himself. "Hopefully, my last, too. I don't think I ever want to know that kind of fear again."

As if she sensed that Angela was his Achilles' heel, Jessie plucked the baby up and practically shoved her into Luke's arms. He had to accept her or allow her to tumble to the floor. One look into those trusting blue eyes and he felt his resolve weaken.

"Say goodbye, Angela," Jessie murmured beside him. "Uncle Luke isn't coming with us."

As if she understood her mother, Angela's face scrunched up. Her tiny lower lip trembled. Huge tears welled up in her eyes.

Luke rocked her gently. "Hey, little one, no tears, okay? Your Uncle Luke will always have a very special spot in his heart, just for you. You ever need anything, anything at all, you come to me, okay, sweet pea?"

As always, the sound of his voice soothed her. She cooed at him. His effect on her gave him a disconcerting sense of satisfaction. He felt as if his sorry existence meant something to somebody.

Jessie seemed to guess what he was feeling. Her gaze, filled with understanding and a kind of raw agony, was fixed on his face. Luke couldn't bear looking into her eyes. She knew too well why he was pushing them away. He looked back at Angela's precious little face instead.

"Goodbye, sweet pea. You take good care of your mommy, okay?"

He held the baby out until Jessie finally had no choice but to claim her.

"Goodbye, Lucas," she said, her voice laced with all the regret he was feeling. "I will never, ever forget what you did for us."

He wanted to tell her it was nothing, but he couldn't seem to force the words past the lump lodged in his throat. He just nodded.

Jessie reached up then and touched her hand to his cheek, silently commanding him to look at her.

When he did, she said softly, "If you ever, *ever* change your mind, I'll be waiting."

"Don't wait too long," he warned. "Don't waste your life waiting for something that can never be."

For an instant he thought she was going to protest, but finally she sighed deeply and turned away. She walked out the kitchen door and never looked back.

It was just as well, Luke thought as he watched her. He would have hated like hell for her to see that he was crying.

Chapter Ten

The commotion caused by their arrival at White Pines was almost more than Jessie could bear, given her already-confused and deeply hurt state of mind.

Harlan gave Doc Winchell the third degree about the baby's health. Mary claimed Angela the minute Jessie set foot across the threshold. Jordan and Cody studied the new baby with fascination, offering observations on which family members she most resembled. A handful of strangers, visiting for the holiday, chimed in.

They had almost nothing beyond the courtesies to say to Jessie, and not one of them asked about Luke. It was hardly surprising, she concluded, that he had refused to set foot in the house at White Pines.

As she stood apart and watched them, Jessie couldn't help wondering why she'd once wanted so desperately to be a part of this family. It suddenly seemed to her that she'd mistaken chaos and boisterous outbursts for love.

Of course, back then she'd had Erik as a buffer. He'd seen to it that she was never left out of the conversation. He'd insisted that she be treated with respect. She had basked in his attention and barely noticed anyone else.

Except Luke.

Thinking of him now, all alone again on his ranch, she regretted more than ever leaving him, despite his cantankerous behavior. She should have risen above it. She should have listened to her heart.

Suddenly she couldn't stand all the fussing for another instant. Reaching for Angela, she startled them all by announcing that the baby was tired from the trip and needed to be put down for a nap. To her astonishment, no one argued. She would have to remember that tone of voice for the next time someone in the family tried to steamroll over her.

"I found an old crib in the attic," Mary said at once. "I had Jordan set it up in your old suite. As soon as the rest of the roads have cleared and it's safer to drive, we'll go into town for baby clothes and new sheets and blankets. In the meantime, I've had Maritza wash a few things I saved from when the boys were babies."

Jessie fought a grin as she tried to imagine sexy, irrepressible Cody, the tall, self-assured Jordan or

Luke ever being as tiny as Angela was now. "Thank you," she said. "I'm sure we'll be fine."

Cody separated himself from the others as she started up the stairs. "How is Luke?" he asked, walking along with her. Lines of worry were etched in his brow that she was sure hadn't been there mere months before. He was only twenty-seven, but he seemed older, wearier than he had when she'd left.

"Stubborn as a mule," she said. "Lonely."

"Why didn't he come with you?"

Jessie met Cody's concerned gaze and gave him the only part of the real answer she could. The rest was private, just between her and Luke. She couldn't say he was staying away because of her. "Because he blames himself for Erik's death, and he thinks the rest of you do, too."

Cody couldn't have looked more shocked if she'd announced that Luke was locked away at home with a harem.

"But that's crazy," he blurted at once. "We all know what happened was an accident. Nobody blames Luke. Hell, if anybody was at fault it was Daddy. He's the one who backed Erik into a corner and made him try to be something he wasn't. Any one of us could have taken a spill on that tractor. Accidents happen all the time on a ranch."

Jessie couldn't have agreed with him more, but she was startled that Cody recognized the truth. Of all of them, he had always seemed to be the least introspective. Cody seemed imperturbable, the one most inclined to roll with the punches. She'd always thought he accepted things at face value, including Harlan's own view of himself as omnipotent. Obviously she'd fallen into the trap of viewing him merely as the baby in the family. The truth was he'd grown into a caring, thoughtful man.

"That's what I tried to tell Luke, but the accident didn't happen here. It happened on his land. He seems to think he should have prevented it somehow." She looked into Cody's worried eyes. "Talk to him. Maybe you can get him to see reason. I couldn't."

Cody looked doubtful. "Jessie, if you couldn't reach him, I don't see how I can. You were always able to communicate with him, even when the rest of us were ready to give up in frustration."

Jessie sighed. "Well, not this time."

At the doorway to the suite she had shared with Erik she paused. Cody leaned down and brushed a light kiss across her cheek. "I'm glad you're back, Jessie. We've missed you around here. I think the last ounce of serenity around this place vanished the day you left."

She was startled by the sweet assessment of her importance to this household where she'd always felt like an interloper. "Thanks, Cody. Saying that is the nicest gift anyone could have given me."

He grinned. "Don't say that until you've opened those packages downstairs. Something tells me everyone's gone overboard in anticipation of your return and the arrival of the baby.'' He winked at her. "One thing this family is very good at is bribery.''

"Bribery?''

"So you'll stay, of course. You don't think Daddy will be one bit happy about his first grand-baby growing up halfway across the state. He's go-ing to want to supervise everything from cradle to college. Hell, he'll probably try to handpick her husband for her. Just be sure he doesn't make her part of some business deal.''

Before Jessie could react to that, Cody was al-ready thundering down the stairs again.

"Cody, for heaven's sakes, remember where the dickens you are,'' Harlan bellowed from some-where downstairs.

"I'm just in a hurry to get another slice of Maritza's pie,'' Cody shouted back, unrepentant.

"No more pie until dinner,'' Mary called out. "There won't be a bit left for the rest of us.''

"Mother, Maritza's been baking for a month,'' Cody retorted. "There must be enough pies in the kitchen to feed half of Texas. You've only invited a quarter of the state at last count. One slice won't be missed.''

Jessie stood for a moment longer, listening to the once-familiar bickering and decided that this, too, was what it meant to be part of a family. Somehow, though, with neither Erik nor Luke here the atmo-sphere had lost something vital—its warmth.

Feeling thoughtful and a little lonely, she opened

the door to her suite, took a deep breath…and walked back into her past.

The house was empty. Luke found himself wandering from room to room, hating the oppressive silence, hating the sense of loneliness that he'd never noticed before. He'd always been a self-contained man. Hell, any cowboy worth his salt could spend days on end in the middle of nowhere, content with his own thoughts.

Suddenly he didn't like his own company all that much. In a few short days, he'd grown used to Jessie invading his space at unexpected moments. He'd come to look forward to his own private time with Angela, their one-sided conversations, her sober, trusting gaze.

He stood at the doorway to his own bedroom and tried to force himself to cross the threshold. For some idiotic reason, he felt as if he were trespassing on Jessie's private space, rather than reclaiming his own.

She'd left the room spotless, far neater than it had been when she'd arrived. The bed had been made up with fresh sheets. He knew because he'd heard the washing machine and dryer running and investigated. He'd found sheets and towels in the dryer, a load of his clothes in the washer.

He sighed. He almost wished she had left the old sheets on. Perhaps then, when he finally crawled back into that lonely bed of his, he might have been surrounded by her scent. Now, he knew, it would smell only of impersonal laundry detergent and the too-sweet fabric softener.

As he stood there he caught the glint of something gold on the nightstand beside the bed. The last rays of sunshine spilled through the window and made the metal gleam, beckoning him. Instinctively he knew whatever it was, it wasn't his. Puzzled, he crossed the room to see what Jessie had left behind.

Even before he reached the nightstand, he realized what it was: a ring. Her wedding ring. His heart skipped a beat at the sight of it. He picked up the simple gold band and let it rest in the palm of his hand. Even though he knew what it said, he read the engraved message inside: Erik and Jessica—For Eternity.

What had she been thinking? he wondered. She must have taken it off when she was cleaning and simply forgotten it, he decided because he wasn't sure he wanted to consider any other implications. He didn't want to believe that she'd been deliberately making a statement, leaving him an unmistakable message that would force him to act or forever damn himself for his inaction.

Eventually he pocketed the ring and returned to the kitchen and poured himself a cup of coffee. He put the ring on the table in front of him as he sipped the rank brew that had been left since morning.

What the devil was he supposed to do now? He could mail it to her at White Pines. Unfortunately, the arrival of her wedding ring in the mail might stir up a hornet's nest, if anyone in the family happened to notice. Heaven knew what interpretation they might place on her leaving it behind. He hadn't even figured out his own interpretation of its significance.

If an outsider saw him, he'd think Luke had lost his mind, Luke acknowledged dryly. He was studying that tiny ring as if it were a poisonous snake, coiled to strike. The truth was, though, that the ring's presence in his bedroom was every bit as dangerous as any rattler he'd ever encountered.

"Seems to me like there are two choices here," he finally muttered, his gaze fixed on the gold band. "Send it off and quit worrying about it or call her up and ask what the devil she had in mind. Sitting here trying to make sense of it isn't accomplishing a blessed thing."

It was also leading him to talk to himself, he noted ruefully.

He carried the coffee and the ring into his office, where he'd left the cellular phone. He sat behind his desk for several minutes, trying to figure out what he could say that wouldn't make him look like an idiot. Finally he just dialed the damn number, taking a chance that Jessie would be in her old suite and that it would still have the private line Erik had had installed. She answered on the first ring.

"Jessie?"

There was the faintest hesitation before she asked, "Lucas? Is that you?"

Something inside him suddenly felt whole again

at the sound of her voice. It was a sensation that probably should have worried him more than it did. "Yeah, it's me," he confirmed. "How was your flight? Any problems?"

"No, everything went smoothly. Angela never even woke up."

"That's good. I imagine everyone there made quite a fuss when they saw her."

"That's an understatement," she said. "According to Cody, your father will probably want to plan out her entire life, up to and including her choice of a husband."

Luke found himself laughing at the accuracy of his youngest brother's assessment. "Listen to him. He has the old man pegged."

That said, he suddenly fell silent.

"Luke?"

"Yes."

"Was that all you wanted, to see if we'd arrived okay?"

He sighed. "No." Without quite realizing that he'd reached a decision on his approach, he blurted out, "Actually, I wanted to let you know that you'd forgotten your wedding ring. You must have taken it off when you were cleaning or something."

"I didn't forget it," she said, a note of determination in her voice.

Her response left him stymied. "Oh," he said and then fell silent again, struggling with the possibilities, fighting a flare of hope he had no business at all feeling. Finally he asked, "Why, Jessie?"

"Think about it, Lucas," she said softly and he could almost see her smiling. "You're a bright man. You'll figure it out."

"Jessie…"

"Goodbye, Luke. Merry Christmas."

She hung up before he could get in another word. He sat staring stupidly at the phone in his hand. He closed his eyes and wished with all his heart that he'd gone to the Caribbean for the holidays. Or maybe taken a trip to Australia. Or even the South Pole.

Then he remembered that Jessie would have found the house empty when she'd gone into labor on the highway. Who knew what might have happened then. He couldn't regret having been here for her. No matter how much pain his feelings for her caused him in the future, he couldn't regret these few days they'd had.

He just had to figure out how to make them last a lifetime.

Jessie gently placed the telephone receiver back in its cradle and turned to the wide-awake baby on the bed beside her.

"That was your Uncle Luke," she whispered, unable to keep a grin from spreading across her face. Just hearing his voice made her pulse do unexpected somersaults.

Angela understood. Jessie was absolutely certain of it. She waved her little fist in the air approvingly.

"How long do you figure it's going to take him to show up here?" Jessie wondered aloud.

She was far more confident now that he would turn up than she had been when she'd ridden away from his ranch with Doc Winchell. Leaving her own car there had been her ace in the hole. If Luke didn't make the trip to White Pines, after all, she knew she could always go back to get her car and have one last chance at making him see what they could have together.

She rolled onto her back, only to have her wedding picture catch her eye. It was still sitting on the dresser, just as it had while she and Erik had lived in this suite.

"You understand, don't you?" she whispered with certainty. "You've forgiven Luke and me for falling in love and that's all that really matters."

A soft tap on her door quieted her. "Jessie?" Mary called softly. "We'll be serving dinner in half an hour."

"I'll be right down," she promised.

"Bring the baby. I've found a carrier for her. I'll leave it outside the door."

"Thanks, Mary."

Jessie listened as her mother-in-law's footsteps faded, then she glanced down at her daughter. "Showtime, angel. It's time to go and dazzle your family."

The baby waved her arms energetically, an indication that she was more than ready for anything the Adams clan had in mind for her—now or in the future. Jessie wished she could say the same.

She had no sooner reached the bottom step, when Jordan appeared to take the carrier from her. At thirty, he was a successful businessman, one of the few to weather the Texas oil crisis and come out ahead. He was considered one of the state's most eligible catches, but he had remained amazingly immune to any of the women who chased after him.

"You look lovely, Jessie." He glanced down into the carrier, his expression faintly nervous as if he weren't too sure what to do with a baby. He seemed worried she might be breakable. "Everyone's anxious to see the newest addition to the family."

Jessie hesitated. "By everyone, I assume you mean that this isn't just a family celebration tonight."

Jordan's mouth quirked in a grin that reminded her so much of Luke, she felt her heart stop.

"Nope. The usual cast of thousands," he said. He leaned down and whispered, "Stick close to me and I'll protect you from the multitudes."

"And what about your own date?" she whispered right back. "I know perfectly well you must have one here. I've never seen you without a beautiful woman on your arm."

A flicker of something that might have been sadness darkened his eyes for just an instant, before his ready smile settled firmly back in place.

"I decided even I deserved a night off," he replied.

"Tired of small talk?" Jessie asked.

"Tired of all of it," he admitted. When Jessie would have questioned him further about whether this indicated an end to his days as Houston's most available playboy, he prevented it by taking her arm and propelling her into a room already crowded with guests.

"Behold the heir apparent," he announced, holding the baby carrier aloft as everyone applauded. That said, he seemed only too anxious to turn the baby over to the first person who asked to hold her. He wandered off without a second glance, his duty done.

For the second time since her arrival at White Pines, Jessie was gently shunted aside by people anxious to get a glimpse of the newborn. She heard the story of her being stranded at Luke's ranch told over and over. She heard her own bravery magnified time and again.

What she never heard, though, was any mention of Luke's incredible role in any of it. Just when she was prepared to climb halfway up the stairs and demand that everyone listen to her version of the events, Harlan folded a strong arm around her shoulders and called for silence.

"A toast," he announced. "Everybody have some champagne?"

Glasses were lifted into the air all around them.

"To Jessie and Angela," he said. "Welcome home."

The toast echoed around the room, as heartfelt from strangers as it was from the family. Even so, the welcome left Jessie feeling oddly empty. White Pines no longer felt like home. What saddened her more was that she wasn't sure whether it was the loss of Erik or the absence of Luke that made her feel that way.

When the cheers had died down, Harlan announced that the buffet supper was ready. The guests moved swiftly into the huge dining room to claim their plates and a sampling of the food that Jessie knew Maritza and the rest of the staff had been preparing for weeks now. She recalled from past years how bountiful and diverse the spread would be, but her own appetite failed her.

She surveyed the room until she finally spotted Cody holding her daughter and went to join them.

"I'll take her," she offered. "Go on and have your dinner."

Cody grinned. "I don't mind. I'm practicing my technique. I figure if I can charm 'em when they're this little, I'll have no problems with the grown-up ladies."

"Well, Angela's certainly fascinated," Jessie agreed as she observed her daughter's fist tangled in Cody's moustache. The baby tugged enthusiastically and Cody winced, but he didn't give her up. He simply disengaged her fingers as he chattered utter nonsense to her. Like Luke, he seemed totally natural and unselfconscious with the infant in his arms.

"You might have to work on your conversational skills," Jessie teased, after listening to him.

"You're not the first woman to tell me that," he admitted with a wicked grin that probably silenced most women on the spot, anyway. Jessie was immune to it, but she found herself amused by his inability to curb the tendency to flirt with any female in sight.

"I guess it's what comes from spending most of my days with a herd of cows," he added. "They're not too demanding."

"And what about Melissa?" she inquired, referring to the young woman who'd been head over heels in love with Cody practically since the cradle. "Is she too demanding?"

Cody's eyes lit up at the mention of the woman everyone assumed he would one day marry, if he ever managed to settle down at all. "Melissa hangs on my every word," he said confidently.

The touch of arrogance might have annoyed some people, but Jessie knew that Cody's ego wasn't his problem. The young man was simply a textbook case of a man who was commitment phobic. Melissa had contributed to the problem by wearing her heart on her sleeve for so long. Cody tended to take her for granted, certain she would be waiting whenever he got around to asking her to marry him.

One day, though, either Melissa or some other

woman was going to turn Cody inside out. Jessie smiled as she envisioned the havoc that would stir.

"What are you grinning about?" Cody asked.

"Just imagining how hard your fall is going to be when it comes. Yours and Jordan's."

"Won't be any worse than Erik's," he teased. "Or Luke's," he added, shooting her a sly look.

Jessie swallowed hard. "Luke's?" she said, feigning confusion.

"I'm not blind, Jessie. Neither is anyone else around here, for that matter. Why do you think they were so appalled when they realized where you were when you had the baby? Luke never did have much of a poker face."

She was stunned. "What are you saying?"

"That my big brother is crazy in love with you. Always has been. Luke may be the strong, silent type, but he's transparent as can be where you're concerned."

Even as her heart leapt with joy at his confirmation of her own gut-deep assessment of Luke's feelings, Jessie denied Cody's claim. "You're wrong," she insisted.

Cody shook his head, clearly amused by her protest. "I'm not wrong. Why do you think he's not here?"

"I explained that earlier. It's because he's feeling guilty about Erik's death."

"He's feeling guilty, all right, but it's not because of Erik's death. At least, that's only part of it,'' he told her emphatically. ''Luke's all twisted up inside because he's in love with Erik's widow.''

Jessie practically snatched Angela out of Cody's arms. When she would have run from the room, when she would have hidden from Cody's words, he stopped her with a touch.

''Please, Jessie, I didn't mean to upset you. I, for one, think it would be terrific if you and Luke got together. Erik's gone. We can't wish him back. And if you and Luke can find some kind of happiness together, then I say go for it. Jordan agrees with me. He seems to be looking for happy endings these days. Don't say I told you but I think the confirmed bachelor is getting restless,'' he confided. ''He needs you and Luke to set an example for him.''

Once more, Cody had startled her, not just with his assessment of the undercurrents that she thought had been so well hidden in the past, but with his blessing.

''I don't know what the future holds,'' she said quietly, the words as close to an admission about her own feelings as she could make. ''But I will always be grateful to you for speaking to me so honestly.''

Cody draped an arm around her shoulders and squeezed. ''Hey, Luke might be stubborn as a mule, but he is my big brother. I want him to be happy. As for you, the whole family lucked out when Erik found you. We want to keep you. And there's Angela to think of,'' he said, touching a finger gently to the baby's cheek. "She deserves a daddy and I think Luke would make a damned fine one."

Only after he had walked away did Jessie whisper, "So do I, Cody. So do I."

Chapter Eleven

Luke could see only one way to push Jessie out of his life once and for all. If she had chosen Erik because she wanted a family to call her own, if she clung to him now for the same reason, then he would give her one. Not his, but her own. Her biological family.

He'd been awake half the night formulating his plan. First thing in the morning on the day after Christmas, he was on the phone to a private investigator he'd used once when he'd suspected a neighbor of doing a little cattle rustling from his herd. He supposed finding a long-lost family couldn't be much trickier than tracing missing cattle.

"Her adoptive family's name was Garnett,"

Luke told James Hill, dredging up the surname from his memory of the first time Jessie had been introduced to the family, practically on the eve of the wedding. Erik hadn't risked exposing her to too many of his father's tantrums or too many of his mother's interrogations. It was probably one of his brother's wisest decisions. Jessie might have fled, if she'd realized exactly what she was getting into. The surface charm of the family disintegrated under closer inspection.

"What else can you tell me about her?" Hill asked.

"What do you mean?"

"Where was she born? Where did she grow up? Her birth date? Anything like that?"

Luke listened to the list and saw his scheme going up in flames. For the first time he realized how very little he actually knew about Jessie. He'd fallen in love with the woman she was now. It had never crossed his mind that he might want to be acquainted with the child she had been or the lonely teenager who'd longed to discover her real family.

"I don't know," he confessed finally.

"You'll have to find out something or it'll be a waste of my time and your money," the private investigator informed him. "With what you're giving me, I can't even narrow the search down to Texas."

Luke sighed. "I appreciate the honesty. I'll see what I can find out and call you back. Thanks, Jim."

"No problem. If I don't talk to you before, have a Happy New Year, Luke."

"Same to you," he said, but his mind was already far away, grappling with various ideas for getting the information he needed about Jessie without her finding out what he was up to. He didn't want her disappointed if he failed to find answers for her.

To his deep regret, he could see right off that there was only one way. He would have to follow her to White Pines. The only way he could ask his questions was face-to-face, dropping them into the conversation one at a time over several days so she wouldn't add them up and suspect his plan. If the thought of seeing her again made his palms sweat and his heart race, he refused to admit that his reaction to the prospect of seeing her had anything at all to do with his decision to go. The trip was an expediency, nothing more.

For the second time that morning, Luke made a call he'd never in a million years anticipated making.

"Hey, Daddy, it's Luke."

"Hey, son, how are you?" Harlan asked as matter-of-factly as if Luke initiated calls to White Pines all the time. If he was startled by Luke's call, he hid it well.

"I'm fine."

"What's up?"

He drew in a deep breath and finally forced himself to ask, "Can you send the plane for me? I'm coming home."

Dead silence greeted the announcement, and for the space of a heartbeat Luke thought he'd made a terrible mistake in calling, rather than just showing up. It had been less than twenty-four hours since he'd flatly declared he wouldn't be coming to White Pines. If his father started one of his typical, if somewhat justifiable, cross-examinations, Luke didn't have any answers he was willing to share. He waited, unconsciously holding his breath, to see how his father would handle this latest development in their uneasy relationship.

"I'll have the plane there in an hour," his father said finally. It was as though he'd struggled with himself and decided to give his son a break for once.

Luke heaved a sigh of relief. "Thanks."

"No problem," Harlan said. He paused, then added, "But if you go and change your mind on me, though, I'm warning you that you'll pay for the fuel."

Luke laughed at the predictable threat, relieved by it. Obviously Harlan hadn't mellowed that much. "That's what I love about you, Daddy. You never allow sentiment to cloud your thinking about the bottom line."

By the time Jessie got downstairs for breakfast on the morning after Christmas, only Mary remained at the table. She looked as stylish and per-

fectly coiffed as she had the night before, despite
the fact she couldn't have had more than a few
hours sleep.

Last night, surrounded by family and old friends,
by the famous and the powerful, she had been in
her element. She was equally at ease at the head of
the table with only her daughter-in-law to impress.
Jessie found that polish and carefully cultivated
class a bit intimidating.

Her reaction to Mary Adams had a lot to do with
the older woman's unconscious sense of style. In
fact, Jessie couldn't ever recall seeing Erik's mother
in anything more casual than wool slacks, a silk
blouse and oodles of gold jewelry. Nor had she ever
seen her with a single frosted hair out of place.
Mary eyed Jessie's jeans and pale blue maternity
sweater with obvious dismay.

"We must take you shopping," she announced,
without a clue that her expression or her innuendo
were insulting.

"I have plenty of clothes," Jessie protested.
"Unfortunately, the baby arrived before I'd
planned, so I didn't bring anything except maternity
clothes along. The pants can be pinned to fit well
enough."

"Not to worry," Mary said cheerfully. "I'll ask
Harlan if the plane's free. The pilot can take us over
to Dallas for the day. We can shop the after-
Christmas sales at Neiman-Marcus. I have half a
dozen things that I need to return and you certainly

won't be needing those new maternity outfits we gave you now.''

She shook her head, an expression of tolerant amusement on her face as she confided, ''Harlan hasn't gotten my size right once in all the years we've been married. I've become used to these post-holiday exchanges.''

Jessie tried again. ''Maybe another day,'' she said a little more forcefully. Deliberately changing the subject, she asked, ''Where are Jordan and Cody this morning?''

''Jordan's already flown back to Houston. He had business to attend to, or so he claimed. He's probably chasing after some new woman. I think Cody is off somewhere with his father,'' she said without interest.

She regarded Jessie thoughtfully. ''That shade of blue isn't quite right for you. I believe something darker, perhaps a lovely royal blue, would be perfect with your eyes.''

Jessie had been so certain she'd ended the subject of the shopping excursion. Apparently she hadn't. ''I'm not sure I have the energy yet to keep up with you,'' she confessed as a last resort.

Finally something she'd said penetrated Mary's self-absorbed planning.

''Oh, my goodness, what was I thinking?'' Mary said, looking chagrined. ''Of course, you must be exhausted. I remember when the boys were born, I didn't even leave the hospital for a week and here it's only been a few days since Angela was born.

How on earth are you managing? Young women today are much more blasé about these things than my generation was.''

Since Mary's question seemed to be rhetorical and she appeared to have fallen deep into thought, Jessie concentrated on spreading jam on her perfectly toasted English muffin. She'd once wondered if the kitchen staff at White Pines had been told to toss out any that weren't an even shade of golden brown. Her own success was considerably more limited. She burned as many as she got right in the old toaster she had in her apartment.

''A nanny,'' Mary announced triumphantly, capturing Jessie's full attention with the out-of-the-blue remark.

''A nanny?'' Jessie repeated cautiously.

''For Angela.''

She'd hoped for a new tangent, but this one was pretty extreme even for Mary. ''Please, it's not necessary,'' she said firmly. ''I can take care of the baby perfectly well. Besides, you couldn't possibly find anyone on such short notice. And I'll be going back home next week, anyway.''

''Nonsense,'' Mary said dismissively. ''You'll be staying right here.''

When Jessie started to argue, Mary's expression turned intractable. It was a toss-up whether Luke and the others had gotten their stubborn streaks from Harlan or their mother. The combined gene pool was enough to make Jessie shudder with dread.

"I won't take no for an answer," Mary said just as firmly. "Even if you insist on going back to that tiny little apartment and that silly job eventually, you have to take a few weeks of maternity leave. You'll spend it right here, where we can look after you."

Jessie bristled at having the life she'd made for herself dismissed so casually, but she bit her tongue. She honestly hadn't given any thought to the fact that she was entitled to maternity leave. It was on her list of things to worry about closer to the baby's arrival. Angela had thrown that timetable completely off.

"I don't know how much time I'm entitled to," she admitted.

"I believe I've heard six weeks is the norm," Mary said distractedly, jotting herself a note on the pad she always had at hand at breakfast for writing down the day's chores. She dispensed them to the staff as merrily as if they were checks. They weren't always received in quite the same spirit, but Jessie doubted if Mary noticed that.

Her mother-in-law glanced up from her notes. "Of course, three months would be better. Why don't I have Harlan call your boss and make the arrangements?" She made another note.

The thought of Harlan Adams negotiating anything with her boss gave Jessie chills. "Absolutely not. I'll make the call later today. After that I suppose we can talk more about how long I'm staying."

She gazed directly at Mary and tried to recall the precise tone of voice she'd used so successfully the evening before. "But no nanny. It wouldn't be fair to hire someone and then turn right around and fire them again."

"Well, of course not," Mary agreed far too readily. "We'll send her home with you. It will be our gift."

Jessie felt as if she were losing control of her life. "You said yourself that my apartment is tiny. When you visited, you complained you could barely turn around in it. It can hardly accommodate a live-in nanny."

Mary didn't even bat an eye at that complication. "Then we'll find you someplace larger," she said at once. She picked up her cup of tea. "If you decide to go back, of course."

"I thought we had settled that," Jessie began, then sighed. Clearly she would be better off saving this particular fight for another day. She didn't have the strength for it this morning. She stood. "I think I'll go back up and check on Angela."

"No need, Jessica. I believe Maritza's sister is sitting with her now."

She had married into a household of control freaks, Jessie decided, fighting her annoyance. Erik had quite likely been the only one in the group whose personality didn't demand that he take charge of every single situation. She had learned her lesson from observing him, though. If she didn't stand up to them, they would dismiss her opinions and her plans as no more than a minor nuisance.

"There's no need for her to stay with the baby," she told Mary forcefully. "I have a few letters to write this morning and some calls to make, so I'll be with her."

With that she turned and headed for the stairs, fully expecting yet another argument. For once, though, Mary was silent. Well, almost silent, Jessie amended. She thought she heard her mother-in-law sigh dramatically the instant she thought Jessie was out of earshot.

Back in her suite, she found a beautiful, young Mexican woman sitting right beside Angela's crib. Apparently she had taken her instructions to watch the baby quite literally, because she didn't even look away when Jessie entered the room.

"Buenos dias," Jessie said to her.

The young woman glanced her way and smiled shyly.

"Do you speak English?" Jessie asked.

"Yes."

"What's your name?"

"Lara Mendoza."

"Lara, thank you for looking after the baby. I'll stay with her now."

Lara seemed alarmed by the dismissal. "But it is my pleasure, *señora.* It is as Señora Adams wishes."

Jessie bit back a sharp retort. "It's not necessary,'' she insisted gently. ''I'll call for you, if I need you, Lara.''

Lara's sigh was every bit as heavy as the one Jessie had heard Mary utter. Apparently she was testing everyone's patience this morning.

Still, she had to admit that she was relieved to be on her own. Perhaps the decision to come to White Pines had been a bad one, after all. All of the things she'd hated most—the control, the dismissal of her opinions, the hints of disapproval— were coming back to her now.

She realized that for all of her hopes and dreams when she'd married Erik, this still wasn't her family. Jordan and Cody seemed to like her well enough. Even Harlan appeared to be fond of her. But Mary was another story. Every time her mother-in-law addressed her, Jessie couldn't help concluding that the older woman found her sadly wanting.

Suddenly she was filled with a terrible sense of despondency. Perhaps there was no place she really belonged anymore, not here and certainly not with Luke. He'd made that clear enough. Perhaps it was time she accepted the fact that she and Angela were going to have to make it entirely on their own.

A tap on the door interrupted her maudlin thoughts. She eyed the door suspiciously. She didn't think she could take another run-in with Mary just yet.

''Who is it?'' she called softly, hoping not to wake the baby.

"Open the door and find out," a masculine voice said.

The sound of that unmistakable voice gave her goose bumps. She practically ran to fling open the door, relieved and elated by his timely arrival.

"Luke," she cried and propelled herself into his arms without considering his reaction.

Despite his startled grunt of surprise at her actions, he folded his arms around her and held her close. Suddenly she no longer felt nearly so alone. Breathing in the familiar masculine scent of him, crushed against his solid chest, she felt warm and protected and cherished. Those feelings might be illusions, but for now she basked in them.

After what seemed far too brief a time, Luke gently disengaged her and stepped back just far enough to examine her from head to toe. His expression hardened, as if something he saw angered him. She couldn't imagine what it could be.

"What's this?" he demanded, rubbing at the dampness on her cheeks. "What's wrong, Jessie?"

Jessie hadn't even been aware that she'd been crying before his arrival. Or maybe they were tears of joy at seeing him. Or perhaps simply the overly emotional tears of a woman who'd just given birth. She couldn't say. She just knew that at this moment she had never been more grateful to see someone in her life.

"Jessie? What's going on?" he asked as he led her away from the door and shut it behind him. A worried frown puckered his brow as he waited with obvious impatience for answers. "What has my family done to you now?"

"Nothing," she said. "Everything. Oh, Luke, they're taking over. I'm trying so damned hard not to let them. I am not a weak woman. You know that."

"No mistake about it," he agreed.

Jessie barely noticed the sudden return of a twinkle in his eye. She was too caught up in trying to explain her frustration. "But they're bulldozing right over me," she said, giving full vent to her exasperation. "They don't listen to a word I say. They don't even hear me."

To her astonishment, Luke chuckled. "Darlin', that's nothing to get all stressed out about. That's just Mother and Dad. Talk louder and stand your ground. Sooner or later, they'll get the message."

Jessie recognized the wisdom of his advice. She'd even seen how well it worked in action. She'd just lost her strength to fight there for a minute. She gazed up at Luke, tears still shimmering in her eyes, and offered a watery grin. "Quite a welcome, huh?"

He grinned. "Can't say I've ever minded having a woman hurl herself into my arms," he teased.

His gaze captured hers and held. Suddenly the teasing light in his eyes died out, replaced by something far more serious, something far more compelling. Jessie's breath snagged in her throat.

"Luke," she began huskily, then cleared her throat and tried again. "Luke, what are you doing here? Yesterday you flat-out refused to come. Did something change your mind?'' She thought of the ring she'd left behind and the odd call he'd made the day before when he'd discovered it.

''I suppose you could say I came to take the pressure off you.''

She regarded him uncertainly. It wasn't exactly the response she'd been anticipating. ''In what way?''

He shrugged. ''With me around, Daddy will be so busy trying to take charge of my life again, he won't have time to go messin' in yours.''

''That's what you think,'' she said dismally. ''Harlan could fiddle with the lives of an entire army platoon without missing a beat. As for your mother...'' She sighed heavily.

Luke grinned. ''Don't I just know it,'' he said, matching her sigh with apparent deliberation. ''Maybe we should both just hide out in here for the duration.''

An intriguing idea, Jessie thought. She was stunned, however, that Luke had suggested it, even in jest. Or, perhaps that was the point. Perhaps he intended to tease and taunt her as he might a younger sister, robbing her of any notions that he thought of her in any kind of sexual way. She searched his gaze for answers, but whatever emotions had been swirling there a moment before had given way to pure amusement.

''I have an idea,'' he said. His voice had dropped to a daring, conspiratorial note.

"What?" she asked suspiciously.

"I saw this very bored young woman sitting right outside your door. I have a feeling she would be more than glad to baby-sit for a bit."

Jessie rolled her eyes. Obviously Lara had decided to stay within shouting distance. "I'll bet," she muttered. "She's there under orders from your mother."

Luke chuckled. "Don't look a gift horse in the mouth. Let's let Lara do her thing. You and I can go to lunch."

"I just ate breakfast," Jessie protested.

"Obviously you haven't noticed the roads into town. By the time we get there, it will definitely be lunchtime."

"Won't your family be expecting you to eat lunch here? Have you even seen your father or mother yet? Or Cody?"

"Not hide nor hair of them. I snuck in the back way," he admitted. "You can help me keep it that way a little longer. Are you game?"

Jessie would have hopped a bus to nowhere if it would have gotten her away from White Pines for a little while, long enough to get back her equilibrium. A trip into town with Luke sounded perfect.

"You tell Lara," she said. "I'll get my coat."

As he started toward the door of the suite, Jessie called after him, "Luke?"

He glanced back.

"I don't have any idea what really brought you here, but I'm very glad you came."

An oddly wistful expression came over his face for an instant. It was gone in a heartbeat.

"Maybe I just heard your prayers for a knight in shining armor," he taunted. "My armor's a bit tarnished, but I can still stand up to a common enemy."

Hearing him expressing the view of Harlan and Mary that she'd been thinking to herself only a short time earlier made Jessie feel suddenly guilty. For all of their bossiness, they had always been kind to her. The huge pile of Christmas presents stacked in the corner—everything from a silver teething ring to a car seat for the baby, from a golden locket to a filmy negligee and robe for her—attested to their generosity.

"They're not that bad," she countered.

"Don't need a hero, huh? Want me to head on home, then?"

Jessie had the feeling he would be only too relieved to comply. For a multitude of reasons, she wasn't sure she could bear it if he left.

She leveled a challenging glare at him. "Just try it, Lucas. You'll have to walk through me."

He winked at her. "An interesting idea."

That wink stirred ideas in Jessie that could have gotten her arrested in some parts of the world, she was sure. Harlan and Mary would certainly have been scandalized by her thoughts. She grabbed her coat before she was tempted to act on any one of them.

As if he'd read her mind, Luke inquired lazily, "In a hurry, darlin'?"

"You have no idea," she replied in a choked voice.

"Oh, I'll bet I do." He touched a finger lightly to her lips. "Hold those thoughts."

Jessie had no problem at all complying with that rather surprising request. She doubted she could have banished them with a solid whack by a crowbar. What she couldn't comprehend to save her soul was why Luke had suddenly taken it into his head to torment her like this. Whatever his reasons, though, she intended to make the most of his presence.

He might walk away from her and from White Pines eventually, but if he went this time it wouldn't be without putting up the fight of his life for his heart. Jessie intended to claim it, this time for good.

Chapter Twelve

Luke was having a great deal of difficulty remembering what it was that had originally brought him to White Pines. Sitting across from Jessie in a booth at Rosa's Mexican Café, his mind kept wandering to that desperate, hungry kiss they had shared in his truck. Just thinking about it aroused him. She had been hot and yielding in his arms, every bit as passionate as he'd ever imagined.

Now, as he watched her gasp with each bite of Rosa's lethally hot salsa, he was just as fascinated by her passion for the spicy food. Her eyes watered. Sweat beaded on her brow. He thought she had never been more appealing, though he wondered if she was going to survive the meal.

"They have a milder version," he said, taking pity on her.

She waved off the offer. "This is delicious," she said as she grabbed her glass of water and gulped most of it down before reaching for another chip and loading it with the salsa. "The best Mexican food I've ever had. I wonder why Erik never brought me here."

Luke didn't have an answer to that, but he couldn't help being glad that they were sharing her first experience with Rosa's Café, a place he'd always preferred to the fanciest restaurants in the state. Rosa, yet another of Consuela's distant cousins, had been bossing him around since his first visit years before. Coming here felt almost more like coming home than going to White Pines. He was delighted that Jessie liked it.

In fact, he was discovering that he was captivated by her reactions to everything. It seemed to him that in many ways Jessie took a child's innocent delight in all of her surroundings. Her responses to the simplest pleasures gave him a whole new perspective on the world, as well. Each time he was with her, his jaded heart healed a bit. Each time she chipped away at his resolve not to get more deeply involved with his brother's widow.

Remembering his resolve reminded him at last of why he'd broken his vow never to return to White Pines. He had come not simply to see Jessie again and indulge his fantasies about her, but to ply her for information about her past. It was a mission from which he couldn't afford to be distracted. He wanted to give her the gift of her family before he walked out of her life.

"It doesn't bother you at all, does it?" she asked, snagging his attention.

"What?"

"The food."

"Why? Because it's hot? I grew up on Mexican food. Consuela put jalapeño peppers in everything. I'm pretty sure she ground them up and put them in our baby food."

Jessie grinned. "No wonder you're tough as nails. This stuff will definitely put hair on your chest, as my daddy used to say."

There it was, Luke thought. The perfect opening. "Tell me about your family," he suggested. "Did you always know you were adopted?"

She shook her head. "No, I didn't have a clue until I was a teenager. One night I was talking about a friend who was adopted and who'd decided to search for her birth mother, and my mother suddenly got up and ran from the room. I had no idea what I'd said to upset her so. Daddy looked at me like he'd caught me torturing a kitten or something and went rushing after her. I sat there filled with guilt without knowing why I should feel that way."

Luke couldn't begin to imagine her confusion and hurt. "Is that when they told you?"

"Later that night. I'd cleaned up the supper they'd barely touched and done the dishes when they finally came into the kitchen and told me to sit down. They looked so sad, but stoic, you know what I mean?"

Luke nodded. He'd actually seen a similar look in her face the day before, when he'd sent her away.

He wondered how much of this she'd shared with Erik. A pang of pure jealousy sliced through him, and he cursed himself for being a selfish bastard, for wanting more of her than his brother had had.

Oblivious to his reaction, Jessie went on. "Anyway, they told me then that they had adopted me when I was only a few days old. They said they didn't know anything at all about my birth mother, that they hadn't wanted to know. They'd made sure the records were sealed and never looked back."

"You must have felt as if your whole world had been turned on its ear," Luke suggested.

"Worse, I think. It wasn't just that I wasn't who I'd always thought I was—Dancy and Grace Garnett's daughter. It was that they had lied to me for all those years. If you knew how Dancy and Grace preached about honesty above all else, you'd know how betrayed I felt when I learned the truth. It was as though they weren't who they'd claimed to be, either." She looked at him. "Am I making any sense here?"

"Absolutely." Since she seemed to be relieved to be sharing the story with him, Luke remained silent, hoping that would encourage her to go on.

"I begged them to let me find my biological mother, but Grace started crying and Dancy got that same accusing look on his face again."

Even now, she sounded guilt ridden, Luke noticed. "Do you realize that when you talk about them in casual conversation, you refer to them as Mother and Father, but just now, talking about that time, you instinctively started calling them by their first names?''

She seemed startled by the observation. "I suppose that's true. Like I said, I started thinking about them differently then.'' She gave him an imploring look. ''Please, believe me when I say that no one could have had more wonderful parents. I loved them with all my heart. I grieved when they died. But something changed that night. I didn't want it to, but it did.''

''Not because they were your adoptive parents, but because they'd lied.''

She nodded. ''The very thing they'd always told me was one of the worst sins a person could commit.''

Luke felt a shudder roll through him and wondered if his own devious plan would fall into the category of lying and whether she would forgive him when she discovered what he was up to.

''But you gave up the idea of looking for your birth parents, didn't you?''

''At first I was so angry that I didn't care what they wanted, but then, after a few days, I realized how deeply hurt they would be. I told myself that they were my real parents in every way that mattered, so, yes, I dropped the idea.''

''Where would you have looked?'' he asked.

''Dallas, I suppose. It was the closest big city.'' She shrugged. ''I was sixteen. This hit me out of the blue. I had no idea how to start.''

''And they never told you anything more, just that you had been born in Texas?''

"Nothing." She sighed and broke the chip she was holding in two and put it aside.

When she glanced up again, Luke saw that her eyes were shimmering with unshed tears. His resolve stiffened. He would find her biological parents for her. She would have her family. She would have an identity that belonged to her, something he realized with sudden intuition was probably just as important to her as family.

No longer would she be Grace and Dancy Garnett's adopted daughter. Or Erik Adams's widow. Or even Angela Adams's mother. She would know her roots, her heritage. That, above all, was something Luke could understand. It was something no one in his family ever lost sight of. He'd been raised on tales of his ancestors and their struggles and accomplishments. They'd been held up as role models, tough in body and indomitable in spirit. Luke and his brothers had been expected to surpass their examples. The pressure had been unceasing.

It was odd, he thought. Jessie had so little family history. He sometimes thought he and his brothers had had too much. The legacy had shaped them into the men they were. He had wanted to shape his own legacy. Cody had fought to claim the one they shared. Jordan was, quite possibly, the most fiercely independent of all of them.

He reached across the table and claimed Jessie's hand. It was cold as ice. Clearly startled by his touch, she met his gaze.

"Just wanted to bring you back to the present, darlin'," he said softly.

Color rose in her cheeks. ''Oh, Luke, I'm sorry. I never talk about the past like that. I can't imagine what got into me. You've probably been bored to tears.''

''Anything but,'' he assured her, resisting the urge to run straight to the pay phone and call Jim Hill with the few bits of new information he had. He needed one last thing, though, the only thing he could think of that might help and that Jessie was sure to know, despite her doubts about so much else. He needed to find out her exact birthday. He knew how old she was—twenty-seven. And he recalled that her birthday was sometime in summer.

In fact he would never forget the celebration they'd thrown at White Pines her first year there. Erik had insisted on a real, old-fashioned Texas barbecue with neighbors coming from miles around and a live band for square dancing. He remembered every minute of it. That, in fact, was the night he'd realized that he was falling for his brother's wife, that what he'd dismissed as attraction went far deeper.

Jessie had been his partner for a spinning, whirling, breath-stealing square dance. Her cheeks had been flushed. Her bare shoulders had shimmered with a damp sheen of perspiration. Her lush lips had been parted, inviting a kiss. He had obliged before he'd realized he was going to do it. The quick, impulsive kiss had been briefer than a heartbeat, but it had shaken him to his core. Jessie had looked as if she'd been poleaxed.

The band had shifted gears just then and played

a slow dance. Jessie had drifted into his arms, innocently relaxing against him, oblivious he was certain to the fact that his body was pulsing with sudden, urgent need. Desperate to keep her from discovering just how badly he wanted her, he had spotted Erik across the dance floor and maneuvered them into his brother's path. Erik had been only too eager to claim his wife.

If there had been regret in Jessie's eyes, Luke had blinded himself to it. He'd taken off right after that dance and from that day on he'd steered as far away from Jessie as he possibly could without drawing notice.

Glancing at her, he wondered if she recalled that night as vividly as he did. Bringing up the memory was one way to learn the last piece of information he figured he could get for the detective—or so he told himself.

"Hey, darlin', do you recall that shindig we threw for your birthday your first year at White Pines?"

Her blue eyes sparkled at once. "Goodness, yes. I'd never had such a lavish birthday party. Your parents actually had a dance floor installed under the stars, remember?"

"Oh, I remember," he said, his voice dropping a seductive notch.

"I'd never square danced before."

"You sure took to it."

"It was exhilarating," she said softly, and her eyes met his, her expression nostalgic.

If she was saying more than the obvious, Luke

couldn't be sure. He decided for his own sanity it would be best to steer away from the minefield of any more intimate memories.

"Was that July or August? All I remember was how hot it was." Of course, he conceded to himself, his memory of the temperature might have had nothing to do with the weather. Jessie could have had his blood steaming with a look back then. She still could, he admitted. Air-conditioning hadn't been manufactured that could cool him off in her presence.

"August second," she said. "It was the day before my birthday."

That nailed it down, Luke thought, rather proud of himself. He glanced at his watch, then slid from the booth. "Excuse me a second, Jessie. There's a phone call I was supposed to make. I just now remembered it."

She regarded him oddly, but said nothing. Feeling like a sneak, Luke practically raced to the phone booth. He reached the detective on the third ring.

"I was able to come up with a little more information," he said and gave him what he had. "Does that help at all?"

"Some," Hill said. "I ran the name through the computer after we talked, just to see if anything turned up based on what you had this morning."

Luke sucked in a breath. "And?"

"Nothing much beyond the usual, social security number, credit rating, that kind of thing. There was one thing I found a little odd, though."

"What?"

"Looks to me as if she's been investigated before. There are some inquiries on the credit history."

"Couldn't that have been for a car loan or a job reference or something?"

"Possibly. It just didn't seem to track that way."

"How recently?"

"A few years back."

Luke felt his heart begin to thud dully. "In the fall?"

"As a matter of fact, yes. Most of the inquiries seemed to be around September or October."

Erik and Jessie had been married on November first. Her name had started coming up at White Pines only a month or two before as someone about whom Erik was serious.

"Do you know something about that?" Hill asked.

"Not for certain, but I'd put my money on Daddy," Luke said, fighting his anger. He'd known that Harlan suspected Jessie's motives in marrying Erik, but he'd had no idea he'd gone so far as to check her out. "My guess is that Harlan was doing some checking before Erik and Jessie got married. He probably wanted to be sure that the Adams name wasn't about to be sullied or that she wasn't going to take Erik for a fortune."

The detective didn't react to Luke's explanation except to say, "Maybe you can get the information you're after from your father, then. He was probably pretty thorough. Do you want me to wait until you check it out?"

"No, get started. Even Daddy probably couldn't bust his way into sealed adoption records."

"What makes you think you can?"

"Because you're going to tell me exactly how to go about it, and then I'm going to tell Jessie. She's probably the only one who can get through the legal red tape."

"If she wants to," Hill reminded him.

Luke thought of the sad expression he'd seen on her face earlier. "She'll want to," he said with certainty.

"She might not like what she finds."

"I'll be with her every step of the way," he vowed. "It'll be okay."

"You're the boss," the detective said. "I'll be in touch as soon as I have anything. Where will I find you?"

"At White Pines."

"Home for the holidays?"

"Exactly," Luke said dryly. "Just your typical family get-together."

It would be a lot less typical when he cornered his father about having Jessie investigated before the wedding. He was filled with indignation on her behalf. In fact, he might very well do something he'd been itching to do for years. He might wring Harlan's scrawny old neck.

Luke's expression looked as if it had been carved in stone when he came back from making that phone call. Whatever it had been about, the call had obviously upset him.

Jessie watched his profile warily on the ride home, wondering if she should try to probe for an explanation for his change in mood. She supposed she ought to be used to his sullen silences, but having caught a few tantalizing glimpses of the other, gentler side of his nature, she wasn't sure she could bear this return to an old demeanor, an old distance between them.

"Bad news?" she inquired eventually.

"You could say that," he said tersely.

"Can I help?"

He glanced her way. "Nope. I'll take care of it."

Jessie's gaze narrowed. "You jumped in this morning when you saw I had a problem," she reminded him. "Why won't you let me return the favor?"

"Because I can solve this myself."

"I could have solved my problem myself, but that didn't prevent you from butting in, because you cared."

Luke's gaze settled on her and his mouth curved into the beginnings of a smile. "You saying you care, Jessie?"

"Well, of course I do," she said hotly. "Luke, you know how I feel about you…" At the warning look in his eyes, her voice trailed off. Then, irritated with him and herself, she added determinedly, "And about what you did for me and Angela."

"Let's not start that again."

"Well, dammit, it's not something I'm ever likely to forget."

"Stop cursing. It's out of character."

She lost patience with all the verbal tap dancing. "Lucas, you are the most exasperating, mule-headed man it has ever been my misfortune to know. It's no wonder I'm cursing."

He grinned at her outburst. "I care about you, too," he conceded, his voice gentler. "If I really needed help with this, Jessie, I swear you'd be the first person I'd turn to."

Ridiculously pleased, she said, "Really?"

"Cross my heart."

"So does it have something to do with the ranch?"

He laughed. "Give you an inch and you go for the whole damned mile, don't you?"

"You know a better way to get what you want?"

An oddly defeated expression passed across his face. "No, darlin', I can't say that I do."

"Luke?"

"Drop it, Jessica. There's nothing for you to worry about." He glanced at her. "Except maybe how you're going to bring Mother and Daddy to heel."

She heaved a sigh. "I'd rather tackle your problem."

"No," he said with a grim note in his voice. "I can just about guarantee that you wouldn't."

Before Jessie could respond to that cryptic remark, he'd parked the fancy four-wheel-drive car in front of the garage and climbed out. Before she could move, he had her door open. He reached out, circled her waist with his hands and lifted her down from the high vehicle.

He was close enough that she could feel his warmth, close enough that his breath whispered against her cheek. She would have given anything to stay just that way, but the reality was they were at White Pines and there were far too many prying eyes.

Besides, judging from the grim, determined set of Luke's jaw, he would not have allowed it.

"Come on, darlin'. Let's go show 'em who's in charge of our lives."

"I was thinking maybe I'd slip away and take a nap," Jessie said wistfully.

"Resting up before the big battle," Luke noted. "A good idea."

"You could do the same," she suggested daringly, casting a sly look up at him. If the way his jaw was working was any indication, he did not mistake the seductive intent of the invitation.

"Darlin', believe me, that would be a declaration of war," he advised her.

Jessie was up for it. And Luke, she knew with every fiber of her being, was tempted. She winked at him. "One of these days you're going to take me up on it," she taunted him.

"Not in this lifetime," he said emphatically.

Jessie just grinned. She had a feeling deep inside that he was wrong. He was going to cave in far sooner than he thought. She could hardly wait.

Chapter Thirteen

With Jessie resting in her suite, Luke paced up and down in his own, trying to cool off before confronting his father with what he'd discovered. Walking into a room and hurling accusations after months of separation would hardly get their relationship back on track. Still, he couldn't help wondering if Harlan made a habit of investigating any woman with whom any of his sons were involved. If that were the case, Jordan and Cody would probably send him into bankruptcy. Luke took a sort of grim pleasure in the prospect. He'd often wondered if his father would ever have to pay the price for his attempted control of his sons.

When he finally considered his temper calm and his approach reasonable, he bounded down the stairs two at a time and headed straight for Harlan's office.

He found his father seated behind a massive desk piled high with files and spread sheets. Wearing a pair of reading glasses, he was squinting at a computer screen, a sour expression on his once-rugged face. Except for the glasses and perhaps a new wrinkle or two, the scene of his father engrossed in work was so familiar that it made Luke's heart ache.

The glasses and the faint signs of aging, though, reminded him of just how long he'd been away. It wasn't just since Erik's death, but all the years since he'd declared his independence from Harlan's manipulations and moved to his own ranch. He wondered how many other subtle changes there had been since he'd gone.

Harlan glanced up at Luke's entrance. "So, there you are," he said.

His pleasure at seeing Luke was betrayed by his eyes, even though his tone was neutral. He almost sounded uncertain, Luke thought with surprise. It was a far cry from the usual arrogance. He couldn't help welcoming the change.

"About time," Harlan grumbled, his tone more in character. "I wondered where the hell you'd disappeared to. Your mother didn't even know you'd arrived. Wouldn't have known it myself except one of the trucks was missing."

"I had an errand in town. Jessie came along and we had lunch," he added with his usual touch of defiance. Even after all this time, it was a knee-jerk reaction, he realized with a sense of chagrin. If his father commented on the weather, Luke found some reason to counter his claim.

His father nodded, ignoring the testiness. "Fresh air probably did her good. She looked a mite peaked to me last night."

"She just had a baby," Luke reminded him.

His father's expression finally shifted to permit a small hint of approval. "Cute little thing, isn't she?" he said with a note of pride. "Looks like an Adams."

"I was thinking she looked like Jessie," Luke countered, just to be contrary...again.

Harlan shrugged, not rising to the bait. "Who can tell at that age?" he admitted. "You boys all looked exactly alike when you were born." His expression turned thoughtful. "Not a one of you turned out the same, though, in looks or personality. I never could make sense of how that happened."

"We all got your stubborn streak, though," Luke reminded him.

Harlan chuckled at that. "I like to blame that particular trait on your mama. Makes her crazy."

"I can imagine."

Harlan settled back in his chair and studied Luke intently. "You look tired. Why'd you really come home, son? You have something on your mind?"

"I just thought it was about time for a visit," Luke replied noncommittally.

"Your mother's going to be mighty glad to see you."

Luke doubted it. Mary Adams was too caught up

in her own social whirl and in her husband to pay much mind to the comings and goings of her sons. He was more interested in his father's reaction. They had never parted without some sort of petty squabble, probably just the clash of two strong wills. Since Erik's death the tension had been greater than ever.

"And you?" he asked, watching his father's expression closely.

His father seemed taken aback by the question. "That goes without saying," he said at once. "This is your home, boy. Always will be."

Luke sighed, relieved yet still incapable of fully believing the easy answer. "I wasn't so sure you felt that way after the way Erik died," he said cautiously. "It's understandable that you might blame me for what happened."

"Is that what's kept you away from here?"

Luke shrugged. "Part of it."

"Well, you were wrong. Your brother died because he was a reckless fool," his father snapped angrily, "not because of anything you did."

Luke was startled by the depth of emotion. He suspected there was a heavy measure of guilt behind the anger, but hell would freeze over before Harlan would admit to it. Still, the reaction worked to his advantage. With his father's usual control snapped, it seemed like the perfect moment to get an honest answer from him.

"I wonder how he would have felt if he'd known you had Jessie investigated," Luke inquired casually, his gaze pinned to his father's face. "It might have given him the gumption to go after the life he really wanted.''

Harlan's skin turned ashen. ''What the devil do you know about that?'' he demanded indignantly, unsuspectingly confirming Luke's suspicions. ''And what business is it of yours, if I did?''

Luke refused to be drawn into an argument over ethics, morality or just plain trust. He had his own agenda here. ''Find out anything interesting?'' he inquired lightly.

''Nothing worth stopping the wedding over, which you obviously knew already.'' He leveled a look at Luke. ''Like I asked before, what business is this of yours? It happened a long time ago. If anyone should have told me to mind my own business, it was Erik, but he never said peep.''

''Maybe because he was too damned trusting to suspect you'd do something like that. I'm not nearly so gullible where you're concerned. I know how manipulative you can be. I like Jessie. I don't like to think that you don't trust her.''

''Is that it?'' Harlan demanded with a penetrating look. ''Or is it something more?''

Luke felt as if he were standing at the edge of a mine field with one foot already in the air for his next fateful step. ''Like what?''

''Like maybe your interest in her is personal.''

''Well, of course it's personal,'' he snapped, hoping to divert his father from making too much of his defense of Jessie by admitting straight out that he cared for her as he would for any other family member. It was a risky tactic. It appeared his father had been far more attuned to the undercurrents around White Pines than he'd realized.

"She's my sister-in-law," he pointed out. "She just delivered my niece in my bed a few days ago. I'd say that gives me cause to take an interest in her."

"And that's all there is to it?" Harlan inquired, skepticism written all over his face.

"Of course." Luke uttered the claim with what he hoped was enough vehemence. His father still didn't exactly look as if he believed him, but to Luke's relief he appeared willing to let the matter drop.

"You found out she was adopted, didn't you?" Luke prodded.

"Already knew that. Erik told us."

"Did you find out anything about her family?"

"Now who's asking too many questions?"

Luke scowled at him. "Just answer me. I have my reasons for asking."

"So did I," Harlan said testily.

Luke stood. "Never mind. I can see this was a waste of time."

"Oh, for goodness sakes, settle down. Yes, I found out about her family. They were good, decent, church-going people. Paid their bills on time. Gave her a good education. There was nothing to find fault with there."

"I meant her biological family."

An expression of pure frustration spread across his father's rough-hewn features. "Couldn't get anywhere with that. Didn't seem worth chasing after, once I'd met her. My gut instinct is never wrong and it told me right off that Jessie's honest as they come. If I hadn't known it before, there was no mistaking it when she walked away from here without a cent after Erik died. She's a gutsy little thing, too stubborn for her own good, if you ask me."

"An interesting assessment coming from you," Luke observed.

Harlan's expression turned sheepish. "So it is."

Luke decided he'd better get out of his father's office before Harlan picked up the issue of Luke's feelings for Jessie and pursued it. He'd diverted his father once, but Harlan was too damned perceptive for Luke to keep his emotions hidden from him for long. A few probing questions, a few evasive answers and the truth would be plain as day.

"I think I'll go hunt down Mother," he told his father.

"I believe you'll find her in the parlor reading or planning some social schedule," Harlan said with a grimace. He turned back to his computer and sighed. "You know anything about these danged things?"

"Enough to get by," Luke said.

"Maybe you could give me a few pointers later. At the rate I'm going, this year's records won't even be programmed before next year."

Surprised by the request, Luke nodded. "I'd be happy to." It was the first time he could ever recall his father admitting that one of his sons might have an expertise he didn't. That single request went a long way toward mending fences, hinting that perhaps they could finally find a new footing for their relationship, one of equals. Respect was all he'd ever really craved from his father. He'd known he had his love, but true respect had been far harder to come by.

Just as Luke reached the door, his father called after him. "It really is good to have you home again, son. This house was built for the whole family. Never realized how empty it would be one day."

Luke felt an unexpected lump form in his throat. He'd discovered the same thing about his own house recently, as well. For a few brief days it had felt like a home. "Thanks, Daddy," he said. "It's good to be here."

Oddly enough, he realized as he walked away, it was true. It was unexpectedly good to be home. He wondered just how much of that could be attributed to Jessie's presence upstairs and whether from now on "home" to him would always be wherever she was.

That night as he dressed for dinner, Luke conceded that his prediction of his mother's reaction to seeing him had been right on target. She had been superficially pleased when she'd greeted him, but within minutes she'd been distracted by a flurry of phone calls from friends confirming holiday plans. He'd been only too glad to escape to his suite, where he waited impatiently for some news from Jim Hill. He doubted his mother had even noticed when he left the parlor.

Upstairs, he spent a restless hour wishing he still had a right to head out to his father's barns and work the horses. He needed some hard exercise to combat the stress of being home again, of being so close to a woman he hungered for and couldn't have. His shoulders ached with tension. His nerves were on edge. He would have gone out and chopped wood, if he hadn't seen a woodpile big enough to last till spring.

He supposed the real truth was that he'd been feeling tense and out of sorts ever since Jessie had appeared on his doorstep. It was as if he were being ripped apart inside, torn between desire and honor. If he'd thought his emotions were frayed at his ranch, he realized now that the necessity for watching every word, every glance while under his father's roof only compounded the problem. His conscience, never something he'd worried too much about before Erik's marriage to Jessie, was taking a royal beating.

Eventually he tired of pacing. Worn out by tangling with his own thoughts, he started back downstairs. Outside Jessie's door, he heard Angela crying and Lara's unsuccessful attempts to quiet her. He hesitated, wondering where Jessie was. Perhaps she had already gone downstairs.

He tapped on the door and opened it. The young Mexican girl, her cheeks flushed, her hair mussed, was frantically rocking the crying baby. The jerky movement was not having a soothing effect. Quite the contrary, in fact.

"What's the problem?"

"I cannot get her to sleep," Lara whispered, sounding panicked. "No matter what I do, she cries."

"Where's Jessie?"

"With the *señora*."

"Has the baby been fed?"

"*Sí.* Only a short time ago."

Luke crossed the room in a few quick strides, then reached down and took the baby from Lara. She fit into his arms as if she belonged there, her warm little body snuggling against his chest. Her gulping cries turned to whimpers almost at once.

"Shh," he whispered. "It's your Uncle Luke, sweet pea. What's with all the noise? Were you feeling abandoned there for a minute?" He glanced at Lara and saw that an expression of relief had spread across her face. "How was she while we were out this afternoon?"

"Like an angel, Señor Luke. She slept most of the time. I thought she would go to sleep again as soon as she had eaten."

Luke rubbed the baby's back. A tiny hand waved in the air, then settled against his cheek. As if she found the contact familiar and comforting, she quieted at once. That strange sense of completeness stole over him again.

Luke made a decision. "Lara, why don't you take a break for a few hours. I think our little angel ought to join the rest of us for dinner."

"But *la señora* said…"

Luke tried to recall exactly how many times he'd heard his mother's edicts repeated in just that way by Consuela, by his father, even his teachers. Mary Adams's influence had been felt everywhere in his life, at least when she chose to exert it. "Let me worry about my mother. Have your dinner. Go on out for the evening. We can manage here."

"*Sí*, if that is your wish," she said with obvious reluctance.

"It is," he assured her.

He found a soft pink baby blanket, obviously a new addition since he doubted there would have been anything pink in the assortment of items his mother had saved from her sons. Wrapping Angela loosely in the blanket, he cradled her in one arm and gathered a few spare diapers and a bottle with his other hand. He eyed a can of baby powder, debated a couple of toys, but abandoned them when he couldn't figure out how to pick them up.

"Remind me to get you one of those fancy carry things," he told the baby, who regarded him with wide-eyed fascination. "I don't have enough hands to carry this much paraphernalia. Things were a whole lot less complicated at my house, before you got outfitted with the best supplies money could buy."

Angela gurgled her agreement.

"You know what I love most about you, sweet pea? You go along with everything I say. Be careful with all that adoration, though. It'll give a guy a swelled head. I don't want to give away any trade secrets. After all, we men should really stick together when it comes to women, but for you I'll make an exception. If there's any heartbreaking to be done, I want you to be the one who does it. You need advice about some jerk, you come to me. Is it a deal?''

The baby cooed on cue. Luke grinned.

''You understood every word, didn't you? Well, now that we've settled how you should go about dealing with men, let's go find your mama and your grandparents. Not that I'm so crazy about sharing you, you understand, but the truth is I'm not always going to be around. You need to have other folks you can count on, too. Your mama's one of the best. And nobody on earth will protect you from harm any better than your granddaddy. He's fierce when it comes to taking care of his own. Just don't let him bully you.''

Angela yawned.

''Okay, okay, I get the message. I'm boring you. Let's go, then.''

Downstairs, he located the rest of the family in the parlor. He found the varying reactions fascinating—and telling. His mother looked vaguely dismayed by the sight of Angela in his arms, just as she had when any of her own children had slipped downstairs during a grown-up party. His father grinned, unable to hide his pleasure or his pride, just as he had when showing off his sons to company. Jessie seemed resigned at the sight of her daughter comfortably settled against Luke's chest.

''Where on earth is Lara?'' his mother demanded at once. ''I am paying that girl to look after the baby.''

Before Luke could say a word, Jessie jumped in.

"Don't blame Lara. I suspect your son is responsible for this. Is that right, Luke?"

Luke shrugged, refusing to apologize. "She was crying."

"Babies cry," his mother said irritably. "Picking them up will only spoil them."

"Oh, for goodness sakes, Mary, she's a newborn," Harlan countered. "There's nothing wrong with giving her a little extra attention. Besides, I want to get to know my first grandbaby. Bring her here, Luke."

He eagerly held out his arms. Luke placed the baby in them and wondered at the oddly bereft feeling that instantly came over him. He moved over and took a seat by Jessie, gravitating almost unconsciously to her warmth as an alternative to the strange sort of serenity he felt when holding the baby.

As soon as he sat down, though, he realized his mistake. Jessie represented more than warmth. She exuded heat and passion, at least to him. His body responded at once, predictably and with the kind of urgency he hadn't known since his teens.

"Sherry, Lucas?" his mother asked.

"Hmm?" he murmured distractedly.

"She's asking if you would like a drink," Jessie explained as if she were translating a foreign language. There was a look of knowing amusement in her eyes he couldn't mistake.

"No thanks," he said.

"I'm very surprised to see you here, Lucas," his mother commented.

"But we're delighted, aren't we, Mary?" his father said, a warning note in his voice.

His mother seemed startled by the sharp tone. "Well, of course, we are. I'm just surprised, that's all. He hasn't been here for months. And," she added pointedly, "he told me quite plainly that he couldn't get here over the holidays. As I recall, he told you the same thing just yesterday."

Luke refused to be drawn into a quarrel. "Plans change," he said.

"Will you be staying long?" his mother asked.

"Mary!" Harlan protested. "You'll make the boy think we'd rather he stayed home."

His mother flushed. "Well, of course, I didn't mean that. For goodness sakes, Harlan, I was just trying to think ahead and make some plans. I was wondering if we should have another party, perhaps for New Year's Eve."

Luke shuddered at the thought. "Not on my account," he said with absolute sincerity.

"I think a quiet celebration is more in order this year," Harlan said, regarding him with something that might have been understanding. "I think we had enough chaos around here last night to last till next year."

"Chaos?" Mary repeated, red patches of indignation in her cheeks. "I worked for weeks to make sure that we had a lovely party for our friends on Christmas and you thought it was chaos?"

Harlan sighed. "I didn't mean any disrespect, dear. Your parties are always well attended. They're the high point of the social season around the whole state of Texas. Everyone knows that. I just think one is enough.'' As if he sensed that his fancy verbal footwork hadn't yet placated her, he added, ''Besides, I know first-hand how much the planning takes out of you.''

Mary sighed heavily, her expression put-upon. ''I suppose a quiet family occasion would be nice for a change. Perhaps for once Jordan and Cody can be persuaded to leave their current paramours at home.''

''I doubt that will be a problem,'' his father said. ''Jordan claims to be fed up with the social whirl and Cody's trying to put a damper on Melissa's enthusiasm for a spring wedding. I suspect they'll be happy to come alone.''

''That was certainly the impression I got from them, too,'' Jessie chimed in. ''I never thought I'd see the day when those two would turn up anywhere without a woman, but they seemed almost relieved to be on their own last night.''

After the initial awkwardness and minor bickering, the rest of the evening settled into something astonishingly comfortable. Dinner passed quickly with quiet conversation about old friends and plans for the next few days of the holidays.

''The McAllisters' annual party is tomorrow night,'' Mary reminded them. She looked at Luke and Jessie. ''I'm sure you'll both want to come.''

''Not me,'' Jessie said at once. ''I'm not quite up to partying yet, but the rest of you go.''

Luke noticed that Jessie claimed a lack of energy only when it suited her purposes. She'd always hated the stuffy McAllisters and the collection of rich and powerful they dutifully assembled periodically to prove their own worth to the neighbors.

"I believe I'll stay here, too," he said, studiously avoiding Jessie's gaze.

His mother opened her mouth to protest, but to his surprise, his father defended his decision. "Mary, leave him be. If it were up to me, I'd stay home, too, but I know you won't have it."

"Well, for goodness sakes, it's social occasions like this that make the kind of business contacts you need," his mother grumbled. "I should think Luke would be aware of that, as well."

Luke settled back in his chair, his decision reinforced by his father's surprising understanding. "I prefer to make my business contacts in an office, Mother. That way there's no confusing my intent. As I recall, the last time I tried to do business at one of these social occasions, Henry Lassiter thought I was going to trade a herd of cattle for his daughter's hand in marriage."

Next to him, Jessie choked back a laugh. Her eyes sparkled with undisguised merriment. "How on earth did you extricate yourself from that?"

"Thank goodness I didn't have to," he said, laughing at the memory. "Janice Lassiter was as appalled as I was. She told her father in no uncertain terms that she was not a piece of property he could trade in to get a prize bull and a few cows. I have to admit I found her a bit more intriguing after she said that."

To his surprise his mother's mouth curved into a smile. "You never told us that story."

"Of course not," Luke said. "Do you realize how embarrassing it was to realize that I'd made some innocent remark that got mistaken for a marriage proposal? It's not something a man wants getting around."

Jessie leaned close and whispered, "There are some women who might even take you up on an innocent remark even without the offer of the cattle. Those are the ones you really have to watch your step with."

Luke shifted and stared at her, his blood suddenly thundering in his veins. He could feel his cheeks flush and prayed that his very observant father was watching something else at the moment. If Luke meant anything at all to Angela, who was sound asleep in her grandfather's arms, the little munchkin would wake up and start screaming right now to divert attention.

She didn't, which meant he had to hide his reactions as best he could.

Why had he never noticed that sweet, demure Jessie was a master of torment? She must have had poor Erik in a daze from the day they'd met. Or perhaps his brother had been made of sterner stuff than he'd ever realized.

"Watch yourself, darlin'," he murmured in an aside he hoped couldn't be overheard. "You're just begging for trouble."

Jessie turned her deceptively innocent gaze on him. "Who's going to give it to me, Lucas?"

Good question. For him to tangle with her in the way he longed to, the way she was taunting him to, he was the one who would be in real trouble. Up to his neck in it, as a matter of fact, and drowning fast.

Chapter Fourteen

If it weren't for the half dozen servants scattered around, Luke and Jessie would have had the house to themselves the following evening, once his parents had gone off to the McAllisters' party. For some reason, Jessie found being alone with Luke at White Pines oddly intimate and very disconcerting. Acknowledging her feelings for Luke at his ranch had been one thing. Admitting them here, where she and Erik had spent their entire married life, was something else entirely.

Frankly, she was still surprised that Luke had conspired to be alone with her. When she'd left his ranch, she had been all but certain she would never see him again unless she arranged it. Now, not only had he followed her to White Pines, he seemed un-

willing to let her out of his sight. She couldn't believe it was because he'd had a change of heart
about their relationship. He was still jumpy as a
june bug around her. To be truthful, she wasn't
much better.

Sitting across from Luke in the huge, formal dining room, with the table set with fancy china, ster-
ling silver and fine crystal, Jessie felt as if the atmosphere were suddenly charged with electricity. In
his kitchen she had been comfortable, even sure of
herself. Here she felt as if she were on a first, very
nerve-racking date. She wondered if he felt the
same uncertainty, the same shivery anticipation.

If he did, it wasn't apparent, she decided with
some regret. He'd worn slacks and a white dress
shirt, left open at the throat just enough to reveal a
sexy whorl of crisp, dark hair and tanned skin. With
his hair neatly combed, his cheeks freshly shaved,
he looked as confident as Jordan, as sexy as Cody
and as at ease as Erik. The combination was enough
to make her palms sweat.

Luke lifted his glass of wine and took a slow sip,
his gaze never leaving her face. The intensity of
that look was deliberate. There was no mistake
about it. Jessie could feel her cheeks flush. Her
pulse skittered wildly.

"Everything okay?" he inquired in a lazy drawl
that sent fire dancing through her veins.

"Of course," she responded in a choked voice.
"Why?"

"You look a little...feverish."

Oh, sweet heaven, she thought desperately, wishing she could pat her cheeks with a napkin dipped in the crystal goblet of ice water. The man was deliberately turning the tables on her. She swallowed hard and searched her soul for the confidence to play his game and win. "No," she said eventually, her voice shaking. "I'm fine."

He nodded politely, but there was a knowing gleam in his eyes. "If you say so."

"I do," she said adamantly.

"Okay."

Fortunately, Maritza came in with the main course just then—beef Wellington. "It is your favorite, Señor Luke, *sí?*"

Luke grinned at her, his attention diverted at last. Jessie used the reprieve to draw in a deep breath and surreptitiously fan herself with her napkin.

"Absolutely," he told the housekeeper. "And not even Consuela does beef Wellington better than you do."

"I will not tell her you said so," Maritza said, her cheeks rosy with pleasure at the compliment.

"Thank you," Luke said, his expression absolutely serious. "She'd put me on a diet of canned soup for a month, if she found out."

When the housekeeper had retreated to the kitchen, Jessie said, "You're very kind to her."

He seemed surprised by the comment. "Why wouldn't I be? She's terrific. The whole family is. Did you know that Rosa who owns the café we went to is another cousin? I believe Lara is Rosa's daughter or maybe she's a second cousin. I've lost track of all the connections."

"And you're nice to all of them." Seeing his skepticism, Jessie tried to analyze what she'd seen in their rapport. "I can't explain exactly," she finally admitted. "It's not that you're just polite, that you say what's expected. You genuinely appreciate what they do. I'm sure that's why Consuela chose to go with you when you left White Pines. I suspect you make her feel like part of the family, while your mother treated her like hired help."

Luke shrugged off the compliment. "Consuela is family to me," he said with surprising feeling. "She's the one who really raised me, raised all of us, for that matter. Mother's single goal in life was to make Daddy's life easier, to give him whatever he wanted. She gave him four sons, then did everything she could to see that we stayed out of his way. If I'm ever fortunate enough to have children, I made a promise to myself that they will never feel the way we felt as kids, as if we were a nuisance to be tolerated."

Jessie was appalled by the assessment, by the trace of bitterness in his voice. Obviously his resentments ran deeper than she'd ever realized.

"Your father certainly never treated any of you that way as far as I could tell," she argued. "He's obviously very proud of all of you."

Luke's expression was doubtful. "You can say that after the way he manipulated Erik, the way he's always tried to control the rest of us?"

Jessie found herself smiling at the concept that anyone on earth could manipulate or control Luke.

"I don't see that he exactly has you under his thumb."

"Because I rebelled."

"Don't you suppose the struggle to become your own man made you stronger?"

His gaze narrowed. "What's your point?"

"That if Harlan had made it easy for you, you might not have fought half so hard to get your own way. All of this could have been yours. You would have had a nice, comfortable life without really struggling for it."

"Are you saying he deliberately battled with us over every little thing just to make us fight back?"

Jessie shrugged, refusing to spell it out any more clearly. She wanted him to look at his past from a fresh perspective and draw his own conclusion. "You know Harlan better than I do."

Luke's expression grew thoughtful. "I never thought about it that way before," he conceded. "I always wanted my own place. I didn't want to follow in his footsteps and simply claim what he'd already built. The harder he fought to keep me here, the harder I fought to go."

"And you succeeded in making the break," she pointed out. "You have a successful ranch of your own now, one you can be especially proud of because you know it's the result of your own hard work, isn't that right?"

He nodded slowly. "Jordan made the break, as well. He and Daddy used to stay up half the night fighting over his future. Daddy was fed up with him wildcatting at oil wells all over hell and gone. Told him it was time to settle down back here. Swore he'd cut him out of the will, if he didn't stay.''

He paused, then suddenly grinned. ''I just remembered something. I was here the night Jordan packed his bags and stormed out to move to Houston. He told Daddy he could take his inheritance and shove it. I came·down when I heard all the commotion and found Daddy standing at a window watching him go. There were tears in his eyes and the strangest look on his face.''

''What kind of look?'' Jessie asked.

''I realize now that it was satisfaction, maybe even that pride you're so sure he feels for us. He was actually glad that Jordan was going after his dream,'' he said, a note of astonishment in his voice. ''Jordan even admitted to me later that he'd had an awfully easy time landing his first desk job in the oil business. He always had a hunch that Daddy had made a call or two.''

''Could be,'' Jessie said. ''Too bad he hasn't tackled Jordan's social life. It's time he settled down. I think he's finally ready.''

''Really?'' Luke shook his head, clearly bemused by the discoveries he was making once he looked past those deeply ingrained resentments. ''That would be something to see. I think Jordan's going to surprise us all when he finally falls in love.''

''What about Cody? How did Harlan deal with him?'' Jessie asked.

''In his heart, Cody was the one who always wanted White Pines,'' Luke said. ''Unlike Jordan or me, Daddy kept pushing him toward the door.

The harder he pushed, the more Cody dug in his heels and made himself indispensable around here. The next thing we knew he'd built himself a little house down the road and was acting as foreman."

Three brothers, Jessie thought, all a little stronger because Harlan had had the wisdom to make them fight for their choices in life, rather than handing them a future on a silver platter.

And then there was Erik.

"Erik was the only one the technique backfired with," she said softly. "He was never like the rest of you. He was gentle, eager to please. You said yourself the other day that he was the diplomat. Whenever Harlan pushed him, he backed down, tried to find a middle ground, hoping to win his father's approval. Instead, Harlan just grew more and more impatient with him."

Luke reached for her hand. Jessie supposed he meant it only as a gesture of comfort, but it made her senses spin. She couldn't have pulled away, though, if her life had depended on it. Fortunately, she supposed, Luke broke off the contact all too soon.

"I suppose the real skill in parenting is understanding each child's personality," Luke said thoughtfully. "Daddy said just last night how amazed he was at how different we were. Maybe if he'd recognized that sooner, Erik wouldn't have suffered so, trying to be something he wasn't. And you wouldn't have lost him."

Jessie took a deep breath and met Luke's gaze. It was time to tell him everything and see where it led them. "I suspect I was destined to lose him one way or another. At least this way he never had to lose me to another man."

Luke choked on the sip of wine he'd just taken. His eyes watered as he stared at her with astonishment written all over his face. "What are you saying?" he demanded.

Jessie drew in a deep breath. She wasn't going to let him mistake her meaning with subtleties. "That I was in love with you long before Erik died," she admitted boldly.

Luke was shaking his head before she completed the sentence. "Don't say that," he protested.

"Why not? It's true." She leveled a gaze into his troubled eyes. "Why do you think I left here after Erik died?"

"Because you couldn't bear to be around me, knowing I'd caused his death," Luke said.

Jessie decided she'd already opened the door. It was time to walk through it.

"No," she told him softly, but adamantly. "Because I was filled with guilt over my feelings for you. From the day Erik and I moved into White Pines, I felt this connection to you. I didn't want it. I couldn't explain it. I certainly could never have acted on it, but it was there, just under the surface, tormenting me."

Tears welled up in her eyes, spilled down her cheeks. "You have no idea how guilty I felt when he died. A tiny part of me was actually glad that I would never have to make a decision to leave him. I don't think I could have, no matter how badly I wanted to. I could never have hurt him that way. For all of his weaknesses, Erik was good to me. He deserved better than he got from me. He deserved my whole heart, instead of just a piece of it.''

She thought back to the few moments she'd had with Erik at the hospital after Luke had come to tell her that her husband was dying. Alert for just a heartbeat, he'd turned that gentle, understanding gaze of his on her.

"Be happy, Jessie," he'd whispered, clutching her hand in his.

"Not without you," she'd insisted, as the life slowly seeped from his body with each weakening beat of his heart.

He'd squeezed her hand fiercely. "Tell him, Jessie." Then more emphatically, he'd said, "Tell Luke."

At first she hadn't realized what he meant. "What?" she'd pleaded. "Tell Luke what?"

He'd struggled for air, then managed to choke out two words. "Love him."

"Of course, I will tell him that you love him," she'd soothed, caressing his cheek.

He'd smiled faintly at that. "Not me. You."

Remembering how stunned she'd been, how consumed with guilt, Jessie thought no man had ever displayed more love, more generosity than Erik when he'd clung to her hand and said, "'S okay, Jessie."

"Oh, Erik, forgive me," she'd pleaded.

That sweet smile spread across his face one last

time. "Nothing to forgive," he'd whispered. "I love you."

She gazed across the table at Luke and wondered how much she should tell him about Erik's final words. Would they free him to love her?

Or, as they had with her, would they merely renew his own deeply ingrained sense of guilt? Knowing that Erik had guessed how they felt about each other, even if neither of them had ever acted on those feelings, was a heavy burden. She could attest to that. It had driven her from White Pines.

In the end she kept silent and the moment to confide passed.

"You're not in love with me," Luke said sharply, cutting into her reverie.

Jessie's head snapped up. She almost choked on the bubble of hysterical laughter that formed in her throat. He seemed to think by saying it enough, he could make it true.

"Lucas, that is not for you to say."

He slammed his glass of wine onto the table with so much force, it was a wonder the crystal didn't shatter. Wine splashed in every direction. He glared at her. "I won't have it, do you understand me?"

She gave him a compassionate look. "Maybe you can control your feelings, maybe you can sweep them under the carpet and pretend they don't exist, but you can't do the same with mine. I won't allow that."

His expression turned thunderous. "You won't *allow* it?" he repeated slowly.

Jessie held her ground. "They're my feelings."

"They're crazy."

She shrugged. "Maybe so. In fact, at this precise moment, I'm almost certain you're right about that. I would have to be crazy to fall in love with such a mule-headed male." She gave him a resigned look. "But, then again, there's no accounting for taste when it comes to matters of the heart."

She watched Luke's struggle to get a grip on his temper. In a perverse sort of way, she almost enjoyed it.

"Jessie, be reasonable," he said with forced patience. "It's not me you're in love with. It's the family. I'm taking care of that."

She went perfectly still. "You're taking care of that?" she repeated carefully. "What exactly does that mean? Did you suggest Harlan and Mary adopt me? What?"

A dull red flush climbed up Luke's neck. "No, I...um, I spoke with a private investigator."

Stunned, she just stared at him. Dear heaven, it was worse than she thought. "About?"

He winced at her curt tone. "It was supposed to be a surprise."

"Tell me now." She bit off each word emphatically. She couldn't think when she'd ever been so furious. He'd denied that this had anything to do with his family. So, if she was interpreting all of the stuttered hints and innuendoes correctly, he had decided to get himself off the hook with her by presenting her with her biological parents. Definitely a tidy solution from his point of view. "What exactly is this investigator investigating?"

Luke heaved a sigh. "He's looking for your mother."

At one time that announcement would have thrilled her. She would have leapt from the table and thrown her arms around him for being so thoughtful. Now all she felt was empty. He was expecting her to trade her very real, very deep love for him for a stranger's possible affection. Couldn't he see it wasn't the same at all?

He seemed genuinely puzzled by her lack of response. "I thought this was what you wanted. You said... You told me how much you'd wanted to find your biological family."

"I did. I still do," she said wearily. When she could manage it without weeping, she met his gaze. "But not if it's going to cost me you."

The instant the words were out of her mouth, she ran from the room. Upstairs in her suite, she sent Lara away and took Angela in her arms.

"Can't he see it, angel? Can't he see that the two of you are the only family I need?"

Well, that had certainly gone well, Luke thought in disgust. Maybe he was every bit as bad as Harlan, trying to manipulate lives and control feelings. He'd only wanted to give Jessie the possible—her real family—to make up for the fact that he could never give her the impossible—himself.

After apologizing to Maritza for spoiling the meal she'd worked so hard to prepare, he slowly climbed the stairs. His thoughts were in turmoil... again.

What could he say to Jessie to make her see that it wouldn't work? No matter how badly he wanted her, no matter how much she professed to love him, Erik would always be between them. There would never be a moment when their passion could flower, free from guilt and the overwhelming sense of having betrayed a man they had both loved. If their own consciences didn't destroy them, the disappointment and indignation of the rest of the family surely would.

He paused outside Jessie's suite and listened. He could hear the faint sounds of movement, the murmur of voices. Or was it only one voice? Jessie's, perhaps, as she soothed Angela back to sleep?

Unable to help himself, he quietly opened the door a crack and peered inside. The suite's bedroom was in shadows. A silver trail of moonlight splashed across the bed.

In a corner of the room the whisper of the rocker drew his attention. Jessie was holding the baby to her breast, nursing her. The glow of moonlight made her skin incandescent. Luke's gaze was riveted, his body instantly throbbing with an aching need.

He realized after a moment that the yearning he felt went beyond the physical. He wanted to claim Jessie and the baby as his own with a fierceness that staggered him. He wanted the right to be in that room beside them, to drink in the incredible sight of mother and child in an act as old as time. He wanted…so much more than words could possibly express.

He could deny it from now to eternity and it wouldn't change the truth. Somehow Jessie had realized that and made peace with it, while he still struggled. He knew, even if she did not, that love did not always conquer the obstacles in its path. She would come to see him as a sorry prize, if he cost her the love of his family.

Suddenly he sensed her gaze was on him. When she looked up, he could see the sheen of dampness on her cheeks, and a dismay worse than anything he'd felt over betraying Erik cut through him.

"I'm sorry," he said in a ragged whisper.

The rocker slowed. "For?" she asked cautiously.

The simple question stymied him. For making her cry? For loving her? For refusing to go down a path that could only lead to worse heartache?

"For everything," he said at last.

He turned away then, a dull sensation of anguish crushing his chest. Knowing he was closing the door on so much more than just the sight of the two people he loved most in the world, he quietly pulled it shut.

Even then, though, he couldn't move. In the gathering silence, he heard Jessie whisper his name. It was no louder than a sigh of regret, but to his ears it seemed louder than a shout. He resisted the longing to open that door—the only shield between him and a wildly escalating temptation—for a single heartbeat, then two.

"Luke?"

He closed his eyes and tried to shut out the sound of her voice, but the echo of his softly spoken name was already in his head, driving him crazy. A sigh shuddered through him and he knew he was lost. He opened the door, stepped inside, then closed it.

And as he did, he knew with every fiber of his being that nothing in his life would ever be the same.

Chapter Fifteen

Jessie watched with bated breath as Luke closed the door to the suite behind him. Her heart seemed to have stilled and then, as he took the first step toward her, it began to thunder mercilessly in her chest.

Dear heaven, how she loved him. Earlier tonight she'd been sure that she had lost him forever. She had run out of ways to combat his stubbornness, or so she had thought.

Apparently all it had taken was the whispered cry of his name on her lips, a soft command he'd been unable to resist. He crossed the room, reluctance still written all over his hard, masculine face, and sank slowly to the edge of the bed beside the rocker, careful not to allow his knees to brush against hers. Too careful. It told her how deeply his feelings for her ran and how much he feared losing control.

His gaze remained fixed on the baby in her arms. A soft, tender smile tugged at the corners of his lips. If she could have, without disturbing Angela, she would have touched a finger to that normally stern, unforgiving mouth. She would have tried to coax that smile to remain in place.

"Was it so very difficult?" she inquired dryly.

His gaze found hers. "What?"

"Walking into this room."

"Not difficult," he said, the smile coming and going again like a whisper. "Dangerous. When I'm around you, I can't think. My common sense flies out the window. No one has ever had such control over me."

"I don't think feelings are something you can dictate with common sense," she said.

"Maybe not, but actions are." He studied her with a rueful expression. "You have the lure of a siren, Jessie. You and your baby."

"Is that so terrible?"

"I've told you all the reasons it is."

"Reasons, yes, but you've never said what was in your heart."

Luke sighed and looked away. When he eventually settled his gaze on her again, there was an air of acceptance about him that she hadn't seen before. It gave her hope.

"My heart," he began, then shook his head. "I'm not sure I can find the words."

She leveled a look at him, then said quietly, "Then show me."

A soft moan seemed ripped from somewhere deep inside him. "Jessie, don't..."

"It's just the two of us here in the dark, Lucas. You can show me what's in your heart. There's no one to object."

She thought she detected the faint beginnings of another wry smile.

"Not just two of us, Jessie. Angela's right here with us. Hardly a proper audience for all I'd like to do to you, all the ways I'd like to show you how I feel."

Jessie wasn't about to let him seize an easy excuse for maintaining the status quo. Her entire body shook with her desperate yearning for his touch.

"She's ready to be put down for the night," she countered. "I'll take her into the other room. After that, Luke, no more objections. No more excuses."

She tucked the baby into her crib, caressing the soft, sweet-smelling cheek with a delicate touch. Suddenly she was overwhelmed with emotions—love for this precious new life, love for the man who waited in the next room. Her fear of the future was diminishing day by day.

Finally it was her love for Luke that drew her back. She was lured by the promise of warmth, by the deep sense of honor that made Luke the man he was, a man worthy of loving. There would be no passion between them, she thought with deep regret. Not tonight. Physically for her, it was too soon. Perhaps emotionally, as well, though she didn't think so.

But there would be commitment at last. She could sense it with everything in her. He would no longer deny his feelings. And with Luke by her side, they could fight the rest of the inevitable battle with his family together.

He stood when she entered, then met her halfway across the room. Fighting, then visibly losing one last battle with himself, he opened his arms to her. Jessie moved into the embrace with the sense that she was finally, at long last, home to stay. The serenity that swept through her was overwhelming.

"It won't be easy," he said, his chin resting atop her head as she nestled against his chest.

"Easy is for cowards," she said bravely.

"Anything this difficult may be for fools," he said dryly.

She stepped back and looked up at him. "Do you love me?"

He cupped her face in his hands, then slowly, so very slowly lowered his head until his mouth covered hers. The answer was in his kiss, a consuming, breath-stealing kiss that seemed to last forever and said *yes, yes, yes* with each passing second. The touch of his lips branded her, the invasion of his tongue claimed her as intimately as she knew his body would some day. Relief and so much more washed through her, filling her with wild exhilaration.

Convinced at last, she dared to insist on an answer to her earlier question. "Do you love me?"

"I thought I'd just told you," he said, a satisfied smile on his face.

"That was just a clue," she said, deliberately dismissing the kiss to taunt him. "A very good clue, but not conclusive. I want proof, Lucas."

His eyebrows rose fractionally. "Oh, really? How far can I actually go under the circumstances."

"I'll let you know when you've reached the limit."

"That's what I'm afraid of, we'll reach yours and test mine beyond endurance."

She stripped him of his shirt with slow deliberation. When his torso was bare, she caressed the hard muscles of his arms in a deliberately provocative gesture, following the shape, learning the texture of his skin. "I'd say you're strong enough to take it."

His gaze narrowed. "Do you have a wanton streak I ought to know about?"

"I suppose that's one of the things you'll learn eventually," she taunted him, delighting in the flare of heat in his eyes, the unmistakable catch of his breath that hinted of sudden urgency.

He reached for the buttons of her blouse then and easily freed them. Beneath the cotton, her breasts were fuller than ever and extraordinarily sensitive. He swallowed hard as his tanned, callused finger traced the pale, rounded flesh, arriving in time at the already throbbing nipple. He leaned down and flicked over the sensitive bud with his tongue. A gasp rose in Jessie's throat as she clung to his shoulders.

With her eyes closed and her head thrown back, there was no knowing where his caresses would come next or how shattering they would be. With each exquisite, daring touch, her body responded in ways she'd never expected it to.

Far too soon, she realized the torment she was putting him—putting both of them—through. There would be no tumbling into bed, no tangling of bared arms and legs, no press of bodies on fire. She had underestimated how difficult it would be to call a halt. Her newly awakened body throbbed with need. Luke's muscles were tensed with the effort of holding back. His eyes glittered with dangerous emotions.

She covered his hands with her own and stilled his touch.

"Enough?" he asked, his voice hoarse.

"Not nearly enough," she replied, still wondering at the discovery that there could be so much more than she had ever experienced with Erik. "But we're dangerously close to the point when I'll lose all reason."

"How long will it be before I can hold you through the night?" he asked, his voice filled with hunger and perhaps just a touch of awe that such a day would, indeed, finally come. They'd reached a turning point and moved on. There would be no going back from this night. They both recognized that.

"There's been no one in my life, Luke. Not since

Erik. I saw no need to ask the doctor about this,'' she confessed with regret. "A few weeks, I believe.''

Luke's expression turned grim. "Just about long enough to put out the wildfire we're about to touch off when everyone figures out what's going on.''

Jessie's confidence faltered for a moment. He still hadn't said the words she'd demanded of him. Every action, every touch told her he loved her, but she wanted him to say the words, wanted to hold the sound of them in her heart. "Luke, exactly what is going on?''

He glanced from her bared breasts to her face and back again. "I'd say that's plain enough.''

"Just sex?''

"Darlin', there's no such thing as *just sex,* where you and I are concerned. I knew the instant I laid eyes on you years ago that it would be like this between us.''

"You know what I mean,'' she said impatiently.

He pulled her back against him, close enough she could feel his warmth, could feel the steady, reassuring beat of his heart.

"We'll work all of that out,'' he promised. "One step at a time, Jessie, we'll find our way.''

He still couldn't seem to bring himself to say the words. But for now, it was close enough. It was a vow that whatever lay ahead, they would face it together.

Harlan was still at the breakfast table when Luke arrived downstairs in the morning. He knew the instant he looked into his father's eyes that he was upset about something. Luke had a sinking feeling deep in his gut that he knew what that something was. He had thought he heard his parents come in the night before just as he'd slipped from Jessie's room well after midnight. He'd been all but certain he had gotten past them undetected, but perhaps he hadn't been as stealthy as he'd imagined.

His father put the paper aside and waited while Luke poured himself a cup of coffee. Luke deliberately took his time.

When he was finally seated, he met his father's gaze. "Everything okay?"

"I was about to ask you the same question."

"Oh?"

"I saw you leaving Jessie's room last night. I wondered if there was something wrong with her or the baby."

The question might have been innocuous enough, but Luke knew his father better than that. Harlan never inquired casually about anything. And their earlier conversation had already demonstrated Harlan's suspicions. Luke could have manufactured a discreet answer, but he had a hunch his father had already figured out the implications of catching him in that upstairs hallway.

"They're fine," he said, focusing his attention on buttering his toast.

"Then there must have been some other reason for you to be sneaking out with half your clothes in your hand."

So, Luke thought dully, there it was, out in the

open. Spelled out in his father's words, it sounded sordid, and his love for Jessie was anything but.

"I love her," he declared defiantly, meeting his father's gaze evenly. "And she loves me."

Harlan sighed deeply, but there was little shock in his eyes. Instead, his gaze hinted of sorrow and anger. "I was afraid of this," he said.

"There's nothing to be afraid of. We're just two people who fell in love. You could be happy for us."

"She's your brother's widow, dammit!"

Luke bit back an expletive of his own. "Erik is dead, Dad. Denying our feelings won't bring him back."

The quietly spoken remarks did nothing to soothe Harlan's temper. "How far has it gone?"

"Not far. She just had a baby."

His father scowled at him. "I meant before."

Luke felt a rough, fierce anger clawing at his stomach. How readily his father was willing to condemn him for a sin he hadn't committed. He supposed that was the price he had to pay for declaring his independence. Despite Jessie's analysis last night, he knew that Harlan would never totally trust him because of that.

"There was nothing between us when Erik was alive," he declared quietly. *"Nothing!"*

"Who the hell are you trying to kid, son? I saw the way the two of you looked at each other. I knew in my gut that was what drove you away, what drove both of you away. You were running from feelings you knew weren't right."

He stared hard at Luke. "Whose baby is it?" he demanded. "Erik's or yours?"

For the first time in his life, Luke honestly thought he could have slammed a fist into his father's face and enjoyed it.

"How dare you?" he said, his tone lethal. "Neither Jessie nor I ever did anything to deserve a question like that. It doesn't say a hell of a lot about your opinion of Erik, either. Whether you choose to believe it or not, he and Jessie had a good marriage. She's not the kind of woman to turn her back on her vows. And I would have rotted in hell before I would have done anything, anything at all to take that away from him."

"Instead, you took away his life."

The cold, flatly spoken words slammed into Luke as forcefully as a sledgehammer. Though he had blamed himself too damned many times in the middle of the night for not doing more to save Erik, the doctors had reassured him over and over that his brother had been beyond help. Hearing the accusation leveled by his father, the same man who'd absolved him from guilt only a day or two before, made him sick to his stomach.

He refused to dignify the accusation with a response. Instead, he simply stood and headed for the door. "I'll be gone before Mother gets down." He glanced back only once, long enough to say, "If Jessie so chooses, she and your granddaughter will be going with me. You can put us all out of your head forever."

"Lucas!" his father called after him. "Dammit, son, get back here!"

Luke heard the command, but refused to acknowledge it. He could not, he *would not* submit to more of his father's disgusting accusations. Nor would he allow Jessie to be put through the same ordeal.

He had known this was the reaction they would face. It was one reason he had fought his feelings so relentlessly. It was why he'd struggled against Jessie's feelings as well, but no more. Those feelings were out in the open now and the fallout had begun. That didn't mean he had to linger at White Pines until his parents poisoned the happiness he and Jessie were on the threshold of discovering.

He was still trembling with rage when he slammed the door to Jessie's suite behind him.

Visibly startled by his entrance and by his obviously nasty temper, Jessie motioned him to silence. "I've just gotten the baby back to sleep," she whispered as she led him into the bedroom. "What on earth's wrong?"

"Pack your bags," he ordered at once. His plan to give her an option in the matter had died somewhere between the dining room and the top of the stairs. He intended to claim what was his and protect them from the righteous indignation they would face if they remained here.

"Why?"

"We're going to my ranch."

To her credit Jessie held her ground. "Why?"

she repeated, her voice more gentle. Worry shadowed her eyes.

Luke muttered an oath under his breath and began to pace.

"Lucas, sit down before you wear a hole in the carpet. Besides you're making me dizzy trying to follow you."

"I can't sit. I'm too angry."

"It's barely seven o'clock in the morning. What could possibly have set you off this early in the day?"

"I just came from having a little chat with Dad. Apparently he saw me leaving your room last night and jumped to all the worst conclusions."

"Meaning?"

He frowned at her. "He assumes you and I are having an affair."

"Luke, if it weren't for certain circumstances, we would be," she said pointedly.

"He assumes it has been going on for some time." When she showed no evident reaction to that, he added, "He wonders if perhaps Angela is mine."

Jessie's eyes widened. Her mouth gaped with indignation. Patches of color flared in her cheeks. She flew out of the rocker and headed for the door.

Luke stared after her. "Where the devil are you going?"

"To have a few words with your father. I will not allow him to insult Erik's memory, to insult all of us with such a disgusting allegation."

Luke caught her elbow and hauled her back into

the room. "It won't help. He's in a rage. He won't listen."

"Oh, he'll hear me," she insisted in a low tone. "Let me go, Luke."

"Not until you calm down." After a moment, she stopped struggling. Her utter stillness was almost worse. "I'm sorry, Jessie. I knew this was the way he would take it. God knows what Mother will have to say when she finds out. She'll probably insist on going into seclusion from the shame of it all. I think the thing to do is get away until they've had a chance to settle down and digest the news. Maybe then we can have a conversation that won't deteriorate into a lot of ugly name calling."

Jessie's chin tilted stubbornly. "I won't leave. Not like this."

"There's no choice. You have no idea what it's going to be like around here in a few hours. I won't let you go through that."

"I'm not leaving," Jessie repeated adamantly. "I thought Angela would bring this family back together. It seemed to me just yesterday that you and your father were putting past differences behind you. I can't allow our feelings to ruin your chances for a reconciliation."

Luke stared at her incredulously. "Jessie, what the hell is going on here? You fought like crazy to get me to acknowledge my feelings for you. Finally, just last night, we agreed to stop fighting how we feel and try to build a future. Now you're willing to put that at risk so my father and I can get along? I don't get it. Where are your priorities?"

"Where they've always been," she said quietly. "With family. Nothing's more important, Luke. Nothing."

He took a step back and studied her as if she were an alien creature. He didn't understand how he had gotten it so wrong. She was still the woman he loved, all right. Her hair was tousled and just begging for him to run his fingers through it. Her cheeks were rosy, her eyes glinting with determination. She was the most incredible mix of soft curves and fierce convictions he'd ever met.

Right now, though, it seemed to him their dilemma came down to a choice between family and him. If he understood her correctly, she was choosing his family.

Raking his fingers through his hair in a gesture of pure frustration, he shook his head. "So that's it, then? After all this, you're choosing them over me."

He had to admit that Jessie looked shocked by his assessment.

"That isn't what I'm saying at all," she protested. "I'm saying we need to stay here and work it out."

"Not me," Luke said stubbornly. "You can make peace with the devil, if that's what you want, but I'll be damned if I'll hang around with people who think so little of you and of me. Frankly, I'd think you'd have more pride, too."

With one last look in her direction, he turned and stalked from the room. Just as he had with his father earlier, he ignored her plea for him to return. As far as he could tell, there was nothing more to be said.

Only after he had his bag packed and was outside did he allow himself to stop for an instant and think about what was happening. When he did, this great empty space seemed to open up inside him.

They had been so close. He had actually begun to believe that dreams could come true. In the end, though, Jessie's love hadn't been as strong as he'd thought.

He threw his bag onto the passenger seat of one of his father's pickups and dug the keys out from under the mat. He'd hire someone to drive it back from his ranch tomorrow. He sure as hell wasn't about to ask Harlan to have the pilot fly him home.

Besides, the long, tedious drive would do him good. He'd have time enough to figure out how he was going to survive not having Jessie and Angela in his life.

He was just about to turn onto the driveway, when a bright red pickup skidded to a halt behind him, blocking his way. Cody leapt from the truck before the engine quieted.

"Luke, what the hell are you doing?" his youngest brother demanded.

"What does it look like? I'm stealing one of Daddy's trucks and going home."

"Without Jessie?" Cody inquired softly.

Luke stilled and stared at his brother. "What do you know about Jessie and me?"

Cody rolled his eyes. "Hell, Luke, anyone who

isn't blind could see how the two of you feel about each other. Don't abandon her now.''

''You've got it backward. She made the decision to stay.''

''You're the one in the truck, about to head down the driveway,'' Cody contradicted. ''That constitutes abandonment in my book. I thought you had more guts.''

A dull throbbing was beginning at the base of Luke's skull. ''Whatever you have to say, Cody, spit it out. I want to get on the road.''

His brother shot him a commiserating look. ''I talked to Jessie a little bit ago. She wasn't making a lot of sense, but I got the gist of it. I know what Daddy said. It was a lousy thing to say. There's no getting around that.''

''So you can see why all I want to do is get the hell away from here.''

''Sure can,'' Cody agreed.

Luke was startled by the unexpected agreement. He studied Cody suspiciously.

''Of course, Jessie also told me a story. She said you'd remembered how Daddy taught us to be strong, how he made us fight for the things we wanted in life. She told me some cockamamy theory that he deliberately puts roadblocks in our paths just so we have to scramble over them. It's his way of finding out how badly we want something.''

Luke closed his eyes. He recalled the exact conversation all too vividly.

''Isn't Jessie worth fighting for?'' Cody asked softly. ''Seems to me like she is.''

His brother's words reached him as nothing else had. Cody was right. He was running away from the most important fight of his life. Luke sighed and cut the pickup's engine.

"When did you grow up and get so damned smart?" he asked as he climbed from the truck and snagged his brother in a hug.

"Not me," Cody denied. "It was Jessie. She gave me all the arguments I'd need."

"She could have tried them on me herself."

Cody grinned. "She said you were too mad at her to listen. She figured since I was neutral, I might have a shot at getting through that thick skull of yours."

"Daddy's never going to approve of me being with Jessie," Luke said. "Mother's going to go ballistic."

"Ought to make life around here downright interesting," Cody said. "Maybe I'll move back to the main house just to watch the fireworks. Jordan will probably want to come home, too."

"Only if you both intend to stand beside me on this," Luke warned.

A crooked grin on his face, Cody held up his hand for a high-five. "That's what brothers are for."

Luke realized that was something he was finally beginning to understand, thanks to Jessie. It killed him to admit it, but it just might be that she was a hell of a lot smarter than he was when it came to matters of family and the heart.

Chapter Sixteen

Her hands clutched tightly together, Jessie stood at the window of her room and watched Luke and Cody's sometimes heated exchange below. When Luke finally shut off the truck's engine and emerged, a sigh of relief washed through her. She had been so afraid that the desperate call she'd made to Cody had been too late. She'd also known he might be her only chance to make Luke see reason.

She knew from her own conversation with Cody on Christmas that he had given her relationship with Luke his blessing. It had been her first hint that not every member of the Adams clan would be opposed to the feelings she and Luke shared.

This morning she had sensed that even more than

Cody's ability to stand up to Luke, what was needed was someone who wouldn't be passing judgment on the original cause of the disagreement between father and son.

As she watched Cody and Luke enter the house, she prayed that all of Cody's skills at persuasion wouldn't be wasted the instant Luke ran into his father.

Drawing in a deep breath, she decided that this was not a battle Luke should have to take on alone. It was their fight. Plucking Angela from her crib, Jessie emerged from her suite and started downstairs.

Halfway down she realized Luke was waiting at the bottom of the steps, his gaze fixed on her. Her pulse skittered wildly as she tried to anticipate what he would say to her. Beside him, Cody shot her a wink and an irrepressible grin.

"I think I'll join Daddy for some coffee," Cody said. "I want a front row seat for the next act."

Jessie smiled at him. "Thanks for coming so quickly."

"No problem. Nothing like tangling with big brother here to get my adrenaline jump started in the morning. Can't wait to get to Daddy now. I might even try to persuade him to let me buy that new tractor I've been wanting."

After he'd gone, Luke finally spoke. "I'm sorry," he said. "I shouldn't have run out and left you to deal with Daddy." The apology seemed to have been formed at some cost. He was watching her uneasily.

Jessie reached out and touched his cheek. "You thought I'd chosen them over you, when nothing could be further from the truth. I chose us, Lucas. We can't have a future if we don't settle this with everyone now. It will eat away at us, until we're destroyed. Hiding away on your ranch is no solution, and in your heart, I think you know that."

His lips curved in what might have been the beginning of a smile. "You play dirty, though, Jessica. Threw my own words back in my face."

"No, I didn't." She grinned unrepentantly. "I had Cody do it. If I could have gotten him here fast enough, I would have had Jordan add his two cents."

He cupped her face in his hands. "You are worth fighting for, Jessie. Never doubt that. The way I felt when I climbed into that truck, the empty space inside me where my heart had been, I hope to God I never feel that way again."

"You won't," she whispered. "I promise."

Angela stirred in her arms just then. Luke glanced at the baby and his expression softened. "Come here, sweet pea," he said and claimed her.

A look of resolve came over his face as he clasped Jessie's hand. "Shall we go face the enemy on his own turf?"

She halted in her tracks, forcing him to a stop. "We won't get anywhere, if you keep thinking of your father as the enemy."

"How else should I be thinking of him? He's standing square between me and the woman I love."

The declaration made her smile. "Try thinking of him as a father who's defending the honor of his son who died."

Luke sighed heavily. "In too many ways that makes it all the harder, darlin'. It's almost impossible to fight a ghost."

Jessie said nothing, just squeezed his hand. She thought she knew how to disarm Harlan Adams, though. And when the time came, she would use Erik's own words to do it.

With Angela in his arms and Jessie at his side, Luke felt his strength and courage returning. He felt whole again. That gave him the resolve he needed to walk back into that dining room and face his father.

His lips twisted into a grim smile as he overheard Cody and Harlan arguing over the need for a new tractor. Cody was cheerfully enumerating a list of reasons to counteract every one of Harlan's opposing arguments. Their words died the instant Harlan spotted Luke and Jessie in the doorway.

"Cody, go and take care of that matter we were discussing," his father ordered brusquely.

For an instant, Cody looked confused. "I can buy the tractor?"

His father shrugged. "Might as well let you do it now, before you drive me crazy."

The tiny victory gave Luke hope. He could see once again that sometimes all Harlan really wanted was a good fight. He wanted to be convinced that a decision was right. If his sons couldn't make a strong enough case, they lost. It might have been pure contrariness, but he sensed that it really was his father's way of seeing that they learned to fight for what they believed in. Maybe underneath that tough exterior, his father really did want only what was best for his sons.

Luke made up his mind then and there that his case for claiming Jessie and Angela as his own would be a powerful one.

"Thought you'd taken off," Harlan said, his tone cool.

His avid gaze carefully avoided Luke and settled on his granddaughter. Luke watched him struggling with himself, fighting his obvious desire to stake his claim on the baby he believed Luke had no right to.

Luke kept his voice steady. "I decided running wouldn't solve this problem."

"Did you reach this decision all on your own, or did Jessie's refusal to go force you into it?"

Luke shot a wry look at his father. "Does it really matter? I'm here now." He glanced at Jessie, seated so serenely beside him. "We're here now."

"You two are going to break your mother's heart," his father said bluntly.

"Why?" Luke demanded. "We've done nothing wrong. Neither of us ever betrayed Erik. We never even let on to each other how we felt until a few days ago. I've been fighting it ever since, out of a sense of honor. It made me crazy, thinking of how Erik would feel if he knew. I couldn't even grieve for him the way I should, because I thought I didn't have the right.''

He felt Jessie's gaze on him, warming him with her compassion.

''I think there's something both of you should know,'' she said softly.

Luke started to silence her, but she cut him off. ''No,'' she insisted. ''This is my fight, too.''

She leveled a look at Harlan. ''I'm fighting for a future for me and for Angela. That doesn't mean we're turning our backs on the past. It doesn't mean we care any the less for Erik. Neither of us will ever forget that he's Angela's father. Choosing to be together just means we're moving forward. That's something Erik understood.''

Harlan's face turned practically purple with indignation. ''How dare you tell me what my son would or would not have understood! Do you think you knew him any better than I did?''

''Yes,'' Jessie said.

The quiet, single-word response seemed to startle Harlan as a full-fledged argument might not have. Luke was astonished by her quiet serenity, her composure and their effect on his father.

''Okay, go on and say your piece,'' Harlan grumbled. ''Get it over with.''

''I was with Erik when he died,'' she reminded them. ''He knew he wasn't going to make it.''

Luke saw tears forming in her eyes, watched as they spilled down her cheeks. She seemed oblivious to them. Her entire focus seemed to be on making Harlan hear what she had to say.

"He knew," she said softly. "He knew how Luke and I felt about each other, possibly even more clearly than I'd admitted up to that point."

"Dear God!" Harlan swore. "That's what killed him, right there. Knowing his wife was in love with another man would be enough to cost any man the will to live."

Jessie shook her head. "No, he gave us his blessing. He said he wanted me to be happy."

"You're making that up," Harlan said. "Damned convenient, since he's not here to speak for himself."

If Luke hadn't seen the agony in her eyes, he might not have believed her himself. He could tell, though, that the memory of those final moments with her husband had tormented her for months now, twisting her up with guilt and self-recriminations.

"It's true," she said evenly. "And if you don't believe me, you can call Doc Winchell. He was right by Erik's side at the end. He heard every word."

A stunned silence settled over the room. Harlan was clearly at a loss. Luke was torn between anguish and an incredible sense of relief that his brother had known about his feelings for Jessie and forgiven him for them. It was as if the last roadblock to his complete sense of joy had been removed. He could feel tears sliding down his cheeks. Unashamed, he let them fall as he watched his father. Not until this moment had he realized how desperately he wanted forgiveness from him, not just for his brother's death, but for this, for loving Jessie.

Harlan finally sank back, his shoulders slumped in defeat. "I don't suppose there's anything I can do to stop you from getting on with a life together," he said grudgingly. "You're both adults. You'll do what you want whether I approve or not."

Luke thought he heard an underlying message in his father's words, a cry for reassurance that their love was deep enough to be worth the cost. He nodded.

"That's true, Daddy. We can get married the way we want. No one can stop us. We can raise Angela and any other children we might be blessed with. We can live happily ever after." He looked straight into his father's eyes then. "But it won't be the same if you're not in our lives. We don't need your approval, but we do want your love."

Jessie's hand slid into his. He folded his own around it and held on tight as they waited for his father's decision. He knew giving in wouldn't come easily to him. It never had. But, as Jessie had reminded him time and again, his father was a fair man.

"It'll take a bit of time," Harlan said eventually. "Some getting used to." A tired smile stirred at the corners of his mouth. "I suppose there's something to be said for keeping Jessica and Angela in the family. She could have gone off and married some stranger."

Luke grinned at him. "I knew you'd find a way to put a positive spin on this sooner or later."

Harlan sighed heavily. "I just hope that's argument enough to keep your mother from going straight through the roof.''

Luke stood and settled the baby against his shoulder. ''Maybe I'll leave that one to you.''

''Sit down!'' Harlan ordered.

Luke grinned at them despite himself. ''Bad idea, huh?''

Jessie patted his hand. ''Remember, Luke, it's a family matter.''

For better or worse, it looked as if the whole clan was going to be together through thick and thin. He just hoped like hell that Cody and Jordan settled down soon and took some of the pressure off him. He glanced at Jessie.

''Happy? You got what you wanted.''

''We got what we needed,'' she corrected. ''I love you, Luke Adams.''

''I love you. And I'll find your family for you, if it's the last thing I do.''

''No need,'' she said. ''I've found the only family I'll ever need.''

''If you two are going to keep this up, I'm going to leave the room and take that grandbaby of mine with me,'' Harlan warned. ''It's not proper for her to be a witness to your carrying on.''

Luke was already leaning toward Jessie to claim a kiss. ''Goodbye,'' he murmured, distractedly.

'''Bye,'' Jessie said just before her lips met his.

Luke was hardly aware of Harlan's exaggerated sigh or of the moment when his father lifted Angela out of his arms. He had something far more important on his mind—the future.

* * * * *

NATURAL BORN DADDY

Prologue

"Hey, boss, the barracuda...excuse me, your fiancée is on line two," Ginger Drake announced from the doorway.

Jordan glowered at his impudent secretary. "I've told you not to call her that."

Undaunted, Ginger merely strolled into his office and perched on the corner of his desk, an act that hiked her skirt to midthigh. Jordan shook his head. If she weren't the most efficient, most incredibly loyal young woman who'd ever worked for him, he would have fired her months ago for her tart remarks and her unrepentant intrusion into his personal life.

"You've also told me to be honest and truthful, no matter how much it hurts," she informed him now. "That's my job around here."

"Your job is taking dictation and typing."

"And keeping you happy," she reminded him. She gestured at the blinking phone line. "*She* does not make you happy. She is a b—"

"Don't say it," he warned, reaching for the phone.

Ginger shrugged. "Well, she is, which you could see for yourself, if you weren't blinded by the size of her—"

"Ginger!" He pointed toward the door. "Out!"

"Just doing my job," she said, and sashayed from the room with a provocative sway of her hips.

Unable to resist, Jordan watched that motion with an appreciative eye. If he hadn't known that she was blissfully married to a linebacker for the Houston Oilers, he would have assumed that Ginger was trying to get his attention. Instead, he knew perfectly well that feminine provocation came as naturally and unselfconsciously to her as flirting with the opposite sex did to him. The difference was, he had tired of it.

Being named one of the city's most eligible bachelors the past five years in a row had lost its charm. He was ready to settle down. The woman on the phone was the candidate he'd chosen six months ago from the string of female acquaintances who accompanied him to the various charity functions that made up the bulk of his social life.

"Hey, darlin', how are you?" he said to Rexanne Marshall once Ginger was out of hearing range with the office door firmly shut behind her. "How was the convention?"

"Interesting," Rexanne said in that deliberately smoky voice that oozed sensuality and, as she well knew, sent goose bumps dancing down his spine.

He settled back in his chair and asked, "Did you make any big deals?" Rexanne really got turned on by her deal making. He could practically envision their passionate reunion.

"You could say that."

Jordan thought he heard something odd in her tone, a hint of strain that was rare for the supremely confident, highly successful owner of a small but thriving Texas cosmetics company. It was a company poised to make a major move into the national marketplace with his financial backing.

"Rexanne, is everything okay?"

"Jordan…"

He could hear her swallowing and suddenly his body went absolutely still. She had bad news. He could tell from that increasingly evident note of uncertainty in her voice. He sat up a little straighter.

"Whatever it is, just tell me," he instructed. He'd meant to sound patient and concerned, but even he recognized the drill-sergeant command in his voice.

"Actually, it was the most amazing thing," she began with a nervous little giggle.

Rexanne was quite possibly the most sophisticated woman he'd ever met. She never giggled. His suspicions tripled as he waited for her to go on.

"I ran into this man, an old friend, actually, from high school, as a matter of fact."

Now the woman who never wasted a word was

babbling. Jordan's sense of dread kicked in. He stood and began to pace, phone in hand. "And?"

"Well, the truth of it is...Jordan, I'm really sorry about this, but..."

"Just spit it out, Rexanne."

"Randall and I got married," she blurted at last. "In Vegas."

Rexanne and Randall? How alliterative, he thought with an uncharacteristic edge of sarcasm. Married? How considerate of her to give him fair warning. The same society page columnists who'd been gushing about their engagement would be gossiping about this turn of events for weeks. It was only one step short of being left at the altar. He didn't like the prospect of being the subject of speculation and innuendo. He didn't like it one damned bit.

"I see," he said coldly. Not entirely sure of the protocol for the circumstances, he went with his gut reaction, which was liberally laced with more sarcasm. "Thank you so much for calling, Rexanne. Have a nice life."

"Now, Jordan, please don't be like that," she whined.

Why had he never noticed that she whined? he wondered. Probably because he'd given in to her every request, showered her with gifts and never once in the months since they had announced their engagement exchanged a cross word with her. Of course, that was probably because Rexanne had tucked herself so neatly and cheerfully into his life, he'd had no reason to complain.

"Darling, I know it's a shock and I wouldn't have hurt you for the world, but this was, like, fate or something," she said in a more familiar, smoky, cajoling tone.

"Fate?" he repeated numbly. "Yes, I suppose it was." *Fate* had benevolently prevented him from having to listen to that whine for the rest of his days. She could ooze sensuality from now to doomsday and he would never stop hearing that whine. It would lurk in his memory like the sound of chalk squeaking across a blackboard.

"Darling, you can't let this change in our personal status interfere with the business arrangement we have," she protested. "You're too much of a businessman. You and I are going to take Marshall Cosmetics to the top around the globe. We're going to make a fortune."

Ah, now they were getting to her real concern, not his feelings, but her future plans for Marshall Cosmetics. "Sorry, *darlin'*, I'm afraid that's going to be up to you and Randall."

"But you promised," she whined.

The sound of her voice was really getting on his nerves. "So did you," he reminded her icily. "Goodbye, Rexanne."

He hung up before she could launch into an attempt to sugarcoat the now-obvious truth—that she had wanted his money and his connections to Wall Street more than she had ever wanted him.

As he sat staring out at the sweeping view of the Houston skyline, he wondered at his lack of emotion. Shouldn't he have felt more than this vague irritation that his plans for settling down had been disrupted? Shouldn't he be feeling empty in side? Shouldn't he be throwing things? He hefted a Baccarat crystal paperweight consideringly, then shrugged and lowered it to his desk. She wasn't worth it.

Maybe he was incapable of the kind of passion that his older brother Luke had found with Jessie. Maybe, he conceded, he'd gone about finding a wife too methodically.

Or maybe the incredible judgment that had propelled him to the top of the oil industry didn't carry over into personal matters. Maybe he was doomed to make the same mistakes over and over, trusting the wrong women.

It wasn't, he admitted to himself ruefully, as if Rexanne had been the first. There had been a whole damned army of poor choices, starting back in college and continuing right up through this latest debacle. Oddly enough, he realized he couldn't even recall the names of most of them. Obviously his heart had never been as engaged as he'd thought it had been.

Finally, dragging in a deep breath, he pushed the problem aside for further consideration on the weekend. He was almost tempted to make a notation to himself on his calendar, so he wouldn't forget. *Women* ought to be enough of a reminder. He reached for his daybook and dutifully jotted it down. He would matter-of-factly dissect his love life as he would a business proposition to see if he could pinpoint where he was going wrong.

He turned back to his desk just in time to see Ginger poking her head into his office. The grin on her face made him wonder if she'd been eavesdropping on his conversation. She'd apparently seen all along what he hadn't, that Rexanne was a barracuda. No doubt that smile meant she was delighted that the woman was out of his life.

"Hey, boss, didn't you hear me buzzing you?" she asked.

"If I had, I would have answered," he retorted irritably.

Her grin widened. She knew, all right, he decided with a sinking feeling. It appeared his latest humiliation was complete. There would be weeks of hearing *I told you so* from her, interspersed with renewed attempts at matchmaking. Maybe he'd finally give in. Ginger's taste couldn't possibly be any worse than his own, though she did seem to know a disturbing number of professional cheerleaders.

"Line one," she prompted him. "It's Kelly."

For some inexplicable reason, Jordan found himself smiling back at his secretary. If there was one person on the face of the earth who could take his mind off his troubles, it was Kelly Flint. She was his best friend, his confidante, his conscience. She had an angel of mercy's sense of timing .

As he reached for the phone the most incredible thought flashed through his head. Why the devil couldn't he marry a woman like Kelly? She was sweet, not the least bit temperamental, funny and, though he'd never really stopped to think about it

before—at least not since the days when they'd
gone swimming in the creek together back in west
Texas—sexy. In fact, just thinking about her sex
appeal made him wonder why he hadn't settled on
Kelly as the perfect solution long ago.

"Why, indeed?" he murmured thoughtfully, pic-
turing her in his head and liking what he saw—
clean-scrubbed, basic beauty with absolutely no ar-
tifice about her. Better yet, he knew for a fact that
she didn't have a duplicitous bone in her body. She
would never betray the man she loved.

"What was that, boss?" Ginger asked, regarding
him with a puzzled look.

"Nothing," he said, because confiding in Ginger
would only draw more advice than he could handle
right now. "Nothing at all."

Something told him, though, that the disclaimer
was more than a massive understatement. He had a
feeling he had just reached the most significant
turning point in his entire life. He mentally
scratched the subject of women from his calendar
and replaced it with one word: *Kelly.*

By the end of the day he would have his plan
for marrying her formulated and by the weekend
he'd be ready to put it into action. Unless something unforeseen popped up, he and Kelly could be
married and settled down by fall. He wouldn't even
have to alter the schedule he'd set for himself when
he'd asked Rexanne to marry him.

Pleased with himself, he finally poked the blinking light on his phone. "Hey, darlin'," he said,
taking what he perceived to be the first step on the
road to the rest of his life.

Chapter One

Jordan drove up the dusty, shaded lane to Kelly's ranch in west Texas with a rare knot in his stomach. Once he'd gotten the idea of marrying her into his head, he hadn't been able to shake it loose. It had been like a burr, sticking to him and snagging his attention at the oddest times.

The only thing that had prevented him from impulsively proposing to her on the phone when she'd called his office earlier in the week was Ginger's fascinated expression as she stood beside his desk the whole time he was on the phone. He had a gut-level feeling that even though his secretary might have applauded Rexanne's replacement, there was something vaguely tacky about proposing to a woman not five minutes after being dumped by the previous fiancée.

Over the next few days the previously implausible idea of marrying his best friend had begun to take shape in his head. He could actually envision Kelly at his side for the rest of his life.

As he'd reminded himself when the idea first came to him, she was calm, sweet and beautiful, at least when she wasn't covered head-to-toe in filth from a rough day on the range. Of course, that wouldn't be a problem once they were married and she was living with him in Houston. She'd have endless hours to pamper herself.

With her glowing skin, her hair the color of wheat in sunlight, and her unexpected brown eyes, she would knock the socks off of Houston society. With her warmth, she would be an asset as a hostess for the kinds of functions that were required of a corporate president. His friends and associates would find her tales of running her own ranch intriguing, if something of an oddity for a woman alone.

Well, not alone, exactly, he reminded himself. There was Danielle. The preschooler was the by-product of Kelly's unfortunate marriage to Paul Flint, a philanderer of the first order, a man who had taken Kelly's tender, trusting heart and broken it into pieces.

Hands clenched and temper barely contained, Jordan had witnessed most of that particular debacle. He'd provided the shoulder for Kelly to cry on when she'd finally decided to end the marriage and take her daughter home to Los Pinos, the tiny west

Texas town where they'd grown up on neighboring ranches.

Danielle was a bit of a complication, he had to admit. He was lousy with kids. He had no idea what to say to them. In all of his plans for settling down, he rarely considered the next step—kids.

He thought back to the previous Christmas. When his sister-in-law had shown up at the family ranch with his infant niece, he'd been completely stymied about what to do with that fragile little baby. Even the prospect of holding her had made his palms sweat. He'd tried not to let his reaction show, but he had known that he had negotiated multimillion-dollar business deals with less display of nerves.

Danielle was equally perplexing to him, even though in a fit of sentiment he'd allowed himself to be persuaded to be her godfather.

The child was barely three feet tall, he reminded himself. At five, she already had an astonishing and precocious vocabulary. Surely he could find a way to communicate with her. If nothing else, he could always buy her half the stock at Toys Unlimited. She'd be so busy with all those new playthings, she wouldn't require any attention at all from him.

Satisfied that he'd dealt with that potential problem in his usual decisive way, he drew in a deep breath and rehearsed what he would say to Kelly to persuade her to marry him. For all of his planning, this part had never quite solidified the way it should have. He kept envisioning her laughing in his face, amused by his out-of-the-blue proposal after all these years of platonic friendship.

Perhaps he should simply tell her that she was the answer to his prayers, someone he liked, someone he trusted.

Someone who could keep him out of the clutches of the wrong women. Even as the words formed, he groaned. Telling her that would certainly go a long way toward charming her. No matter how unemotional she might be, even a woman who'd been chosen as the solution to a problem of sorts wanted to be wooed a little. As a practical matter, he knew Kelly would see the sense of his proposal, but he would definitely have to dress it up with a little romance.

Damn, how was he going to pull this off? Kelly was the most fiercely independent woman he'd ever met, especially since her divorce. She might not want to marry anyone after her experience with Paul, especially not a man who, at one time or another, had been pictured on the society pages with half of Houston's eligible female population. His track record, though certainly not immoral, might be a too vivid reminder of her ex's habits.

Since the divorce, Kelly had taken charge of her life. She had returned to the falling down ranch her family had left her and tackled the task of making it work with the kind of gritty determination he couldn't help but admire.

For the past two years she had worn herself ragged, working from before dawn until well after dark, seven days a week. The ranch hardly had a look of prosperity about it, but there was no mistaking that her efforts were paying off. There was fresh paint on the old house, inside and out, and her herd of longhorns was growing. Even now the livestock was visible in the distance, grazing on newly acquired pastureland she had bought with every penny of her divorce settlement.

The hard work should have taken its toll, but, he was forced to admit, in recent months Kelly had never looked healthier or happier. She no longer had the haggard, tight-lipped, stricken look of a woman who'd been betrayed by the man she'd loved. In fact, she glowed, radiating a sense of serenity and bone-deep satisfaction that had made visiting her the highlight of his trips home.

Whenever the weighty sense of family that Harlan Adams imposed on all of his sons grew too burdensome, Jordan slipped away from White Pines and spent time in Kelly's kitchen, sipping the herbal tea she preferred and talking of inconsequential things that somehow all added up to a kind of tranquillity he found nowhere else in his life. The thought of spending the rest of his days around a woman capable of creating such a peaceful atmosphere soothed him.

Okay, so they wouldn't be marrying for love. Neither of them had had much luck with messy emotions anyway. An old-style marriage of convenience struck him as the sensible way to go. Kelly would never have to worry about money for herself or her daughter again and he would never have to deal with another female barracuda.

As he walked toward the front porch of the ranch house, a porch that sagged and dipped from years of use and sloppy construction, he noted the huge pots of bright flowers she tended with such care in the evenings. They were thriving, the blossoms providing vivid splashes of color against the front of the white house.

Already anticipating their life together, he sighed with contentment. Kelly was a nurturer. Like those flowers, he and any children they ultimately might have would thrive in her care. Assuming he got over this uneasiness he felt with these pint-size enigmas, that is.

He fingered the small jewelry box in his pocket and smiled, pleased with his decision. Kelly's fat gray-and-white cat wound between his legs, purring and shedding on his navy pants. Jordan glanced down, felt a momentary touch of annoyance, then sighed. The old tomcat was part of the package and at least he seemed delighted by Jordan's presence.

With a rare twinge of trepidation, he knocked on the screen door and called out, "Hey, darlin', it's me."

He heard the thunder of tiny feet as Dani came careering around a corner and raced down the hallway. She skidded to a halt, her blond curls bouncing.

"Hi, Jordan," she said, swinging the screen door wide and coming out to join him. "Mommy's in the barn. Francie's having kittens. A lot of kittens."

Jordan cringed. "Really?"

"Want to come see?"

He would rather eat dirt, but the sparkle of anticipation in Dani's eyes was too powerful to resist. "Sure."

To his astonishment, Dani tucked her hand trustingly in his and tugged him around the side of the house toward the barn. "You could have one, if you wanted," she told him.

"I work very long hours. I'm not sure what I'd do with a kitten in Houston," he said, trying to sound as if he regretted it when the truth was he couldn't have been more relieved.

"Cats don't mind if you're not home very much. They're very independent," she informed him. "We hardly ever see Francie, except when she's going to have kittens."

Old Francie reminded him of certain types of people who only turned up when they were in trouble. He hoped Kelly wasn't going to view his visit that way.

Dani stopped on the path in front of him, her face turned up, her brow knitted with concern. "Mommy says we have to give all of them away," she told him.

Her eyes suddenly and, Jordan thought, rather suspiciously filled with tears.

"What if we can't find homes for them?" she asked, sounding pathetic. "Will we have to drown them in the creek?"

The little minx was pulling out all the stops. Jordan choked back a chuckle at the preposterous notion that Kelly would allow harm to come to a single kitten. "No, Dani, I seriously doubt that your mother would drown them in the creek. Where would you ever get such an idea?''

"That's what Daddy said should happen to kittens."

"But you didn't do it, did you?"

"No, because I found homes for every single one." She looked up at him speculatively. "Maybe they'd like a new kitten at White Pines. I'll bet there are mice there and everything. A kitten would be a big help."

"I'll ask," he told her, wondering what his mother would have to say about a kitten scratching her precious antique furniture.

"Promise?"

"Cross my heart."

A radiant smile spread across her face. "Thanks, Jordan. I really, really think you should take one, too. So you won't be lonely."

Actually, he had another idea for staving off loneliness. He glanced up and saw the very woman he had in mind standing in the barn, hands on slender hips, a challenging spark in her eyes as she regarded her daughter.

"You have your work cut out for you, young lady," Kelly announced, barely sparing a glance for Jordan. "There are seven kittens in here. Francie's tuckered out and so am I. See to it that Francie has some fresh food and water."

"Cream, Mommy. Don't you think she deserves cream just this once? Having kittens is hard work."

"Fine, bring her some cream."

Dani tore off across the lawn as fast as her churning little legs could carry her.

"And don't put it in a good china bowl! Use plastic," Kelly shouted after her. Finally she glanced at Jordan. "What brings you by on a Friday night? You didn't mention anything about coming home when we talked earlier in the week."

Jordan shrugged. He was struck by an uncharacteristic twinge of uncertainty. He tucked his hand into his pocket and tightened his grip around the jewelry box for reassurance. "Just an impulse."

"Come on in. I'll make us some tea. Chamomile, I think. You look almost as frazzled as I feel."

"You don't look frazzled," he noted even though it was a charitable remark. Her hair was tousled, her makeup nonexistent, her clothes caked with mud and hay and other stains that didn't bear too close a scrutiny.

Inside the cozy kitchen, which was shadowed in the gathering twilight, she smiled at him. She took down two china cups and placed them on the kitchen table. "And you're a lousy liar, despite all that practice you get dispensing your charm all over Houston. How's the oil business?"

"Challenging."

Attuned as always to his moods, she paused while filling the teakettle with water. "Bad week?"

"No worse than most."

Her gaze narrowed. "That doesn't sound convincing, old chum."

Jordan picked up the empty cup and turned it slowly in his hands. The fine porcelain was cracked and chipped, but he found the delicacy oddly enchanting. Flaws, he'd discovered over time, often made people, like china, more interesting. He wondered what flaws Kelly had. After all these years, he could think of none. Discovering them suddenly struck him as a fascinating pastime.

"Jordan?"

He looked up from the fragile cup and saw that Kelly was regarding him with a puzzled expression. Those huge brown eyes of hers were filled with concern.

"Everything okay?" she asked.

"Rexanne broke the engagement," he announced casually.

"Good," Kelly replied without the slightest hint of sympathy.

"Damn," he muttered irritably. "Did everybody dislike her except me?"

"I didn't dislike her," Kelly corrected. "I just thought she was all wrong for you."

"Why?"

"She was using you."

"Weren't they all," he said dryly.

"As a matter of fact, yes," she said as she poured the boiling water into the pot, tossed in a handful of tea leaves and waited for it to steep.

"Have you ever approved of any woman I've dated?"

Kelly took the question he'd intended to be sarcastic seriously. "There was one, back in college. I think her name was Pamela. You dumped her after the first date."

"And she was right for me?"

"I didn't have all that long to check out her sincerity," she reminded him, "but, yes, I think she could have been. She was sweet."

Jordan scowled. *Sweet?* Perhaps innocuous would have been a better description. He didn't even remember a Pamela, which didn't say much for either her or him.

"Actually, I think my taste is improving," he said, his gaze fixed on Kelly's face. There was no immediate reaction beyond a faint flicker of something in her eyes, something he couldn't quite identify. She seemed slightly more alert, perhaps even a little wary.

"You've already found a replacement for Rexanne? Isn't that a little cavalier?"

"Not really. I told you a long time ago that I thought it was time for me to settle down."

"Right, so you proposed to the first woman to cross your path after that, and look where that got you."

"She wasn't the first woman to cross my path," he protested. "I was seeing several women at the time. Rexanne seemed like the best choice."

"Maybe out of that lot, but did you ever stop to consider there was slim pickings in that bunch?" She waggled a slender finger at him. "I'll answer that. No, you did not. You just decided you wanted to be married and filled the opening as methodically as you would have a position at your company. You probably had a stupid checksheet."

She wasn't all that far off the mark, though he

wouldn't have told her that for another gusher in his oil fields. "Well, I'm not going to be so hasty about it this time," he said.

"You just told me you've identified the woman you want to marry. It's been what? Two days? Maybe three since your engagement broke off?"

"Four, actually."

She rolled her eyes. "Definitely long enough," she said with a touch of unfamiliar sarcasm. "Jordan, why can't you just relax and let nature take its course?"

He gave her a disdainful look. "I don't have a lot of faith in nature."

She gave him a wry look. "You would if you'd been in that barn with me an hour ago."

"I don't think the fact that your tomcat can't keep his paws off of Francie is a testament to nature in its finest moments."

She shrugged, a grin tugging at the corners of her mouth. "Okay, you may have a point about that. So, who's the latest woman to capture your fancy?"

He leveled a look straight into her eyes and waited until he was sure he had her full attention. "Actually, it's you."

Kelly—calm, serene, unflappable Kelly—succumbed to a coughing fit that had her eyes watering and Jordan wondering if he'd gone about this in an incredibly stupid way. It wouldn't be the first time the direct method had failed him.

Still, he was determined to make her see the sense of this. All of those lectures he'd given himself about dressing it up with a little sweet talk flew out the window. He set out to hammer home the logic.

"It's a perfectly rational decision..." he began.

"You're not serious," she said when she could finally speak.

He pulled the jewelry box from his pocket and placed it on the kitchen table in front of her. Since she was eyeing it as if it were a poisonous rattler, he flipped it open to reveal a stunning three-carat diamond that pretty well proclaimed him to be dead serious. Despite its impressive size, it was simpler than the engagement ring he'd purchased at Rexanne's urging. She'd wanted flashy. Kelly struck him as the kind of woman who would admire simplicity. Gazing into her eyes, however, he had the sinking feeling that admiration for his taste in rings was the last thing on her mind.

"You've obviously lost your mind," she said, but her voice was softer now and laced with something that might have been regret.

"Quite the contrary. It's the only rational decision for both of us."

"Rational," she repeated as if it were a dirty word.

There was an ominous undercurrent he didn't quite get. "Actually, yes. I've given it quite a lot of thought. We've known each other forever— there won't be any nasty surprises. We've both had more than our share of those. I can give you the kind of life and financial security you deserve."

"And I can give you…what? A hostess? A cook, perhaps? A bed partner on cold nights?"

Jordan could feel the blood climbing into his cheeks as she enumerated some of the very thoughts that had occurred to him. They'd sounded better in theory than they did spoken out loud by a woman who was clearly insulted. She wasn't taking this well at all. He searched for a new approach. "Now, Kelly…"

Unfortunately he never got to finish the sentence. Kelly was already shaking her head, rather emphatically, it seemed to him.

She stood and glowered down at him. "Not a chance. No way. Forget it, bud. Take a hike." She seemed to be just warming up.

The flare of unexpected temper just might be one of those previously hidden flaws he'd been hoping to discover. He tried to calm her. "You're saying no without giving the matter any consideration at all," he advised her. "When you do, I'm sure you'll see—"

"Not if we both live to be a hundred and ten and we're the only two people tottering around on the face of the earth," she assured him.

Jordan was beginning to get an inkling that she meant it and that nothing he was likely to say tonight was going to change her mind.

"Okay, okay," he said, defeated for the moment. "I get the picture."

"I doubt it."

A hasty exit seemed in order. "Maybe I'd better let you sleep on it. We can talk again tomorrow."

Kelly drew herself up and squared off in front of him. Fire sparked in her eyes, amber lights bringing that normally placid shade of brown alive. "We can talk tomorrow, if you like," she said emphatically, "but not about this."

Jordan edged carefully around her and made his way to the front door. "See you in the morning."

"Jordan?"

Her voice halted him in his tracks. She had obviously followed him.

"You forgot something."

He turned back. She was holding out the box with the engagement ring. "Keep it here," he said, refusing to accept it. "Try it on. Maybe you'll get used to the idea."

She tossed the ring straight at him. He caught it in midair and sighed. "I'll bring it with me tomorrow."

"Don't," she warned angrily. "I'm not some poor substitute you can call on when the first string doesn't show."

Jordan was shocked by her assessment, even though he had to admit there might be just the teensiest bit of truth to it. "I'm sorry. I never meant it like that," he insisted.

She sighed heavily. "Yes, Jordan, I think that is exactly how you meant it."

That said, she quietly closed the door in his face. He was left standing on the porch all alone. Oddly enough, it was the first time in all the visits he had paid to this house that he was leaving feeling lonelier and far, far emptier than when he had arrived.

He made up his mind as he drove the few miles back to White Pines that night that that wouldn't be the last of it. After all, hadn't he wooed some of the most sought-after women in all of Texas? Maybe approaching this as a business proposition hadn't been the wisest decision. He'd try roses and, if that didn't work, billboards along the highway, if he had to. Nobody said no to Jordan Adams. Kelly would weaken sooner or later. What struck him as slightly worrisome was the fact that it suddenly seemed to matter so much. Somewhere deep inside him he had the troubling impression that she was his last and best chance for happiness.

"The man is impossible!" Kelly declared, leaning against the front door and listening for the sound of his car driving off before she budged. She didn't want to move until she knew for certain he wasn't coming back. She seriously doubted she could hold out against his ludicrous proposal for very long. She'd been in love with the man practically since the cradle.

Unfortunately he had never once in all these years given her a second glance. She doubted he would be doing it now, if he hadn't suffered a defeat in his blasted plan for his own life. Who in hell had a timetable for getting married? No one she knew except Jordan Adams. Well, he could put that plan into action without her.

"Mommy, are you okay?" Dani asked, peering up at her.

"I sure am, munchkin," she said with more exuberance than she felt.

"You look funny."

She grinned at the honest assessment. Bending over, she scooped her daughter into her arms and swung her high. "Funny?" she repeated indignantly. "Mommy is beautiful, remember?"

Dani giggled from her upside-down vantage point. "Very beautiful," she confirmed. "Let me down, Mommy. My head's getting dizzy."

"Mine, too, sweetie," she murmured, glancing through the window and watching the red glow of Jordan's taillights disappear into the night.

Suddenly she thought of all the times she'd watched Jordan drive away, her heart thudding with disappointment once more because he hadn't recognized how perfect they were for each other, because his kiss had been nothing more than a peck on the cheek.

She'd married Paul Flint only after she'd finally faced up to the fact that Jordan was never going to view her as anything more than his pal. Her world had fallen apart after that stupid, impulsive decision. Not right away, of course. It had taken a month or two before Paul had started spending more and more time away from their home. She wasn't even certain when he'd started seeing other women.

When she finally accepted the fact that Paul was having affairs, she asked for a divorce. Jordan had been there to pick up the pieces. He hadn't even said he'd told her so as he'd transported her and then three-year-old Dani to the ranch where Kelly had grown up.

From that moment on they had fallen into their old pattern of frequent phone calls and visits whenever he came home from Houston. She looked forward to their talks more and more. She had dreaded the day when his marriage to Rexanne would force an end to the quiet, uncomplicated time they spent together.

At least that wasn't a problem any longer, she thought with another sigh.

"Mommy? Are you sad?" Dani inquired with her astonishing perceptiveness.

"Just a little," she admitted.

"I know just what you need," her daughter announced, giving her a coy look that Kelly recognized all too well.

"What's that?"

"A new kitten."

Kelly grinned at her child's sneaky tactics. The suggestion was certainly a more rational one than Jordan had offered. A kitten was a whole lot less complicated than taking on a husband who'd selected her for marriage for all the wrong reasons.

"I'll think about it," she promised. "Now, go take your bath and get ready for bed."

Dani bounced off toward the stairs, then halted and looked back. "Mommy?"

"Yes."

"Think really hard, okay?"

"Okay."

It was the second time that night that she'd been asked to carefully consider a decision that could change her life. Instinct told her to say no to both requests. Her heart was another matter entirely.

Chapter Two

Jordan lingered over coffee at White Pines the morning after his proposal to Kelly. He'd been up since the crack of dawn, in the dining room since six-thirty. All that time he'd been pondering a new approach to the problem of getting Kelly to take his declaration of his intentions seriously. For the first time in his life, he was at a loss.

He heard the sound of boots on the stairs and glanced toward the doorway. Harlan Adams appeared a moment later, looking as fit as ever despite the fact that his fifty-sixth birthday was just around the corner. He regarded his son with surprise. Jordan suspected it was feigned, since nothing went on around White Pines that his father didn't know within minutes.

"Hey, boy, when did you turn up?" his father asked as he surveyed the lavish breakfast buffet their housekeeper had left for them.

"Last night."

"Must have been mighty late."

"I'm too old for you to be checking my comings and goings," Jordan reminded his father.

"Did I ask?"

Jordan sighed and battled his instinctive reaction to his father's habitual, if subtle, probing. Harlan loved to goad them all, loved the spirited arguments and loved even more the rare wins he managed against his sons' stubbornness.

According to Luke, the oldest, their father battled wits with them just to get them to stand up for what they wanted. Jordan supposed it might be true. He'd practically had to declare war to leave White Pines and its ready-made career in ranching to go into the oil business. Yet once he'd gotten to Houston, the path had miraculously been cleared for him. He'd promptly found work at one of the best companies in the state before striking out on his own a few years later.

"Everything okay around here?" he inquired as his father piled his plate high with the scrambled eggs, ham and hash browns that were forbidden to him except on weekends. He noted with some amusement that Harlan gave wide berth to the bran flakes and oatmeal.

"Things would be just fine if Cody didn't decide he has to have some newfangled piece of equipment every time I turn around," Harlan grumbled.

"How many have you let him buy?" Jordan asked.

His father shrugged. "Put my foot down about some fancy computer with those little disks and intergalactic communications potential or some such. I can't even figure out the one we've got. Luke spent a whole day trying to show me again the last time he and Jessie were over here, but if you ask me, pen and paper are plenty good enough for keeping the books."

Jordan hid a smile. He knew that his father's pretended bemusement covered a mind that could grasp the most intricate details in a flash. Any trouble he was having with his computer was feigned solely to grab Luke's attention.

"Daddy, you're practically in the twenty-first century," he chided. "You have to keep up with the times."

"A lot of nonsense, if you ask me." He grinned. "Leastways, that's what I tell Cody. Keeps him on his toes."

The youngest of the Adams brothers, Cody was the one who'd fought hardest for his place as the head of the White Pines ranching operation. Harlan had pushed just as hard to get him to leave and strike out on his own. Now there was little question in anyone's mind that Cody was as integral to the family business as his father was.

"One of these days the two of you are going to butt heads once too often," Jordan warned his father.

"Not a chance," Harlan said with evident pride.

"That boy's stubborn as a mule. Might even be worse than you or Lucas and he's a danged sight ornerier than Erik."

He sounded downright happy about his youngest's muleheadedness. He studied Jordan over the rim of his coffee cup. "You never did say what brought you home."

"No," Jordan said firmly. "I didn't."

"Wouldn't have anything to do with that Flint woman, would it?"

Jordan's head snapped up and he stared at his father. "Why would you ask that?"

"Because you make a beeline for that ranch every time you drive into the county. Can't be sleeping with her, since you do wind up in your own bed here at night."

Jordan's jaw tightened at the too personal observation. "My sleeping arrangements are none of your concern. Besides, Kelly and I are just friends. She's had a rough time of it these past couple of years. I try to look in on her every once in a while to make sure she's okay." At least, that had been his motivation until last night's visit.

His father nodded. "She's getting that place of hers on its feet, though. She's got a lot of gumption and that girl of hers is a real little dickens. She called here last night to see if you'd asked yet about whether we want a kitten."

Despite his annoyance with his father, Jordan couldn't help chuckling at Dani's persistence. The remark was also proof that his father had known he was back in town and had also known exactly where he was the night before. All the questions had been designed just to needle him.

"Did you agree to take one?" he asked, referring to the kittens Dani hadn't trusted him to save.

"How could I say no? The child was worried sick about her mother drowning them all in the creek. She mentioned that you'd reassured her that wouldn't happen, but she wasn't taking any chances." He eyed Jordan speculatively. "Does that pitiful excuse for a father of hers get by much?"

Jordan wasn't surprised that his father knew the whole ugly story. It was hardly a secret, but even if it had been, Harlan made it his business to know about the folks around him, including those on neighboring ranches. He was even more persistent when it came to the women in his sons' lives.

"Not that I'm aware of," he told his father.

"Can't understand a man who wouldn't be proud to call a little one like that his own."

"Neither can I," Jordan said grimly. He'd expressed his views on Paul Flint more than once to Kelly, long before she'd finally decided on divorce as her only option. He'd even offered on occasion to pummel some sense into the man.

"Shame to go through life without a daddy," Harlan observed.

Jordan regarded him intently. There was no mistaking that his father had a point to make. "Meaning?"

"Just what I said," he insisted, sounding a little too innocent. "A child deserves two parents. Of course, a situation like that is all wrong for a man like you."

"Now what's your point?" Jordan's voice contained a lethal warning note.

"Just that I understand you. You're not looking for some country gal and a ready-made family. I've seen your type, glossy, sophisticated, like that... what's her name?"

"Rexanne," Jordan supplied automatically, used to his father's refusal to get the names of the women in his life straight.

"Right," he said. "Now she's the perfect wife for a big oil tycoon."

Jordan was beginning to wonder exactly how much his father knew about his broken engagement. It seemed to him that the digs were a little too pointed for him not to have heard about it. He'd always despised Rexanne, just as he had every other woman Jordan had brought to White Pines. His sudden defense of her was clearly part of some Machiavellian scheme of his. He'd probably been on the phone to Ginger during the week and gotten an earful about his son's social life—or sudden lack thereof.

"I'm afraid Rexanne is out of the picture," Jordan said tersely.

Harlan tried for a sympathetic look, but the effort was downright pitiful. There was a gleam of pure satisfaction in his eyes. "Sorry, son," he said without much sincerity.

"She was the wrong choice. I'll get over it."

Sooner than anyone imagined, if he had his way about it.

"It's not surprising, then, that you were over to visit Kelly last night. She always has had a sympathetic ear, especially where you're concerned."

"We weren't lamenting my love life last night," Jordan said.

Curiosity blossomed on his father's transparent features. "Oh?"

"We were just...talking," he finally concluded weakly, unwilling to broach the actual subject matter of their conversation. Once Harlan got that particular bit in his teeth, there'd be no controlling his efforts at manipulation.

"Just don't go letting her get the wrong idea now, son. You said yourself, she's been through a lot. No point in getting her hopes up now that you're on the rebound. No telling what a woman might do when a man is vulnerable. They can be downright sneaky when they're out to get their hooks into a man."

"There's nothing the least bit sneaky or underhanded about Kelly," Jordan snapped.

"If you say so, son. You certainly know the woman better than I do."

Jordan didn't think he liked the direction this conversation was heading. Any minute now his father was going to say something truly offensive about Kelly and he would leap to her defense. There was no telling what would happen after that. His mother would probably find them tussling on the dining room floor.

He tossed his napkin down on the table and stood. "I've got to get out of here."

"Going for a ride?" his father inquired, his expression perfectly innocent.

"Yes," he said tightly, and slammed out of the house.

Only much, much later did he wonder what he would have seen if he'd looked back. He had the strangest feeling he would have caught a complacent smile spreading across his father's face.

With Dani visiting a friend for the day, Kelly had spent the entire morning checking on her livestock and inspecting her fences. Of course, given her state of distraction an entire section of fence could have been down and it would have slipped her notice. Fortunately the ranch hand she'd been able to afford just a month ago had been riding with her most of the day. Now, though, she was alone again, riding at a more leisurely pace.

She kept glancing toward the horizon, looking for some sign of Jordan's car. Her ears were attuned to the sound of approaching hooves, as well, since he sometimes chose to borrow one of his father's horses and ride over.

He still looked incredibly well suited to horse and saddle. In fact, she'd always thought he looked far more impressive and a hundred percent sexier in jeans and a chambray shirt than he did in those outrageously expensive designer suits he wore most of the time in Houston. Every time he put one of those suits on, it was as if a barrier went up between them. Sometimes she didn't even recognize the man he'd become in Houston.

More than his clothes had changed. As if fitting himself to a role, he'd been transformed into a sophisticated executive, driven and sometimes, it seemed to her, a little too coldly dispassionate.

His proposal the night before had certainly fit the new Jordan. The old Jordan, the sensitive man who often sat in her kitchen talking until dawn, the exuberant daredevil who'd ridden over every square inch of her ranch and his own with her at midnight, would never have made such a proposition. He'd had more romance in his soul, even if little of it had been directed her way. Now she had to wonder if he'd wasted it all on that string of unsuitable gold diggers who'd spent the past few years trying to catch him.

She knew without a doubt that he wasn't going to give up on this crazy idea he'd gotten into his head about marrying her. One of his most attractive traits was his tenaciousness. To ready herself for the next assault, she had spent the entire morning reminding herself of all the ways to say no—and mean it.

She was so busy concentrating on shoring up her defenses, she missed the plane the first time it flew over. The second time the sound of its engine drew her attention to the vivid blue sky. There was nothing especially unusual about a small plane overhead. Many of the more successful ranchers actually had their own planes to check out the far reaches of their land. Jordan's family was one of them. Many more ranchers hired them on occasion. There was a small but active private airport nearby.

What was unusual about this particular plane was the message trailing through the clear blue sky behind it: Marry Me, Kelly.

She stared at it with a sort of horrified fascination. She supposed a case could be made that it was exactly the sort of impulsive, outrageous thing the old Jordan would have dreamed up, the sort of thing she'd claimed only moments ago to miss. Her heart, in fact, turned a somersault in her chest, a slow loop-de-loop that very nearly made her giddy.

Her gaze riveted on that message, she bit back a groan. The whole blasted county was going to know about Jordan's proposal now. Well, maybe not that Jordan was behind it, though that news would come quickly enough. Los Pinos was small enough that nothing ever stayed secret for long, including the identity of the man who'd taken his family's plane up from the local airstrip to make his proposal in such an outrageous way. Her phone was probably ringing off the hook already.

Even as she watched, the plane made another slow loop and circled back. Just when it reached a spot directly overhead, she saw something being scattered through the sky. Like confetti falling, it drifted down until the first touch of pink landed on her cheek. Rose petals, she realized at its silky touch against her skin. The man had filled the sky with rose petals.

She sucked in a deep breath, inhaling the sweet scent of them, then lowered her head and rode de-

liberately away from the cascade of pink. Tears
stung her eyes. He was making it awfully damned
hard to say no. So far, though, he hadn't come close
to the one thing that would have guaranteed a *yes*.

She reached the house just in time to see him
settling his tall, lanky frame into a rocker on the
porch. At the sight of her he stilled and waited, his
expression oddly hesitant. That was a new side of
Jordan altogether, one that stole her breath away.
Not once in all the years she'd known him had he
ever appeared the least bit vulnerable. He'd always
been terribly, terribly sure of himself.

"You have rose petals in your hair," he said quietly.

"Funny thing about that," she said just as quietly, her gaze caught with his. "They were falling
from the sky."

His mouth curved into a slow smile. "Amazing."

"Not many men could make that happen."

"Maybe not. I suppose it takes a man intent on
making an impression."

Kelly sighed. "Jordan, you've never needed
messages in the sky or rose petals to make an impression on me. Don't you know that?"

He seemed to sense that she hadn't been as impressed as he'd hoped. "What does it take?" he
asked.

She reached up and patted his cheek. "I think
I'll let you think about that awhile longer."

Undaunted, he followed her into the house, heading straight for the kitchen as always. This time,

though, he maneuvered past her and reached for the cups himself. He looked as if he needed to stay occupied, so Kelly washed up at the kitchen sink, then settled herself at the table and waited.

He filled the kettle and put it on the stove, then lingered over her selection of herbal teas. "Which one?"

"Orange spice, I think. The situation seems to call for a little *zing*."

"What situation would that be?" he inquired, leaning against the counter, his gaze on her steady and unrelenting.

She really hadn't wanted to get into this again today. In fact, she had warned him the topic was off-limits. Those blasted rose petals had made that impossible. "This notion you've gotten in your head," she said.

"About marrying you?"

She grinned at his quick-wittedness. "That's definitely the one. It appears to me that this breakup with Rexanne has hurt you more than you're willing to admit. Perhaps it's addled your brain."

His eyebrows rose a fraction. "Oh, really?"

"Yes, really. Did you really love her, Jordan? Was I mistaken in thinking that she just came along at the right time, at the precise moment when you'd decided you needed a wife to complete your transformation into solid citizen?"

He went very still. "Transformation?"

Kelly almost chuckled at his expression. "I seem to recall a boy who ran away from home at seventeen to be a wildcatter on the oil rigs. Then there was the disruption you caused at the high school when you got on the public address system and performed a rock song you had composed. The lyrics, as I recall, had every teacher blushing. The principal had to take the rest of the day off, she was so stunned. And let's see now, there was the summer you rustled a few of your own daddy's cattle, so you could start your own herd.''

A once-familiar impish grin tugged at the corners of his mouth. ''Not fair,'' he accused. ''I was only seven when I did that.''

''It was, however, the beginning of a highly notable career as the family rebel. I'm sure Harlan despaired of your ever turning into someone respectable.'' She surveyed him closely, from the neatly trimmed brown hair to the tips of his polished boots, and regretted that his hair no longer skimmed his collar and his boots weren't worn and dusty. ''I'd say you beat the odds. A wife would complete the package.''

''You make it sound so cold and calculating,'' he objected.

She shrugged. ''If the shoe fits…''

''It doesn't. I'm thirty years old. It's just time I settled down.''

''When was it you decided you needed a wife?'' she asked.

''What do you mean, when?''

''What was the precise date?''

''I don't recall,'' he said stiffly. ''Sometime last fall, I suppose.''

''I'll tell you precisely. It wasn't fall at all. It was

January 12, your birthday. You turned thirty with a worse midlife crisis than most men have when they're forty-five. You made your decision. Then you looked around and chose Rexanne. When that didn't work out, you did another survey of the candidates and decided on good old Kelly. Did you figure all alone out here, I wouldn't put up much of a fuss before saying yes?''

He had the grace to look embarrassed by her assessment.

''Well, isn't that exactly how it happened?'' she persisted.

''Something like that,'' he agreed with obvious reluctance. He regarded her with a stubborn thrust of his chin. ''That doesn't make the plan any less sound.''

''Exactly how far have you thought this through?'' she inquired carefully, barely keeping a flare-up of temper in check. ''Have you chosen a wedding date? Picked the caterer? Reserved the church?''

''Not exactly,'' he muttered in a defensive tone, which told her that was exactly what he had done.

She was going to lose it and fling her steaming hot tea straight at him in another ten seconds. ''Let me guess,'' she said. ''You were figuring on the same date you'd set with Rexanne and you figured the caterer could just change one of the names on the cake. The minister wasn't likely to care who was standing next to you, isn't that right?''

''Those are just details,'' he argued. ''You can

pick the date, the church, the caterer and anything else you want. The sky's the limit.''

"How thoughtful!''

"You don't have to be sarcastic.''

"Oh, I think I do. When a man gets the romantic notion of letting me fill in for his originally intended bride, I definitely have to get a little sarcastic,'' she said, clinging to her cup so tightly her knuckles were turning white. The idea of splattering that tea all over him was looking better and better. Unfortunately the stuff was cooling too fast to do much damage and far faster than her temper.

"You have it all wrong,'' he insisted. "It's not like I plucked your name off some computer network. You and I have known each other all our lives. We're compatible.''

"Oh, really?'' she said doubtfully. She seized on the most obvious thing she could think of to point out their differences. "Where did you plan on us living?''

He seemed taken aback by the simple question. "In Houston, of course.''

"I hate Houston,'' she shot back.

"No, you don't,'' he said, as if he knew her better than she did herself. "You just had a bad experience there. Paul colored the way you feel about the city.''

Kelly gritted her teeth to control her exasperation. "No,'' she said eventually, when she could speak calmly. "I disliked it from the first.''

"Then why the hell did you move there?''

She would not tell him in a thousand years that

she had moved there to be near him. "Because it seemed like the right thing to do at the time. There were opportunities there that didn't exist around here."

"And there still are. Even more doors will open up to you as my wife."

It was the last straw. "Dammit, Jordan, don't you know me at all? I will not use you or anyone else to gain acceptance," she said tightly. "Around here I have made my own way. I have earned the respect people have for me."

"I never said you hadn't," he said. Now his exasperation was clearly growing by the second. "I'm just saying things will be easier for you as my wife."

She sighed. "You'll never get it."

His expression suddenly softened and he hunkered down in front of her. His eyes were level with hers and filled with so much tenderness that Kelly wanted to gaze into them forever. "I do get it," he said quietly. "One of the things I admire most about you is your fierce independence."

"Then how could you even think about taking that away from me and making me nothing more than your appendage?"

His lips quirked with amusement. "Plenty of wives are able to exert their independence. Marriage isn't likely to join two people like us at the hip. I am capable of compromise, Kelly." His gaze caught hers. "Are you?"

The question caught her off guard. "Not if it means losing who I am."

"I want to marry you because of who you are," he declared. "Why would I want you to change?"

"That's what marriage does. It changes people."

"Not if they fight it."

She had no ready answer for that. She was beginning to weaken and he knew it. She could read the gleam of triumph in his eyes. With his hands resting on her thighs, with his masculine scent luring her, all of the old yearnings were beginning. Heat flooded her body and made her reason vanish. She had wanted Jordan Adams as far back as she could remember. She had ached for his touch, hungered for just one of the wicked kisses that he seemed to share so freely with other women.

"You've never even kissed me," she murmured without thinking.

She hadn't meant it as a dare, only as an observation, but Jordan was quick to seize the opening. His hands, softer now than they had been when he was working his father's ranch, but still strong, cupped her face. His thumbs gently grazed her lips until they parted on a sigh of pure pleasure. His mouth curved into a half smile at that and, still smiling, he touched his lips to hers.

The kiss was like the caress of warm velvet, soft and soothing and alluring. It made her head spin. The touch of his tongue sent heat spiraling through her, wicked curls of heat that reached places she was certain had never before been touched.

"Oh, Jordan," she murmured on another sigh as he gathered her close and deepened the kiss until she was swimming in a whirlpool of sensation.

In her wildest imagination she hadn't known, hadn't even guessed at the joy a mere kiss could bring. This was Jordan, though, the man she'd always believed to be her other half. If she had known his touch would really be like this, she would have fought for him long ago. She wouldn't have waited, patient and silent, for him to wake up and notice her. She would have overcome her shyness, shoved aside all of her fears of rejection and tried to seduce him.

If only she were more than a means to an end, if only he really, truly loved her, she would say yes to him in a heartbeat, if only to guarantee that incredibly rare moments like this would never end.

When at last he released her, Jordan looked almost as dazed as she felt. His hands lingered on her face as if he couldn't bear to break the contact.

"Was that a *yes?*" he asked.

Kelly listened to her heart and heard *yes* repeated over and over. Her head, though, was louder. "No," she said with more regret than she'd ever felt about anything she'd ever done.

"But..."

She touched a finger to his lips. "Don't argue. This isn't about all the clearheaded, rational arguments you can mount. It's not about bullying me until you get your way."

Jordan looked as lost as if she'd been talking about astrophysics. "What, then?"

"Think about it," she advised him, hiding a grin at his confusion. "I'm sure it will come to you eventually."

Now that he'd really, truly kissed her, now that she knew the first faint stirrings of all the passionate possibilities in his arms, she wasn't sure she'd be able to bear it if it didn't.

Chapter Three

"He is clueless," Kelly declared to Jordan's sister-in-law Jessie a few weeks later.

Kelly hadn't been around when Jessie's marriage to Erik Adams ended with his tragic death in a ranch accident. Jessie had been pregnant with Erik's baby at the time. By the time Kelly had returned to Los Pinos, Luke, the oldest of the Adams brothers, had delivered the baby during a blizzard and he and Jessie had fallen in love and married. Whenever the two of them came home to White Pines with their daughter, Jessie slipped away for a visit and the kind of girl talk they rarely got elsewhere. Over the past months, Kelly had come to consider her a good friend.

"For a man widely regarded as brilliant, I think

his synapses regarding women short-circuited sometime around puberty,'' Kelly added as she kneaded her bread dough with a ferocity that had Jessie grinning.

"You love him, though, don't you?" Jessie teased. Regarding Kelly intently, she reached over to still her flour-covered hands.

Kelly gazed into blue eyes filled with concern and sighed heavily. Eventually she drew in a calming breath and shrugged. ''Depends on when you ask.''

''I'm asking now.''

''Now I'm exasperated, annoyed, perplexed and bordering on murderous.'' Her temper flared up all over again. ''He actually thinks I'll pack up Dani and move back to Houston. Wasn't he even awake during my marriage to Paul? Did he miss every single one of the opinions I expressed about the city during the entire drive from Houston back to this ranch? Has he been oblivious to how hard I've worked to make a go of this place? Can't he see how I love it?''

''Maybe he can see that the work is wearing you out. Maybe he just assumes a wife should want to live where her husband lives,'' Jessie suggested. ''There is a tradition of that sort of thing. Whither thou goest, et cetera.''

''Well, times have changed. I've been there, done that. I'm perfectly happy right here.''

''You look exhausted to me.''

''So what? I didn't say it was easy. I said I loved it. Every little improvement I'm able to accomplish around here gives me a deep sense of satisfaction. How can I give that up to go be some socialite wife?''

"It doesn't have to be an either-or situation. Compromise," Jessie said.

"He used the same word, but he doesn't know the meaning of it," Kelly said with conviction. Jordan was the kind of man who knew exactly what he wanted and assumed the rightness of it. Control was second nature to him. He was more like his father in that respect than he had ever acknowledged.

She sighed. "When I came back here after the divorce, I really needed to figure out who I was. I was no longer the teenager with the crush on the boy next door. I was no longer Paul Flint's cheated-on spouse. I didn't know who I was. I'm still rediscovering myself. I don't want to need anyone ever again."

"Then don't marry him."

"Have you ever tried to say no to Jordan?" Kelly inquired dryly. "Short of barring the front door, disconnecting the phone and never looking out the windows, I can't seem to avoid these declarations of intent he's been dreaming up for the past month. Did you look in the living room? There must be seven dozen roses in there. I sneeze when I walk through the door. Worse, Dani's beginning to ask a lot of questions. I've avoided answering them so far, but that can't go on much longer. She's a very perceptive child and all those roses are hard to kiss off.'' She hesitated. ''That's another thing that worries me.''

''What?''

''Dani. Jordan acts as if he's scared to death of her sometimes.''

Jessie nodded. ''I can believe that. The first time he held Angela, he looked as if he might faint. Obviously he's just not used to being around kids.''

''Maybe,'' Kelly said doubtfully. ''What if it's more than that? What if he just plain doesn't like children?''

''You asked him to be Dani's godfather. Obviously, you trust him instinctively with your child. Give him time around Dani and see how it goes. How does she behave around him?''

''Dani misses her father desperately. She looks at Jordan with so much hope in her eyes sometimes that it breaks my heart. She wants a daddy. I'm not sure she's too particular about who it is. That's another reason to keep all this nonsense from her. If she learns that Jordan has proposed, she'll stop at nothing to make it happen. Have you ever tried to say no to a stubborn five-year-old? Between worrying about her finding out and fending off Jordan, the whole thing is wearing me out.''

''I think it's supposed to wear you down.''

Kelly sighed. ''That, too.''

Jordan was beginning to wonder if Kelly was right, that he had lost his mind. For the past month he'd spent an awful lot of time trying to outguess a woman he had known forever, a woman he'd been certain he understood completely. It was a damned confounding turn of events.

Not that he didn't love a challenge. He did. He'd just never expected his old pal Kelly to provide it. To his everlasting chagrin, he had expected her to say yes to his proposal without giving the matter a second thought. The plan was so sensible, he didn't see how she could say anything else.

As for that kiss they'd shared, his body hardened every time he thought about it. Who would have guessed that good old Kelly had that much passion inside her? Once he'd recovered from the shock, he'd realized that it was a benefit he hadn't even considered when he'd made his choice. Discovering that he wanted her physically was a hell of a bonus.

Years ago, when he'd experienced the first faint stirrings of desire for her, he'd forced them aside. His father had always told him there were women for marrying and women for dalliances. He had known with certainty even then that Kelly was the kind of woman a man married, not the kind he experimented with. That kiss a few weeks back, though, had hinted that she might have shared that early attraction. There had seemed to be a lot of pent-up emotion behind it.

He glanced up just in time to see Ginger taking her usual place on the corner of his desk. Her skirt hitched up a practically indecent three inches, exposing shapely thighs. Her attempt to tug it lower failed dismally. One of these days he really was going to have to have a talk with her about office decorum.

"Don't you ever sit in a chair?" he grumbled.

"Sure," she said easily. "At my desk. At yours, this is better. So, what's it going to be today? Roses? Candy? Balloons? A trip to the moon?"

Jordan sighed. He was running out of ideas. "What would have worked on you?"

"I'm easy. I'd have caved in after the first two or three dozen roses," she said readily. "Of course, DeVonne did have to get a little creative. He actually told me he loved me. Have you mentioned anything along those lines to Kelly?"

He could feel patches of color climbing into his cheeks. Ginger's expression told him she could interpret exactly what that meant. She regarded him with a mix of disgust and pity.

"You haven't, have you? Jordan Adams, you don't deserve a woman like Kelly. You're some kind of throwback to another era. You think you're doing her some great favor just by asking, don't you?"

"Of course not."

Ginger rolled her eyes. "Work on that delivery, boss. It's not believable. You probably told her something romantic like how she'd never have to work another day in her life or how she could attend teas with all the hoity-toity people in Houston society, am I right?"

It was close enough that Jordan could feel another rush of blood up the back of his neck. He scowled at his secretary. "Don't you have work to do?"

"Just taking care of your love life. Once you

make up your mind what you're sending today, I'll place the order. Then I'm out of here. I'm taking the afternoon off.'' Her eyes sparkled with anticipation. "DeVonne is taking me in-line skating tonight. It's our anniversary. I intend to look sexy as hell for the occasion.''

"In-line skating? And you call me unromantic,'' Jordan muttered.

"We met in-line skating,'' Ginger informed him huffily. "Bumped smack into each other. Believe me, when you smack into a professional linebacker, you're down for the count. When I finally caught my breath, I took one look into those big blue eyes of his and it whooshed straight out of me again. The man is awesome.''

She wagged her pencil at him, obviously hinting she was ready to take notes. "So, what's it going to be today?'' she asked again. "Try to be original, boss. Even I'm getting bored and I'm not on the receiving end.''

"More roses, I suppose,'' he said, sounding thoroughly defeated even to his own ears.

Ginger shook her head. "Enough with the roses already. She's bound to be sick of them. I think I'll make it orchids. And if you don't have anything better to do this afternoon, I'd suggest you go to the mall and pick out some outrageously expensive perfume to send tomorrow.''

He stared at her blankly. "What kind?''

"Something French and sexy. Something that will drive you wild when you get a whiff of it.''

He thought Kelly smelled pretty good as it was,

fresh and clean. He wasn't sure he wanted her to smell like a Paris whorehouse. This might be another of those times when it would be best to go with his own instincts and ignore Ginger's. "I'll look around," he promised.

An hour later, after wandering through a mall indecisively, he walked past a lingerie shop. He stopped in his tracks and stared openmouthed at the display in the window. All that silk and lace would definitely drive a man wild. He tried to imagine Kelly's reaction if she opened a box and found something like that inside. Would she slap him upside the head? Laugh at him? Or would her imagination kick into overdrive the way his was doing? Would she finally realize that he truly thought of her as a sexy, provocative woman? He figured it was worth the risk.

After glancing around to see if he was being observed, he sucked in a deep breath and marched inside. He'd never seen so many silky underthings in his life. Each struck him as more daring and sensual than the next.

"May I help you?" a girl barely out of her teens inquired perkily. A Ginger-in-training, he decided.

"I'd like to buy something for a lady."

She grinned. "I'm relieved," she said. "I doubt we'd have anything in your size."

The unexpected joke, which also reminded him of his secretary, released some of his anxiety. "I don't have a clue about sizes and stuff like that," he admitted.

"Is she about my size? Bigger? Smaller?"

"A little taller," he said without hesitation, then paused. The rest seemed downright intimate to be discussing with this total stranger. She was watching him expectantly, though. She was probably used to men fumbling around with embarrassment.

"Maybe a little bigger..." He cleared his throat. "On top," he added in a choked voice.

She grinned again without batting an eye. "Got it. And on the bottom?"

He thought of Kelly's cute, sassy little behind. "Curvy," he said. "But not too big."

The teenager grinned. "Okay. Now, did you want a teddy? A negligee? Bra? Panties?"

He was stymied. His gaze went back to the item that had drawn his attention to the window. Rexanne had owned something similar, but seeing her in it had never seemed to stir him the way just the thought of seeing Kelly wearing one did. He had no idea what it was called.

"What's that?" he asked.

"A teddy. It's from France. Very chic."

Ginger had said he ought to get something from France that was capable of driving him wild. Another glance at the teddy told him that ought to do it. No question about it. With Kelly in it—or mostly out of it—he wouldn't be able to catch his breath for a month.

"I'll take that."

"In red, black, pink or blue?"

"All of them."

The clerk's eyes lit up, which hinted that he

might have made a mistake not asking about the price. He didn't care. "Can you wrap them?"

"Absolutely."

Fifteen minutes later he exited the store with his elegantly wrapped package. An hour later he was driving straight toward west Texas at a speed that openly defied state law. This was one gift he intended to give her in person. Tonight. And he was too damned impatient to waste time waiting around in an airport to be on his way. Besides, a long drive was the only way he could think of to cool off before he scared her to death by making it plain exactly how badly he wanted her.

The pounding on the front door woke Kelly from a sound sleep. She glanced at the clock beside her bed. It was well after two in the morning. She automatically sniffed the air for the smell of smoke. A fire was the only thing she could think of that would cause all this uproar at this hour. The air smelled summer fresh with just a hint of the flowers she'd planted in pots on the porch below.

Grabbing her old chenille robe from the foot of the bed, she belted it tightly around her and glanced outside. She spotted Jordan's car parked haphazardly in front of the house. So much for the who, she thought wearily. All that remained was the why. Why would he be carrying on like a lunatic in the middle of the night? She'd sent him a polite thank-you note for the gifts. Maybe he hadn't considered it adequate, but this was hardly an appropriate hour to discuss her lack of manners.

She hurried down the stairs, pausing only to re-assure a sleepy-eyed Dani that there was no problem.

"Go on back to bed, sweetie. It's just Jordan."

"He sounds mad or something."

"Don't worry about it. I'll take care of it." In fact, she was going to wring his stupid neck.

Downstairs, she switched on the porch light and opened the door a crack, determined not to admit him. "What do you want?" she demanded, noting that he was still wearing a suit and tie. He had at least loosened the tie. Obviously he'd driven all the way across the state straight from work.

He shoved a huge box toward her. It wouldn't fit through the crack. "I brought you this."

The box was intriguing with its gold paper and fancy bow. Still, Kelly determinedly wrapped her arms around her middle and refused to take it. "Jordan, this has to stop."

Her insistent tone seemed to totally bemuse him. He regarded her with evident confusion. "Why?"

"Because I cannot be bought."

Shock registered on his handsome features. "I'm not trying to buy you," he swore. "I'm trying to…"

Words clearly failed him. Kelly could understand why. There was hardly another interpretation for what he'd been doing. "Buy me," she supplied.

"No," he insisted. "I'm trying to court you."

Her heart skittered wildly. "Oh, Jordan," she murmured, feeling her insides turn to mush. "Please don't do this to me."

His gaze settled on her and a once-familiar warmth spread through her.

"Could I come in so we can discuss this?" he asked.

Kelly did not want him in the house, not with her resolve wavering and his determination solidifying. "It's the middle of the night. I have fences to mend in the morning."

"I'll help," he promised.

"When was the last time you mended a fence?"

"Not that long ago," he shot back. "I was raised on a ranch, you know. There's almost nothing I haven't done."

"And hated," she reminded him. "That's why you couldn't leave White Pines fast enough."

"If you're going to analyze me, could we do it over coffee? I'm beat."

"If you're that tired, go home to White Pines."

"Is there some reason you don't want me in the house?" he inquired, studying her with amusement. "You aren't afraid I'm going to persuade you to say yes, are you?"

That was exactly what she was afraid of, but she refused to admit it. She opened the door wider. "Come on in. You get one cup of coffee and a half hour of my time," she said firmly. "That's it."

He grinned. "Whatever you say."

He was already stripping off his tie on his way to the kitchen. He unbuttoned his collar, exposing a hint of the dark hair on his chest. He sat down, elbows on the table, and watched as she started the coffee. Kelly could feel his gaze on her. When she was sure she was totally composed, thoroughly immune to his charm, she turned toward him.

The speculative, heated look in his eyes made her breath catch in her throat. Nothing, she decided, could have prepared her for that. He looked as if he wanted her, as if he truly desired her, not just as if she were an acquisition he was considering to complete his life. It was a turn of events she definitely hadn't considered.

"Can I talk you into opening your present?" he asked in a slow, lazy tone that made her pulse race.

"No," she said in a rush, her gaze fixed on that lavish box with its fancy wrapping.

"It won't bite," he assured her.

"Jordan, I do not want your presents."

"Not even if giving them to you makes me happy?"

She shook her head. "I should have guessed. We're talking your needs here, not mine."

"You have no idea what I need," he commented, a challenging glint in his eyes. "Want to know?"

Kelly swallowed hard. "I don't think so."

"I'll tell you anyway."

He pulled the box toward him and slipped the ribbon off. He slid a finger under the wrapping paper and flipped it away. Then with the slow, tantalizing timing of a stripper, he lifted the top of the box. Kelly couldn't have shifted her gaze away if her life had depended on it.

He folded back the layers of tissue paper and hooked a finger through a narrow strap of red silk. As he lifted his hand, the sexiest, most exquisite teddy she had ever seen emerged from the box. She felt his gaze on her, gauging her reaction. She couldn't stop looking at that obviously outrageously expensive scrap of lace and silk. She thought of all the plain cotton underthings in her drawers upstairs. She wanted that teddy with every feminine fiber of her being. She stared at it, trying to hide her longing.

That, she thought, swallowing hard, was what he saw when he looked at her? When had he stopped thinking of her as denim and plaid? When had he stopped looking at her as a pal and begun noticing her as a woman?

"It's…beautiful," she said in a choked voice, reaching out to skim her fingers over the silk. She jerked her hand back as if that red-as-flame material were just as hot as any blaze, except perhaps the one inside her.

"There are more," he said, dropping the teddy he held into a pool of red on the table.

Sinful black followed, then a wild, hot shade of pink. The last was a vivid, sapphire blue. Kelly loved them all. Never in her life had she owned anything quite so provocative. Her wardrobe of underwear tended toward practical cotton, with a few scraps of lace and silk for special occasions, but there was nothing, *nothing* like this. It hadn't seemed necessary since she and Paul had split. Indulgences were something she couldn't afford.

"Where on earth would I wear them?" she murmured, even as she clutched them to her.

"Why not here?" he asked. "The thought of one

of these under your jeans and an old plaid shirt gives me goose bumps.''

''It's not very practical,'' she said.

''Not everything in life has to be practical,'' he reminded her.

''It does when you're trying to keep a ranch afloat.''

''Then think of me as the impractical side of your life.'' He gestured around the kitchen with its faded wallpaper, old appliances and huge oak table. ''All of this represents reality. Let me fulfill your dreams.''

Tears sprang to her eyes at the sweet, tempting suggestion. ''Jordan, sometimes you say the most incredible things,'' she said.

He seemed alarmed that she was crying. His finger shook as he wiped away the dampness on her cheeks. ''Sweetheart, I didn't mean to make you cry.''

''I know,'' she said, crying harder, then laughing at herself. ''It's so silly. You're making it so hard for me to go on saying no.''

''That's the idea.''

''One of us has to be practical here. Obviously it's not going to be you. Jordan, it wouldn't work,'' she repeated for what seemed the hundredth time. This time, though, even she could tell there was a lot less conviction behind the declaration.

''We're not a couple of kids with stars in our eyes,'' he said. ''We could make it work.''

The remark, so like him, snapped her out of the dreamy, hopeful state of mind he'd induced in her.

"But I want stars in my eyes. If I ever marry again, I want it all." She fingered the piles of silk scattered across the table, then gazed directly into his eyes. "I want it all, Jordan. Nothing less."

He stood slowly, then, the faintest hint of anger in his eyes. "I won't stop trying," he said with a touch of defiance.

"You'll be wasting your time."

Before she realized what he intended, he turned back, leaned down and kissed her, a bruising, hard kiss that stole her breath away. His mouth plundered hers, branding her as his as surely as if she'd been one of those heads of cattle at White Pines.

While she was still dazed, he said softly, "I don't think so, sweetheart. I don't think it will be a waste of time at all."

Chapter Four

Jordan figured he must have gotten less than an hour of sleep the entire night. Despite his exhaustion, he was back at Kelly's just before dawn, expecting to find her dressed and ready to get to all that fence mending she'd talked about the night before. Instead he found the house quiet and dark except for a faint light he thought he detected in the kitchen.

So, she hadn't gotten much sleep, either. He counted that as a positive sign, an indication that perhaps she had spent the remaining hours of the night lying awake thinking about him, just as he had about her.

He walked around toward the back of the house, prepared to taunt her a little about getting a late start. Instead he found only Dani in the kitchen, standing on a chair in front of the sink, carefully pouring cereal into a bowl.

Hiding his disappointment, he tapped on the screen door. When Dani turned toward him and her face lit up, he felt the oddest sensation in the pit of his stomach. It was almost...*paternal,* he thought with amazement, or at least what he took to be some sort of fatherly emotion. Relief that he could experience such a sensation flooded through him. It would certainly make his future with Kelly less complicated.

"Hi, Jordan. Want some breakfast?"

Stepping inside, he eyed the frosted cereal warily. "I don't think so."

"It's really, really good."

She looked so hopeful that he relented. "Okay, maybe just a little."

She stretched on tiptoe, teetering just enough to cause his breath to catch in his throat. Reaching into the cupboard, she withdrew another bowl, a very large bowl. Then she upended the box and dumped in enough cereal to feed an army.

"Hey," he protested, "I said a little bit."

She gave him another of those disarming smiles. "I think you're going to really, really like it."

Leaving the box on the counter, she climbed down while Jordan held his breath and barely restrained the urge to pluck her up and set her feet firmly on the floor himself. He did manage to grab the bowls before she could and put those safely on the table.

She retrieved a carton of milk from the refrigerator and a pair of spoons from a drawer. It seemed to be a routine with which she was disturbingly familiar. It gave him yet another argument to use on Kelly. If they were married, she wouldn't be out of the house so much or so exhausted that her daughter was up before her, as he suspected might be the case this morning. At any rate, if he had his way, Dani would have a full-time mother.

"All set?" he inquired dryly, watching her precise preparations.

Looking an awful lot like her mother had years ago, she bit her lower lip and studied the table thoughtfully. "We need a banana," she decided.

She scampered into the pantry and returned with a banana. With surprisingly deft little fingers, she peeled it, broke it almost in two and plopped the larger piece into his bowl and kept the smaller for herself.

"Maybe we should slice it," Jordan observed.

"I can't. Mommy doesn't let me use knives when she's not here."

"Then it's a good thing I'm here," he said. He opened a drawer and retrieved one.

"How come you know where the knives are?"

"Because I'll bet I've been in this kitchen almost as many times as you have," he told her.

She tilted her head and studied him suspiciously. "How come? I live here."

He grinned at her. "Ah, yes, but I grew up practically next door and I was over here almost every day when your mom and I were kids. Nothing much has changed in here.''

''Oh, yeah, I forgot. You've known Mommy a really, really long time.''

''Forever,'' he agreed, surprised at how easily conversation came with this pint-size version of his oldest friend. Why had he never noticed before that Dani wasn't really so terrifying? She was just a little person with obvious views already forming. He already knew about her powers of persuasion.

''Speaking of your mom, where is she this morning? Still sleeping?''

''No. She left a long time ago. She's mending fences right outside. She says I can come find her when I'm done with breakfast.'' She eyed him speculatively. ''Maybe you should come, too. Can you string wire?''

''With the best of them,'' he affirmed.

She gave a little satisfied nod. ''Good, because I can't really help. Mommy's afraid I'll get barbed wire stuck in my backside.''

''A very real danger,'' Jordan said, trying not to chuckle out loud. He took his first tentative bite of cereal. To a man whose cereal consumption was usually confined to bran flakes, this stuff was sweet enough to make him gag. He noticed that Dani was watching him intently, a worried frown puckering her brow.

''Don't you like it?'' she asked, sounding like an uncertain cook whose very first meal was on the table.

''It's…'' He struggled to find a word that

wouldn't offend, but also wouldn't encourage her to offer him more—ever. "It's different."

She gave a tiny sigh of resignation. "Too sweet, huh?"

"A little bit," he confirmed.

"That's what Mommy says, too. She says it makes her gag. I only get to have it on weekends, so it won't destroy my brain cells."

Jordan grinned. "I don't think your brain cells are in any immediate danger. You seem pretty bright to me."

"Thank you," she said politely.

They ate their cereal in companionable silence after that. The instant Dani had finished hers, she picked up the bowl and carried it back to the sink and climbed deftly back onto the same chair so she could reach the faucets. She rinsed the bowl and stacked it in the drainer. Jordan carried his own bowl to the sink.

"I'll wash it for you," the child offered.

"No way," he said. "Fair's fair. You fixed breakfast. I can at least wash my own bowl."

Dani climbed down without argument. "I'll go brush my teeth and then we can go." She eyed him worriedly again. "Do you have a toothbrush with you? Mommy says it's important to brush your teeth at least twice a day, especially after breakfast, so your teeth won't rot."

"After all that sugar, I can see why it would be a concern," Jordan agreed. "Don't worry about me, though, I'll take care of my teeth."

"You won't leave without me, will you?"

"Nope. I'll be waiting right here."

"Maybe you'd like to see the kittens before we go," she said hopefully. "They're getting really, really big. You might want one, after all. Mr. Adams is taking the tiger-striped one, so you can't have him. And Jessie said she'd take the black-and-white one."

Jordan hid a grin. Obviously his whole family had been taken in by this little con artist. "Did you manage to pawn one off on Cody?"

"Oh, yeah. I forgot. He said he'd take the two that look like twins. They're black with little white noses."

"Two, huh? You must have been very persuasive."

"Not me," she said modestly. "It was the kittens. I told you they're really, really cute. I think you're going to change your mind."

"I don't think so, but we can take a look after we help your mom."

"Okay," she agreed, and ran off, her tiny feet thundering up the stairs.

Jordan shook his head. Maybe kids weren't so mysterious, after all. Maybe, like grown-ups, they just wanted someone to listen and take them seriously. More or less the way he wanted Kelly to take him seriously. Though she hadn't exactly laughed in his face, she didn't seem to think anything he had to say on the subject of marriage was worth listening to. He had to come up with some way to change that before this unexpected desire he'd begun feeling for her drove him out of his mind.

Before he could come up with a new twist on what already seemed like an old theme, Dani raced back down the stairs.

"Let's go."

"Do you know exactly where your mom's working?" he asked, wondering a bit at Kelly's willingness to leave Dani all alone.

"Sure. She's right behind the barn."

About a hundred yards away, more or less, easily within shouting distance. Which meant, Jordan thought dryly, she had definitely seen or at least heard him arrive. Which also meant she was deliberately avoiding him, he concluded with an odd sense of triumph. Kelly only hid out when she was uncertain. Her resolve must be wavering.

With Dani leading the way, they circled around the barn. He spotted Kelly less than a hundred yards along the fence line, the sunlight glistening off her hair. Despite the heat, she was wearing a long-sleeved blouse, jeans and heavy gloves to protect herself from the barbed wire. Even so, as they approached, he could see a rip in one sleeve and a tiny nick on her flushed cheek.

An irrational surge of anger boiled up inside him, followed rapidly by a tide of protectiveness. She shouldn't be doing this. Even if she insisted on ranching, she should have a foreman and half a dozen hands to deal with the heavy labor. He knew in his gut, though, that she wouldn't thank him for suggesting that. With that damned pride of hers, she wanted to do it all herself. It was as much a matter of principle with her as it was a financial necessity.

"Hi, Mommy," Dani shouted, running ahead. "Jordan's here to help."

Kelly's head snapped up at the sound of her daughter's voice, then her gaze sought his. He could see the dark circles under her eyes and knew at once that he was responsible. Oddly, though, he didn't feel the same sense of triumph he'd felt earlier when he'd suspected she might have spent the same sort of restless night he had. This was the reality. She looked exhausted. And on a ranch, people who were exhausted could make dangerous mistakes, as he knew only too well. A careless mistake was what had cost them his brother Erik, when his tractor had overturned at Luke's.

"Damn," he muttered under his breath. He should never have let this happen.

He approached her slowly, then hunkered down next to her. He touched a finger to the torn sleeve, but his gaze went at once to her cheek. The nick there was as tiny as he'd first suspected, but it had bled. "You should clean that out."

"It's nothing," she said, avoiding his gaze. "I'm up-to-date on my tetanus shots. I'll wash it out and put some peroxide on it when I go inside. What are you doing here?"

"I told you I'd be back to help with the fences."

"It's not necessary."

"A promise is a promise." He stood and slid his hands into the pockets of an old pair of jeans he hadn't worn in years and rocked back on his heels.

She fell silent and, for the life of him, Jordan couldn't think of another thing to say, either. He wondered why after years of having so much to talk about, they were suddenly so awkward with each other. The quiet serenity he'd come to count on had vanished. If it was lost forever, he had no one to blame but himself. He'd tried to change things between them and in doing so had cost himself the one thing that had mattered most—Kelly's friendship.

With Dani assigned to walk along the fence line to look for additional breaks, Jordan was left alone with Kelly.

"Get much sleep last night?" he asked eventually.

"Enough," she replied tightly, concentrating on her struggle to stretch the next length of wire taut.

Jordan leaned down to help her. "Doesn't look that way to me," he observed.

She scowled at him. "Thank you."

He grinned at the testy note. "Not that you're not always beautiful," he told her.

She glanced up, her face just inches under his. The nearness was too tempting for Jordan to resist. He dropped a quick kiss on the tip of her nose.

"Jordan!" she warned, casting a harried look in Dani's direction.

"She might as well get used to it," he said. "The same goes for you."

"Not now," she snapped impatiently, jerking on the wire. She lost her grip and the line snapped back, snagging her sleeve. She muttered a colorful expletive under her breath as Jordan reached for her hand.

"Let me see."

"No. It's nothing."

He chuckled, suddenly recalling how often she had reacted just that way to any hint of sympathy whenever she'd taken a spill from a horse or scraped her knees when they were up to their childhood pranks.

"You never did want anyone fussing over you," he said, capturing her hand despite her attempts to avoid his grasp. He couldn't feel the warmth of her skin or its silky smoothness through the thick gloves, but he could imagine it. His body tightened.

"I still don't," she said heatedly.

Jordan ignored the protest and her squirming as he examined the rip in her sleeve and checked to see if the wire had snagged the tender skin beneath. "Just a scratch," he said eventually.

"I told you that."

"Yes, but your diagnosis wasn't nearly as informed as mine. I actually checked your arm."

"Jordan, I was working this fence line long before you showed up this morning and I will be working it long after you're back in your penthouse office in Houston next week."

"Can't deny that," he said agreeably. "But while I'm here, you might as well let me pitch in."

She rocked back on her haunches and sighed. The look she turned on him was filled with exasperation and resignation. "On one condition."

He grinned. "I love it when you bargain."

She fought a smile and eventually succumbed.

"Do you have any idea what a perverse man you are?"

"Is that good?"

"I've certainly never considered it to be a desirable attribute."

"Then I'll change," he promised.

"Pardon me if I don't hold my breath. As for that condition, you will not under any circumstances bring up that ridiculous proposal while Dani's in the vicinity. Got it?" she asked, regarding him with a defiant lift of her chin.

"Why not?"

"Isn't that obvious? I don't want her getting ideas about the two of us. She'll only be disappointed."

Jordan glanced up and searched for some sign of Dani. The fence line apparently forgotten, she was gathering wildflowers. She had an armload. He was struck by a sense of déjà vu.

"Looks as if she has your taste in floral displays," he commented, directing Kelly's attention to her daughter. As he did, he realized where he'd gone wrong. He'd been trying to woo Kelly the same way he would court those shallow, grasping socialites in Houston. Kelly wasn't a hothouse-flower kind of woman. Bluebells or daisies would have pleased her more.

Now that the realization had come to him, he saw that it had always been true. Her favorite gifts as a teenager hadn't been the fancy ones he and his brothers and their friends brought to her birthday parties. She'd always loved most the ones her father and mother had made for her, gifts that had come from the heart.

What could he give her now that would have the same kind of meaning? He studied her as she watched her daughter, saw the delight and love shining in her eyes, and recalled how often she'd worried out loud to him about the absence of Paul Flint in Dani's life. "She needs her father," she had said more than once.

Jordan wasn't convinced that anyone on earth needed a man like Paul Flint, but Kelly's point had registered just the same. She wanted her daughter to have a daddy. Even his father had seen that.

If Jordan could prove to her that he was suited for that role, if he could give her what she wanted most for her child, maybe Kelly would finally accept the idea that she needed him as a husband, as well.

Kelly watched as the sun beat down on Jordan's bare shoulders. He'd stripped off his shirt an hour or so before and she hadn't gotten a thing done since. Every once in a while she managed to tear her gaze away after giving herself a stern lecture about turning into a sex-starved divorcée, but in general she found the play of his gleaming muscles entrancing.

How on earth did he stay so fit sitting in an office all day long? she wondered. His shoulders and chest were thicker than she'd recalled, no longer an adolescent boy's body, but a man's. An intriguing line of dark hair arrowed down his washboard-flat stomach and vanished beneath the snap of his faded, snug jeans.

For years now she had forbidden herself to study him with so much carnal fascination. First of all, she had been married and she would have died before allowing herself even a hint of disloyalty toward a man she'd belatedly discovered didn't deserve it.

Then, more recently, it had seemed like a very bad idea to allow her old feelings for Jordan to stir to life again. She hadn't needed the pain of another rejection. He'd never given her a second glance during all those years when she had worn her heart on her sleeve. There was no reason to believe his feelings toward her had changed.

Now, though, with his proposal on the table— albeit for all the wrong reasons—she felt she had a right to study him from his windblown hair to his dusty boots. The sight of that expensive snakeskin layered with barnyard dirt made her smile. This was the old Jordan, the one she'd missed, the one who didn't give a hang about appearances. The most rebellious of the brothers who'd filled the days of the lonely, only child next door, allowing her to tag along with them and later to compete with them as an equal.

"What are you looking at so intently?" he inquired, his voice laced with amusement.

She could feel herself blushing to the roots of her hair. "I was just worried you were going to mar that beautiful expanse of chest."

His gaze settled on her. "Would you have kissed it to make it better? It might have been worth it."

Dazed by the very idea, she slowly shook her head. "I don't think so," she said in a choked voice.

"Why not?"

"Bad idea," she mumbled, forcing herself to look away.

"What was that?" he taunted.

She stared at him defiantly. "I said you're a flirt and a tease and proper women aren't safe around you."

He nodded seriously. "I thought it might be something like that."

"Don't sound so proud of yourself."

He winked at her. "I'm not the only one around here for whom pride is a character defect."

"Jordan, I..." Her voice trailed off. There was no point in arguing with him, no point in trying to explain that pride wasn't keeping her from accepting his proposal. It just wouldn't work. She couldn't marry a man she loved so desperately and spend the rest of her life pretending that she didn't.

Still, knowing that the one thing she'd always dreamed about—marrying Jordan—was finally within her reach and yet so far away, filled her with wistfulness.

She was so lost in imagining a life with Jordan that she never noticed that the sun was beginning to sink toward the horizon in a blaze of orange. When she felt a shadow fall over her, she looked up and saw Jordan staring down at her. He'd shrugged into his shirt, but left it unbuttoned. The impish gleam that had been in his eyes all day had given way to a look that was far hotter and more dangerous.

When he held out his hand to assist her up, Kelly briefly considered ignoring it. Something inside her, though, longed for some contact, no matter how innocent. His earlier inspection of her arm had made her heart pound. Her blood had sizzled with the memory of his quick, unexpected kiss on the tip of her nose and, despite her best intentions, she wanted him to repeat it.

No, she corrected, what she wanted was a repeat of that spine-tingling kiss they'd shared in her kitchen a month ago. There had been the kind of magic in that kiss she could almost believe in. It was the kind of magic that could make a woman forget that she'd ever been betrayed by a man. It was the kind that inspired wonder and hope for the future. It was the dangerous kind.

Sighing, she put her hand in his and let him help her up. Her muscles ached. Her eyes were scratchy from dust and exhaustion. Her nose felt sunburned, despite repeated applications of lotion and the hat that she'd tried to keep on but had tossed aside more than once as a nuisance.

"Tired?" Jordan asked, his gaze warm and filled with concern.

"A bit," she admitted, wondering at the expression in his eyes that said he thought she was beautiful, despite what she knew to be the truth after a long day of hard work under a hot sun.

''Then I'll take charge of the rest of the night. Shower and change, then you and I and Dani will go into town for pizza.''

She stared at him in openmouthed astonishment. She doubted Jordan had dined on pizza since he'd discovered French cuisine and four-star restaurants. And he had never, ever, indicated the slightest desire to spend any more time than absolutely necessary with her daughter.

''You want to take both of us into town for pizza,'' she repeated, not bothering to hide her incredulity.

''You haven't changed that much, have you? You still love pizza?''

''Of course, but...''

''And Dani?''

''It's her favorite.''

''Well, then, it's all settled. I'll be back to get you in an hour.'' He dropped another one of those innocuous pecks on her nose and headed for his car, leaving her staring after him in bemusement.

Exactly when, she wondered, had her old buddy—steady, safe, reliable Jordan—become so unpredictable? One thing was for certain, the evidence that he had was definitely mounting up.

Chapter Five

The aroma of garlic and oregano, of tomato sauce and spicy Italian sausage filled the tiny pizza parlor in town. Kelly had taken Dani to DiPasquali's Italian Kitchen only occasionally. The visits had been a rare treat on their tight budget. Even so, the old wooden booths with their red vinyl seats, the scarred tables and red-checked napkins were very familiar. They hadn't changed at all since she and Jordan and their friends had come here as teenagers. Just walking through the door evoked all sorts of fond memories.

The owners were the same, as well. Anthony and Gina DiPasquali were still fussing over their customers as they had for three decades now. Now their daughter Liz and their son Tony were slowly taking over the business, but it was Anthony's bois-terous command of a kitchen that turned out con-sistently mouth-watering pizza and Gina's warmth that drew people back.

Gina had obviously caught a glimpse of Jordan even before they came through the door. She was already rushing out from behind the register as they entered. She threw open her arms to envelop him in a smothering hug that had Kelly grinning and Jordan looking faintly embarrassed.

"How many years has it been since you've come to see me?" Gina demanded after a spate of Italian delivered with a Texas twang. No one knew for certain which language was her first, English or Italian, but she managed to keep up a steady stream in both. "I'll tell you how many. Too many. Come, come. You will sit at our very best table, right be-side the kitchen so I can visit with you when it is quiet and Anthony can see you as he goes in and out."

When Kelly, Dani and Jordan were settled in the booth, Gina beamed at them. "It is like old times, yes? The two of you here together. Now, tell me, what can I get you? Is it still the large pizza with everything and the largest soft drinks in the house?"

"No anchovies," Kelly reminded her emphati-cally.

"And I'd like a beer," Jordan added.

She smiled down at Dani. "And for you, little one? A small soda, perhaps?"

Dani shook her head. "A big one, just like them."

Kelly grinned at her daughter. "I think a small might be better. You can have more if you want it."

Dani sighed heavily. "Okay, Mommy."

Jordan laughed. At a quizzical look from Kelly, he said, "She reminds me so much of you. Sometimes it's spooky. It takes me back so many years."

Suddenly nostalgic, Kelly asked, "They were good times, weren't they, Jordan?"

He reached across the table and captured her hand in his. "The best."

Dani studied them intently, moving from Kelly's face to Jordan's and back again. "Tell me," she insisted. "Tell me about way back then."

Jordan finally released her hand and leaned back in the booth. "It wasn't that long ago, munchkin," he informed Dani indignantly. "Your mom and I are hardly old codgers."

"What's a codger?"

Kelly grinned at Jordan's apparent loss for words. Obviously he wasn't used to a five-year-old's insistence on explanations for everything she didn't understand. *Why* and *how come* were among Dani's favorite words.

"A codger," she explained, "is a cranky old person."

Dani nodded sagely. "Okay, you aren't that cranky, I suppose. Except when I forget and leave my markers all over the floor and you slip and fall down."

"Yes," Kelly admitted. "I am definitely cranky then." She leaned close to her daughter's perfect face. "But I am not old!"

"How old are you?"

"You know," Kelly said, not particularly wanting to be reminded that she would turn thirty in a few months. If she had the same kind of early midlife crisis Jordan had experienced, who knew what craziness she was likely to indulge in.

Dani looked at Jordan. "You know how old she is. Tell me," she commanded with all the imperiousness at her disposal.

Jordan waggled a finger to encourage her to come closer. Dani knelt on the seat and leaned across the table.

"She is almost thirty," he confided in a stage whisper.

"Isn't that old?" Dani asked.

"Very, very old," he confirmed.

"You'll pay for that," Kelly warned him. She couldn't really get angry at the lighthearted byplay. Watching the exchange between her daughter and Jordan warmed her heart. If only... She brought herself up short. That way lay heartache.

Jordan looked intrigued by her mild threat. "Oh?"

"When you least expect it," she added.

"Something to look forward to," he noted, clearly not the least bit worried.

A slow, lopsided grin crept across his face. There was a knowing twinkle in his eyes that made Kelly's stomach flip over. Obviously she'd chosen to taunt a master and he'd managed to turn the tables on her with no more than a dangerous look.

The moment might have lasted far longer, if Dani hadn't grown impatient at being ignored. She tugged on Jordan's sleeve. "What was the baddest thing Mommy ever did?"

His eyes were still sparkling. This time, though, it was clearly at some memory Kelly had the feeling she didn't want him sharing with her precocious daughter. Thankfully, Anthony came out of the kitchen just then with their pizza. Kelly prayed that the distraction would get Dani's mind off the past.

It worked, too, for another five minutes. Long enough for Dani to take her first bite of pizza and her first sip of soft drink. Long enough for Anthony and Jordan to spend time catching up, before Anthony retreated to the kitchen. Long enough for Kelly's nerves to get entirely rattled in anticipation of which memories were crowding into Jordan's head and which he might choose to share.

Lord knew, she had her own. She remembered lazy summer days beside the creek, fishing poles in hand, as she and Jordan talked about their hopes and dreams. She'd been the first he'd told about his hunger to work the oil fields. She recalled winter skating parties at the same creek, with a bonfire and mugs of hot chocolate and Jordan's arm casually thrown around her shoulders to keep warm. She recalled the two of them racing each other and the wind on horseback. Jordan always won, but it was the ride itself that was exhilarating, that and being with the boy she knew she loved.

Sometimes it seemed what she remembered most was the sense of anticipation, the belief that at any second Jordan would look into her eyes and discover the woman he loved. She remembered, too, the bitter disappointment at each and every lost opportunity. More, she'd never forgotten the sense of having failed dismally because not even the man who knew her best wanted her.

"Tell me, Jordan."

Dani's command cut through her reverie and Kelly studied the two people she loved most in the world. Dani had a streak of tomato sauce on her face and a faint soda mustache. Jordan wore a faded chambray shirt, open at the collar. He hadn't bothered to tame his hair into the style he wore in Houston. Just from the one day in the sun, she thought she could detect blond highlights scattered in the rich brown. A few more days of outside work and it would be streaked with lighter strands.

Her gaze dropped to his hands, already sporting the beginnings of a golden tan. She knew the strength of those hands. For years, it seemed, she had longed to feel them caressing her, had dreamed of them waking her senses. Instead, it had been Paul Flint's rougher touch that had awakened her sexuality.

"Well, now," Jordan began with a touch of drama in his voice as he responded to Dani's insistent demand. He glanced into Kelly's eyes and a smile curved the corners of his mouth. "Did you know that your mother once locked me in the attic?"

"I did not," Kelly retorted indignantly, recalling the incident vividly, but with a decidedly different spin.

"Did, too," he accused.

"The door stuck. That wasn't my fault."

"You were the one who slammed it so hard it rattled the hinges."

"Because you were tormenting me."

Jordan had the same innocent expression on his face now that he'd had then when he'd explained to her parents why he was hidden away in their attic after suppertime. He'd told only part of the story, just enough to worry her, just enough to get her and not himself into trouble. Kelly scowled at him. "You were a brat then and you're a brat now."

Dani's fascinated gaze clung to Jordan. "What happened then? Did Mommy get punished?"

"She did, indeed," Jordan said with an expression of smug satisfaction on his face. "She was grounded for a whole week and she had to clean the attic. She hated that the most because it was all dusty and covered in cobwebs."

"You mean, there were spiders?" Dani asked. At his nod, she said, "Ugh! That's disgusting." She glanced worriedly at Kelly. "You wouldn't make me clean the attic, would you?"

"Depends on whether you're ever bad," Kelly declared, purposely injecting an ominous note into her voice.

"I'm never bad," Dani protested. "Well, hardly ever and I never, ever, locked anyone in the attic."

"Then we won't have a problem, will we? Now

then, I think that's enough reminiscing for one night. I think it's time we were getting home.''

As they were driving back to the ranch, Kelly sensed Jordan's gaze on her. He'd been in an odd mood ever since they'd left the restaurant, a little withdrawn, maybe a little nostalgic.

''Do you remember what I was tormenting you about that day in the attic?'' he inquired eventually in a lazy drawl.

Kelly glanced into the back seat and saw that Dani had fallen asleep. ''I remember,'' she admitted. Even now the memory had her scowling. ''You wanted to practice kissing.''

''I wanted to be sure I got it right. I didn't want to kiss my first date and get it wrong. It would have been humiliating.''

''And kissing me wrong wouldn't have bothered you?'' she inquired just as irritably now as she had then.

''Nope. I knew you'd forgive me. I was trusting you with my fragile ego.''

''Do you have any idea how infuriating it was to a teenage girl to be considered target practice for some boy? What you were telling me was that I was not good enough for the real thing.''

His expression sobered. ''I never meant for you to see it that way.''

Unexpected tears gathered in her eyes. ''Then why would you be doing the same thing to me now?'' she asked quietly.

He looked over at her, shock written all over his face. ''What the hell is that supposed to mean?''

"Aren't you asking to practice marriage on me, just the way you did with kissing back then?"

"Of course not!"

"Sounds that way to me."

"Marrying you won't be practice, Kelly. It'll be for keeps."

He said it so emphatically that she almost believed him. Still, there was no getting around the point that he had never once, not in all the years she'd known him, said he loved her. Even Paul Flint had given her that much. Maybe the words hadn't meant much in the end, but at least they'd started off with a promise of undying love. If that hadn't been enough to sustain a marriage, how could she possibly trust a commitment that started with anything less?

After he'd dropped Kelly and Dani off, Jordan drove home, pondering the evening. He wasn't exactly sure where he'd gone wrong. He'd thought the entire day was going really well. He'd actually enjoyed being with Dani, answering her endless questions, awestruck by her inquisitiveness. He'd loved teasing bright patches of indignant color into Kelly's too pale cheeks. He'd thought the taunting and the memories had stirred exactly the right kind of amorous thoughts.

But there had been no mistaking the sudden souring of the mood on the drive home. He had no idea how to combat this absurd notion Kelly had gotten that he viewed a marriage between them as practice. That wasn't it at all. When he made a commitment, he kept it. Businessmen he dealt with trusted him on the basis of a handshake. Why couldn't a woman he'd known all his life trust him on the basis of a sacred vow?

He was still mulling over what had happened when he glanced into his rearview mirror and noted a pair of headlights bearing down on his car. Whoever it was was driving erratically and far too fast given the nighttime conditions on the winding country road. Jordan clung to the wheel a little more tightly.

There was a sharp curve coming up just ahead and even though he knew the road like the back of his hand, he felt his palms turn sweaty. That curve was no place to be with a crazy driver on his tail. Opting not to take a chance, he pulled off onto the shoulder of the road to let the car pass. As it whizzed by, he realized with a sense of dismay that the bright red pickup was Cody's.

"What the hell?" he muttered, pulling out behind his brother and speeding up a little.

The truck took the curve on two wheels, causing Jordan's breath to lodge in his throat. A sense of impending tragedy made his stomach tighten. Dear God in heaven, he wasn't sure the family could take another loss. Erik's death had shaken them all, especially Luke, who had been there when that tractor overturned, and their father. Harlan Adams was tough, but they had all known he felt a terrible burden of responsibility for not recognizing that Erik wasn't suited for ranch work. If anything happened to Cody on the heels of that, it would destroy him.

Staying a safe distance behind—not that he was willing to drive fast enough to catch his brother—he followed him all the way to the turnoff that led to the small house Cody had built for himself a few miles from the main house at White Pines.

Dust churned and rocks flew on the unpaved lane. By the time Jordan pulled to a stop, Cody had already leapt from the truck and stormed into the house.

Whatever had him in such a state must have been pretty bad, Jordan surmised. He'd left the truck door and the front door of the house standing wide open. Just to be on the safe side, Jordan leaned inside the truck and nabbed the keys Cody had left in the ignition. His brother wasn't getting back on the road tonight, if he had anything to say about it.

Jordan approached the house cautiously and peered inside. "Cody?"

The sound of objects slamming against walls carried from the bedroom. He followed the clatter. The sight that greeted him almost made his heart stop. Cody's face was twisted in fury. When he wasn't throwing lamps and boots against the wall, he was haphazardly jamming clothes into two open suitcases on the bed. He was cursing a blue streak at the same time.

Jordan tried to make sense of what he was saying, but other than gathering it had something to do with Melissa Horton, the rest was lost in a tangle of expletives.

"Cody!" He had to shout to make himself heard over the racket his brother was making.

Cody whirled as if he'd been shot. "What the hell do you want?" he demanded. "Who let you in?"

"Since there's no one here except you and me, I guess the answer to that is obvious," he said lightly, hoping to calm his younger brother down by staying cool himself. "So, what's going on?"

"What does it look like?"

"It would appear that you're packing."

"A hell of an observation. No wonder they pay you big bucks in Houston."

"Want to tell me what this is all about?"

"Not particularly. I just want to hit the road."

"To go where?"

Cody paused for a minute and a fleeting expression of indecision passed over his face. It was rapidly chased away by an all-too-familiar look of stubborn defiance. It was the one trait the Adams men shared in spades.

"Who knows?" he said.

"Sounds like you've really thought this through," Jordan commented dryly.

"Look, I didn't invite you here," Cody snapped. "And I don't need to listen to any of your pompous sermons."

"You must have me confused with Daddy."

Cody almost grinned at that, then caught himself. "Jordan, just stay out of this, okay?" he said in a calmer, more resigned tone. "Please."

"I don't think I can do that. You're obviously upset about something, too upset to be taking off without thinking things through."

Cody slammed the suitcases shut and headed for the door. "Your opinion is duly noted," he said as he exited.

Jordan watched him go and counted to ten. Cody tore through the front door, steaming mad.

"What have you done with my keys?"

"Tucked them away for safekeeping," he admitted. "I saw the way you were driving earlier. You're not getting back on the road until you cool down."

Cody crossed the room in three strides and stood toe-to-toe with him. Cody was only an inch or so taller, but he was broader through the shoulders. If it had been anyone other than his brother, Jordan might have been intimidated. With Cody, though, he stood his ground. There was too much at stake for him to back down now. He was willing to risk a black eye and a tender jaw, if that's what it took to keep him here, at least for tonight.

"Give me the keys," Cody demanded, his hands balling into fists.

Jordan met his furious gaze evenly. "I can't do that," he said softly. "You know I can't, Cody."

Apparently Cody recognized the note of determination in his voice. As if he were a balloon that had been punctured, Cody seemed to deflate before his eyes. He combed his fingers through his hair and sighed. "Damn."

"Come on, little brother. Sit down and tell me what this is all about," Jordan encouraged. "Did you and Daddy have a fight? You know how mule-headed he is. He'll give in eventually, though."

"This isn't about Daddy." Cody's mouth twisted in a mockery of a smile. "For a change."

"Melissa?"

There was a haunted look in Cody's eyes when he finally lifted his head and met Jordan's gaze. "I caught her out with my best friend," he admitted. Every painful word seemed to be wrenched from deep inside him.

"Maybe it was totally innocent," Jordan said, standing up for the girl he knew absolutely worshiped his brother.

"Trust me, that's not the case," Cody said bitterly. "They were in each other's arms. They didn't have to spell it out for me."

"So you're going to run off and leave the field open for him to move in on her?"

"I'd say it's a bit late to be worrying about him moving in. He's claimed her as his already."

"I don't believe it," Jordan said emphatically. "She's crazy about you."

"Maybe she was," Cody conceded. "Not anymore."

Jordan saw the anguish the admission cost him. Everyone in the family had teased Cody at one time or another about taking Melissa for granted. It appeared his baby brother had finally recognized the depth of his feelings for her, just in time to discover it was too late.

Cody met his gaze. "Will you explain to Daddy?"

"What do you want me to tell him?"

"Just that I had to get away."

"You will be back, though, right?"

Cody's gaze shifted away. "I don't think so. I think it's time I cut the ties to White Pines."

"But you love it here, more than any of us," Jordan protested, realizing at last the depths of Cody's despair. "It's in your blood."

"I know," he admitted, unshed tears visible in his eyes before he turned away to hide them. "Look, you can get out of here now. I'll be okay."

"I'm not leaving," Jordan insisted stubbornly. "Sleep on this. Maybe in the morning things will look different to you."

"Nothing will change," Cody declared grimly.

"Just give it until morning."

Cody tried to stare him down, but eventually he nodded. "If I do, you'll handle things with Daddy?"

Jordan heaved a sigh of resignation at the renewed note of determination he heard in his brother's voice. He knew in his gut that Cody wouldn't be swayed. Under the same circumstances, he probably wouldn't have been, either.

"I'll do my best," he promised. "On one condition."

Cody regarded him suspiciously. "What's that?"

"You'll tell us where you are. You won't cut yourself off from the family."

His brother nodded. "If you'll swear that none of you will ever tell Melissa where I am. I don't want to ever hear her pitiful excuses for what happened tonight. I don't ever want to see her again at all."

Jordan thought his brother was protesting a little too much, but he agreed. "We'll keep your whereabouts from her, if that's what you want. I'll see that the rest of the family agrees."

"Jessie, too?"

Jordan grinned. Their sister-in-law was a soft touch when it came to romance. "Jessie, too," he promised.

He bunked out on Cody's lumpy old sofa. Eventually he went to sleep, still praying that by morning his younger brother would come to his senses. No matter what he'd promised and would do if he had to, he really, really didn't want to be the one to explain to his father that Cody had taken off.

Harlan Adams had a tendency to fly off the handle and go after the messenger when he got bad news. This particular message was very likely to get him blasted with a shotgun.

Chapter Six

Cody was gone when Jordan awoke at daybreak. Obviously his brother had managed to find the truck keys in his pocket or he'd had a spare set hidden away that he'd forgotten about the night before in his fury over his girlfriend's betrayal.

Jordan groaned as he thought about what his father's reaction was going to be to the news. He worried, too, about whether Harlan could still handle all of the ranch's strenuous activities. As vital and fit as his father was, he had been depending more and more on Cody to run the day-to-day operations at White Pines. It was something that would have to be discussed, but to be perfectly honest, Jordan dreaded getting into it. His father hated even the slightest hint that Cody's role at White

Pines had gradually become equal to or even more important than his own.

First things first, though. He had promised Kelly he'd be back this morning to offer more help with the fences. She'd probably be delighted if he failed to show, but he wasn't about to give her an excuse to accuse him of letting her down. Obviously she already had a lot she was blaming him for, garbage from their past he hadn't even been aware was simmering in her head. The workings of the female mind had always been a puzzle to him, except with Kelly. Now it appeared she was falling into that same incomprehensible pattern of behavior.

With some reluctance he reached for the phone and dialed the ranch. To his vague relief, Dani answered. At least with her, he wouldn't have to explain past actions.

"Hi, Jordan," she said so eagerly it made his heart flip over. "Thanks for the pizza. It was scrumpsi-delicious."

He grinned, despite his mood. "I'm glad you liked it."

"Did you and Mommy have a fight after I fell asleep in the car?" she asked, a frightened note in her voice. It was the concern of a child who'd already seen her father walk out of her life, no doubt after more than one angry exchange with her mother.

Jordan's heart thudded dully. How much could she possibly have heard? Why the devil hadn't they been more discreet? They'd both assumed that Dani was sleeping soundly in the back seat. "Why would you think that, munchkin?"

"Because Mommy looks all sad this morning and she yelled at me for watching a video instead of coming to take my bath."

So, Kelly looked sad, did she? He'd have to think about what that meant. As for her attitude toward Dani, he was pretty sure he wasn't the one responsible for that. "How many times had she called you to take your bath?"

"Once," Dani said.

Jordan had his doubts. "Really? Just once?"

"Maybe it was twice."

More likely double that, Jordan guessed. "Don't you think that could have had something to do with why she yelled?"

Dani sighed. "Maybe," she conceded. "She still looks sad, though. Are you coming over?"

"In a bit. Is your mom there?"

"She's in the shower."

The vivid image that appeared in Jordan's mind could have steamed up the whole state of Texas: Kelly naked, slick with water, her body provocatively covered with suds, his hands sliding slowly over her. He nearly moaned out loud, then caught himself. Thoughts like that about Kelly had never occurred to him in the past or, if they had, he had banished them at once. It was getting more and more difficult now to forget such images.

"Okay, munchkin, would you be sure to tell her I called?" He was proud of the steadiness of his voice when his pulse was still ricocheting wildly.

"Tell her I have to spend some time with my father this morning, but I'll be there as soon as I can, okay? Can you remember that?"

"I can remember."

"Tell her the minute she gets out of the shower."

"Okay. 'Bye, Jordan."

"'Bye, munchkin. See you later."

Jordan left Cody's shortly after hanging up. The trip to the main house took only a few minutes, not nearly long enough for him to decide how to tell his father that Cody was gone. He didn't catch a break once he was there, either. He found Harlan already seated in the dining room, the newspaper spread open in front of him.

His father regarded him with open speculation as Jordan poured himself a cup of coffee and plucked a corn muffin he didn't really want off the buffet.

"You didn't listen to a word I said to you, did you?" his father grumbled when Jordan was seated at the table.

"Which words of wisdom are you accusing me of ignoring?"

"You spent the night with that woman."

He noticed that the note of glee in his father's voice contradicted the somewhat negative phrasing of the statement. It simply confirmed Jordan's suspicions that his father had been trying out a little reverse psychology on him by warning him away from Kelly.

"I assume you're referring to Kelly, and no, I did not spend the night with her," Jordan told him irritably, cutting the muffin into precise little sections to avoid having to meet his father's gaze. "I was at Cody's."

That grabbed his father's attention. Harlan's gaze narrowed suspiciously. "What the devil were you doing there?"

"Trying to persuade him not to hightail it away from here."

"Dammit all!" Harlan set his coffee cup down so hard, the coffee splattered all over the tablecloth. He made no attempt to blot it up. "Cody's leaving? Without a word to me? Damn that boy's hide."

"He's already left," Jordan corrected.

"Why would he want to go and do something crazy like that? We have work to do. He couldn't have picked a worse time for a vacation."

"I don't think he sees this as a vacation."

The color drained out of his father's face. "He's taken off for good?"

"So he claims."

He stared at Jordan, disbelief and anger warring on his face. "That's nuts," he protested. "He loves this place. It'll be his one day. You and Luke will get your shares, of course, but the ranch will belong to Cody."

"Which is exactly as it should be. He's the one who always wanted it."

"So, why the hell did he go and leave?" He waved his finger under Jordan's nose. "I'll tell you this, if he doesn't have a darn good explanation, I'll cut him out of my will, that's what I'll do."

His father's face was turning bright red as his anger mounted. Jordan suspected, though, that beneath that anger there was genuine concern. For all of his domineering attitude and his manipulations, Harlan loved his sons.

"Come on now, Daddy, settle down," he soothed. "You don't know the whole story."

"So tell me," his father snapped.

Jordan wasn't sure how much detail Cody would want him going into, but he realized his father wouldn't be satisfied with some evasive answer. "He and Melissa had some kind of a falling out. A pretty bad one. He needed to get his head straight, so he took off."

"To go where?"

"He didn't say. He did promise to let us know where he winds up on the condition that we never share that with Melissa. Who knows, maybe once he has time to cool off, he'll change his mind and come straight back here."

His father's shoulders sagged. "I always knew that boy was going to wake up too late and see what his fooling around and taking her for granted had cost him. Did she leave him for somebody else?"

Jordan refused to say. "I don't know that for sure." He studied his father worriedly. "Will you be okay around here? Have you got enough help?"

As he'd expected, Harlan immediately scowled at the question. "Boy, I was running this place when the whole bunch of you were in diapers. I suppose I'm capable of putting in a few more years of hard work."

"Luke would be willing to help out, I'm sure."

"He has his own place and his own family to

think about." Harlan shook his head. "Dammit, Jordan, I don't want to tell your mama about this. This means some of those trips she has planned will have to be postponed. Besides that, she dotes on Cody. He was her baby."

Jordan wasn't sure there was much truth in that. He'd never noticed that his mother doted on anyone in the household except his father. Still, he asked, "Do you want me to tell her?"

"No, I'll do it." He leveled a hard gaze at Jordan. "There's just one thing I want to know, son. Why the hell didn't you do something to stop him? This thing with Melissa would have passed over quick enough, if he'd stayed here and dealt with it. Now who knows how long it'll fester inside him and keep him from coming home."

Jordan's own sense of guilt was as painful as any accusation his father could throw at him. "I did what I could," he said tersely. He stood. "You're sure you'll be okay?"

Harlan sighed. "I always am."

Despite the assurance, Jordan squeezed his father's shoulder on his way past. "I love you, old man."

His father's weathered, callused hand patted his. "I know you do, son."

"So does Cody."

His father nodded. "I know that, too." He glanced up. "You on your way back to Houston?"

"No. I'm going back over to Kelly's. She needs more help with that fence."

"Exactly how long will you be sticking around here, then?"

"That remains to be seen," Jordan said.

An awful lot depended on how long it took him to get Kelly to agree to his proposal. At some point in the past twenty-four hours he'd resolved not to leave until she said yes. Maybe it was Cody's reaction to losing Melissa, maybe it was his father's to Cody's departure, but suddenly he'd grasped that there was nothing more important on earth than family and he wanted to claim Kelly and Dani once and for all as his.

Kelly hadn't bothered the night before to tell Jordan that she and Dani always went to church on Sunday morning. She hadn't figured it mattered. He probably wouldn't show up anyway, not after the way she'd accused him of using her to fill in until the right woman came along. He'd appeared to be genuinely exasperated with her for reaching that conclusion. She couldn't imagine what else she was supposed to think, but he obviously resented the accusation.

At any rate, she wasn't all that surprised when he wasn't on her doorstep at dawn. All the way to church and back, she told herself it didn't matter, that she wasn't disappointed, that it would be better if he went back to Houston and got on with his life and let her get on with hers. She had too much pride to want to be a practice wife or a convenient hostess, until the right woman came along.

Apparently, however, that particular message

didn't quite get from her brain to her traitorous heart. That blasted part of her anatomy reacted with pure delight when she spotted him rocking on her front porch as she drove up the lane to her house after church. She fought the impulse to race from the car and fling herself into his arms. Dani's reaction, however, was another thing entirely. For the first time Kelly could recall, her daughter didn't look overjoyed to see Jordan waiting on their doorstep.

"Uh-oh," Dani muttered, scooting down in the front seat.

Kelly glanced at her daughter and saw the worried frown puckering her brow. "What's wrong?"

"I forgot something."

Kelly glanced from Dani to Jordan and back again. "Something about Jordan?"

"Uh-huh."

A vague stirring of alarm spread through her. "What did you forget?"

"He called before."

"Jordan called?" She had to battle with herself to keep her voice from climbing. There was no point in letting her daughter know how much that small, seemingly inconsequential piece of information meant to her. "When?"

"When you were in the shower," Dani admitted in a tiny voice. "He said he had to go see his father and he'd be here later."

"Did you tell him we were going to church?"

Dani shook her head. "I'm sorry, Mommy. He

made me promise to tell you, but I just forgot. Don't be mad at me.''

Kelly reached over and rubbed her daughter's cheek with her knuckles. How could she not forgive her? Dani didn't have a mean-spirited bone in her body. And she was obviously contrite. There was, however, a lesson to be learned here.

''I'm not mad,'' she reassured her. ''But Jordan is another matter. You made a promise to him and you didn't keep it. How do you propose to handle it?''

Blue eyes, filled with dismay, gazed up at her. ''I have to 'pologize, huh?''

''I'd say so.''

''Is he going to be really, really mad?''

''Oh, I think Jordan is a fair man. He'll listen to what you have to say. Go on, now. Run and tell him what happened.''

With obvious reluctance, Dani unhooked her seat belt and slipped out of the car. Kelly hid a grin as she watched her daughter crossing the yard, her gaze fixed on Jordan. No criminal heading for the hanging tree had ever walked at a more halting pace. She paused at the bottom of the steps. From the car, Kelly could hear her hesitant greeting.

Jordan's rocker stilled as he listened to the stammered apology. Kelly slowly left the car and went to join them. As she approached, she didn't dare risk a glance into his eyes for fear they'd both start chuckling.

''I see,'' he said quietly when Dani concluded

her explanation for breaking her promise. "Will it ever happen again?"

Dani shook her head emphatically. "Never. I really, really promise. Cross my heart. Next time I'll even write it down, if you'll show me how to spell your name."

Jordan held out his hand. "Then that's good enough for me. Apology accepted. And I'll teach you to spell my name later on this afternoon."

Relief spreading across her face, Dani bolted up the stairs and flung herself into Jordan's arms. After a startled look at Kelly, he picked the child up and hugged her. A wistful expression passed across his face as Dani's arms wound tightly around his neck.

In that instant, watching the two of them with a lump in her throat, something inside Kelly shifted. Suddenly she began to envision possibilities that she'd been staunchly denying for weeks now. If Jordan could accept Dani as his own, if he could love her child as she did, then perhaps his feelings for her didn't really matter. If she could guarantee Dani's happiness by giving her a father, then perhaps she could live with no more than Jordan's affection for herself.

"So, where have you two been?" Jordan inquired after Dani disentangled herself and received permission to go to the barn to check on the kittens as soon as she'd changed her clothes.

Kelly propped herself against the porch rail. "Church."

"You didn't mention anything about that yesterday when I told you I'd be back this morning to help with the fences.''

Kelly shrugged. "We've always gone to church on Sunday, before doing any work. Besides, I thought you'd probably change your mind.''

"Because?''

"Because of last night.''

He nodded slowly. "I'll admit what you said in the car took me by surprise. It never occurred to me that you would think I intended our marriage to be anything less than the real thing. That's not the way I do business.''

Kelly frowned. "Business?''

He had the good grace to wince. "Sorry. Force of habit. I spend an awful lot of time negotiating deals. The terminology is ingrained.''

She tried to cling to the pragmatic way she'd felt only moments ago, but his attitude grated. She couldn't help it. She didn't like being viewed as part of a business deal, something acquired with no more emotion than he might display when gobbling up a new company for his corporation. Maybe marrying Jordan for Dani's sake wouldn't be so smart, after all. She'd have to think about it long and hard, far longer than it appeared he was inclined to give her.

"I'm going in to change," she said, heading for the door.

"Kelly?''

"Drop it for now, Jordan.'' Still holding the screen door open, she glanced back at him. There was an oddly forlorn expression on his face she didn't know how to interpret. "Stay for Sunday dinner, if you like. We'll work afterward."

He brightened at once. "Fried chicken?"

She grinned at his enthusiasm. The way to this man's heart had always been through his stomach, no doubt about it. "Always," she assured him.

"You know something?"

"What?"

"It's really good to know that some things never change. Fried chicken on Sundays is one." He paused, his gaze fixed on her. "You're another. Please don't ever go and change on me, Kelly."

She thought about that remark the whole time she was changing clothes. A few minutes later she met Jordan in the kitchen. He was already setting the table for her, just as he had whenever her mother had invited him to stay for Sunday dinner years ago. He'd even taken out the good china, just as he'd been instructed to do back then.

"Another old habit?" she teased.

"Exactly." His gaze settled on her. "It feels right being here, Kelly."

She nodded, unable to say anything. Having him here felt too darned right to her, too. It was a dangerous sensation, a trap she didn't dare fall into. Nostalgia was no reason to get married.

Getting a grip on her emotions, she put him to work peeling potatoes next. As she prepared the chicken, she watched him closely. Despite his expressed contentment at being there, there was something quiet and distant about him that was out of character.

"Jordan, what's going on with you?" she asked eventually.

He glanced up from the mound of potatoes forming in front of him. "It's Cody."

Kelly's heart thumped unsteadily as she imagined the youngest of the brothers injured or worse. She'd been gone when Erik was killed in an accident on Luke's ranch, but she'd spent time with Jordan after that and seen how devastating it had been for him. It hadn't been easy for her, either. She'd felt as if she'd lost her own brother. If something had happened to sweet, irrepressible Cody... She didn't even want to think about it.

"Has something happened to Cody?"

Apparently he heard the alarm in her voice, because he reached out and touched her hand.

"Nothing like that," he reassured her hurriedly. He went on to tell her about Cody's abrupt departure the night before. "Daddy's fit to be tied, not just at Cody, but at me for not stopping him."

Kelly could just imagine the guilt trip Harlan was capable of laying on Jordan. "Cody's a grown man. He has to handle his problems whatever way works for him. I could shake Melissa, though, for doing something like that. It doesn't make any sense. She's adored Cody forever."

"That's what I thought, but Cody swears he saw what he saw. He couldn't wait to take off. Now Daddy's threatening to cut him out of the will. Whatever he feels right now, it would kill Cody to lose White Pines."

"Would Harlan really disinherit him?"

"I suppose that depends on how long Cody stays away. You know how stubborn Daddy is."

Kelly surveyed him pointedly. "I certainly do. It's a trait he passed along to all of you."

"I'm not stubborn," Jordan denied.

"Oh, please."

"Determined, maybe. Dedicated."

"Bullheaded," she corrected.

He grinned, that lopsided, boyish grin that was so at odds with the sophisticated image he'd projected in recent years. "If you know that, then you should know you haven't got a chance in fighting me on this proposal."

"You're forgetting one thing."

"Which is?"

"I am every bit as bullheaded as you are, Jordan Adams."

"Admittedly a frightening thought," he teased. "But you don't scare me, Kelly Flint. You're weakening already. I can tell."

Kelly swallowed hard against the tide of pure panic that his observation sent through her. "How can you tell a thing like that?"

"Oh, no, you don't. I'm not telling you my secret way of figuring out what's really going on in that head of yours. It's the only advantage I've got."

It wasn't, Kelly thought with a sigh. The real advantage he had was that she was still head over heels in love with him.

Chapter Seven

Kelly spent the rest of the day watching as the bond between her daughter and Jordan miraculously strengthened. It was as if some barrier inside Jordan had fallen and allowed him to open his heart to the child. Always stiff, formal and a little aloof in the past, today he had finally relaxed, reminding her why she had wanted him as Dani's godfather in the first place. Well, one of the reasons, anyway.

To her initial surprise Paul had been delighted with the choice. An ambitious man, she finally realized that he relished the tie to the powerful Jordan Adams. Kelly could hardly criticize his motives, when her own were less than pure. She had asked Jordan to be Dani's godfather, not only because he was the sort of stable, bright, fun-loving influence she wanted for her child, but because it would forever link them all together.

Jordan had balked at first, swearing that what he knew about children would fit on the head of a pin. Kelly had had to use every persuasive skill at her command to talk him into it.

Now, observing the two of them, she was glad she had. Just seeing their heads close together as Jordan tried to teach Dani how to make homemade peach ice cream after they'd worked on the fence for awhile made Kelly's resolve slip another notch. Soon she wouldn't have any reserves of willpower left for resisting him. Dani wanted a father desperately and Jordan was slowly but surely slipping into that role. It was far more natural to him than he had once insisted or she had once imagined.

She closed her eyes against the sight of man and child, but she couldn't stop her thoughts from dashing headlong back to a time when she'd dreamed of seeing Jordan with their child in just such a scene. She'd envisioned a pint-size boy, his thick, sun-streaked hair falling in his face, wearing tiny cowboy boots and trailing after his daddy with the same rolling cowboy gait. She'd imagined a little girl with dark brown curls and big brown eyes cuddled in her father's arms as he rocked her to sleep, crooning a lullaby in his deep, soothing voice.

Dani's excited shouts cut into her reverie.

"Mommy, I did it!" Dani hollered, thundering onto the porch, a bowl in her hand. "Look! I made ice cream!"

It looked more like soup to Kelly, but she didn't

complain as she took the offered bowl and tried a taste. "Wonderful," she declared. "The best peach ice cream I've ever had. Maybe you two will turn out to be the next ice cream magnates."

"Peach is good, but chocolate is better. Jordan says next time we'll make that. It's his favorite, too."

"Oh, really? You and Jordan seem to be making a lot of plans today."

Jordan strolled up to the porch and leaned back against the railing right smack in front of her, a position that put his incredible thighs and other interesting parts of his anatomy practically at eye level. Kelly jerked her gaze up to rest more safely on his face. He shot her a knowing little grin that set her teeth on edge.

"Any objections to our plans?" he inquired, clearly daring her to challenge his determination to weave himself into the fabric of their lives.

Kelly waited until Dani had scampered off to check the ice-cream maker before responding. "Only if you intend to disappoint her," she warned in a low voice. "Paul has done enough of that to last her a lifetime."

"I will never disappoint her or you," he vowed, regarding her solemnly. "You can take that promise to the bank."

As soon as the businesslike words were out of his mouth, he looked chagrined. "Sorry."

"I know, force of habit."

Somehow, though, this time she couldn't work herself into much of a snit over it. With the sun setting into a purple haze of twilight and the fragrance of flowers filling the hot, dry air, she felt too at ease, too comfortable with the camaraderie they'd shared all day long to risk spoiling it with another quarrel over semantics. Jordan would probably always use business terms for describing things. At least he'd formally asked her to marry him, not to enter into a merger.

Besides, it was getting late, too late to squabble and ruin an otherwise perfect day. It was time for Dani to be going to bed and soon it would be time for Jordan to be going back to Houston. She was surprised he'd hung around this long. By Sunday evenings he was usually chomping at the bit to get away from west Texas and back to the big city so he could dig into the piles of work he always brought home from the office.

"You leaving for Houston soon?" she asked.

"Trying to get rid of me?"

"No, just wondering."

"I'm not going back."

Startled, she stared at him. "You mean tonight?"

"I mean, not until you and I reach some sort of compromise."

She knew what compromise meant in Jordan's terms. He wanted her to capitulate completely. She shot him a wry look. "It's a little early for you to think about retiring over here to wait me out."

"Oh, I don't anticipate it taking nearly that long."

After glancing to make sure that Dani was occupied and out of hearing range, Kelly warned him emphatically, "You will not bully me into making a decision."

He shrugged, looking supremely confident. "I didn't plan to."

She sighed. "You're just going to try to wear me down, then, aren't you?"

"I prefer to think of it as winning you over to my way of thinking."

Before she could respond to that, Dani rejoined them, leaning against Kelly's thigh and yawning widely. "Sleepy?" Kelly asked, looping an arm around the child's waist and hugging her close.

"Uh-huh," she admitted.

"Then run up and fill the tub. I'll be up in a minute to give you your bath and tuck you in."

"But I just took a bath before church."

"And you got filthy again today."

"Okay." Dani gazed sleepily up at Jordan. "Will you stay and read me a story?" she asked, an unmistakable wistful note in her voice.

Kelly saw the hesitancy in Jordan's eyes and silently cursed him. Before she could jump in, though, he grinned. "You have anything with horses in it?"

Dani beamed. "*Black Beauty*. It's my favorite."

"Ah, yes, I think I remember that one. It was your mom's favorite, too."

Kelly stared at him. "How on earth do you remember that?"

"There's a lot I remember about you," he taunted. "For a very long time you told me all your deepest, darkest secrets. For instance—"

The devilish twinkle in his eyes caused Kelly to cut him off. There was no telling what story he'd share with her daughter, if she didn't watch her step. "Never mind," she said in a rush. "If you don't mind staying around to read, the bath shouldn't take more than fifteen minutes or so."

"I'll clean up the ice-cream maker." He caught her gaze. "Maybe I'll bunk out on your sofa tonight, so we can get an early start on those fences in the morning."

"You're thinking of staying here?" she repeated weakly.

"Do you have a problem with that?"

She had a problem with it, all right, but it wasn't one she intended to share with him. She simply shook her head and fled inside with her daughter.

As she was bathing Dani, she couldn't help hearing Jordan moving around downstairs. Just knowing he was in the house made her feel different somehow, protected, warmed. Heck, who was she kidding? She felt a shivery stirring of anticipation knowing that he intended to stay the night. He'd suggested the sofa, but there was a perfectly good guest room right next to her own and he well knew it. She would be able to imagine him in that bed, perhaps even hear the steady rhythm of his breathing. The very thought tantalized her.

Sure, they'd all camped out together as kids, with his father or hers along as a chaperon for the whole rowdy bunch of them, but this was different. This meant spending the night under the same roof with a man who claimed to want her as his wife, a man she'd wanted in her bed since she'd first discovered the chemistry at work between a man and a woman.

The thought of testing that chemistry intrigued her, until she realized that would make her no better than Jordan. She had accused him of wanting a practice wife. Surely she shouldn't be considering testing their relationship to see if the chemistry was right between them.

Besides, for her part, she knew it was. She'd been going weak in the knees around Jordan too many years not to know it. As for him, he was too much a sexual being to want to marry her if he didn't intend to sleep with her. That must mean that he found her attractive. In fact, she thought she'd even detected a smoldering look of desire in his eyes on more than one occasion lately, especially when he'd watched her face as he'd displayed all that sexy lingerie he'd bought her.

A timely splash of cool water hit her square in the face.

"Mommy, you're not paying attention to me," Dani accused. "I could drown."

"Who are you kidding? You can swim like a fish."

"Not in the tub," Dani declared. "Am I clean yet? I want to go hear *Black Beauty.*"

"I suppose you're clean enough," Kelly agreed, holding open a towel and folding her daughter into it and rubbing her briskly. She picked up a blue-and-white cotton Dallas Cowboys T-shirt that was Dani's favorite sleepwear. "Put this on and then hop into bed. I'll get Jordan."

She opened the bathroom door and practically tripped over his booted feet. "Jordan!"

"Thought I'd save you the trip down to get me."

"How thoughtful!"

He grinned unrepentantly as he followed her to Dani's room. "By the way, I like the decor."

Kelly glanced around at the Winnie the Pooh wallpaper and stuffed animal collection that filled half a dozen shelves. "Somehow this doesn't strike me as you."

"I was referring to your room."

Her gaze shot up. Her pulse skittered crazily. "You were in my room?"

"The door was open. I peeked." He rocked back on his heels. "Expecting company?"

Hands on her hips, Kelly glared at him. "What is that supposed to mean? Any company I have stays in the guest room. And," she added pointedly, "that includes you."

"But that king-size bed is really something. Doesn't it get lonely?"

She continued to scowl and said pointedly, "It hasn't yet."

"Liar," he whispered in her ear just as Dani came bounding in and plucked her book from the shelves. She thrust it into Jordan's hands.

"Read," she ordered imperiously.

"My pleasure," he told her, but his gaze was still fixed firmly on Kelly's blushing face. Apparently satisfied that he'd completely disconcerted her, he settled down onto a chair beside the bed and dutifully began to read.

Kelly stared at him and at her daughter. Dani was obviously enraptured by the dramatic telling of her favorite story. She sighed. She wished a bedtime story were all she wanted from Jordan. She wanted more than that, though, much more. And very little of what she hungered for was nearly so innocent as a bedtime story.

And every time he snuck beneath or over or around her defenses, she wanted it all with a desperation that stunned her. Not sure she could bear it another minute, she slipped from Dani's bedroom and retreated downstairs.

Away from him, away from the two of them, she struggled to get her bearings. Unfortunately, she suspected that there weren't enough hours in the day or weeks in the year for her to ever build up adequate resistance to the man upstairs.

Jordan found Kelly in the kitchen an hour later, stirring her cup of tea distractedly, even though he knew perfectly well she had put neither sugar nor cream nor lemon in it. Nervous habit, he guessed, and hid a smile.

He noticed she'd swept her hair up off her neck into a loose ponytail. Escaping tendrils curled softly against her skin. Suddenly he wanted very badly to press a kiss to that tender spot on the back of her neck. He weighed his desire against the temperature ofthat steaming cup of tea she was likely to heave at himand decided against it. He still had to go slowly here or lose what little ground he had gained with her.

He poured himself a cup of tea from the pot on the table and took a seat next to her. Beneath the table, their thighs brushed. Alarm sparked in her eyes, but he knew she had too much pride to let him know he was getting to her. Aside from the sudden rigidity of her posture, she gave no other hint of how desperately she wanted to flee. Those delectable, stiff little shoulders told him he was on the right track, though. From now on he intended to crowd her a bit, literally and figuratively.

"Is Dani asleep?" she asked.

He noticed the thready huskiness in her voice. It confirmed that the tactic was working. She was not nearly as immune to him as she wanted to pretend. Of course, being this close to her without sweeping her into his arms was also killing him, but it was a torture he was willing to endure if it accomplished his goal.

"She's out like a light," he confirmed. "I was so caught up in the story, I read all the way to the end of the chapter before I noticed."

"I could loan you the book," Kelly offered, amusement dancing in her eyes.

"I think I'll just stick around for a while and finish it here."

"Jordan..." She sighed and fell silent, the protest left incomplete.

"Go on, say it," he urged. "We can't settle this, if we aren't open and honest."

He saw the familiar quick temper flare in her eyes again.

"This is not a damned business negotiation," she

reminded him for the umpteenth time. She held up her hands. "Never mind. I don't want to talk about this again anyway."

Jordan caught one of her hands in midair and lifted it to his lips. The kiss clearly caught her off guard. Her gaze shot to his and she struggled to yank her hand away. He held on for one more soft brush of his lips over her knuckles. Despite the gloves she wore for work, there were tiny nicks scattered across that pale skin. He touched his mouth to every one. He could feel her pulse scamper wildly. Her hand in his trembled. He finally took pity on her and released the hand.

"What are you doing?" she demanded indignantly. She shoved both hands under the table out of view, but, as they both knew, hardly out of reach.

He chuckled. "You're not that naive."

"No, I'm not," she snapped. "Which is why I want to know what you're up to."

"No secret there. I'm trying to get you to marry me. I'll use most any means I have to, fair or foul, to persuade you. I am willing to compromise, though, on certain points," he said, deliberately using the business terminology he knew she hated. Predictable fire danced in her eyes.

"Compromise?" she repeated, her tone ominous.

"Of course. I'm a reasonable man." He was pleased with himself for having thought of this, to say nothing of feeling downright noble.

"And what exactly are you willing to compromise about?"

"For starters, you hate Houston. I hate ranch life." The last was an understatement, which made his willingness to reach a middle ground all the more indicative of how serious he was about this. Kelly had listened to him ranting and raving about getting away from west Texas for years before he'd finally gone. She had to know how significant this particular compromise was for him.

"True. What do you suggest?" Kelly asked, regarding him doubtfully. "That we move to Boston?"

She sounded testy. He figured that was because she knew she couldn't argue with his logic. "Don't be absurd," he chided. "We'll commute. Weekdays in Houston. Weekends, holidays and vacations on the ranch."

She didn't look nearly as bowled over by the proposed arrangement as he'd hoped.

"Uh-huh. And who is supposed to work the ranch while I'm in Houston?"

He hadn't considered all the details, but he'd learned long ago to be quick on his feet in a discussion of this importance. "You have a hand working for you already. We'll hire an experienced foreman."

"I can't afford to hire someone."

Jordan was getting a headache. Clearly Kelly didn't know the meaning of the word compromise. She wasn't shifting her position by so much as an inch as near as he could tell. "But I can."

She was already shaking her head. "I promised

myself that I would make a go of the ranch on my own," she insisted.

"Why does it have to be totally on your own? Why can't you accept a little help?"

"Because it's my fault it's in the state it's in," she snapped, then looked shocked by what she'd revealed.

"Why on earth would you think you're to blame?"

"Because if I'd stayed here and helped out instead of running off to Houston, things would never have gotten this bad."

"That's ridiculous," he declared. "Besides, that's all in the past. Let's deal with the here and now."

"Okay," she said agreeably. "Maybe by next year I could afford help, but not now. That's the reality of the here and now."

The woman was stubborn as a mule. He wondered if she'd been born that way or if she'd picked it up from hanging around with him and his brothers. Goodness knew, they all had stubbornness to spare.

"Oh, for pity's sake," he snapped impatiently. "I'll loan you the money."

"No bank would take a risk on me," she countered coolly. "Why should you?"

"Because it's the only way I know to get you to budge from this place," he said, thoroughly exasperated.

There were moments—and now was definitely one of them—when he thought he might have been deranged to suggest this whole marriage idea. He and Kelly hadn't had a quiet, serene exchange in weeks. He hadn't had a decent night's sleep.

And too damned many of his waking moments he'd been rock-hard just thinking about her. He supposed that feeling passion for the woman he'd decided to marry was a good thing. It was just that it had come about so unexpectedly. One minute he'd been planning to lead a nice, tame existence with a safe, uncomplicated pal, a woman who shared his values and his history. The next he hadn't been able to stop thinking about seducing her, about running his hands over her body, about the taste of her lips, the shape of her breasts, the texture of her skin.

He groaned. Talk about complications! If he so much as looked at her tonight, he was liable to make love to her here and now, on top of the kitchen table. His decision to crowd her had clearly backfired. He was the one in turmoil, while she looked calm as could be.

He shoved his chair back from the table and abruptly stood. "I have to go," he said, his voice choked, his gaze very carefully averted.

"I thought you were going to spend the night here."

On the sofa? Or, as she had suggested, in the guest room? Less than thirty feet from that king-size bed of hers? Not if there was an armed posse surrounding the place and he was the target. He bolted for the door, not certain exactly where he was headed. He wasn't sure he was up to one of his father's inquisitions about Cody.

"I'm going to stay with Luke and Jessie," he announced. The drive to their place ought to be just about long enough to cool him off and it would keep him out of range of his father's anger for another night.

Kelly didn't offer another protest. Oddly enough, he thought he caught the faintest hint of a smile right before she closed the door behind him. He had the feeling he didn't want to know what *that* had been about.

Chapter Eight

"Ginger, I want you to cancel all my meetings for the rest of the week," Jordan told his secretary when he called Houston first thing on Monday morning. It was only 8:00 a.m., but he knew she'd already been at her desk for at least half an hour. Most of the time she even beat him to the office and he was an early starter.

"You're going on your honeymoon," she guessed, sounding far more pleased than she had when he'd told her about his engagement to Rexanne. "You must have finally talked Kelly into getting married. Congratulations, boss!"

"I wish," he said dully.

"She hasn't said yes yet?"

The shock in Ginger's voice gave him some encouragement. Obviously she thought he was a catch, even if Kelly did not. "Not even maybe," he admitted.

"Well, for heaven's sake, boss, you can't just shut down business on a whim. How long do you expect it to take to persuade her?"

"You're a woman. You tell me."

"Did you do like I said? Did you buy some of that French perfume? Did you tell her you loved her?"

Jordan supposed his silence was answer enough, because Ginger gave a little snort of disgust. "Jeez, boss, you're missing the most obvious things. Perfume is equated with sex, at least the right one is. And every woman wants the man she's marrying to be crazy in love with her. Stop being so stodgy and do something over the top for a change. Dazzle her."

"But this is Kelly," he protested. "We've known each other forever. She doesn't expect all that hearts and flowers sentiment. She'd probably laugh in my face."

Ginger sighed heavily. "Boss, I hate to say it, but you deserve to remain single. You might as well come on back to Houston now, because if Kelly has a brain in her head, which she obviously does, she'll boot you out of there sooner or later anyway. You'll wind up with one of those dull, grasping socialites, who won't care how you woo them as long as you ultimately give them access to your bank account."

"Thanks for the vote of confidence," he said,

thoroughly demoralized. "Just cancel the meetings, okay? Or see if one of the others can take them. Mark could probably handle the one with the equipment manufacturer." He listed others that could be turned over to key members of his staff. "You'll have to postpone the rest."

"And what am I supposed to tell people?"

"Tell them I'm working on a major acquisition and it's taking more of my time than I'd planned."

Ginger gave another derisive sniff. "Tell Kelly that, why don't you? That'll really win her over."

Jordan wasn't about to admit to her that his lack of romanticism was already a major bone of contention between Kelly and him. "Just do what I asked, please. I'll see you next week."

"Bet it'll be sooner," Ginger muttered.

"Goodbye," he said pointedly. "Call me at Kelly's if you need me."

"I think maybe I'll try reaching you at White Pines first. Odds are that's where you'll be."

She hung up before he could respond to her final, stinging taunt. Damn, what was with women, anyway? They all stuck together. He suspected Jessie would be no different.

Now that he thought about it, maybe that was the real reason he'd driven all the way to Luke's the night before. He'd wanted a chance to test his thinking on his brother's wife.

Jessie had always struck him as a sweet, practical, no-nonsense kind of woman. She was very fond of Kelly. Surely she would see the sense in the arrangement he was proposing to Kelly. Like him,

Jessie would want what was best for her friend. Someone who would look after her and Dani.

He found Jessie downstairs in the kitchen. The baby was propped up in her high chair and Jessie was spooning something that looked like watered-down oatmeal into her mouth. Most of it appeared to be on Angela's face and the floor with a goodly portion streaked from Jessie's face all the way down the front of her blouse. Oddly enough, she didn't seem to mind.

The minute Jessie spotted him, she stood and shoved the tiny spoon into his hand. "Feed her, would you? I need to check the laundry."

"Can't she wait?" he inquired, staring helplessly from Jessie to the baby and back again. Before the words were out of his mouth, Angela balled her tiny hands into fists and began whimpering. Jessie didn't even glance back.

"Okay, okay," he murmured, taking a seat opposite the baby. He dipped the spoon into the cereal, if that's what it was, and aimed at Angela's mouth. Unfortunately the target moved. The cereal dribbled down her cheek. She seemed pleased, though, that he'd tried. She smiled happily, displaying what might have been the beginnings of a tooth.

"Let's try this again," he said, bolstered by that smile. The next spoonful actually made it into her mouth, then dribbled out. He had the strangest suspicion that this was a game she enjoyed playing. Another perverse woman in the making, he decided with a sigh of resignation.

He scooped up more of the disgusting cereal and aimed again. This time she hit the spoon and splattered it back on him. Globs of the white stuff stuck to his shirt. He was forced to admit to a certain admiration for her muscle tone. She'd whacked that spoon with real strength.

Babies were obviously more of a challenge than he'd originally thought. He made up his mind to get the hang of dealing with them. After all, he supposed that sooner or later he and Kelly would want children of their own, baby brothers and sisters for Dani. He hadn't given a lot of consideration to kids in the past, but his experiences with Dani lately were changing his mind.

"Do you really want this stuff?" he inquired. "Frankly, it looks pretty disgusting to me."

"You're not the one eating it," Jessie retorted, coming back from the laundry room just in time to hear him trying to get out of feeding her child. She glanced at his shirt. "Maybe I'd better put that in with the next load of laundry."

"Do you do one after every meal?" he inquired, glancing around at the diaper she'd used to mop up previous spills, at Angela's filthy romper and Jessie's own spotted clothes.

"Actually, I've threatened to wear a plastic garbage bag with a slit in the top for my head," she admitted. "It's not always this bad, though." She grinned. "And sometimes it's much worse. Spinach is the pits."

"How reassuring. No wonder Luke has taken a powder and left you in charge."

"He's been gone since sunrise. He swears it's because there's work to be done, but I have my doubts. I think you may be right. He took one look at his precious daughter after her first experiment with baby food and decided not to show up for mealtime until she reaches her teens. He has this illusion that she's perfect and perfect does not include this particular image."

Jordan heard the tolerant amusement in her voice and saw the sparkle in her eyes. There was no mistaking the love radiating from her when she talked about her baby or his brother. He wondered if he and Kelly would ever have that kind of emotion between them. Probably not the way he was going about things, he was forced to admit. Ginger might have a point about that, though he'd sure as hell never tell her that. She was impossible enough as it was.

"Can I ask you a question?"

"Sure," Jessie said as she carefully spooned the remaining cereal into Angela's mouth. "Does it have something to do with Kelly?"

He wasn't all that surprised that she'd guessed. Harlan had probably mentioned his suspicions to Luke. Or, more likely, Kelly had told Jessie herself. He knew they talked regularly.

"What did she tell you?" he asked.

"About?" she replied noncommittally.

"Us."

Jessie spared him a glance. "Us? As in you and Kelly?"

"You don't have to act so innocent. I'm sure she told you I'd proposed."

Her expression turned quizzical. "Is that what it was?"

Jordan moaned. "Not you, too?"

"Well, you have to admit your technique lacked finesse."

"I sent flowers. I had a message flown over the ranch. I had thousands of rose petals dropped from the sky. I brought her sexy lingerie. The stuff damned near drove me wild imagining her in it. She didn't even take it out of the box."

Jessie's eyes widened at the mention of the lingerie. "Oh, really? She didn't mention that."

Jordan thought of how embarrassed Kelly had been by that particular gift. "I'm not surprised." He stared at Jessie, feeling totally bemused and helpless for the first time in his life. He didn't like the sensation at all. "I even offered to compromise on where we live."

Jessie put aside the bowl of cereal and leveled a penetrating look straight at him. "Before I answer, may I ask you a question?"

"Of course."

"Do you love her?"

Ginger had essentially asked the same thing and he'd been unwilling or unable to answer. He saw that he couldn't evade Jessie so easily. He had the feeling she could read between the lines of whatever answer he chose to give.

"I don't know what I feel," he admitted candidly. "She's always been a part of my life. I never thought of her in any way other than the best friend I ever had until recently.''

''After your engagement to that awful Rexanne person fell apart?''

Another vote weighed in against his ex-fiancée. He must have been blind. ''Exactly,'' he said.

''So you decided to rebound straight to the woman who'd been the one safe, secure constant in your life.''

It didn't sound nearly so sensible or laudable when Jessie described it. ''Something like that.''

''She ought to knock your teeth down your throat,'' Jessie said succinctly.

His eyes widened. ''Thanks.''

''I'm serious. Of all the selfish, pigheaded decisions, Jordan Adams, that takes the cake. I'd say you'd better think long and hard about what you really want out of this relationship before you push Kelly's back to the wall. She's my friend and I don't want to see her hurt again. If you can't admit you love her, I'll stand up and shout my objections right smack in the middle of the service when the preacher asks if anyone knows just cause why you shouldn't be wed. I guarantee I'll make it the most humiliating moment of your life.''

He saw evidence of the fiery temper Luke had mentioned on occasion, but no one else had ever seen in calm, serene Jessie. ''You would, wouldn't you?'' he said in amazement.

''Damn straight.''

He grinned despite himself. ''I'm glad she has you for a friend.'' He stood and headed for the door. "Fair warning, though. If I ever do manage to convince her to marry me, I may put a muzzle on you before I let you near the church."

Jessie didn't even flinch. "Tell her you love her and you won't have to."

The words echoed in his head all the way back to Kelly's ranch. After stopping in town to buy a picnic lunch, he sped the rest of the way to her house. He parked beside her car, checked the house for her even though he knew it was unlikely she'd be there in the middle of the day, then saddled up a horse and rode off in search of her.

As he rode, with the sun beating down on his shoulders and fluffy white clouds scudding across the vivid blue sky, he tried to analyze why he was so determined to marry Kelly. Was it pure cussedness because she'd said no and no one ever turned down Jordan Adams? Or was it something more, some feeling deep inside he'd never before analyzed too closely? Had all those times he'd gravitated to her house, ostensibly just to check up on her, been indications that she fulfilled some need in him?

He looked to his own parents for some clue about what love was all about. Harlan and Mary Adams had been married nearly thirty-five years. His father's eyes still shone whenever his wife walked into a room. As for his mother, she wasn't an especially warm woman, except when it came to her husband. With him, she radiated charm and laughter and the heat of desire even after all these years. They shared common goals and an abiding affection. Their marriage had been an example to all of their sons, even if Mary Adams's parenting skills had left something to be desired.

Surely, he thought, he and Kelly felt some of those same things. Maybe he'd just never put a label to them before. Maybe he'd repeatedly come back to west Texas, back to her, because he knew that with her he felt whole as he did with no one else on earth. Was that love?

He'd called himself in love with Rexanne and with others before her. He'd tacked the label on his feelings, because it seemed to be expected. But whatever emotions he'd felt then now seemed pale in comparison to the depth of what he felt when he was with Kelly and with Dani. He felt passion with Kelly, but he also felt a rare contentment, the kind that would endure. It was that, he knew, that had drawn him back to her.

Maybe he could say he loved her and say it in all honesty. Damn, but it was complicated, though. He didn't want to lie to her about something this important. He didn't want her to marry him under false pretenses. He'd been fooled before by love. So had she. He didn't want to make a mistake like that again, especially not with Kelly. She deserved only words he could back up with total conviction. One man like Paul Flint was more than any woman deserved.

It would be easy enough to say what she expected, to utter those three little words that would end this stalemate, but would it be fair? Would it be honest, when he was filled with so many doubts and questions?

He resolved to his regret that it would not be. If she accepted his proposal, it would have to be with the understanding that his feelings were still unclear, even to him. She would have to say *yes* knowing that while the commitment was as solid as granite, his emotions were more like quicksand, riddled with uncertainty.

He spotted her off in the distance just then, the sun glistening off her hair, the hat she wore only under duress dangling around her neck. Dani was seated on the saddle in front of her, a tiny cowboy hat perched on her head, her short legs clinging to the sides of the horse. Something inside him melted at the sight of them. If what he felt wasn't love, it was something darned close to it.

Dani saw him first and waved. "Hi, Jordan," she shouted, the greeting carrying on the still, hot, dry air.

Kelly's head snapped up. She was obviously startled to see him riding toward them. "I thought you'd be long gone by now," she said when he neared.

There was an uneasiness in her eyes that he deeply regretted. He knew he'd put it there with all of his pushing. Yet he knew this was too critical to their future for him to back off.

"I still have a very important matter pending," he said, his gaze even with hers and unrelenting.

She seemed to squeeze Dani a little more tightly against her body, the protective instinct of a mother with her endangered child. Or was it the mother who felt endangered in this instance?

"Jordan, this isn't the time," she said briskly, warning him to silence with a glance at Dani, then adding pointedly, "I have work to do."

"And I'll help," he promised. "But you have to break for lunch sometime. Why not now? I see the perfect spot over there under that old cottonwood." He gestured toward the basket he'd filled with sandwiches and ice-cold lemonade. "I brought a picnic."

"With potato salad?" Dani asked, oblivious to the undercurrents between the two adults. "And peanut butter and jelly?"

"You bet," he said, relieved that he'd thought of a child's tastes and included the peanut butter and jelly. "Cookies, too."

Kelly shook her head. "At this rate, you're going to win by default," she accused, relenting and turning her horse toward the shady spot to the west. "The ranch will fall apart because the work's not getting done, then where will I be?"

"You'll always have a place with me." He gazed directly into Kelly's eyes again as he set Dani down and sent her off to unpack the picnic basket. "Would it be so awful?" he asked when Dani was out of hearing.

A glint of determination flashed in her eyes. "Under those circumstances? Yes," she said without hesitation. "I told you that fixing this place up is important to me."

Jordan couldn't help admiring the streak of pride

that kept her focused on making a go of this ranch entirely on her own, even if it was making his task a whole lot harder. "Then I'll just have to help ensure that it doesn't fall apart, won't I?"

She frowned. "We've been over this already. I won't take your money, Jordan."

"How about my help?" he retorted softly.

She hesitated, then sighed. "No rancher ever turns down an offer of help," she said. "As long as there are no strings attached."

"No strings," he assured her. Just when she appeared to relax slightly, he added, "For now."

Kelly was losing the battle. Every time she turned around all week long, Jordan was there, offering support, muscle and laughter. Every night Dani crawled into his lap after dinner and begged to be told a story about when he and her mother were little like her. Jordan seemed to enjoy the reminiscing almost as much as Dani did.

Even the old tomcat had turned traitor. He'd taken to curling up at Jordan's feet, purring loudly whenever Jordan deigned to rub his stomach.

More often than not, though, his gaze would cut to Kelly, rocking slowly in the chair next to his on the porch. Whenever she dared to meet his eyes, she saw something there that stunned her, something that might have been love, something that unmistakably was pure, raw desire.

And yet he hadn't touched her. There'd been no more bone-melting kisses, just spine-tingling, sizzling looks. He was so careful to avoid even the most casual contact that she almost screamed with frustration. Her skin heated with anticipation whenever he neared. Her entire body ached with longing. These old, familiar, unfulfilled yearnings were driving her flat-out crazy.

"You okay?" Jessie asked when Kelly called her on Friday. Five days of skirting Jordan had taken their toll and obviously it showed in her voice.

"No," she said succinctly.

"Uh-oh, what's Jordan done now?"

"Nothing."

"Isn't that what you wanted?" Jessie asked, sounding vaguely confused.

"Yes…no." She sighed heavily. "Dammit, Jessie, I don't know anymore."

Instead of offering the sympathy she'd anticipated, her friend chuckled. "Oh, sweetie, I'm sorry, but watching the pair of you doing this dance of seduction is wearing me out."

"How do you think I feel?" Kelly retorted.

"Let me ask you something. You admitted to me that you love him, so that's not the issue, is it?"

Leave it to Jessie to cut straight to the chase. "No."

"And he obviously cares enough about you to want to spend the rest of his life with you and to raise Dani as his own. He may not call it love, but it's definitely a commitment, right?"

"Yes. What's your point?"

"Don't get mad at me for asking this, but do you think you might be holding out to punish him for all those years when he never gave you a second glance?''

''That's absurd,'' Kelly said indignantly. ''What would be gained by that?''

''Satisfaction, maybe,'' Jessie offered. ''Tormenting him might be a kind of sweet revenge for all those years you spent silently suffering.''

''Absolutely not. That's not the kind of person I am.''

''Not normally, I know, but these are unusual circumstances. It might be natural to want to exact a little revenge because he flaunted all those other women in your face. I'm not saying that's what's behind your indecision here, I'm just suggesting you think about the possibility.''

Jessie's suggestion angered her. She didn't like thinking she was capable of exacting revenge for deeds she thought she'd long since forgiven, deeds that had never been meant to hurt her in the first place. Still, she knew her friend wouldn't have mentioned it if she didn't think there might be some validity to it.

''I'll think about it,'' Kelly agreed.

In fact, she thought about little else for the rest of the day. She recalled all the instances when Jordan had spent hours on end talking about the hottest girls in high school and asking her advice on how to get them to go out with him. Not that he'd had that much trouble. Even as teenagers, girls had gravitated to him because of his good looks and fun-loving personality. It hadn't hurt that he was a star athlete, too.

He'd been equally sought after during his one year in college, chased when he'd been working the oil fields, and on every year's most eligible bachelor list once he'd settled in Houston. He'd had more relationships than she could count, but when each one had ended for one reason or another, he'd always come back to her to lick his wounds. She'd consoled him, boosted his ego with her nonjudgmental adoration, made him laugh again.

And all the while, her own heart had ached.

When she'd finally tired of the pattern, she had turned to Paul Flint and impulsively married him, determined to put Jordan and her wasted emotions behind her once and for all.

But Jordan had refused to stay out of her life. He had befriended Paul, even though he couldn't stand him. He'd stayed on the fringes of their lives, close enough to pick up the pieces when the marriage had fallen apart. The divorce had taken a long, messy year or more after she'd returned to her family's ranch. Jordan had stuck by her through every terrible minute of it.

She'd experienced a wild moment of hope then, sure that it was finally their turn. Within weeks, however, he had announced his engagement to Rexanne. Though Kelly had known better than to hope for the impossible, she had been devastated just the same. She'd shored up her defenses so securely after that that the marines couldn't have penetrated.

All that night she lay awake considering Jessie's question. Was it possible that she was cutting off her nose to spite her face, just to get even with

Jordan for not turning to her sooner? Was she holding out for moonbeams, when what he was offering was much more solid?

From practically the first moment she'd ever set eyes on Jordan she had known in her heart that he was the man she would one day marry. That sense of inevitability had taken a very long time to shake. Now, when she'd least expected it, her chance was finally here and she couldn't seem to bring herself to say yes. Was that nothing more than pure perversity?

As Jessie had pointed out, he might not have said the words she desperately wanted to hear. He might not have said he loved her, but he was willing to stand up in front of God and everyone and declare his intentions to love, honor and cherish her for the rest of their days.

In that moment, she made up her mind. If Dani had no objections, if Jordan's determination hadn't wavered, she would say yes.

And then she would dedicate the rest of her days to making sure that neither of them ever regretted the choice they had made.

Chapter Nine

"Mommy, is Jordan going to be my new daddy?" Dani asked the following morning while shoving her French toast around in a puddle of syrup.

The unexpected question brought up the subject that had kept Kelly awake all night long.

"If he has his way, he is," Kelly muttered before she could catch herself.

She hadn't anticipated getting into this before she'd even had her first cup of coffee. In fact, she hadn't intended to get into it with her daughter at all, at least not until the matter was more settled with Jordan himself.

"When?"

"That's hard to say, sweetie. There are some things we have to work out."

"Like what?"

Kelly thought of all the doubts that had chased through her mind. None of them were things she could share with her daughter. "Just things," she said evasively.

Dani studied her intently and apparently concluded Kelly still wasn't convinced that Jordan would make a proper daddy. "I like Jordan," she informed her mother firmly. "I think he would make a very good daddy."

Kelly wondered if her daughter had insights into Jordan that hadn't come to her yet. "Why is that?" she asked.

"He brings me candy."

Kelly refrained from labeling the candy what it was—bribery. Hadn't he tried the very same tactic on her? She'd already told Jordan half a dozen times to cut it out or he'd be paying Dani's dental bills.

"Don't you like Jordan?" Dani inquired worriedly. "You used to be bestest friends, that's what you said."

"Most of the time I like him very much," Kelly conceded.

"More than Daddy?"

Ah, now there was a mine field if ever Kelly had seen one. She had prepared an answer to that long ago, knowing sooner or later that rather plaintive question or one very similar was going to come up. Dani was too precocious not to ask difficult questions about the man who had sired her but spent very little time in her life.

"Your father is a fine man," she said, almost by rote. "He and I just weren't well suited. We were very young and we made a mistake getting married."

Dani contemplated that for a while, then turned a troubled look on Kelly. "Was I a mistake, too?"

Tears sprang to Kelly's eyes. She wrapped Dani in a hug and squeezed, peppering her worried little face with kisses. "Never, not in a million years. You are the very best part of my life. I wanted you more than anything."

"Daddy, too? Did he want me more than anything?"

Kelly cursed the man she'd once been married to for putting her on more tricky turf. Paul had never been inclined to have children, had agreed to Kelly getting pregnant only after frequent arguments. It had been yet another mistake on Kelly's part. She had thought Paul would love being a father, once he'd gotten over being terrified by the idea of it. She'd been convinced he would take to it. He hadn't. It was one reason she'd watched Jordan's behavior with Dani so closely, one reason she had fretted over how well the two of them would get along. Now, thankfully, she knew there was no comparison.

All of which didn't give her an easy answer to Dani's question.

"Your father loves you very much," she said, forcing a note of conviction into her voice that Paul didn't deserve. She wouldn't be the one to ruin his relationship with his child. He was doing that very nicely all on his own. She hoped someday he would wake up and realize how much he'd missed and suffer regrets for the rest of his life.

"Then why doesn't he ever come to see me?" Dani asked.

"Because he's very busy." The excuse came automatically. She'd been uttering it since the day of the divorce. And for a long time before that, for that matter.

"Jordan's busy, too," Dani stated. "He has a great big company to run and he comes. He's been here a whole week now. He even reads me a bedtime story every single night. Daddy never does."

Kelly thought of her ex-husband's difficult childhood, a childhood he'd used to excuse his need for excess, for more money and more women, just to prove his own worth.

"I don't think anyone ever read to your father when he was little," she said, trying to give Paul the benefit of the doubt one more time. "He doesn't realize how important it is."

Dani shot her a confiding look. "Jordan says he likes to read to me."

Kelly had noticed that herself. After his initial reservations, Jordan had seemed to enjoy the quiet evening time with Dani as much as she always had. "Does he now? Did he say why?"

"Because he likes all those stories, but grownups look silly reading fairy tales to themselves. He says he's going to teach me to read one all by myself for the times when he's not here." She turned her dark, velvet blue eyes on Kelly. "I really, really hope you make Jordan my new daddy fast."

In an unfortunate bit of timing, Kelly heard the screen door open just then.

"I really, really hope so, too," Jordan chimed in, winking at Dani, who bolted from the table and threw herself into his arms. They both regarded Kelly hopefully.

Kelly might have been able to hold out against Jordan's powers of persuasion for a little longer, just to assure herself that the decision she'd reached in the dark of night made sense in daylight. Teamed up with her daughter, though, he was an irresistible force. She could do a lot worse than Jordan Adams. In fact, she already had.

She lifted her gaze and met his eyes and saw something there that stunned her—uncertainty. Jordan was vulnerable where she was concerned. It was hardly a declaration of undying love, but it was a start, something to build on.

"Set the date," she said.

He didn't bat an eye. "Next weekend," he said, his serious gaze never wavering from hers. "We'll fly to Vegas."

What an appalling idea! Kelly regarded him indignantly. "Not on your life. This may not be a traditional marriage, but we are going to have a traditional ceremony. We'll have the service and the reception right here."

Jordan turned and cast a dubious look around the house, which for all of her hard work was undeniably shabby in spots. "Here?" he protested mildly. "I can't see the governor..."

"The governor can come here or he's not invited," she said flatly. "This is our wedding, not a business dinner. We don't have to impress anybody." She shot him a challenging look. "Do we?"

A grin spread across his face. "Not a soul, sweet pea."

Filled with the first faint stirrings of hope at the quick capitulation, Kelly crossed the kitchen and patted his cheek. "This could work out yet, *sweet pea*."

Jordan glanced at Dani. "Munchkin, wouldn't you like to go out and check on the kittens?"

"But I haven't even finished my French toast," Dani protested. "'Sides, I want to talk about the wedding, too. Can I be a flower girl? My friend Megan was one. She told me all about it."

Kelly didn't think talking was what Jordan had on his mind. Frankly, at this precise moment, it was the last thing on hers, as well. She needed to feel his arms around her, needed to fit her body against his. She wanted desperately to feel all the passion that marriage was supposed to promise, to be reassured that she wasn't making a terrible mistake.

"Sweetie, of course you can be a flower girl," she promised her daughter. "Remember, though, that today's the day we promised to take a kitten over to Jordan's daddy. You have to decide which one."

"And Cody? Don't forget he wanted two."

Jordan winced. "We'll have to talk about that.

Cody's gone away for a while. We'll have to find another home for the two he'd picked out.''

Dani's face fell. Her lower lip quivered. "But what if we can't?"

"We will," Jordan promised. "If we don't, they can live with us."

Kelly stared at him. "But you said…"

He shrugged. "I can't let you go drowning them in the creek, can I?"

"I would never drown them in the creek," she said, shocked by the very idea of such a thing. "Where on earth would you get such a notion?"

He glanced at Dani, who had hung her head. Kelly had never seen a clearer portrait of guilt.

"Danielle Flint, is that what you've been telling everyone?" Kelly demanded. "No wonder everyone's been so eager to claim these kittens."

Dani's expression of guilt quickly fled. Her chin tilted defiantly. "I had to do something. Besides, they're really, really cute. I knew everyone would like them once they got to know them."

Kelly looked up from her daughter's belligerent face to find Jordan's lips twitching with amusement. "Are you sure you're up to a lifetime of this?" she asked him.

"Oh, I think I'll manage," he said confidently. "You've never scared me."

"More's the pity," she said with feeling. "But I was thinking of Dani."

"She's just the icing on the cake," he assured her.

Dani looked from one to the other, clearly puzzled. "What cake?"

"Never mind, munchkin. Go check on those kittens," Jordan said. "Your mom and I have wedding plans to make."

Dani finally climbed out of her chair and ran from the house. The minute she was out of sight, Jordan cupped Kelly's face in his hands. He studied her intently.

"Are you sure?"

"I have been since I was eight," she admitted, suddenly breathless. "You're the one who took a very long time to come around."

He didn't even begin to deny the accusation. "I guess I had to mine through a lot of fool's gold before I could tell I had the real thing right here."

She held the words to her heart. It was as close to an *I love you* as he'd come. "How are your parents going to react?"

"Oh, I suspect Daddy's been figuring on this for weeks now, maybe even years. If he's content with the decision, Mother will be, too."

Kelly sighed with regret. "I wish my parents had lived long enough for this. They always adored you. As hard as they tried, they never warmed up to Paul."

Jordan tilted her head up. "And you? How did you feel about me?"

"Jordan, I said I'd marry you. Don't get greedy."

"Suddenly I want it all," he whispered softly, just before he slanted his mouth across hers.

Kelly was swept away by the kiss, swept away to a time and place where dreams became real and magic filled every hour of the day. It was a place she'd never thought to reach, because she'd always known only one man could take her there.

And now, out of the blue, it was real and every bit as incredible as she'd always imagined.

The wedding plans were completely out of control. Kelly latched onto Jordan's arm when he walked through the door the following Wednesday and dragged him into the kitchen.

"This has to stop," she insisted.

He regarded her warily. "What?"

"Your mother has taken over. A decorator steamrolled through here this morning as if she were preparing for the Normandy invasion." She glared at her fiancé of less than a week. "I will not have it, Jordan. I won't!"

"What exactly was she here to do?"

"She is designing the wedding," she said, a note of disgust in her voice. "Between now and Saturday, she intends to transform this house into a summer garden. She wants to put trellises with roses in the middle of my living room."

He seemed almost as bemused by the concept as she was. "And you don't want them there?"

"I want my living room to look like a living room, not a damned fake garden!"

The expletive apparently convinced him she was at the end of her patience. Jordan reached out and snagged her hand. Somehow she wound up in his lap, with his arms reassuringly settled around her waist and his lips on hers.

"Kissing won't make it better, Jordan!" she warned at one point.

"Are you sure about that?" he inquired, brushing his lips back and forth against hers until her blood sizzled. It did pretty much wipe thoughts of anything else out of her mind.

"It could be helping just a little," she admitted as his lips found a sensitive spot on her neck. A shudder washed through her. "Okay, more than a little."

"Are you distracted yet?"

"From what?" she murmured, giving herself up to the sensations spinning through her.

A knock on the screen door interrupted. Kelly's sigh only deepened when she spotted Mary Adams, her soon-to-be mother-in-law, on her doorstep. She was wearing her going-into-battle shopping outfit of linen pants, a silk blouse and sufficient gold jewelry to impress the most difficult salesclerk. As stifling hot as it was, she looked cool and unrumpled.

"Enough of that, you two," Mary said briskly as she entered without waiting for permission. "It's ridiculous enough that you've only given a week's notice for this wedding, we can't go wasting time on nonsense."

Kelly gazed helplessly into Jordan's eyes and mouthed, Do something!

Jordan stood. He towered over his petite mother, but his size clearly didn't intimidate her.

"Out of my way," she commanded. "I need to see the kitchen."

"Why?" Kelly inquired suspiciously.

"To let the caterer know what's possible and what isn't."

"I was thinking we'd have those little cocktail wieners and maybe some potato chips," Jordan said. "Maybe a big old platter of barbecued ribs."

His mother simply scowled at his teasing as she breezed past. Kelly trailed along in her wake, tugging Jordan with her. Why hadn't they eloped to Vegas as Jordan originally suggested? It would have been better than this armed invasion of strangers that Jordan's mother had planned.

Mary Adams glanced at Kelly. "What about your dress? Perhaps we should have Harlan's pilot fly us over to Dallas this afternoon. I'm sure we could find something on short notice at Neiman-Marcus."

The suggestion explained Mary's attire. Kelly balked at going anywhere to buy anything. "I have a dress," she said adamantly.

Mary looked aghast. "You're planning to pluck something out of your closet? This is your wedding, for heaven's sake, and Jordan does have a certain status to maintain. What you wear will reflect on him."

The comment grated. "Jordan," Kelly said sweetly, "could I see you in the living room?"

She noticed when she finally had him alone that his eyes were sparkling with pure mischief.

"A problem, sweet pea?"

"If your mother does not back off, I swear to you that I'm going to wear jeans for this wedding and serve lemonade and store-bought cookies."

Jordan pulled her against him. "Sounds perfect to me."

She studied him intently, not sure whether she could trust the dead-serious note in his voice. "You wouldn't mind?"

"Actually, I'd rather like to see the governor's face as he sips lemonade and munches a handful of Oreo cookies. He'd probably prefer it over the rubber chicken and hard little peas he usually gets."

Kelly sighed. "He might be perfectly content, but your mother's likely to flip out."

"Sweetheart, it's our wedding. The details are entirely up to you. Just tell me what time you want me here and I'll show up. I could care less about the rest."

"Are you sure?"

"Absolutely."

"Any idea how many people your mother has invited?"

"Nope," he admitted.

"Maybe I'd better ask that before I get too independent here," she said, calmer now that she knew Jordan was in her corner no matter what she decided.

She went back to the kitchen where she found her future mother-in-law tsk-tsking at the size of the stove and refrigerator.

"Kelly, I think it's time for new appliances, don't you?"

"Absolutely," she agreed without hesitation. Her parents had bought the current ones years ago and they were clearly on their last legs. "But I thought fixing the roof and painting were more important."

The concept of budgetary constraint was clearly beyond Mary's comprehension. "Yes, but this is something you can't put off. I can't possibly have the caterer do anything the least bit elaborate without a decent stove or refrigerator." She jotted a note to herself. "I'll take care of it this afternoon. Do you want white again?"

Kelly moved in front of her. "No new stove and no new refrigerator," she said quietly, even though her stomach was churning and her blood was heating to a boil. "This is a wedding, not a home show."

"But what about hot hors d'oeuvres? And your freezer won't even hold a spare pint of ice cream, much less the ice sculpture I've ordered."

"It's ninety degrees outside. Why would you order an ice sculpture in the first place?"

Mary Adams stopped in her tracks and stared. "You intend for everyone to eat outside? My dear, people will be perspiring," she declared as if that were the worse tragedy that could possibly befall anyone. "You simply cannot ask them to deal with all the dust, to say nothing of this sweltering hot weather. Their clothes will be ruined."

"How many people have you invited?" Kelly countered.

Mary avoided looking her in the eye. "Just a few. You did say you wanted it kept small."

"How many?"

"A hundred, more or less."

Kelly gulped. It was even worse than she'd suspected. "That's what you consider small?"

Mary seemed oblivious to Kelly's distress. "Of course, given Jordan's status, there are business considerations, as well as old friends and family," she informed her future daughter-in-law. "I cut it as best I could."

Kelly had guessed the number would be half that high, which was precisely why she'd considered the possibility of an outdoor celebration. This clinched it.

"I see," she said, rather proud of how calm she managed to sound. "And where do you expect these hundred people to fit inside the house? If you think it would be stifling outside, imagine them all crammed in here without air-conditioning."

"Without air-conditioning?" Mary sank down onto a kitchen chair. "Oh, my, I suppose that is a problem, isn't it?" She fanned herself with her little leather notebook. "Darling! Jordan, come in here at once!"

Jordan, who'd apparently taken refuge in the living room rather than get caught between his mother and his bride, came into the kitchen. He glanced warily from his mother to Kelly and back again. "What now?"

"I really think there is only one thing to be done," his mother said briskly, clearly recovered from her momentary shock. "We will have to move the wedding to White Pines."

"Absolutely not!" Kelly insisted, just as Jordan hurriedly said after one glance at her face, "Now, Mother, let's not be hasty."

Mary scowled at the pair of them. "Well, I simply don't know what else to do," she said in that haughty tone Kelly knew she could come to hate. She gestured around her. "This house is simply not big enough or equipped for a wedding. White Pines has all of the latest, industrial-size appliances and the staff is used to dealing with caterers and a large number of guests. This is the most important day of your life, after all. It should be something to remember."

"It's the most important day of *our* lives," Kelly said, her voice tight.

Jordan clearly heard the stress in her tone, because he hurried his mother out of the kitchen. "Mother, let me discuss this with Kelly and we'll get back to you."

Kelly could hear his mother protesting even as she was hustled away.

"Jordan, the wedding is in three days," Mary complained. "You can't possibly wait another moment before deciding."

"We're waiting, Mother. I'll be in touch."

Kelly thought the screen door slammed rather emphatically behind her. She was resting her head on top of her folded arms when Jordan returned to the kitchen and pressed a kiss to the back of her neck.

"Don't get fainthearted now," he murmured.

She looked up at him and tried to blink back

tears. The most incredible day of her life was going to turn into a nightmare. It was on a fast track to calamity and she could see no way to stop it.

"Jordan, I do not want to get married at White Pines," she said emphatically. "I do not want to wear a dress your mother has picked out. I do not want a swarm of caterers and strangers around us."

He sat down opposite her and took her hand in his. "What do you want? Just tell me and I'll take care of it."

Something in his voice told her she could trust him to do exactly that. "I want a small wedding. Just family. I want to wear my mother's wedding gown."

At his startled look, she added, "I didn't wear it when I married Paul. I saved it all these years so I could wear it if you and I ever got married." She sniffed and wiped at the tears tracking down her cheeks.

"Consider it done," he promised.

"Just like that?"

"Just like that."

Suddenly she was uncertain. "Is that selfish? Is your mother right about this being important to you for business reasons?"

He laughed. "Sweetheart, my mother thinks every occasion is an opportunity to solidify business relationships. Don't give that a second thought."

"But she's already invited the governor."

"And I'm equally certain the governor has

enough events to attend that he won't mind if I call up and tell him we've decided to elope.''

''Elope? I didn't say…''

''In a manner of speaking,'' he added hastily. ''I think perhaps we should plan the ceremony for Friday, tell the family they're simply coming here for a rehearsal dinner and let 'em know after it's over that it was the real thing.''

Kelly chuckled as she considered how that news would go over with Mary Adams. ''Your mother will kill us.''

''The most important thing is you and me getting married, right?''

No doubt about that, Kelly thought. She'd been waiting a lifetime for it to happen. ''Right.''

He stood and dropped a kiss on her forehead. ''Then leave the rest to me. Six o'clock, Friday evening, you and I are getting married.''

Kelly flew off of her chair and wrapped her arms around him. ''Jordan, I do love you.''

As soon as the impulsive words were out of her mouth, she regretted them. She hadn't intended to let him see so soon that her heart was on the line. It would have been far better to let him go on thinking that he was making a business acquisition of sorts.

He folded her into his arms and rested his chin on her head. She thought his heart was beating a little faster than usual, thought she detected a faint shudder sweeping through his body. Small signs, but they gave her hope. In time, surely Jordan would be able to say those words. In time…

Chapter Ten

The wedding was going to be as unconventional as the reasons behind it. An hour before the scheduled ceremony Jordan glanced around Kelly's living room and surveyed the hastily accomplished preparations with a sense of amazement. Admittedly he was no judge of such things, but it looked perfect. Informal, romantic and unique, just like the woman he was marrying.

Dear heaven, he was getting married tonight! He had actually won the battle to claim Kelly's heart. He was marrying a woman who'd been a part of his life for so long that he couldn't remember a time when she hadn't been important to him.

His proposal might have been impulsive, but he sensed without a doubt that he'd made the right decision. He and Kelly were a good match. Marriage wasn't nearly so intimidating or confusing when it was approached in a logical manner. Obviously she'd seen that, as well.

"Nervous?" Luke asked, amusement in his dark eyes as he watched Jordan pace amid the bouquets of wildflowers set on every available surface.

"About marrying Kelly? Not in the least," he said candidly. "About Mother's reaction when she finds out this is the real thing, you bet. She's going to pitch a fit. But if this will make Kelly happy, it will all be worth it. Frankly, I'm glad to be getting it over with. I keep thinking Kelly's going to change her mind."

Luke patted him consolingly on the shoulder. "Don't worry about Kelly. She's been in love with you ever since I can remember. As for Mother, she won't stay mad, not for long, anyway. Daddy will be so pleased by all of this, he'll see to it she handles this with her usual aplomb. And as long as he's happy, she won't bat an eye."

Jordan had his doubts, not about his father's powers of persuasion, but about his mother's flexibility. "I hope you're right. I don't want her and Kelly getting off on the wrong foot."

"Standing up to her is the only way to get off on the right foot," Luke said. "Jessie figured that out early on, while she was still married to Erik. She really had to take a stand once the baby was born or Mother would have taken over Angela's upbringing. Mother finds Jessie a challenge, but she doesn't dislike her. Besides, have you had any indication after all these years that Mother has anything at all against Kelly? It's not as if you're marrying some stranger.''

Jordan wondered about that. Kelly had seemed more perplexing to him lately than she had in all the previous years he'd known her. "If you say so," he said, glancing anxiously toward the stairs. "I wish they'd hurry up."

"You don't want them down here before Mother and Daddy arrive, do you? Once Mother sees Kelly in her wedding dress and you in your tuxedo, she's going to know something's up. In fact, it might be a good idea for you to hide out in the kitchen for a while with Consuela," he suggested, referring to his housekeeper.

Consuela had been more mother than hired help to Jordan and all of his brothers. When Luke had elected to build his own ranch, rather than remaining at White Pines, Consuela had gone with him after assuring herself that she was leaving Harlan and Mary in the capable hands of her cousin Maritza. She had always loved Kelly, who'd been in and out of the Adams kitchen as a child. The minute she'd heard about the change in wedding plans, she'd insisted on coming along not just as a beloved guest, but to fix the wedding dinner and bake the cake. Unfortunately, she'd lost patience with his hovering hours ago.

"She's already thrown me out of the kitchen once," Jordan admitted. "She said I was in her way." He sighed and looked at his older brother.

"I wish we could have talked Cody into coming back for this."

"I know," Luke said. "I tried. I think Daddy did, too. Cody is still hurt and angry and his pride's at stake. To top it off, he's the most stubborn of all of us and he's dead set against ever setting foot in Texas again as long as Melissa Horton is here. At least we can be grateful he found another job in ranching. He's not just bumming around, hell-raising and licking his wounds."

Jordan didn't find much comfort in that. "But Wyoming is a long way from home," he noted.

"He'll be back one of these days," Luke said with the certainty of an older brother who'd had time to observe the behavior patterns of his siblings. "Cody is as tied to this family as any of the rest of us, maybe even more so. He's the one who took the most interest in our ancestors, the one who cared the most about being an exalted Adams. He got Mother's powerful sense of family and Daddy's mule-headedness. Sooner or later his anger at Melissa will fade and he'll recognize that this is where he really belongs."

Jordan wished he were as sure. He'd seen Cody the night he'd discovered Melissa with his best friend. Luke hadn't. "I hope so. I think Daddy's missing him a lot. As much as Daddy grumbled about being displaced on his own ranch, I think he was really looking forward to having more time to travel with Mother."

"Maybe, but he's too damned young to retire," Luke commented. "He hasn't taken a real vacation in all these years because his heart's been in running White Pines. How much traveling do you think he really would have done before he'd gone nuts?''

"One trip," Jordan agreed with a chuckle. "Maybe two, especially when he figured out how much money Mother could spend in Paris in a week. His willingness to indulge her might have suffered a major setback after that.''

They were interrupted by the sound of a car driving up the lane. Jordan peered anxiously through the screen door.

"Mother and Daddy?" Luke asked.

"The minister, thank goodness. At least we'll all be in our places when they show up. Maybe we can even get through the 'I do's' before they guess what's going on.''

"Optimist," Luke taunted. His expression suddenly sobered. "I'm happy for you, little brother. Kelly's one in a million, after Jessie, of course. And I can vouch for the joy of starting off with a readymade family. It's not nearly as intimidating as I imagined.''

"I'm relieved to hear it," Jordan said, hugging his brother. "Thanks for helping me pull this off. No one could have ever had a better best man.''

"I'm just glad you finally woke up and asked the woman. Jessie was driving me nuts to give you a push, but we both knew you'd just rebel. You've already wasted too many years chasing after the Rexannes of the world.''

"Mother liked her," Jordan acknowledged as he went to open the door for Reverend Garrison, who'd been officiating at family ceremonies as far back as Jordan could remember.

"That should have been your first warning," Luke shot back dryly. He grinned at the minister. "How are you, Reverend?"

"Delighted to see another one of you lads tying the knot," he said, shaking Jordan's hand. "Explain to me again about this being a surprise service. Have to say I've never performed a wedding quite like that before. Who's not in on the secret? Surely not the bride."

"Oh, no," Jordan reassured him. "She's most definitely in on it. It's Mother and Daddy. Things were getting a little out of hand with the planning, so Kelly and I decided to do this our own way. As fast as Mother invited people, we turned around and uninvited them. We promised them a huge reception at White Pines in a few months, assuming Mother's started speaking to us again by then. At least she'll be able to plan that exactly the way she wants to."

The minister chuckled. "Seeing how your daddy likes to think he's the one running things in the family, I can't wait to see Harlan's and Mary's expressions when they find out."

Luke and Jordan exchanged a look of complete understanding. "Us, either," Jordan admitted with more than a little trepidation.

He peered out the door again and spotted dust flying at the far end of the lane. "Guess we'll know soon enough how it's going to go over. Luke, you want to warn the bride and get Consuela in here? I don't want to waste a second.''

It already seemed as if he'd wasted far too much of his life.

As Kelly gazed at herself in the mirror, Jessie stood back and admired the creamy lace and silk wedding dress that had been Kelly's mother's. ''You look beautiful,'' she told her. ''You'll knock Jordan's socks off.''

Dani peeked around from behind her mother and stared at her reflection in the mirror. Her eyes widened. ''Mommy, you look like a princess, just like the one in my book.''

The compliments were exactly what Kelly needed. They calmed the butterflies in her stomach.

''I feel like a princess,'' she admitted, her cheeks flushed. She had never felt this way before, not even on the day she had married Paul.

She'd had half a dozen attendants then and a church filled with friends and family. They'd even had a string quartet playing as the guests arrived. It had been a fantasy, storybook wedding, but she'd participated without this nervous sense of anticipation, without so much as a flutter of pure excitement. Now, just thinking of Jordan waiting downstairs, her pulse hammered.

''All set?'' Jessie asked. ''I saw Harlan and Mary drive up a second ago. Luke will be putting 'The Wedding March' on the stereo any minute now.''

Kelly reached over and clasped her friend's hand. ''Thank you for being here for me.''

Jessie smiled. "Where else would I be? I've been waiting for this day for a long time, too. You two were made for each other. Jordan's softer around you, less driven. Given a little time, I think it's entirely possible the man will get his priorities in order."

Kelly wasn't quite so convinced the leopard could change his spots. "I hope you're right. I really don't want to spend any more time in Houston than I absolutely have to."

"Then you'll just have to convince him that modern communications are such that he can run his business perfectly well from right here in west Texas. Give him a modem as a wedding present."

"An interesting idea," Kelly said slowly, giving it serious thought. "There really isn't any reason he couldn't operate the company from here, is there? I'm sure all those vice presidents and administrators he has running around over there would be glad to be out from under his thumb. Maybe I'll have a little chat with Ginger one of these days. She could probably tell me how tricky the logistics would be."

"She's his right arm, isn't she?" Jessie asked. "If you could win her over, it seems to me that would be half the battle."

"I've spoken to her several times when I called Jordan at the office. Her husband is from this part of the state," Kelly said, beginning to see how it could all work out. "From what I gather he's been bugging her to live over this way during the off-season. Says he wants to get back into ranching before he retires from football. She's held out because she loves her job. She doesn't want to be stranded way out here with nothing to do.''

"There, you see,'' Jessie said triumphantly. "All it'll take is a little ingenuity.''

"And perhaps a little of Harlan's skill at manipulation,'' Kelly admitted. "Think he'd give me lessons?''

"I doubt anything would thrill him more. It killed him to see Jordan move that far away. Nothing makes Harlan happier than being surrounded by family.''

Before they could get any more carried away with their plans, Dani piped up, "I hear the music, Mommy. I hear it!'' She started spinning around. Flower petals scattered from her basket as she twirled.

Jessie picked up Angela, who'd been sleeping peacefully during the preparations. She gazed at Kelly. "Ready?''

Kelly drew in a deep breath, then nodded. "Ready.''

Jessie bent down to Dani. "You know what you're supposed to do, right?''

Dani's expression turned serious. "I go down the steps and sprinkle rose petals all the way to the living room until I get to Jordan.''

"Exactly right,'' Jessie confirmed, and opened the bedroom door. "Let's have a wedding!''

Kelly watched as her daughter descended the stairs, then began her slow walk into the living room, self-consciously scattering the flower petals.

When Luke winked at Dani as she passed, Kelly could see the familiar, impudent grin spreading across her child's face.

Then, from the living room, she heard Harlan's exclamation of pride and Mary's enthusiastic praise of their soon-to-be granddaughter.

"Oh, how darling!" Mary Adams exclaimed. "Dani, you look absolutely precious."

Kelly didn't hear what was said after that, because suddenly Jessie was moving down the steps in her pale blue dress and her own grasp on the banister tightened into a death grip. This was it. After all these years of waiting and hoping, after all the disappointments, her wedding to Jordan was finally only a few minutes away. She had more than enough trepidations, but as many as there were, they were no match for the joy that was radiating through her. She was sure her smile was as big as Texas as she began the walk to Jordan's side.

She took each step slowly, savoring the anticipation of the instant when Jordan would see her, praying that he would be pleased, praying even harder that the cool deliberation behind his proposal would be transformed into pure emotion on this day. When he vowed to love her, she desperately wanted to see in his eyes that he meant it.

Then, practically before she knew it, her hand was in Luke's and he was walking her into the living room. With no one to officially give her away, he was serving double duty as best man and her escort. He patted her hand reassuringly and leaned down.

"You'll make him happy," he whispered with conviction. "Never doubt that." He winked then. "And if he doesn't do the same for you, let me know and I'll beat him up for you."

Impulsively Kelly stopped where she was and stood on tiptoe to kiss the cheek of this man who'd been her champion since childhood. "I'm so glad I'm going to be part of your family."

"It should have happened long ago," he said, his expression suddenly serious. "But you know how stubborn we Adams men are. One thing about us, though, once we make up our minds, we're steady as the Rock of Gibraltar."

"I'm counting on that." She drew in a deep breath, then made the turn into the living room.

She was dimly aware of Mary's soft gasp of astonishment, vaguely aware of Harlan's whispered exchange with his wife. It was one thing for Dani and Jessie to be dressed up for the rehearsal, another entirely to see the bride in her wedding gown. Superstition alone would have precluded it.

"What on earth?" Mary exclaimed, gazing from Kelly to her husband and back again.

Kelly was oblivious to whatever Harlan said in response. Her gaze was locked with Jordan's. His eyes shone when he saw her. She suspected his throat had gone dry, because he swallowed hard.

And then he smiled. Heavenly days, what that smile did to her. Her stomach flipped over, her pulse skipped crazily. Suddenly, as Luke placed her hand securely in Jordan's, her heart was filled to overflowing.

"Dearly Beloved..." the reverend began.

The rest was a blur. Kelly knew she made the appropriate responses because no one had to prompt her. Still, the only thing that seemed at all real was Jordan's firm grip on her hand and then the cool slide of gold as he slipped the wedding ring on her finger. She noticed, too, that his hand trembled ever so slightly when she slid a thicker, matching band of gold over his knuckle to rest in the place where it would remain for the rest of their days.

"I now pronounce you husband and wife," the reverend intoned. "You may kiss the bride."

Jordan's warm lips grazed hers, lingered, then claimed her mouth more hungrily. Kelly's knees went weak. She looked up and met Jordan's intent gaze. Rock-solid, dependable Jordan. Her husband! Just looking into his eyes steadied her. There was no uncertainty in his expression, no hint of doubt in the depths of his eyes.

They had done it, she realized as Jessie kissed her cheek and Luke pumped his brother's hand. They had actually gotten married just the way she'd envisioned, surrounded by those dearest to them and no one else.

Dani held up her arms to Jordan, who promptly lifted her up. "You're my daddy now, right?" she demanded, clearly dismissing the man who was biologically responsible for her birth but had done nothing to earn a secure place in her heart.

"I am your daddy," he concurred, an unmistakable note of wonder in his voice. Pride shone in his eyes.

Well satisfied with the incredible bond that had formed between Dani and Jordan, Kelly dared a glance at her new mother-in-law. Confusion was written all over her face. Kelly left Jordan's side and went to speak to her. She took Mary's cool hands in her own.

"Please, don't be too angry with us."

"You're married?" Mary said, sounding faintly bemused, rather than furious. "You're actually married?"

"We really are. We both wanted a quiet, intimate celebration. We talked about eloping, but we very much wanted all of you here. I hope you're not too disappointed."

Mary shook her head, as if trying to shake off her confusion. "But all of the guests, the arrangements..." Her voice trailed off helplessly.

Still holding Dani, Jordan came over and dropped a kiss on his mother's cheek. "All taken care of," he assured her. "I spoke with everyone and told them they'd receive an invitation to a reception at White Pines later." He regarded her intently. "If you're still willing to plan a party for us."

Mary stood there, her expression uncertain, until Harlan moved in.

"Of course, we will. We'd be proud to, wouldn't we, Mary?" He tugged Kelly into a tight embrace. "Welcome to the family, girl. It took too damned long to make you one of us. I for one couldn't be more pleased."

He glanced over at Dani, who was still clinging

to Jordan's neck as if she was afraid to let loose of this new, attentive daddy she'd just acquired. "As for you, young lady, I think you've got all the makings of a real Adams," Harlan declared. "You bargain with the best of them. Next thing you know you'll be running that oil company of Jordan's. As for that kitten you talked me into taking, she's already queen of the barn."

"Want another one?" Dani inquired. "I think maybe Francie is going to have kittens again."

Jordan shot a horrified look at her that had his father and Kelly laughing. "Oh, no," he muttered. "I'm having both of those cats fixed first thing tomorrow."

The old tomcat, who'd slipped out of the kitchen to wind between Jordan's legs, meowed a violent protest at the threat.

"What a disgusting conversation for your wedding day," Mary chided, clearly recovered from her initial shock. "Jordan, I do wish you'd remember the manners you were taught."

He leaned over and kissed her again. "Are we forgiven for not telling you about the wedding ahead of time?"

Kelly watched her mother-in-law closely, saw the momentary indecision, then caught Harlan's quick squeeze of her hand. Mary rallied at once, her impeccable breeding and her adoration and respect for her husband overcoming whatever disappointment she was feeling.

"Of course you're forgiven, darling. A surprise wedding will have everyone talking. People will be absolutely desperate to receive invitations to the party your father and I will throw for you.''

As Jordan and Luke had predicted, their mother was clearly in her element. She would be able to plan exactly the sort of celebration she wanted. All Jordan and Kelly would have to do was show up. It seemed like a suitable arrangement to Kelly. She surely would have bungled something crucial and Mary would never have forgiven her. Now the burden of pulling off the reception would be totally on Mary's capable shoulders.

''Come, come,'' Consuela called from the doorway to the dining room. ''The wedding dinner is ready.''

As the others went off to sit down, Jordan held Kelly back. She shot a questioning look at him. ''Everything okay?''

''I just had the most incredible need to kiss my bride.''

She tilted her chin and met his gaze. Those butterflies in her stomach took to doing somersaults. ''Any particular reason?''

''Because you're beautiful and because that official kiss at the end of the ceremony was over far too quickly to suit me,'' he murmured as he settled his mouth firmly against hers.

As always, it was the touch of velvet and fire, inflaming her even as she tried to think about the guests who were waiting for them a few feet away. ''Jordan,'' she whispered dazedly.

''Mmm?''

''Your family.''

"They're our family," he corrected. "And they can wait. We're newlyweds, remember? We're expected to spend a lot of time kissing."

His lips claimed hers again. His tongue invaded her mouth, teasing, inviting, sending her senses whirling. Finally, when she could barely stand, he ended the kiss, though he continued to hold her pressed tightly against his body. His heat surrounded her, drew her in. His masculine scent, counterpointed by the aroma of the flowers that filled the room, made her heady with longing.

"I had no idea," he murmured.

"No idea about what?"

"That I could ever want anyone this desperately."

He sounded shaken by the sudden discovery, shaken and more than a little pleased, she observed.

He was no less pleased than she. She'd spent years all too familiar with the desperate yearning that had just struck Jordan for the first time. And, she realized with both astonishment and anticipation, in a matter of hours a lifetime of longing would finally be fulfilled.

Chapter Eleven

It was amazing how quickly Jordan managed to rush everyone through a four-course meal and a wedding cake. Kelly almost felt sorry for their guests, who were hustled out of the house with all the finesse usually reserved for door-to-door salesmen.

As bad as she felt, though, she did absolutely nothing to delay their departure. Ever since that kiss had practically knocked her stockings and her traditional wedding garter off, she'd been counting the minutes until she could finally be alone with the man she had loved for so many years. They'd planned a few days here all alone as their honeymoon.

To her chagrin, she'd barely spared a glance for

her daughter, who'd gone off eagerly with Luke and Jessie, excited about her first opportunity to help baby-sit her new cousin Angela. She knew Dani would be in good hands with Jessie and Consuela there to look out for her. For the first time since Dani's birth, she was able to be purely selfish for just a little while. She intended to cherish these few days of quiet, private time with Jordan right here in the home she intended to share with him for the rest of their days.

As the last car drove off, she was finally left alone with her brand-new husband. Suddenly she felt absurdly shy. She glanced at Jordan as if he were a blind date she'd never seen before. Given the haste with which their status had changed from friends to mates, she realized belatedly that she hadn't yet fully made the mental adjustment to their new, untested relationship.

Marrying a best friend shouldn't have been nearly so scary, she thought, battling unexpected panic. Perhaps if they'd had a normal courtship, perhaps if they'd been intimate or at least shared more than a few deep, steamy kisses, she wouldn't have felt like blushing every time she looked at him. Somehow, though, going from best friend to lover in a heartbeat filled her with uncertainty. She felt as if her entire world had shifted crazily and she'd been left off-balance.

All of the insecurities that had welled up in her when she'd discovered her ex-husband had been turning to other women returned now with doubled intensity. Failing Paul had been one thing. Failing this man she loved so deeply was something else entirely. She wasn't sure she'd be able to bear it if she disappointed Jordan.

As if he sensed her turmoil, Jordan took her hand in his. "We're going to be okay," he reassured her.

Kelly lifted her gaze to his. "It's just that this feels so strange," she confided.

"Scared?"

"A little."

"Why?"

Since he seemed honestly interested in the answer, she began to relax just a little. She kicked off her shoes, settled herself on the sofa and accepted the glass of wine he held out. Seated beside her, he waited patiently as she struggled to find an explanation that would make sense to him.

"I think what scares me the most is the possibility that we'll mess up what we already have," she began cautiously. "You're the very best friend I've ever had. You've always been there for me. You can practically read my mind. It seems like we're putting that at risk for something that's far less certain."

His lips twitched. Amusement danced in his eyes. "Do you mean sex, by any chance?"

Kelly swallowed hard and nodded. "It changes things, complicates them."

"Or enhances them," he suggested quietly. "Sweet pea, we can take this slow, if that's what you want. I know I pushed hard for you to make this decision. I hardly gave you any time at all to think, probably because I was afraid you'd say no if you really thought it over. If you're not ready to make love, we'll settle into being married awhile first.''

His understanding made her want to weep. He was being so damned nice, so *reasonable*. Perversely, she wanted to smack him. Why wasn't he sweeping her off her feet, using his considerable experience to seduce her?

"Don't you want..." she began uncertainly, all of her fears crashing down on her and filling her with dread.

Shock spread across his face as he apparently realized what she was most afraid of. He reached for her then and pulled her into his arms. The gesture alone began to dispel her doubts, but it wasn't enough. She waited, breath caught in her throat, to hear what he had to say.

"Of course, I want to make love," he reassured her. "I've been wanting to for weeks now. Do you know how many times I've left here aching for you?" He took her hand and pressed it lightly against his arousal. "See, that's what being close to you does to me. I seem to have developed this craving for touching you."

Stunned by the discovery that Jordan really did want her, Kelly's irrational fears fled as rapidly as they'd escalated. Panic gave way to frantic desire. She twisted to face him and cupped his face in her hands. Her thumbs skimmed over the faint stubble on his cheeks, relishing the rough texture that she'd yearned for so long to feel.

"It will be okay, won't it?" she asked, a note of pleading in her voice.

"More than okay," he promised. "This marriage of ours is going to last forever and it's going to be filled with passion and laughter. I'm going to make you happy, Kelly."

She smiled at the determination she heard in his voice. "You already have," she whispered against his lips. "You already have."

With Kelly snuggled next to him on the sofa, still wearing the wedding dress that had once been her mother's, Jordan felt more serene, more complete than he had in months, maybe even years.

He understood the doubts and uncertainties that had assailed her after everyone had left. Her lousy marriage had robbed her of the confidence she'd once had in spades. He intended to give it back to her.

Admittedly, though, he'd had his own moment of panic earlier, when he'd seen her coming down the stairs in a swirl of silk and lace. The tomboy he'd grown up with, the best friend he'd always relied on had been transformed into a fairy-tale princess, just as Dani had confided to him seconds before her mother had appeared.

The hope and trust he'd seen shining in Kelly's eyes at that moment had frightened him. What if he couldn't be the husband she deserved? What if his impulsive decision to claim her for himself short-changed her? He'd been thinking mostly of himself when he'd proposed marriage. He'd tired of the chase, of the unceasing test of wills with women he never seemed to understand. He'd been anxious to settle down. Most of all, he'd wanted to do that with someone he knew and understood, someone uncomplicated.

From that instant on, however, he'd discovered that Kelly was perhaps the most complicated of any of the women he'd ever known and his feelings for her were far more complex than he'd ever imagined. When she'd appeared before him in her wedding gown, a vision of unexpectedly fragile loveliness, he'd wondered for the space of a heartbeat what he'd gotten himself into, if he was up to the challenge of making her happy.

And then she had been beside him, her hand tucked trustingly in his and he had known not another second's doubt. He smiled to himself, satisfied that the gut instinct that often led him to take quick, decisive action in business had served him well in choosing a mate.

She stirred slightly in his arms, drawing his attention to the way her breasts shifted against his chest. Her wedding dress was hiked well up her shapely calves.

He thought again of her misplaced doubts and smiled to himself. Oh, he wanted her all right! For days now he'd been able to think of little else but making her his. He'd wanted to caress and explore and inflame. He'd wanted her to come apart beneath him and he wanted to see the flare of excitement and satisfaction in her eyes. He wanted to discover all of the facets to this woman, who'd suddenly become so incredibly intriguing to him, so sweetly, unexpectedly desirable.

"Jordan?"

"Hmm?"

"This is nice."

"What is?"

"Sitting like this, with your arms around me."

Nice? It was killing him. "Aren't you hot with that dress on?" He'd stripped off his tuxedo jacket and tie long ago, but the room still felt stifling to him. To be honest, though, maybe the heat was emanating from him. Each time Kelly squirmed even a little, his body temperature rose another degree. Given the flush in her cheeks, she had to be feeling the same sort of heat, as well.

"I am hot," she confirmed. "But I'm too comfortable to move."

"What if I were to carry you upstairs?" he suggested in a choked voice.

"An interesting idea," she replied, a teasing glint in her eyes.

"Was that a yes or a no?"

"I think a yes," she said, then hesitated, before bestowing a tremulous smile on him. "Definitely a yes."

Jordan's heart was suddenly beating so hard he wasn't sure he'd heard her correctly. "Now?"

"Now."

With an eagerness that was far too telling, he scooped her into his arms. Cuddled against his chest, she looped her arms around his neck and settled her head against his shoulder. Her sweet breath fanned against his cheek. He was so stunned by the sensations spinning through him, he almost dropped her. A primitive need combined with an instinctive protectiveness swelled inside him.

Tightening his hold on her, he carried her up the stairs and headed straight for her bedroom. In the doorway, he came to a shocked and dismayed halt. The room was in chaos, filled with the scattered, feminine debris of two women and one child getting ready for a wedding.

"Whoops!" she murmured, then chuckled at the sight. "I'm sorry, Jordan. Put me down. I'll have it all cleaned up in no time."

"Isn't there a guest room?" he asked, not even trying to hide his sense of urgency.

She grinned. "Sure there is. You know this house as well as I do, Jordan."

"Well, then?"

"Twin beds," she reminded him.

He groaned. "We'll manage."

"Jordan, you're over six feet tall and I'm not exactly petite. If you think I'm sleeping in a twin bed with you, you're nuts."

"Who's talking about sleeping?"

"Okay, doing anything with you in a twin bed. One of us is bound to topple to the floor."

At the image she'd created, he felt a chuckle begin deep in his throat. "Exactly how energetic, are you?"

She blushed to the roots of her hair. "Jordan!"

"Okay, okay, I'll help you straighten up in here." He reluctantly lowered her to her feet. Before she could even move, he was tossing things off the bed and onto the floor. To his sincere regret, she was trailing along behind him, picking up each item and folding it neatly before tucking it away in a drawer or closet or laundry basket.

"Do you have to do that now?" he demanded impatiently.

"Jordan, you have waited years to get me into bed. In fact, for years, you didn't appear the slightest bit interested in getting me to bed. Can't you wait a few more minutes so it will be perfect?"

He found the equation between tidiness and perfection a bit disconcerting. "As long as you don't decide to start ironing, too, I suppose I can wait." He caught her gaze and held it. "And just so you know, I did think about getting you in bed back then. I just figured your father or mine would aim a shotgun straight at my backside if I did. I thought I was displaying admirable restraint in treating you like a lady."

She grinned at him, obviously pleased by the discovery that she had the upper hand over him in this. In fact, she looked downright smug all of a sudden.

"Go downstairs and find some candles," she ordered every bit as imperiously as her daughter might have.

"It's still daylight."

"Twilight," she corrected. "It'll be dark soon and I want candles."

He sighed. "Anything else?"

"Bring back the wine, too."

"Got it," he said, heading out the door.

"And some flowers," she called after him. "Lots and lots of flowers."

He poked his head back into the room. "You're enjoying this, aren't you?"

"What?" she inquired with a look somewhere between pure innocence and very feminine satisfaction.

"Tormenting me."

"Is that what I'm doing?"

"Yes, dammit," he shot back, but there was little venom in his voice.

He actually found her playfulness another delicious surprise. The delay was tantalizing. As if he didn't already want her badly enough, his body was practically throbbing with need now. There was no way she could possibly have any doubts at all, after this, about how hungry he was for her. Torment was a small price to pay for reassuring her on that point.

To even the score just a little, though, he took his own sweet time to gather up the candles, flowers and wine she'd requested. Let her stew a little, too, he thought as he finally made his way back upstairs. If the sexual tension mounted another notch or two, they would probably burst into flames on contact.

Back upstairs, at the doorway to the room, he came to a screeching halt for the second time that evening, stunned by the sight in front of him.

She had used the time very efficiently. Not only was the mess cleared away, but she had somehow managed to shed her wedding gown and exchange it for a filmy white negligee that skimmed over her curves, revealing details about her body he'd only imagined before. Her back was to him, the fading light from outside just enough to enhance the intriguing vision before him.

"Dear heaven," he murmured, stunned into immobility. His throat went dry.

Turning to look at him over her shoulder, she gave him the kind of soft, knowing smile women had been bestowing on infatuated men for eons. It sent a shudder of pure desire sweeping through him.

"I thought you were beautiful before, but I was wrong," he said in a strangled voice. "You are magnificent."

Surprisingly, the comment drew a look of uncertainty. "You don't have to say that."

"I do," he insisted, hastily setting flowers, wine and candles on the nightstand beside the bed and reaching for her. "You are magnificent."

She came into his arms without hesitation, fitting her body to his with an eagerness that turned his breathing ragged. Her anxious fingers worked at the studs on his shirt. As it came open, she pressed hot, quick kisses against his bared chest. The touch of velvet soft lips and warm breath sent his pulse spinning wildly.

"Whoa," he murmured. "Slow down, sweetheart. We have all night."

He glanced into her eyes then and read more than desire there. He detected once again that uncertainty and realized that until he claimed her in a rush of uncensored passion, she would be filled with doubts. About him. About whatever seeds of uncertainty Paul had planted in her brain with his shabby treatment of her.

There would be time enough later for long, slow, deliberately sensual seduction, for discovery. There were years ahead of them for lazy caresses and deep, passionate kisses. Thousands of nights lay before them, nights of sultry breezes and whispered exchanges as they learned intimate secrets about each other's body.

When her trembling fingers reached for the button on his pants, he helped her, shucking them off along with his briefs, after kicking aside his shoes.

Pulling her tightly against his hard, anxious body, he tumbled carefully onto the bed with her. He rolled her on top of him as they fell, exulting in the natural fit of soft curves and hard angles.

He never took his eyes from hers, not when his hands skimmed over her full, sensitive breasts, not when her hands reached for his aroused manhood. He saw the moment when her eyes darkened with passion, saw the instant of surprise when he fit his body to hers, entering her with a hard, fast stroke that had her gasping and her hips lifting to meet each thrust.

And he witnessed in the depths of her eyes the precise second when her body shattered in a climax that rocked them both. The satisfaction that streaked through him then, the wonder of giving her pleasure, was like a miracle. He'd had no idea that making love could be like this.

She was still panting, still exhilarated when he took her on another, slower climb that had her eyes widening with astonishment and then pure delight as they reached the pinnacle together and dove off into yet another whirlwind of sensation more magnificent than anything Jordan had ever experienced before.

He wasn't sure which was more heady, watching Kelly reach the heights of joy or sharing it with her. Together, they brought him immense gratification.

Eventually, exhausted and satiated, he settled Kelly more tightly against his body, his arms around her waist, her head resting on his chest.

She was certainly full of surprises, this woman he'd married. Once again, he indulged in a moment of smug satisfaction with his decision making. Obviously it was possible to use cool logic when choosing a bride. The passion they'd just shared reinforced his confidence.

Kelly propped herself up on her elbow and stared down at him. Her fingers tangled in the hair on his chest, then skimmed over bare, still damp skin.

"What are you thinking?" she asked.

"About us," he replied without hesitation.

She appeared instantly fascinated. "What about us?"

"How well suited we are. In bed and out. It just goes to prove my point."

A shadow crossed her eyes. "What point would that be?"

"That people should use their brains more often when choosing a mate."

"As opposed to what?"

He heard the edginess in her tone too late. By

the time he met her gaze, her eyes were frosty, the brown glinting with angry amber lights. He tried to back off the quicksand he'd inadvertently wandered onto. "Never mind," he muttered and tried to distract her with a caress.

She brushed away his hand and sat up, clutching the sheet to her. "I think you'd better tell me, Jordan."

He saw that he was way too far into this now to escape. "Come on, Kelly, you know what I mean. We both used our heads in deciding to get married. We didn't have a lot of silly illusions. We made a sensible decision that will benefit both of us."

"In other words, a successful merger." Her voice was heavily laced with chilly disdain. She gestured at the rumpled bed. "And this? I suppose this is just one of the perks for the executives?"

Actually, it was, but he was wise enough to keep that particular observation to himself. "Now, Kelly…"

She climbed out of the bed, dragging the sheet with her. He was certain no one had ever exited a marriage bed with more dignity, with more icy contempt.

"Don't you 'now, Kelly' me," she said, waggling a finger under his nose. "I made love to you tonight, Jordan Adams. I did not seal a damned business deal!"

With that she stalked from the room, the sheet trailing after her like the train of an impromptu bridal gown. Unfortunately, Jordan had the distinct impression that not only the honeymoon, but quite possibly the marriage, as well, was over.

Chapter Twelve

Kelly was still steaming at dawn when she heard Jordan coming slowly down the stairs, his steps heavy. She'd been on the front porch most of the night, wrapped in her sheet, rocking in an attempt to calm her fury.

It hadn't worked. Now, anticipating him joining her on the porch made her blood boil and her palms sweat. She'd wanted another hour or two to get her temper under control and all of her defenses solidly into place. When she faced him again, she had hoped to be cool, calm and collected. She was nowhere near that when he appeared.

Dressed in a pair of faded jeans, unsnapped at the waist, his hair becomingly tousled, his eyes still sleepy, Jordan opened the screen door and stepped outside. Looking at him made her heart climb into her throat. She refused, however, to let the mere sight of him get to her. Loving him so desperately, wanting him, was what had made her suspend judgment and agree to marry him when she'd known better.

Discovering that he still thought of their marriage as some sort of twisted business arrangement within seconds of also discovering that their passion was extraordinary had left her reeling. It confirmed every dire prediction she had made for a future built on such flimsy turf.

Even though he was waiting, she refused to meet his gaze.

"Good morning," he said eventually, sounding wary.

She remained stubbornly silent.

"Still mad, huh?"

Huddled in the rocker, she refused to utter a word.

Jordan was not a man easily defeated. He walked in front of her so she couldn't ignore him and hunkered down. He put his hands on her thighs to still the rocker. The touch guaranteed her attention.

"I'm sorry," he said. "I swear that I didn't mean to upset you."

She scowled at him. "But you did mean what you said, right?"

He stood and raked his hand through his hair in an impatient gesture. "Yes, no… Hell, what do you want me to say? Do you want me to lie to you?"

A good white lie might be welcome about now, she thought irrationally, then sighed. "No, I suppose not."

"Sweet pea, we just need a little time to adjust. This is new to both of us. Once we're settled in Houston..."

Warning bells went off in Kelly's head. "'Settled in Houston'?" she repeated very slowly. Her gaze locked with his. "I am not settling in Houston. We agreed to split our time. Weekends, holidays and vacations here. Weekdays there. That was the deal."

She made sure there was no mistaking where she put the emphasis. She managed to make the time they would spend in Houston sound like exile in Siberia. Jordan blinked at her adamant tone.

"We did discuss that, but—"

"No buts," she insisted, cutting off any speculation that there was room for more negotiation. "We agreed."

"Let's be reasonable," he began again.

She wasn't in the mood to be reasonable. Being reasonable and practical and pragmatic—to say nothing of caving in to her hormones—was what had gotten them into this disastrous situation.

"We had a verbal contract," she said, throwing his favorite sort of terminology back into his face. "Are you trying to wriggle out of it?"

He winced, but didn't back down, either. "Now, Kelly..." he began in a placating tone that set her teeth on edge.

"Forget it. We can end this marriage just as quickly as we arranged it," she warned.

Even as she spoke, she spotted the stubborn thrust of his chin and recognized that she might have pushed Jordan too far. She didn't much care. If this marriage wasn't going to be a partnership, if his promise of compromise had been so much hot air, they might as well discover it now.

"We are not ending this marriage," Jordan said quietly, eyes blazing. "As for where we live, we'll work it out."

"We already have," she said again.

His jaw tightened. "Fine. Pack your bags. We'll pick up Dani first thing tomorrow and drive back to Houston."

Kelly was shaking her head before the words were out of his mouth. "Not tomorrow. I can't leave the ranch with no one in charge."

"No problem. I'll call Daddy. He can deal with your hand to make sure chores get done until we make other arrangements."

"But the cats…"

"The damned cats will be taken care of. Weekdays in Houston," he reminded her, throwing her own words back in her face. "We'll settle anything having to do with the ranch next weekend. Daddy can screen some candidates for foreman while we're gone."

Backed into a corner now, he wasn't going to budge on this. If she intended to hold him to the letter of their verbal agreement, then he clearly planned to hold her to it, as well. Kelly could see that from the fire in his eyes and the clenching of his jaw. The gene for stubbornness, carried by both Harlan and Mary Adams, had clearly doubled in Jordan. Kelly tugged the sheet more tightly around her and rose as regally as any queen.

"Why wait? I'll be packed in an hour."

He scowled. "Fine, if that's what you prefer. I'll make some coffee and some breakfast. As soon as we've eaten, we can drive to Luke and Jessie's."

Kelly could only begin to imagine what those two would have to say about Kelly and Jordan appearing on their doorstep first thing in the morning after their wedding night. The prospect was damned humiliating, but she refused to back down and ask Jordan to at least delay their departure until Sunday after all.

Let him explain why their honeymoon had ended so abruptly. He thought he had all the answers. Let him see how well they held up to his brother's scrutiny. Maybe she'd even take Luke up on his offer to punch his brother out for her. No doubt he hadn't imagined there would be a necessity for it quite this soon.

Still seething, she threw clothes into suitcases with almost as little care as she'd displayed when leaving Houston after her divorce. She gathered up a few of Dani's favorite toys and resolved that her daughter would be allowed to pick out a new selection for the Houston house. If they were going to be shuttling back and forth, then each home needed to have its own set of clothes, toys and books. She refused to pack and repack every few days. The same went for everything from cosmetics to toothbrushes. Two complete households, she decided firmly. Let Jordan put that in his pipe and smoke it.

And, first thing on Monday morning, she intended to have a very long talk with Ginger about the logistics of moving Jordan's primary business offices home to west Texas.

In fact, she might very well take the secretary to lunch and probe her brain for the secrets of tolerating her husband's high-handedness. She had always considered herself to be an expert on Jordan, but she'd seen a new side of him in the past few weeks—a man all too used to getting his own way—and she had a feeling Ginger knew far more about that side than she did.

Refusing to ask for assistance, she hauled the luggage downstairs and piled it by the front door. Lured by the aroma of coffee, she reluctantly headed for the kitchen and another confrontation with her husband.

Jordan glanced up from the morning paper at her entrance. "I have pancakes and bacon staying warm in the oven. Sit down. I'll get it and pour you a cup of coffee."

"Just coffee and juice for me, and I'll get it."

He scowled at her as he stood. "Sit, dammit. I said I'd get it."

Kelly rolled her eyes at the testiness and sat. He poured the coffee, filled a glass with juice and then reached into the oven to retrieve the breakfast he'd prepared. Suddenly he yelped in pain and jerked his hand back. His bare hand.

Kelly sighed and stood. Jordan obviously wasn't thinking any more clearly this morning than she was.

"Let me see," she said, reaching for his hand.

"It's fine," he growled.

"Let me see," she said, and clamped her hand around his wrist. There was a nasty streak of red across his palm that was destined to blister. She tugged him toward the sink. "Here, run cool water on it and I'll get some salve."

He stood stoically while the water cascaded over his burned hand. She retrieved the ointment she kept on hand for burns. Taking his hand in hers again, trying not to notice the way her pulse jumped at the contact, she gently applied the soothing salve, then wrapped the wound lightly in gauze.

She was so intent on bandaging his hand that she didn't notice the intensity of his gaze for some time. When she finally glanced up, the fire banked in his eyes was every bit as hot as the plate he'd tried to pick up.

She released his hand at once and turned her back on him, busying herself with getting the offending plate from the oven, turning off the stove and then sitting down at the table to eat the breakfast she'd claimed not to want. It might as well have been sawdust for all the attention she paid it as she swallowed bite after bite mechanically.

"We can't avoid talking about it forever," he observed eventually.

He'd tilted his chair back on two legs and clasped his hands on top of his flat stomach in a posture that screamed of relaxed confidence. She risked a look directly into his eyes. "Talking about what?"

"The fact that we've gotten off to a lousy start."

She shrugged. "We both know it. Why talk about it?"

A look of annoyance passed across his face. "So that we can resolve the problem and move on."

Kelly's temper flared. "How...businesslike!"

He stood up so fast, then, that his chair toppled over. Before she realized what he intended, he was leaning over her, bending down, his mouth unexpectedly plundering hers in a bruising kiss clearly meant to wipe all other thoughts out of her head. After a brief struggle of wills, it succeeded in doing just that. Her mind emptied of everything except the way Jordan made her senses swim. She abandoned the battle and gave herself up to that devastating kiss.

His lips gentled, then, coaxing, persuading, reminding her of the way they'd been together in the middle of the night—hot, slick sensuality, mind-altering pleasure, gentle sharing. They were good together, as instinctively attuned as two people who'd been married for decades. Jordan was the kind of sensitive, intuitive, giving lover women dreamed of finding. He had gauged her reactions time and again and suited his lovemaking to her needs. He was doing the same thing now.

Eventually he released his grip on her shoulders and stood back, his gaze fixed on her in a way that told her he was taking in her flushed cheeks and the kiss-swollen lips that clearly told him the effect he had on her. For once, though, he seemed more dazed than smug.

Observing him, Kelly thought how ironic it was that they were so instantly attuned physically, while all the years of straight talk had abandoned them and left them suddenly incapable of communicating in words without bickering.

She gathered her composure and drew herself up. "I think it's time to go," she said in a voice that shook.

For a moment she thought he might argue for staying right here, for settling their differences in bed, but he didn't. After a bit, he just nodded curtly.

"I'll get the bags into the car," he said.

"I'll clean up in here and be right with you."

It was all so cool, so polite and civilized that she wanted to scream. Instead, the instant he was gone and she was left alone with soggy pancakes and cold coffee, she felt tears welling up in her eyes.

She'd had the wedding of her dreams the day before. She was married to the man she'd always loved. She'd discovered a passionate side to herself and to him that had filled her with ecstasy.

And she'd never been more miserable in her entire life.

Jordan would rather have faced a firing squad than Luke and Jessie's worried, accusing looks. Their gazes darted between him and Kelly, their eyes filled with questions that only Dani's presence had kept silent since their arrival.

"So, you're driving back to Houston?" Jessie said with obviously feigned cheer, her gaze penetrating. "Do you have to be back in the office first thing Monday? You are supposed to be on your honeymoon, after all. Surely the incomparable Ginger could hold down the fort a few days longer."

Jordan glanced at his wife. Kelly's cheeks were flushed with embarrassment. She'd looked everywhere but at him since they'd arrived. He couldn't decide whether he wanted to console her or to shake her.

Dammit all, he hadn't wanted to head back to Houston today any more than she had. He still wasn't quite sure how it had happened, except that she'd dug in her heels and then he'd dug in his and their disagreement had escalated from there. Somehow he'd forgotten how often that used to happen to them as kids. They were both quick to anger and stubborn as mules. It had always taken Luke or Cody to coax them out of their funks.

He glanced at his older brother and caught a grin tugging at Luke's mouth. Obviously he was recalling the same thing. The amused reaction left Jordan feeling faintly disgruntled. Clearly he couldn't count on much help from that direction. Luke seemed perfectly content to let him and Kelly work this fight out all on their own.

"I'm sure Jordan and Kelly have their reasons for going to Houston today," Luke observed, confirming Jordan's opinion of his brother's intention to stay the hell out of this argument.

Jessie didn't appear to have the same reticence. "What reasons?" she demanded, frowning. "Dani's perfectly fine here with us, aren't you, sweetie?"

Dani nodded. "I'm helping Consuela take care of Angela. She's messy."

The comment drew a faint smile from Jordan. "I can vouch for that," he murmured.

"Hey, that's my daughter you're maligning," Jessie said. "Dani, honey, why don't you go check on her? She's with Consuela."

As soon as the child had run off to the kitchen, she turned her determined gaze back on Jordan. "Okay, explain."

Jordan swallowed hard under the scrutiny. "I don't think so."

Jessie looked from him to Kelly. "Kelly?"

"Ask Jordan."

Luke laughed out loud at that. "Maybe their reasons are none of our business," Luke suggested.

Jessie did not seem pleased by her husband's observation. "Of course, it's our business. We're talking about your brother and my friend."

"That doesn't give us inalienable rights to interfere," Luke shot back.

Suddenly, to Jordan's astonishment, Kelly chuckled. "Stop it, you two. The next thing we know, you'll be fighting and you won't even know why."

Jessie regarded her intently. "Do you know why you're fighting?"

Kelly considered the question thoughtfully. "I know," she said. "I'm not so sure Jordan does."

He frowned at that. "Hey, don't make me into the bad guy here."

Luke gazed heavenward. "How many times have I heard those words from you two? You'd think after all these years, you'd learn to fight fair."

"I'm not the one…" Kelly began.

"Whose side are you on, big brother?" Jordan demanded.

"Ah, the sweet sound of two stubborn personalities butting heads yet again," Luke said. "Jessie, maybe we should back off and let them fight it out."

"Not in my living room," she countered. "I do have a compromise, though."

At the mention of compromise, Kelly's gaze caught his. He wasn't sure but he thought he detected amusement dancing in her eyes. "Bad idea," he told Jessie. "I'm afraid compromise is what got us into this argument."

Jessie wasn't about to be put off so easily. "That's not possible. Compromise is good."

"Not necessarily," Kelly muttered.

"Well, you'll just have to listen to mine," Jessie declared. "If you two absolutely must go to Houston, wait and leave in the morning, let Dani stay here until you come back. At least you'll have some privacy for the next week or so. It may not be a honeymoon in the Caribbean, but it's the best I can offer on short notice."

Jordan glanced hopefully at Kelly. Given time,

he knew they could work this disagreement out. It would go much more smoothly if they didn't have Dani to worry about. It was Kelly's call, though. He wasn't about to start their marriage by forcing her to leave her daughter behind. He didn't ever want her to think that he wasn't interested in all of them being a family. Unfortunately, she didn't look overjoyed by the suggestion.

"I don't know…" She looked at him, clearly struggling with the prospect of abandoning her child even for a few days. "Jordan?"

"It's up to you."

"Come on," Jessie urged. "It's the perfect solution. She's having a wonderful time here and she's no trouble at all. You were planning for her to be here a few days anyway. Besides, you don't want her caught up in the middle of your argument, do you?"

Jordan watched Kelly debating with herself, clearly aware of the sense of Jessie's suggestion, but resisting it just the same. He kept silent and let her work it out on her own.

"I suppose it would be okay just this once," Kelly agreed eventually. She shot a determined look at Jordan and added, as if daring him to contradict her, "We'll pick her up Friday evening."

"Absolutely," he agreed.

Still looking worried, she gazed at Jessie. "Are you sure it won't be an imposition?"

"Absolutely not," Jessie said. "Right, Luke?"

Luke cast a quick look Jordan's way. Jordan gave his older brother an almost imperceptible nod.

"Right," Luke agreed.

"And you'll stay the night," Jessie prodded.

Clearly Kelly would have preferred to eat dirt, but she nodded. Jordan figured he had till morning to think how to mend fences.

They were on their way at daybreak. Dani hadn't batted an eye at their departure, but Kelly had been misty-eyed ever since.

"Are you sure you don't mind leaving Dani here?" Jordan asked after he'd made the turn onto the highway. "There's still time to change your mind."

"No, I think it's best that you and I resolve some things before we try to get on with having any kind of normal family life. Jessie was right. Dani heard enough fighting between Paul and me. I don't want her to go through that again."

Jordan studied her intently. "Are we going to fight?"

She sighed and met his gaze. "It seems inevitable, doesn't it?"

"What seems inevitable to me is being married to you," he said at once. "The rest of it is just details."

Kelly's startled expression gave way to something that might have been relief. "Do you really mean that?" she asked.

"I never say anything I don't mean," he assured her. "Sometimes I don't phrase things tactfully enough. Ginger's always getting on me about that.

Sometimes I cut to the chase too soon, but I always, always mean what I say.''

He slowed the car and eased it onto the shoulder of the road, so he could look directly into her eyes. ''When I stood in front of that minister night before last and promised to love, honor and cherish you all the rest of our days, I meant every word.'' He leveled a gaze straight at her. ''Did you?''

Tears shone in her eyes and her lower lip trembled as she nodded. ''I did.''

''Then, like I said, sweet pea, all the rest is details.''

Chapter Thirteen

The very first detail Kelly intended to deal with was getting the two of them out of Houston permanently. She had forgotten how heavy and oppressive the air there could be in midsummer. Clothes clung damply the minute they stepped out of the car. The movement between stifling heat and air-conditioning was capable of inducing pneumonia, especially since Jordan kept his home at Arctic-level temperatures. A chill sped through her at the blast of cold air that hit her the instant he opened the huge, carved front door.

Other than the frigid temperature, Kelly really had nothing against Jordan's house. She'd been in it dozens of times when she had lived in Houston. She'd always admired the neat sweep of perfectly tended lawn, the cool turquoise waters of the pool, the thick, lush wall-to-wall carpeting, the decorator-chosen selection of fine paintings and antiques.

None of it, though, seemed to have anything to do with Jordan, at least not the man she knew. What frightened her was the possibility that it might reflect this other Jordan, the shrewd businessman she wasn't nearly so fond of, the man who bargained for a bride with the same single-minded determination with which he'd go after an oil contract.

Only his study, with its book-lined walls, its slightly faded Southwestern decor, its original Remington bronze sculpture, seemed to fit his personality or his taste. The rest was too formal, too sterile.

And she could just imagine how long it would take Dani to destroy all those yards and yards of white carpeting that had clearly been chosen by someone without children or, worse, by someone who never intended to have children.

Children? Dear heaven, they hadn't even discussed them except in the most passing way. What if Jordan really didn't want more? What if all that white carpet had been the idea of a man who saw his house as a showplace rather than a home? What had happened to her brain? Why hadn't she asked the most basic question of all? *Do you, Jordan Adams, want a family?* Paul had certainly taught her that was something that couldn't be taken for granted.

Seeing Jordan with Dani must have reassured her, but she'd been a fool not to ask anyway. Making assumptions was the worst sort of mistake a woman could make, especially when it was a lesson she should have already learned.

Standing in the doorway, her thoughts in turmoil, she was startled when Jordan lifted her off her feet to carry her across the threshold. She was struck anew by the enormity of what they had done. Somehow, even more than the vows they'd taken, the traditional act of being carried across the threshold into Jordan's home, onto Jordan's turf, reminded her of all the unanswered questions, of the compromise she had agreed to to be with this man she loved. A renewed sense of panic set in.

Apparently oblivious to her shift in mood, Jordan set her carefully back on her feet in the huge foyer, then took her hand as he led the way upstairs for the first time.

It was late. The drive had taken forever and they had stopped often, rarely talking, just grabbing a bite to eat or a tall, cool, soft drink to soothe their parched throats. Going to bed seemed only logical, but Kelly wasn't ready for that. She couldn't seem to form the words, though, that would halt their inevitable progress up that wide, winding staircase. Being alone with Jordan in Luke and Jessie's guest suite sure had been hard enough. This was awful.

At the doorway to the master suite, he paused. "Kelly?"

She heard an unfamiliar note of uncertainty in his voice and met his gaze. "What?"

"I want you to be happy here. I want us to be happy."

He seemed to be imploring her to reassure him that their quick, impulsive marriage was moving onto more solid ground. Unfortunately, she had too many uncertainties herself to be able to say exactly what he clearly wanted to hear.

Instead she gazed across this threshold into a room she hadn't seen before. In all of her previous visits she'd studiously avoided so much as a peek at a room that had seemed emotionally off-limits to her as Jordan's friend, rather than his lover. She hadn't wanted to see the bed to which he took other women but never her.

Now, she surveyed the dark furnishings that had been someone's idea of a bachelor's taste and opted for a touch of humor. "You could go a long way toward making that happen by getting rid of the fur bedspread and the waterbed."

As she'd hoped, he grinned. "The fur's not real."

"No, but without it, you could probably raise the thermostat another ten degrees."

"Too cold in here?"

"Not if you're wrapped in that thing."

He chuckled. "Okay, I get the message. Now, about the waterbed. Have you ever slept in one?"

"No."

"Don't knock it till you've tried it."

"Jordan, I get seasick. You couldn't even take me out on the creek in a rowboat, remember?"

He turned an interesting shade of green at the memory. "I'll have it out of here in the morning," he promised. "Of course, we should check to make absolutely sure it's a problem."

Kelly regarded the bed doubtfully, but there was such a gleam of pure anticipation in Jordan's eyes that she kept her doubts to herself. "If you say so."

She approached the king-size waterbed tentatively. There was something incredibly seductive about it, especially with that expanse of soft, fake fur spread across it. She sat down and tested her stomach as the bed shifted beneath her. The ebb and flow of the water was disconcerting, but not entirely unpleasant.

"Well?" Jordan asked, his expression hopeful.

"So far, so good," she admitted.

"Mind if I join you?"

She eyed the bed nervously. "Not as long as you don't fling yourself on the bed and set off a tidal wave."

Clearly amused, he dropped down beside her. His weight set off another softly rolling wave.

"Ready for the next step?" he inquired.

"Which is?"

"Getting out of our clothes."

She stood hastily and backed off a step. "I think I'll do that on firm ground, thank you very much."

"But you will be back?"

She gazed into worried blue eyes and sensed a deep concern for getting things off to the right start here in his home. "I will be back," she promised, then amended, "Tonight."

"And tomorrow?"

"Maybe we ought to take one night at a time,"

she said, casting a suspicious look at the bed. "You might not even want me back in there tomorrow if this doesn't go well."

"Maybe not in *this* bed," he agreed with a mischievous smile that reminded her of the Jordan of old. "But, like I told you before, this can be out of here first thing in the morning and one more to your liking in its place."

His expression sobered. "I want you to make this your home, to make whatever changes are necessary to make you and Dani comfortable here."

Kelly kept silent about her intention to see that this was their home for as brief a time as possible. Instead she inquired, "Can I get rid of the white carpet?"

"Every boring inch of it," he agreed readily.

His response, indicating his distaste for it, surprised her. "Exactly whose idea was that?"

He sighed. "Rexanne's."

"I should have known. Obviously she wasn't the maternal type."

"Do you really want to waste time discussing my former fiancée?"

"Did you have something else in mind?" she asked, even though she could see perfectly well by the gleam in his eyes exactly what he was thinking.

"Getting you back into this bed would be a start."

Kelly pushed aside the memory of all of the angry exchanges earlier in the day. She deliberately squashed any thoughts of that terrible moment when she'd realized that Jordan's perception of their marriage hadn't changed drastically from the moment he'd first gotten the idea into his head and pursued her with single-minded determination.

In fact, she suspended thinking at all, clinging only to the promise that they could work out the details and make their marriage a real one.

She stripped quickly out of her clothes and moved into the waiting circle of his arms, into the heat emanating from his body. She lost herself to the gentle movement of the bed and the swell of anticipation in her heart as his hands caressed and stroked until every inch of her was on fire, burning with need.

She welcomed him into her, lifting her hips to meet him, opening her mouth to his tongue, then gasping with the sweet, sweet shock of coming apart in his embrace.

Worries and fears didn't vanish in that moment of surrender, but, for a time, they hardly seemed to matter at all. All that mattered was being close to Jordan, fulfilling the hunger that had been building inside her since she'd first discovered the chemistry that was possible between a man and a woman.

The rest would still be there in the morning. She could tackle the problems then with a clearer head and a lighter heart. Or so she told herself as she drifted off to sleep, still resting her head against Jordan's chest, reassured by the steady rhythm of his heart and the unmistakable strength in the arms that held her tight.

Jordan thought the first night in their Houston home had gone rather well, all things considered.

He had no doubt at all that the basic disagreement between them still existed, but when they were in each other's arms, little else seemed to matter.

That was what kept him from rolling out of bed at first light and heading to the office as he routinely would have done. He was reluctant to leave this haven they seemed to have found away from their differences.

Propped on an elbow beside her, he watched as Kelly slowly came awake. A soft smile came and went as she blinked, saw him, then closed her eyes again. A pleased, sensual expression remained on her face. He realized it was the first time he'd ever watched her wake up in the morning. She did it slowly, easing into the day in a way he found thoroughly fascinating.

"What time is it?" she murmured eventually, eyes still tightly shut.

"Six-thirty."

"I should be up."

"Why?"

"There's work..." she began, then let the sentence trail off.

"Nope," he reminded her. "You're on vacation."

She sat up, bringing the sheet with her and tucking it around her breasts. Jordan reached over and tugged it down. "Don't be shy with me," he said. "Please."

Though color climbed into her cheeks, she left the sheet where it had fallen, exposing her breasts to the chill air. The nipples puckered and hardened even as he watched. He swallowed hard against the tide of raw desire rolling through him. He couldn't resist, though, touching a finger to each sensitive peak. He was thrilled by the shudder that instantly swept through her.

"You are amazing," he whispered hoarsely. "Your body is so responsive."

"Jordan, don't you have to go to work?"

He couldn't tell from the ragged note in her voice if she was anxious for him to go or stay. "Sooner or later," he murmured.

"Wasn't that the reason we came to Houston?" she asked.

He was too fascinated with the way the morning sun was casting highlights and shadows on her smooth skin to pay much attention to the note of determination in her voice. "Hmm?"

"I asked if the reason we are in Houston is so that you can go to your office," she said.

This time it would have been impossible to miss the edge of exasperation in her voice. "Actually, we are in Houston because you made an issue of that damned compromise."

As soon as he'd snapped out the retort, he realized his mistake. Up went the sheet...and the wall between them. He sighed heavily and climbed out of the suddenly cold bed. This time he didn't intend to stick around to repair the damage.

"If you want me later, I'll be at the office," he said stiffly. He took his clothes into the bathroom. "As you made clear, that is the only reason you agreed to come here." With that, he slammed the door.

It appeared they were destined to have a far more volatile marriage than he'd ever anticipated, at least if he kept opening his mouth. Every time he did, he managed to put his foot squarely in it.

Kelly refused to linger in that huge waterbed all by herself, not with Jordan slamming things around in the bathroom and cursing a blue streak. She seemed to be testing his patience, which was just fine with her. Hers had snapped a long time ago.

Downstairs, she snatched up the phone and dialed his office. As she'd anticipated, Ginger was already at her desk.

"Hey, Kelly," the secretary said at once. "How's it going?"

Kelly wasn't about to give her the earful that question deserved. "Fine."

"If you're looking for Jordan, he's not in yet. In fact, I thought he was still over at your place trying to talk you into marrying him."

"He won that battle," Kelly said dryly. "We're into the full-scale war now."

"Uh-oh," Ginger murmured. "What can I do?"

"Are you free for lunch?"

"Why, sure. I'm getting sick of eating those little cartons of yogurt at my desk. You want to meet me here at noon?"

"I think we'd better meet at the restaurant." She named one close to Jordan's office. It was the same one he had traditionally taken her to when they'd met to catch up on each other's lives in what now seemed a far simpler time in their relationship. "Is that okay?"

"Sure thing. See you there at noon."

"Meanwhile, prepare yourself. My husband is in a snit."

"Well, damn," Ginger said. "I was hoping marriage to you would mellow him out."

"Not so far," Kelly admitted grimly.

She spent the next half hour staying out of Jordan's path. It wasn't all that difficult. He appeared to head straight from the bathroom out the front door without so much as a backward glance. It was an interesting route given that the more logical access to the garage was through the kitchen where she was seated drinking her coffee. She was beginning to wonder if perhaps she shouldn't have had this little meeting with Ginger *before* the wedding.

She sighed. Too late for second thoughts now. She just needed a refresher course in what made her husband tick. All those tips she'd stored away since childhood needed to be updated to deal with the grown-up idiosyncrasies.

A few hours later, after taking a taxi into town, she was seated in a booth across from the perky, sensible redhead who was Jordan's right arm at the office. Ginger was scrutinizing her with obvious fascination.

"Okay," she said finally, "how'd he talk you into it?"

Kelly shrugged. "I wish I knew. One minute I

was saying no, no, no, and the next thing I knew I was standing in front of a minister saying I do.''

Ginger nodded. "He has that effect on people. I can't tell you the deals that seemed on the verge of falling through, only to turn completely around at the last possible second. You've known him forever, though. You should be immune to his tactics.''

"He's never tried these particular tactics on me before." She chuckled. "And frankly, I doubt he's used the same ones in business.''

"Ah," Ginger said knowingly. "*Those* tactics.''

"Among others. He got Dani on his side, too, and that pretty much sealed the deal.''

"How's he taking to being a daddy?''

"Oddly enough, that seems to be the part of all this he has nailed. He's a natural. He and Dani are like co-conspirators, always making plans and whispering secrets.''

"Sounds as if you feel left out," Ginger observed.

"Not at all. I'm thrilled they get along so well. I just wish he and I could communicate as easily.''

Ginger's face fell. "But you two were always able to talk. I envied you. DeVonne's not big on communication." She grinned. "Not verbal communication, anyway. You and Jordan, though, could always talk about anything. He used to say that all the time.''

"I guess that must have been before the stakes got to be so high.''

"Meaning that marriage changes things," Ginger

concluded. "Maybe that's because it's almost impossible to lose a best friend, but people are getting divorced all the time. You've already been through that, so you know it's a real possibility. That makes you start pulling your punches, being less honest than you ought to be, am I right?"

Kelly gave her a rueful grin. "I'm not sure Jordan would agree that I've been pulling any punches, but actually you're exactly right."

"Seems to me like that's the perfect way to ruin the best thing you two had going for you."

"It is, isn't it?" Kelly murmured thoughtfully. "Ginger, you're a genius."

The young woman grinned back at her. "Well, of course I am." She sighed. "Now if you could just convince Jordan to move our offices to west Texas."

Kelly laughed. "You're reading my mind. That was the other thing I wanted to talk to you about today. Is that feasible?"

"Why, sure it is. He might have to fly here for meetings every so often, but half of what he does can be done by phone and fax. I've been telling him that for ages now, but he's too bullheaded to listen. If you ask me, he was just afraid if he moved back, he'd be under his daddy's thumb again."

"Harlan's not even in the oil business," Kelly protested, though she didn't doubt for a second that Ginger was exactly right.

"You know, I love that man, but Harlan does have his opinions. It doesn't seem to matter that he's not in oil. He still manages to offer Jordan unsolicited advice about a dozen times a week.''

''And what does Jordan do?''

''Sometimes he puts him on the speaker phone, mumbles an appropriate response when the occasion arises and gets on with his paperwork. Those are the good times. Then there are the times when he slams the phone down so hard it breaks. I've taken to keeping a new stock of telephones in the supply closet. The phone company loves those calls. It's probably paying Harlan to make them.''

Kelly couldn't help chuckling at the image. It was vintage Jordan and Harlan. They'd always scrapped like willful, territorial puppies. She was still laughing when she heard a polite, masculine cough and looked up to find her husband's watchful, suspicious gaze focused straight on her.

''Something amusing?'' he inquired.

Kelly swallowed hard. ''Actually, yes.''

Ginger, the little traitor, bounced out of the booth as if she'd heard a fire alarm. ''Thanks for lunch, Kelly. Congratulations, again!''

Kelly nodded distractedly, her gaze locked with her husband's as she tried to gauge his mood. ''Thanks for…everything.''

Ginger scooted past Jordan. '''Bye, boss.''

''Ginger,'' he acknowledged coolly. He slid into the space his secretary had vacated. ''You two catching up?''

''Yes.'' Suddenly the booth felt very crowded. It wasn't just Jordan's size, but all those suspicions he clearly had.

"Or conspiring?" he asked.

"Now what on earth would we have to conspire about?"

He shrugged. "Beats me. Maybe moving the office to west Texas?"

Kelly groaned. "You heard."

"Every word," he confirmed. "And I do not break phones when I talk to Daddy."

"Oh?"

"I break them after, when I throw them across the room."

She chuckled. "You're not really furious at me for talking to Ginger, are you?"

He sighed. "Why would I be furious? You were asking a question, one that unfortunately plays right into Ginger's hands. She's been bugging me to make the same move for ages, so she can keep her job and her marriage."

Kelly figured he hadn't exploded yet, so she might as well pursue the point. "So why haven't you considered it?"

"It never made sense. My life was here."

"Your business life or just Rexanne and all of her predecessors?"

His mouth twisted into a wry smile. "Probably the latter more than anything."

"But that's no longer true. Now your social life—your family life—is clear across the state." She reached over and put her hand on top of his. "Please, won't you just think about it?"

He studied her intently. "Does it mean that much to you?"

"Yes," she said firmly. "It does."

"Do you hate Houston so much? Is it because of Paul?"

She shook her head, not entirely willing to explain the whole truth of it. Her disastrous marriage was one element, but actually a very small one. Then she recalled what Ginger had said about pulling punches.

"I never wanted to live in Houston," she admitted finally. "I love the ranch, always have."

"But you moved here years ago, right after I did."

"Exactly," she said softly. "Right after you did."

She saw the precise moment when the explanation registered.

"You moved here *because* of me?" he asked, clearly astonished. In fact he couldn't have looked any more shocked if she'd announced she wanted to take up stripping.

"Yep. Pretty crazy, huh? Half the time you didn't even notice I was around." She had abandoned her father to struggle along alone for a man who hadn't even paid attention to her presence. The knowledge of that betrayal of her dad had eaten at her for years.

"But I always thought…" He shook his head, as if to clear it. "I guess I don't know what I thought."

"You just took my presence for granted," she said, unable to hide the note of resentment, even after all this time.

He nodded slowly. "I suppose I did." He lifted his gaze and looked her squarely in the eyes. "I'm sorry. If I'd known—"

She stopped him with a touch of a finger to his lips. "If you'd known, you wouldn't have done anything differently. My heart was always on my sleeve, Jordan. You just didn't want to see it."

He closed his eyes and sighed. "I was a fool, wasn't I?"

She nodded, not letting him off the hook easily. "I always thought so, but then, I was a bit biased in my own favor. Those women you were choosing over me were airheads."

He brought her hand up to his lips and kissed the work-roughened knuckles. "Will it really make you happy for me to move the company headquarters?"

"West Texas is home, Jordan. It's where our family is, where our roots are."

"More's the pity," he said dryly.

She chuckled at his expression. "Stop worrying about Harlan. You've been standing up to him for a long time now and I haven't noticed either of you suffering too much as a result."

"I suppose not," he conceded. "Okay, sweet pea, we'll give it a try. I'll keep the Houston office space for meetings that can't be held elsewhere, but I'll look for space for a new headquarters when we're home this weekend. I'll have to see how the rest of the staff feels about relocating to determine how much space we need, but a lot of the people would probably prefer a small-town atmosphere for raising their families."

Kelly regarded him with astonishment. He'd agreed. Just like that, and all because she'd worked up the courage to tell him straight out what was in her heart. Perhaps if she kept it up, they could work out the rest of those complicated details, starting with whether or not Jordan wanted to have more children.

Before she could tackle that subject, though, she met his gaze and caught the rising heat in his eyes. He wanted her, again, after all those times during the night. Her pulse skittered crazily and her self-esteem as a desirable woman soared.

"Do you have to go back to the office?" she asked.

He grinned. "You were reading my mind."

He took care of the check with the speed of a man very anxious to make love to his new bride. He had them in the car and home before Kelly could gather her thoughts.

Much, much later, wrapped in his arms, she teased him about kidnapping her from the restaurant.

"Hey, you were the one who asked if I had to go back to the office," he protested.

"How do you know I wasn't going to suggest a shopping excursion?"

The look he directed at her was almost comical. "You wanted to go shopping?"

"Maybe."

"You did not." He slid his hand between her legs. "Would you rather buy a dress than do this?"

She grinned. "Maybe."

His touch intensified. "Really?" he taunted. "I don't believe you."

"I haven't shopped for a fancy designer dress in quite some time. It would take a lot to compete with trying on all those fancy, sexy clothes," she managed to gasp. His mouth closed over her breast. "Of course, this is nice," she murmured.

"Nice? Nice!" His voice climbed indignantly.

"Very nice."

He lifted himself above her and entered her with exquisite slowness, the slow slide a sweet torment. The retreat left an agony of yearning. "How nice?" he demanded.

"Incredibly, wickedly nice," she declared.

And then, for quite some time, she couldn't speak at all.

Chapter Fourteen

The next few days in Houston turned into a honeymoon, after all. It was a time of revelation for Jordan. His bride turned out to be a woman of limitless and astonishingly inventive passion. She held nothing back.

Except, perhaps, for love, he realized despondently as he sat alone in the dark sipping a cup of coffee just before dawn on Saturday morning. They had driven back to the ranch via Luke and Jessie's the night before, arriving late. Kelly and Dani were both still sleeping upstairs. He'd been too restless to sleep, troubled by something he couldn't quite pin down or put a name to.

The past few days should have left him feeling ecstatic. He should have been filled with contentment, delighted with the way his decision to marry Kelly had turned out. Instead he had the uneasy feeling that he'd lost more than he'd gained.

For a woman who had stunned him with her claim just a few days before that she had loved him forever, Kelly had suddenly turned surprisingly silent on the subject of her own emotions. He certainly couldn't complain about their lovemaking. She was stunningly sensual in bed, as generous with her body as she had once been with her compassion and her affection. He told himself that should be more than enough, that the words didn't matter, but deep inside he recognized something she had known all along—they did matter.

He couldn't help wondering—and worrying just a little—about her reticence. Something crucial seemed to be missing from their relationship. There was some part of her that she wasn't sharing, that she was holding back as if she feared he might trample on something she held dear.

What more could he do, though? He thought he had made it clear to her that he believed in them, believed in their marriage. He had even agreed to look for a new headquarters for his company, one closer to home, just because she had told him how important that was to her. Surely that gesture should have reassured her that his intentions toward their future were serious.

Dammit, he should have been on top of the world. He had gotten exactly what he wanted. He had a family now, a defensive barrier against another stupid mistake with the wrong woman. He had been granted the unexpected gift of a warm, passionate wife. He even had a precious little girl, whom he couldn't have loved more if she'd been his own.

What was happening to him? Why did it suddenly seem to matter so much whether Kelly cared half as deeply for him as he was beginning to suspect he did for her? They were married, committed to vows they both held sacred. Still, he wanted more, some indefinable thing he didn't know how to describe, much less fight for.

He had seen it, though. He had seen it between his parents, a glow that came over them whenever they were in the same room. He had felt it every time he'd been with Luke, Jessie, and little Angela. He had seen the radiance on Jessie's face whenever she glanced at Luke. He had caught the unmistakable pride and adoration on his brother's face each time Luke glimpsed Jessie or the baby. As with his parents, the air around Luke and Jessie hummed with the electricity of their love. No one lucky enough to be in their presence could ever doubt the depth of their feelings for one another. *That* was what he wanted.

There were times like now when Jordan wondered if he'd truly gotten married or, as Kelly had often accused, merely made a bargain. The irony, of course, was that a few weeks ago he hadn't known the difference, no matter how often Kelly had tried pointing it out to him. Apparently he should have listened to her more closely. Maybe then he would have grasped the distinction, maybe then he wouldn't have set himself up for this unfamiliar emptiness deep inside him.

Now he wondered if it was too late to change the ground rules. He thought of all the unexpected things Kelly had brought into their marriage, along with being a woman he knew he could trust with his life. He thought of what the future might be like without her in it and realized that losing her was a risk he could never take. Just as Cody had blown it with Melissa Horton, he had taken Kelly for granted. As much as he disliked what that said about him as a man, he knew it was true. He also knew he would never do that again.

Sitting there as the sun rose and brightened the kitchen, he examined the dilemma with the same methodical logic he would apply to a business problem. He considered every angle, weighed every option. When the solution finally came to him, he was astounded he hadn't recognized it sooner.

The answer was a baby, a link that would bind them together more snugly than the vows they'd taken.

A baby! The very thought filled him with unexpected anticipation. The role of daddy had turned out to be one for which he was surprisingly well suited, after all. A little brother for Dani, maybe a little sister, too. The perfect family.

Contentment stole through him as he contemplated the image. Pleased with himself, he charted a course. Now all that remained was to get Kelly thinking along the same lines.

Surely, it would be easy. She adored Dani. From

the day of Dani's birth, Kelly had thrived on motherhood. In fact, Paul's disinterest in being a parent had been the primary cause of trouble between them, along with his philandering, of course. Jordan predicted she would be thrilled with his thinking, as ready to embark on this new, shared commitment as he was.

Of course, he warned himself, as he began preparing a breakfast feast to get her in the proper mood, Kelly hadn't exactly been predictable lately.

No matter, he told himself blithely. When he set his mind to something, he could be very persuasive. He'd gotten her to marry him, hadn't he? By comparison, this battle ought to be little more than a skirmish, an easy victory.

"You want to have a baby?" Kelly asked.

She knew she was staring at Jordan as if he'd announced a desire to bring an elephant into their lives, but she couldn't help it. If he had made such an announcement, suggesting the adoption of a huge gray beast, she couldn't have been any more astounded.

She abandoned the special waffles he'd prepared, obviously to set the tone for this conversation, and pushed aside her plate. She laid her fork carefully back on the table, buying time, hoping to figure out what the devil was going on with her husband this morning.

"Why?" she demanded eventually. The question wasn't all that complex, but it certainly cut to the heart of the matter.

Jordan seemed dumbfounded that she'd asked. She could see by the darkening of his eyes that it wasn't the reaction he'd been hoping for. At this precise moment, however, she was more interested in a little honesty and straight talk than she was in catering to some whim of his. The man hadn't once mentioned children except in the most passing way. In fact, she had worried about his silence on that very topic. Now he expected to snap his fingers and produce a child in nine months.

Rather than being eager to agree, she found herself filled with caution.

"Why?" she repeated more emphatically, since he seemed to be ignoring the original question.

Patches of color darkened his cheeks. "Isn't that what couples do?" he said defensively. "You always said you wanted a houseful of kids. Have you changed your mind?"

The last of her foolish eagerness fled at his tone. Kelly shook her head. "No. I love children," she said dully.

"Well, then, that settles it."

The man clearly didn't have a clue about the fine art of holding a conversation, much less a discussion. He was much better at issuing edicts. "Do you really think it's that simple?" she asked.

"I think it can be, if we're both agreed."

Exasperated, she waved aside the too quick answer. "Are we both agreed? What do you want?"

"A baby," he repeated, clearly bemused by what he apparently considered her pigheadedness.

"Why?" she persisted, trying one more time to

get to the real reason for this sudden interest in procreation.

Heaven knew, she would give anything to have Jordan's baby, but not without exploring the subject in a little more depth. She'd been too eager once before and discovered too late that Paul had gone along with her only to get her off his back. That might not be the case with Jordan, but perhaps he was only anticipating her desires and trying to settle the matter before it became an issue between them. After all, he'd witnessed firsthand the way the same topic had affected her marriage to Paul.

In so doing, though, he was the one to make it an issue. She studied him intently and waited for his answer.

"The usual reasons," he grumbled.

"And what would those be?" she inquired stubbornly, drawing a ferocious scowl.

"Dammit, do you or do you not want to have a baby?" he snapped.

I want you to love me, she cried to herself. *I want a baby that is a product of our love.* "I do," she said finally, "but not until we're sure we're ready."

"I'm sure."

"You keep saying that, but you haven't said why."

"Isn't that obvious?"

"Not to me."

He glowered at her irritably and stood. "I'm going for a walk."

Kelly nodded curtly. "You do that. And while

you're gone, perhaps you'll come up with an explanation for this sudden decision of yours.''

Judging from the way he slammed the door behind him on his way out, she had a feeling he was going to be too busy cooling off to think clearly about much of anything.

Blast it all, when was he going to learn that he couldn't just make unilateral decisions for the two of them and expect her to fall into line? He'd done it when he'd decided on marriage. She was determined he wouldn't get away with it when it came to electing to have a baby. They would not bring a child into this world until Jordan could say without reservations that he loved her.

She sighed at that and resigned herself to a long wait. He was as clueless now about what would really make her happy as he had been weeks ago.

''Mommy, where's Jordan?'' Dani asked sleepily as she wandered into the kitchen, once again wearing her favorite Dallas Cowboys T-shirt.

''Cooling off,'' she said dryly, gesturing in the direction in which he'd gone.

Dani blinked. ''Outside? Isn't it hot out there?''

Not half as hot as it had been in the kitchen a few moments before, Kelly thought. ''It is,'' she said, and scooped her daughter up, tickling her until she convulsed with giggles. ''That was just an expression.''

Dani seemed content with the explanation. She wound her arms around Kelly's neck and delivered several smacking kisses to her face. ''I really, really missed you, Mommy.''

"Not half as much as I missed you."

Her daughter frowned. "Do you think Jordan missed me?"

"I know he did."

"How do you know?"

"Because he bought you a present every single day," she said, thinking of the pile of stuffed animals and dolls that had accumulated in the room that would be Dani's for however long it took for Jordan to relocate the business.

"Where are they?" Dani demanded, scrambling down.

"Most of them are in your new room in Houston, but I think he did bring one thing back for you. As soon as you eat your breakfast, you can run outside and track him down. I know he's very anxious for you to see it."

Dani headed for the door. "I want to see it now."

Kelly blocked her way. "After you eat and get dressed, young lady." She handed her a glass of orange juice. "Drink this, while I make pancakes."

"Can't I have cereal?" Dani pleaded, bouncing up and down. "It's faster."

"Okay, fine." She poured a bowlful of corn flakes, added milk and slices of banana. "Here you go."

As she spooned up the cereal, Dani tried speculating on what Jordan had brought her. "I'll bet it's a dollhouse," she said, her gaze fixed on Kelly's face.

"I'm not saying," Kelly said, forcing herself to remain expressionless. "It's Jordan's surprise."

"Is it a new teddy bear, a great big one?"

Kelly grinned at her persistence. "I'm not saying," she repeated.

"Please, Mommy, my tummy will get all inside out, if I don't know really, really soon."

"Then you'd better stop asking so many questions and finish that cereal," Kelly advised.

Dani fell silent and concentrated on her breakfast. The instant she'd spooned the last bite into her mouth, she climbed down from her chair and raced for the back door.

"Whoa! Clothes, remember?"

Dani managed to exchange her T-shirt for shorts and a top in record time. She waved as she ran past Kelly. "'Bye, Mommy."

On the other side of the screen door, though, she hesitated. "Mommy?"

"What?"

"Can I call Jordan *Daddy?* I know he said at the wedding that he was my new daddy, but he didn't say what I should call him."

Kelly's heart swelled with emotion at the plaintive request. If only Jordan really were her daddy, she thought with regret. "That's up to you and Jordan. Why don't you discuss it with him?"

"Will my real daddy be mad?"

Kelly doubted Paul Flint would much care one way or the other. Given how seldom he showed his face, it was doubtful he'd ever even know.

"I don't think so, munchkin. I think he'd want you to do whatever makes you happy."

It was a blatant lie, but Kelly would do whatever

it took to keep Dani from ever discovering that, at least not until she was old enough to judge her father's behavior for herself. She would have to be the one to put the labels—selfish and uncaring came to mind—on it.

"All right!" Dani enthused. "I can hardly wait to see Jordan. He's the very bestest daddy in the world."

Maybe not the bestest quite yet, Kelly thought, smiling as she watched Dani go racing off in the direction of the barn. But he was working on it. By the time they had a baby of their own—*if* they had a baby of their own, she corrected—she was convinced he'd have it down pat.

First, though, he had to give some serious thought to his motivation for parenthood. Hopefully, he would come back from his walk with all the right words. If he didn't, if his reasons were as muddy as the ones behind his decision to marry her, she resolved that hell would freeze over before she would have his child.

And there would remain this huge empty space inside her, a space meant to be filled by all the love she had to share with Jordan's children.

Jordan heard Dani's shouts long before he spotted her. She was racing down the lane as fast as her churning little legs could carry her. He stooped down and held out his arms. She ran into them and flung her arms around his neck. Why hadn't he ever guessed how being a parent would make him feel?

"I was sleeping when you came to get me last

night and I never, ever, woke up until this morning," she said.

"I noticed," he said, loving the way she smelled of bubble bath, loving even more the fierce protectiveness she aroused in him.

"Did you miss me?" she demanded.

"Every single minute," he confirmed. "But I'll bet you didn't miss me and your mom at all."

"Sure I did. I even drew you a picture. Want to see it?"

"Of course, I want to see it," he said as she reached into her pocket and pulled out a piece of paper that had been folded and refolded into a small, rumpled square. Jordan took it and spread it open. Tears sprang to his eyes as he saw what she'd depicted.

There, drawn with the brightest crayons in the box, were Kelly and Dani, standing in front of a lopsided house that was recognizable as this one. He was standing between them. In case the drawing itself wasn't clear, she had labeled each of them in crooked letters—Mommy, Dani and Daddy. A fat black cat—or something that vaguely resembled one—was at their feet. A striped cat was clutched in Dani's arms. Kelly was also holding something.

"What's that?" he asked, though he had a pretty good idea.

"That's my baby sister," she said. "See the pink blanket? That's how you know it's a girl."

Jordan nodded solemnly, since he couldn't seem to squeeze a word past the lump lodged in his throat. Across the top Dani had written in large, tilting letters, My Family.

"Did you show this to your mom?"

"Not yet. I made it for you. Will you hang it in your office?"

"You bet I will," he promised.

"Are we going to have a baby?" Dani asked worriedly. "I really, really want a sister."

Jordan saw an opportunity to probe this pint-size genius's mind for an argument he could offer Kelly on the same topic. "Why?"

"So we can play with our doll's together," she said at once. "I tried with Angela, but she's pretty little. She couldn't even hold the doll."

"Babies generally start out pretty little," he mused.

"Couldn't you and mommy have a big one?"

He chuckled. "I don't think it works that way. So, tell me why else you want a sister?"

Dani's face scrunched up as she gave serious thought to the question. "So we can love her to pieces. Mommy always says she loves me to pieces." She looked up at him. "I think she loves you to pieces, too."

An interesting tidbit of news, Jordan thought. "She does? What makes you think so?" he asked, pushing aside how pitiful it was to be pumping a five-year-old for information on his own wife.

Dani gave him a disgusted look. "Because she married you, silly."

Realistically, Jordan supposed that was one explanation for Kelly's decision, even if she'd never flat-out said it. His spirits rose a fraction. "Anything else?"

"She thinks you're a saint."

Jordan stared. "A saint? What makes you think that?"

"'Cause she always said the only way she'd ever get married again was if a saint came along. And we learned in Sunday school that you should love saints, right?"

He found the logic a little convoluted, but essentially correct. It was certainly a topic worth discussing with his wife.

"Jordan?"

"Yes, munchkin?" he said distractedly, his thoughts already leaping ahead to the conversation he would have with Kelly the instant he got back to the house.

"I been thinking."

"Oh?"

"I think maybe I should call you Daddy," she said, gazing at him soberly. "What do you think?"

He gave her a fierce hug. "I think there's nothing that would make me any happier."

"Really?"

"Really, really," he confirmed. He took her hand. "Why don't we go back to the house and I'll show you what I brought for you?"

"You brought me a present?" Dani asked, looking a little too innocent.

"I did, indeed," he said. And in another nine months or so, he intended to see that another of her dreams came true. She would have that baby sister—or a brother, if nature got the order mixed up.

As they reached his car he paused and opened the trunk, removing a huge box that had taken up every square inch of room. He watched in delight as Dani saw the picture on the side and a grin spread across her face.

"It's a baby buggy," she said. "Hurry, Daddy. Open it up."

The minute he had the small pink carriage out of the box, Dani grabbed the handle and began propelling it straight toward the barn. Jordan stared after her in bemusement.

"Where are you going?" he shouted.

"To get Francie and the kittens. I'm going to take them for a ride."

"It's supposed to be for your dolls."

"But I know that Francie really, really wants to go for a ride."

Jordan had his doubts, but he let her go. He had more important things to settle.

He found Kelly inside doing laundry. She'd changed to a pair of incredibly provocative shorts and a halter top. The dryer had made the laundry room steamy. Her skin glistened with a sheen of dampness. With all of the noise from the washer and dryer, she didn't hear him approaching. He slipped up behind her, wrapped his arms around her waist and sprinkled kisses across her bare shoulders.

"Nice," she murmured, and turned in his loose embrace to claim a real kiss.

Her body fit snugly against his. Heat shot through his veins. On any other occasion the distraction would have worked. Today, though, Jordan had something more than sex on his mind, even though he was relieved by the discovery that she no longer seemed to be quite so furious with him.

"Dani and I have been having quite a chat," he told her.

"Really? How'd she like the carriage?"

"She's out in the barn even as we speak, gathering up Francie and the kittens for a ride."

Kelly grimaced. "I'm sure Francie will love that. Maybe we should go rescue her."

"Francie can take care of herself," he said. "Right now, I want to talk about a picture Dani drew for me." He showed her the folded paper.

"And this is?" Kelly inquired, pointing to the pink bundle in her arms.

"Her baby sister."

Kelly's gaze shot to his. "Did you put her up to this?"

"No, but the picture got me to thinking. The one thing the family in this picture has that we haven't talked about is love."

"Evidenced by all the hearts, I suppose?"

"Exactly." He kept his gaze fixed on Kelly's face and thought he read something that might have been uncertainty in the depths of her eyes. As if he'd been struck by a bolt of lightning, the last piece of the puzzle suddenly came clear. Kelly did love him still, just as she once had and just as Dani had said. She'd just been waiting for him to wake up and discover that he loved her.

"I realized something when I saw this. I do love you," he admitted, finally finding the right words to express all the things he'd been feeling over the past weeks and months. As soon as the words were out, he realized exactly how right they were.

"That's why I want to fill this house with our children," he explained, trying to make her see all that he'd discovered in his heart. "There are so many more reasons, too. Dani shouldn't be an only child. Any child who is a part of you will steal my heart."

He grinned at the transformation he saw on her face. "Am I getting warm?" he asked, even though he could read the answer in her smile.

"I don't know about you, but I'm getting very warm." She searched his face. "Are you sure this is what you want? If we have a child, there's no turning back."

"There was never any chance of turning back," he said with certainty. "To borrow a phrase from your daughter, I love you to pieces." He gave her a lazy smile. "I may be slow, sweet pea, but once I get there, I never, ever, change my mind. Guaranteed."

Epilogue

"**I** think we should get the whole family together and go into town for dinner tonight," Kelly announced on a Sunday in mid-June, almost ten months after their marriage. "I've already called Jessie. She and Luke will drive over this afternoon. Do you want to call your parents or should I?"

Jordan regarded his wife warily. "You never want to get together with my parents. You always say my mother gives you hives."

"I can tolerate her criticism for one night. And I adore Harlan."

He nodded. "So, what's the occasion? It's not your birthday." She had turned thirty without mishap a few weeks before. "It's not mine. It's not our anniversary."

"You sure about all that?" she taunted.

"I'd like to claim total credit, but believe me, Ginger never lets me forget. She says there are certain things that are inviolate in a good marriage and special occasions top the list. She puts every important date on my calendar and circles it in red."

"A wise woman," Kelly enthused.

"You still haven't said what's going on."

"It's a surprise."

Her reticence was making Jordan extremely nervous. Every once in a while, Kelly devised some scheme that threw the wonderful, quiet routine of their marriage into chaos. He had a hunch this was going to be one of those times. He was still reeling from the discovery that in seeking serenity, he'd found a woman filled with surprises.

"Does Dani know?" he inquired innocently.

Kelly chuckled. "Absolutely not. I know she can't keep a secret, especially from you. Do you bribe that child or what?"

"Never."

"Are you calling your parents or not?"

He sighed. "I'll call them. What time and where?"

"DiPasquali's at seven."

Jordan spent the rest of the day surreptitiously observing his wife and trying to figure out what was going on in her head. The predictability he'd once cherished in Kelly had obviously vanished sometime after puberty without his noticing. She'd become a totally perplexing, complicated—okay, fascinating—woman. There wasn't a day that passed that he didn't thank his lucky stars that he'd been smart enough to marry her.

When they arrived at the Italian restaurant that night, Gina and Anthony had already pushed several tables together for them in the middle of the room. Jordan had the distinct impression that they, too, were in on this hush-hush secret.

In fact, only the men in the family seemed to be left out. Luke and his father seemed as bemused by all the fuss as he was. The women were all smiling conspiratorially—even his mother—which only added to his nervousness. He was tempted to run out and call Ginger just to make sure a special occasion hadn't slipped his mind, after all.

Kelly seemed inclined to prolong his agony, too. Not a word about what had drawn them together was spoken all during the noisy, laughter-filled dinner. Only after they'd finished the pizza did he glance at the other end of the table where Kelly was seated next to Jessie and her almost-two-year-old daughter, Angela. Kelly was whispering to Gina, who smiled broadly and nodded.

"I will get dessert now," the restaurant owner said.

"Bring me some of that Italian ice cream," Harlan said. "What's it called? Spumoni?"

"Not tonight," Kelly said. "I've arranged for something special."

Jordan's gaze shot to hers. Her expression was unreadable and she refused to meet his eyes.

"Anyone like coffee?" Gina DiPasquali asked.

"Another beer for me," Harlan said.

"I'll take the coffee," Luke told her. He leaned over and kissed Jessie's cheek. "What about you? Coffee?"

Jessie nodded.

As soon as the order was complete, Gina vanished into the kitchen. A moment later she returned, dispensing cups and filling them with coffee. She brought Harlan's beer from the bar, then disappeared again.

A few minutes after that the restaurant lights inexplicably dimmed. Jordan started to get to his feet, but his father stopped him with a firm grasp of his arm and a gesture toward the kitchen. He looked up and saw Gina carrying a cake ablaze with candles. Once again, his heart climbed into his throat. Whose birthday was it? And why the hell hadn't Kelly or Ginger, either one, just told him? He felt like an idiot.

To his complete consternation, Gina seemed to be heading his way. She lowered the cake to the table in front of him.

His startled gaze sought out his wife. "It's not my birthday," he said.

"Read the inscription," she suggested.

He glanced down at the huge white cake with its pink roses and blue writing. Happy Father's Day, Jordan, it read. Love Kelly, Dani And ???

Father's Day? Wasn't that one of the ones Ginger was supposed to remind him about? And shouldn't this cake be for Harlan?

He looked around the table and saw everyone grinning expectantly. *Father's Day?* Question marks? His name, not his father's on the cake? The implication finally sank in. All of the breath whooshed out of him.

His gaze shot up. "Is this... Are you..."

Kelly's head bobbed up and down. "We're going to have a baby," she confirmed as the entire table erupted into applause.

Jordan's pulse raced. His eyes locked with his wife's and stayed there as he moved from his chair and headed straight for her. A baby? They were going to have a baby! Suddenly he was afraid his heart might burst from sheer joy.

Kelly stood and hurried into his arms.

"I love you," he whispered against her soft, fragrant hair. "More every single day."

"I love you."

"Me, too, Mommy. Me, too," Dani said, tugging on their shirtsleeves.

Jordan reached down and hefted her into his arms. "You, too, munchkin. We love you, too." He glanced around at the others and a smile spread across his face. "Happy Father's Day, everyone!"

He saw his mother reach for his father's hand and squeeze it. Tears glistened in his father's eyes as he looked from his wife to his two sons and back again. Luke's hand had settled possessively on Angela's tiny shoulder. Jessie rested her hand on top of his. Angela's birth had brought them together. Today they were happier than ever.

During his entire life, Father's Day had been one of those occasions that Jordan acknowledged dutifully but without much thought or emotion. Ginger usually picked out the card and gift for his father, often sending it without even getting his signature. It had happened just that way this year, he was sure.

He doubted that he would ever treat the occasion so cavalierly after today, though. From now on, he knew that being a father would give him the kind of emotional fulfillment he had once despaired of ever feeling. Maybe it was true what Kelly had once said to him, maybe he really was a natural born daddy.

In the midst of their celebration, he happened to glance across the restaurant. Melissa Horton was sitting in a booth all alone, her expression forlorn as she watched the family she had once wanted so badly to be a part of. Even across the room, he could detect the tears shimmering in her eyes.

Jordan was about to go and ask her to join them when she hurriedly stood, then bent over to retrieve something from the booth. To his astonishment, he saw that it was a baby carrier.

Stunned, he was drawn across the room despite himself. Perhaps he was thinking of the news he'd just received. Perhaps he was thinking of his brother, settled now on a ranch in Wyoming and determined never to set foot in Texas again because of this woman.

"Melissa," Jordan acknowledged, stopping her in her tracks with the quiet command in his voice.

She blinked hard, fighting those unmistakable tears, then finally faced him, her chin tilted defiantly. "Hello, Jordan."

He automatically glanced at her hand, wondering

why he'd never heard that she had married. It would have been the kind of news that his family would surely have been aware of. Her ring finger was bare.

He turned his attention to the carrier. "May I see? I just found out that I'm going to be a father in a few months. When I saw you had a baby, I couldn't resist."

She looked as if she'd rather sink straight through the floor, but she eventually nodded and put the carrier onto the table. By this time Kelly had wandered over to join him, tucking her hand into his.

"She's darling," Kelly said when Jordan stood there in stunned silence, unable to form a single word.

He didn't know much about babies. He'd heard they all looked the same, but he was absolutely certain that the infant with the huge brown eyes and dark tuft of hair looked exactly like an Adams. Except for the pink bow tied around the hair, she was a dead ringer for pictures he'd seen of Cody, chubby little cheeks and all.

Alarm darkened Melissa's eyes as she watched his reaction.

"She's Cody's, isn't she?" he said more harshly than he'd intended. Kelly stared at him in shock, then looked again at the baby.

Tears spilled down Melissa's cheeks. "Don't tell him. Please. He'll just hate me. Promise you won't tell him."

Jordan couldn't make any such promise. Nor, from the expression he saw in Kelly's eyes, was she willing to guarantee her silence, either.

"Not without talking to you," Kelly said quietly, giving the young woman a hug. "I'll be in touch."

Apparently satisfied with the answer, Melissa picked up her baby and fled.

"We have to tell him," Jordan said, keeping his voice hushed so the others wouldn't hear. Harlan would have a fit, if he ever found out.

He glanced back toward the table, where no one else seemed to have taken much notice of the exchange. They'd all taken Cody's side against Melissa and obviously considered her presence here tonight not worthy of their attention. "What do we tell them?"

"Nothing until we've had a chance to think about all of the ramifications," Kelly said sensibly. "Now let's go back to the others and celebrate our news, okay? I don't want anything spoiling this moment."

Jordan forced his anxieties about his brother and this baby Cody knew nothing about from his mind. He leaned down and kissed his wife. Whatever they decided to do about Melissa and Cody, they would decide it together.

"I love you," he said again, thinking how incredibly lucky he was. "Love me?"

"Always." She touched her hand to his cheek and met his eyes. "Always."

* * * * *

THE COWBOY AND HIS BABY

Chapter One

Damn, but it was cold, Cody Adams thought as he chased down the last of the herd of cattle he was rounding up. Texas had never been this frigid, not even in the middle of January. He was surprised half the livestock hadn't flat-out frozen in the harsh Wyoming winter. They'd lost a few head of cattle, but nothing like what he'd anticipated the first time the temperatures had dropped below zero and the snow and ice had swirled around him.

The bitter cold and the frequent blinding snowstorms did serve one useful purpose, though. They kept him so busy—kept his brain cells so frozen, for that matter—that he hardly ever thought about home. He'd freeze his butt off and suffer frostbite on most any part of his anatomy for the blessing of a blank memory. He didn't want to think about Texas or his family. Most of all, he didn't want to think about sneaky, conniving Melissa Horton and the way she'd cheated on him.

It had taken him a long time to block out the image of his longtime girlfriend wrapped in his best friend's arms. Even now, more than a year later, that terrible, gut-wrenching moment sneaked up on him when he least expected it and reminded him that that kind of pain might hide out, but it seldom went away.

With the last of the herd rounded up and dusk falling, Cody gestured to one of the other hands that he was leaving and headed back toward the small but cozy line shack he'd insisted he preferred to the bunkhouse. He'd claimed it kept him closer to the cattle for which he was responsible, but the truth was, he craved the isolation.

For a man who had been a very social creature back in Texas—okay, a notorious flirt—it was quite a change and, for the time being, a welcome one. It was the only surefire way he could think of for staying out of trouble and avoiding the sort of heart-ache that falling for some woman just about guar-anteed.

His boss, impressed by the fact that for years 28-year-old Cody had been running White Pines, his family's ranch back in Texas, hadn't argued with his idiosyncratic decision. Lance Treethorn had in-sisted only that a phone be installed so he could reach Cody on business. He was the only one with the number. He rarely used it. Cody dropped by the ranch house often enough to stay in touch.

On the tiny porch Cody stomped the snow off his boots, gathered up an armload of firewood and went inside. Within minutes he had a fire roaring and had shucked off his skeepskin jacket. He stood in front of the blaze, letting the heat warm his chilled body. Unfortunately, it couldn't touch the cold place deep inside him.

He'd been standing there for some time, lost in thought, when he noticed the stack of mail sitting on the table in the kitchen area of the one-room cabin. It was sitting atop a foil-covered pan that he suspected from the sinful, chocolaty aroma, contained a batch of freshly baked brownies. He grinned and ripped off the foil. Sure enough, brownies. Apparently, Janey Treethorn had been by again.

The fifteen-year-old daughter of his boss had a giant-size crush on him. Thankfully, though, she was painfully shy. She limited her overtures to dropping off his mail, always with a batch of brownies or his favorite apple pie. In the summer it had been fresh fruit cobblers. She was usually careful to stop by while he wasn't home. On the one occasion when he'd caught her, she'd blushed furiously, stammered an apology for intruding, and fled on horseback before he could even say thanks.

Unable to resist, he grabbed one of the brownies and ate it as he sorted through the few pieces of mail she'd left, putting the bills aside to be paid later. A small blue envelope caught his attention.

Turning it over, he recognized his sister-in-law's handwriting.

As always, when anything came from a member of his family, his heart skipped a beat. Letters were rare enough to stir a pang of homesickness each time one arrived. Jordan's wife had been dutifully writing to him once every two weeks or so from the moment she and Jordan had gotten married. For a man who swore he wanted nothing to do with anyone or anything back home, it was downright pitiful how he looked forward to Kelly's chatty letters and the family gossip she shared with such humor and telling insight. This one was more than a week overdue. Since the others had come like clockwork, he'd been trying not to admit just how worried he really was.

He could tell right off there was something different about this one, too. It was stiffer, more like a card than a letter. He grabbed a second brownie, then carried Kelly's latest correspondence with him back to his chair in front of the fire.

When he ripped open the envelope, a tiny square dropped out of the card inside. He grabbed for it instinctively and found himself staring at an infant swaddled as tight as a papoose in a blue blanket. He caught himself grinning at the sight of that tiny, red, scrunched-up face.

So, Jordan was a daddy, he thought, amazed by the shaft of pure envy that shot through him. He'd known the baby was due any day now. Kelly had kept him apprised of every detail of her pregnancy, including his older brother's bemusement at the natural childbirth classes she'd insisted he take with her. He wondered if Jordan had made it through the delivery or if he'd fainted at Kelly's first big-time contraction.

He closed his eyes against the tide of longing that rolled over him. He was missing so damned much, he thought, once again cursing Melissa for the betrayal that had made staying in Texas where he belonged impossible.

He was missing seeing his other brother Luke and his wife Jessie's little girl grow. Angela had turned two back in December. Kelly had sent a picture of her with her face streaked with icing and her fist in the middle of the chocolate birthday cake with its two, fat pink candles. He'd tucked it in his wallet, along with the snapshot of Kelly's daughter from her first marriage, Dani, a little con-artist-in-training who could persuade penguins to buy ice, if she was of a mind to. Now he opened his wallet and inserted the tiny picture of this latest addition to the family.

He stared at the brand new baby one last time and wondered if he'd ever see him. He'd been named Justin James, according to the information on the birth announcement.

"We're going to call him J.J.," Kelly wrote in the note accompanying the card. "We can't wait for you to see him. Jordan swears he hasn't slept a wink in the past week. I don't know how that can be, since I'm the one up every time the little monster screams in the middle of the night. I haven't noticed Jordan pacing the floor alongside me. I think he's been sleeping with a pillow over his head deliberately, so he can claim he never hears J.J. crying. He swears he only wakes up after I've already left the bed. The silver-tongued devil says it's missing me that wakes him. He thinks a line like that will make me more sympathetic to him. Fat chance.

"No, seriously," he read on, "your big brother has been a huge help. I think he's a little awed by fatherhood…or maybe it's just that mountain of diapers he's expected to wash every night."

Cody chuckled at the image of his button-down brother, the big-time oil company executive, changing diapers and warming bottles. Maybe he was taking to it better than any of them had anticipated, including Jordan himself.

"We're scheduling the baptism for the end of the month and we expect you to be here," the letter continued. "No excuses, Cody. It's time to come home."

It's time to come home. Kelly's words echoed in his head, taunting him, reminding him that nothing would ever make this beautiful, sprawling Wyoming ranch into home. Lance Treethorn was a kind, decent man. He'd become a good friend. His daughters were real little angels and they treated Cody like one of the family. Even so, it wasn't the same. Not that a little thing like being homesick mattered. Even though his heart ached for the life he'd left behind, he knew he could never go back. He'd rather eat dirt than get within a hundred miles of the traitorous Melissa ever again.

It had been over a year since he'd left Texas, eighteen months to be exact, but not even time had cured him of the rage that had sent him away from everyone and everything dear to him.

Mention Texas and he didn't think of his beloved White Pines, didn't think of his parents or his brothers, much as he loved them all. The only image that inevitably came to mind was of Melissa Horton. Sometimes not even an entire bottle of the best liquor in the store could blot out the memories of the woman who'd betrayed him with his best friend.

Even now the vision in his head of Melissa was so vivid he could practically feel the silky texture of her skin and the soft flow of dark auburn hair through his fingers. He could practically smell the sweet summer scent of her.

But along with the sensual memories came the blinding rage, as powerful now as it had been on the day he'd left Texas for good. Accompanying that rage was the anger and frustration of realizing that he was, in part, responsible for what had happened. Maybe if he'd told her he loved her, she wouldn't have turned to Brian Kincaid in the first place. Maybe if he'd had a clue just how much she mattered to him, instead of taking her for granted, he wouldn't be lying awake nights aching for her. He'd been a fool. She'd been a cheat. Quite a pair, the two of them. Maybe he deserved to be this miserable. She certainly did, though he had no idea if she was. She could be happily married to Brian now, for all he knew.

Before he'd realized what he was doing, he'd

ripped the note inviting him to the baptism of Jordan and Kelly's baby to shreds. He couldn't allow himself to be tempted back, not even by something as important as this. He would not go back to Texas. Not now. Not ever.

The decision was firm, but it left him feeling heartsick and more lonely than he'd ever felt in his life. He was almost glad when the ring of the phone shattered the silence. He grabbed the receiver gratefully.

"Hey, boss, what's up?" he said, knowing it would be Lance Treethorn on the other end of the line.

The widowed father of three young girls, Treethorn had his hands full with trying to run the ranch and raise his daughters to be proper young ladies. He'd succeeded with the oldest. Janey was as prim and proper and dutiful as a father could ever want, but the two younger ones, ten and twelve, were terrors. Cody didn't envy the thirty-five-year-old man trying to get them raised and married without calamity striking.

"We got the herd rounded up today," he told Lance. "We only lost one more to the cold."

"Thanks, Cody, but I didn't call for an update."

Something in Lance's voice triggered alarm bells. "What's wrong?" he asked at once. "Are there problems with the girls?"

"No, it's nothing like that. We're all fine, but you had a call here at the house."

"I did?" He'd given the Treethorn number only to Jordan, with a direct order that it never be used except for a dire emergency. He knew his brother would never break that rule. His heart thudded dully as he waited for whatever bad news Jordan had imparted.

"Call home," his boss told him. "It sounded pretty urgent. Your brother asked how quickly I could get a message to you. Obviously Jordan still doesn't know you have a phone in your cabin."

"No," Cody admitted, grateful that his boss had never asked why he insisted on having such a buffer between him and his family. Lance was the best kind of boss, the best kind of friend. He was scrupulously fair. He lent support, but never asked questions or made judgments. There had been no hint of criticism in his voice when he'd commented just now on Cody's decision to keep his private phone number from his family.

"I'm sorry he bothered you," Cody apologized anyway.

"You know damned well it's no bother. I just hope everything's okay at home. Give me a call if there's anything I can do to help."

"Thanks, Lance."

Cody hung up slowly, thinking of the tiny picture that he'd placed in his wallet only moments earlier. Had something happened to Justin James? Or to Kelly? Why else would Jordan call? Damn, but he hated being so far away. What if... He allowed the thought to trail off.

"Stop imagining the worst and call," he muttered out loud, finally forcing himself to dial his brother's number, knowing that this call, whatever it was about, would shatter whatever distance he'd managed to achieve from his past.

Jordan picked up on the first ring. His voice sounded tired and hoarse.

"Hey, big brother," Cody said.

"Cody, thank God. I was worried sick you wouldn't get the message for days."

Jordan, the most composed man Cody had ever known, sounded shaken. The alarm bells triggered by Lance's call were clanging even louder now. "What's wrong?"

"It's bad news, Cody. Real bad."

Cody sank onto a chair by the kitchen table and braced himself. The last time Jordan had sounded that somber was when their brother Erik had been killed in an accident on Luke's ranch.

"Is it Dad?" he asked, hating even to form the words. Harlan Adams was bigger than life. He was immortal—or so Cody had always tried to tell himself. He couldn't imagine a world in which Harlan wasn't controlling and manipulating things.

"No, he's fine," Jordan reassured him at once, then amended, "Or at least as well as can be expected under the circumstances."

"Dammit, Jordan, spit it out. What the hell has happened?"

"It's Mother," he began, then stopped. He swallowed audibly before adding, "She and Daddy were out riding this morning."

He paused again and this time Cody could hear his ragged breathing. It almost sounded as if Jordan were crying, but that couldn't be. Jordan never

cried. None of them did. Harlan had very old-
fashioned ideas on the subject of men and tears. He
had set a tough example for them, too. He hadn't
shed a single tear when Erik died. He'd just retreated into stony, guilt-ridden silence for months
after the loss of his son. The rest of them had coped
with their grief dry-eyed, as well. If Erik's death
hadn't caused Jordan's cool, macho facade to crack,
what on earth had?

"Jordan, are you okay?" he asked.

"No. Mother took a bad fall, Cody."

Cody felt as if the blood had drained out of him.
Hands trembling, he grabbed the edge of the table
and held on. "How is she? Is she…"

"She's gone, Cody," Jordan said with a catch in
his voice. "She never woke up. She was dead by
the time the paramedics got to the ranch."

"My God," he murmured, stunned. Forbidden
tears stung his eyes. Ashamed, he wiped at them
uselessly. They kept coming, accompanied by a terrible sense of loss. "Are you sure Daddy's okay?
Why aren't you with him?"

"Luke and Jessie are over at White Pines now.
Luke's got the funeral arrangements under control.
Kelly and I will be going over right after I get off
the phone. I wanted to stay here until you called
back. How soon can you get here?"

Cody noticed his brother asked the question as if
there were no doubt at all that he would be coming
home. "I don't know," he said, struggling between
duty and the agony that going home promised.

Disapproving silence greeted the reply. "But you

will be here,'' Jordan said emphatically. "I'm telling Daddy you're on your way."

Cody rubbed his suddenly pounding head. "I don't know," he repeated.

"Look, this is no time to be indulging in self-pity, little brother," Jordan snapped impatiently. "Daddy needs you here, probably more than he needs any of the rest of us. He'll need you to take up some of the slack at White Pines while he pulls himself together. He's always depended on you. Don't let him down now."

Cody said nothing.

Jordan finally broke the silence with a sigh. "We're scheduling the funeral for Saturday," he said. "Be here, Cody."

He hung up before Cody could reply.

Cody sat in the gathering darkness, silent, unchecked tears streaking down his cheeks. He had no choice and he knew it. Mary Adams might not have been the kind of warm, doting mother a child dreamed of, but Harlan Adams had worshiped her. He could not let his father go through this kind of grief without all of his sons at his side. It was the kind of loyalty that had been ingrained in him since birth. As badly as he wanted to pretend it didn't matter, he knew better. Nothing mattered more at a time like this.

He took some small comfort in the odds that said he would probably never even see Melissa. He doubted she would have the nerve to show up at the funeral. She certainly wouldn't have the audacity to show up at White Pines afterward. It would be okay. He could slip in and out of town before temptation overtook him and he sought out so much as a glimpse of her.

At least, that's what he told himself on the long, sad drive back to Texas after he'd cleared his departure with Lance. He'd chosen to drive to delay his arrival as long as possible. Maybe to come to grips with what had happened in private. He'd spend a few days with his family to grieve. A few days to do whatever he could for his father. A few days to spoil his nieces and hold his brand new nephew. A few days to soak up enough memories to last a lifetime.

With all that going on, Melissa would be the last thing on his mind.

The very last thing, he vowed with grim determination as he finally turned into the lane to White Pines.

He slowed his pickup and looked around at the land that he loved, the land he'd hoped one day would be his since Luke's mile-wide independent streak had sent him chasing after his own dream and his own ranch and Jordan was only interested in oil.

Even in the dead of winter, it was starkly beautiful, at least to him. He was home and suddenly, despite the sorrow that had drawn him back, he felt at peace for the first time since he'd driven away more than eighteen months before.

Melissa Horton took a break from her job behind the lunch counter at Dolan's Drugstore and perched on a stool with the weekly newspaper and a cup of coffee. Her attention was riveted to the story of Mary Adams's tragic riding accident.

The 55-year-old woman had always been incredibly kind to her. Melissa had figured Mary pitied her because she'd been mooning around Cody for most of her life. Once Mary had even tried to give her some advice. It had turned out to be lousy advice, but Melissa was certain Mary had thought she was doing her a favor.

Mary had sat her down one afternoon over tea and told her that Cody was taking her for granted. Not that that was news. At any rate, Mary had claimed that the only way Melissa would ever win him would be to make him jealous. Tired of being ignored except when it suited Cody, and taking the well-meant advice to heart, Melissa had tried to do just that by going out just once with Cody's best friend.

What a disaster that had been! Had she chosen anyone else, maybe the plan would have worked, but she'd foolishly selected the one man she'd figured wouldn't get hurt. Brian had known her heart belonged to Cody. He'd known their date meant nothing, that it was only a ploy to shake up Cody. He'd even tried to argue her out of it, warning her it could backfire, but her mind had been made up. She had risked everything, certain that Mary Adams was right. She'd seen it as the only way to get Cody to finally make a commitment to her.

She should have guessed that Brian understood Cody even better than she did. Every time she thought of the anger and hurt in Cody's eyes that night, it made her sick to her stomach. He had stared at them for the space of one dull, thudding heartbeat. He'd looked not at her, but through her. His gaze riveted on Brian, he'd said, "A hell of a friend you turned out to be."

He had spoken with a kind of lethal calm that had been more chilling than shouted accusations. Then he'd turned on his heel and walked away. He had taken off the next morning and never once looked back.

For the past eighteen months she'd had no idea at all where he was. Brian hadn't heard from him, hadn't expected to, for that matter. She hadn't had the courage to ask Cody's family for information. Her shame ran too deep.

There had been times when she'd considered being in the dark a blessing. It had kept her from chasing after him, from destroying what few shreds of pride and dignity she had left.

Now, though, she had no doubts at all that Cody would be coming home. She might have driven him away with her betrayal, but his mother's death would surely bring him back.

Had he changed much? she wondered. Had he lost the flirtatious, fun-loving nature that had charmed her and half the women who'd crossed his path? Would she have to live with regrets for the rest of her life for turning him into a bitter, cynical man?

"No good'll come of what you're thinking," Mabel Hastings advised, coming up behind her to peer over her shoulder at the front page of the newspaper.

"How do you know what I'm thinking?" Melissa asked defensively.

Mabel shook her head, her tight gray curls bouncing at the movement. When Mabel had a permanent, she meant it to last. She'd been wearing the exact same hairstyle as far back as Melissa could remember. It did not suit her pinched features.

"I been reading you like a book ever since you set eyes on Cody Adams way back in junior high school," Mabel informed her huffily. "You seem to forget how many times you sat right here at this very counter making goo-goo eyes at him."

Melissa chuckled despite her irritation at the unsolicited interference. "'Goo-goo eyes'? Mabel, exactly how old are you? A hundred, maybe? Not even my mother would use an expression like that."

The older woman, who was probably no more than sixty, scowled at her. "Don't matter what you call it, the point is you've been crazy about that boy way too long and just look where it got you."

Melissa sensed the start of a familiar lecture. Listening to it was the price she paid for having a job that paid enough in salary and tips to keep her financially afloat and independent. She didn't have to take a dime from her parents.

"Okay, I get your point," she said, trying to avoid the full-scale assault on her sense and her virtue. "Drop it, please. I probably won't even see Cody."

She was bright enough to know it would be far better if she didn't. Her life had taken some unexpected twists and turns since he'd left, but it was settling down now. She was at peace with herself. There were no more complications, no more tears in the middle of the night over a man who didn't love her—at least, not enough—and no more roller coaster ups and downs.

No way did she want to stir up old memories and old hurts. One look into Cody's laughing brown eyes and she couldn't trust herself not to tumble straight back into love with him. She'd clearly never had a lick of sense where he was concerned.

Now, though, the stakes were way too high. Now she had more than her own heart to consider. She had someone else to protect, someone more important to her than life itself—Cody's daughter, the child he didn't even know he had.

Chapter Two

The entire family was walking around in a daze. Cody had never seen them like this, not even when Erik died. He supposed they were all following Harlan's lead. His father hadn't spoken more than a word or two to anyone. He hadn't eaten. He wasn't sleeping. He had refused a sedative prescribed by the doctor. Not even his unusually subdued grandchildren, tugging on his sleeves and competing for his attention, drew so much as a smile. He looked haggard and lost.

On Saturday morning Cody found Harlan in his office, staring at nothing, his complexion a worrisome shade of gray. Cody walked over and perched on a corner of his desk.

"Hey, Daddy, are you doing okay?"

Harlan blinked, his gaze finally focusing. "Cody, have you been here long?"

The vague question startled Cody. Normally nothing went on at White Pines that Harlan didn't notice. "Actually, I got here yesterday."

His father's lips quirked for a fraction of a second. "Hell, I know that. I haven't lost my marbles. I meant now. Have you been standing there long?"

Relief sighed through Cody. "Nope. Just walked in. Everyone's been looking for you."

"Must not have been looking too hard," Harlan grumbled in a manner that was more in character. "I've been right here all night long."

Cody was dismayed. "You didn't sleep?"

"Off and on, I suppose."

"Daddy, you should have been resting. Today's going to be rough enough without facing it exhausted."

His father shrugged. "I couldn't go upstairs."

"Damn," Cody muttered. Why hadn't any of them thought of that? Of course it was going to be hard for their father to spend time in the suite of rooms he had shared for so many years with his wife. It was hard for the rest of them just being in the house where their mother had reigned over every last detail. "I'm sorry. I'll go upstairs and bring some clothes down for you. It'll be time to go to the church soon."

He had barely reached the door when his father's voice stopped him.

"How could a thing like this happen?" Harlan murmured.

His choked voice sounded too damned close to tears. Cody was shaken by that as he hadn't been by anything else in his life.

"We were supposed to have so many years left," Harlan went on. "I had promised your mother we'd travel, that we'd see all the sights she'd been reading about over the years." He glanced at Cody. "Did you know she gave up a trip around the world for her college graduation to marry me? I promised to make it up to her one day, but I never got around to it."

Guilt sliced through Cody. His departure had kept them from going on those trips. His father had had to take over the running of White Pines again, just when he'd been ready to indulge all of his wife's fantasies.

"You can't think about that," Cody told him, partly because he couldn't bear to think about it, either. "You'll make yourself crazy. Think about the years you did have. You made Mother very happy. She loved being your wife. She loved being mistress of White Pines. She was wild about all those fancy ancestors of yours."

"She loved you boys, too," Harlan added quietly. "Oh, I know she didn't pay you the kind of attention she did me. I regret that. I regret that you all thought that meant she didn't love you."

At Cody's expression of shock, he added, "Don't deny it, son. I know you boys couldn't help feeling that way. Catering to me was just your mama's way. When you were little, I don't think she knew quite what to make of you. She was an only child.

She wasn't prepared for the chaos of four rambunctious boys. But she cared about you and she was so very proud of the way you all turned out.''

"Even me?" Cody asked, unable to prevent the question from popping out. He hated what it said about his insecurities. He had feared that turning his back on White Pines would cost him whatever affection either of his parents felt for him.

Harlan chuckled. "Are you kidding? You were her baby. There wasn't a day since you've been gone that she didn't worry about you and how you were getting along, when she didn't tell me how she missed hearing you thundering down the stairs or raising a ruckus in the kitchen.''

"She hated it when I did those things," Cody protested.

"Only until they stopped," Harlan said softly. Sorrow had etched new lines in his face. The sadness behind the comment emphasized them.

Cody watched with amazement and new respect as his father visibly pulled himself up, gathering strength from some inner reserve that had been severely tested in the past few days. He stood, crossed the room and put a comforting arm around Cody's shoulders, sharing that strength with his son.

"Come on, boy. Help me figure out what to wear, so I won't put your mama to shame.''

Together they climbed the stairs and went to prepare for the funeral of the woman Cody had adored and on occasion admired, but until just this morning had never understood.

* * *

Melissa watched the clock above the soda fountain ticking slowly toward noon. She would not go to Mary's funeral. She would not! If she did, she would be going for all the wrong reasons.

Drugstore owner and pharmacist Eli Dolan came out from behind the prescription counter, then peered at her over the rim of his reading glasses. "You going?"

"Going where?" Melissa asked.

He muttered something about women and foolishness under his breath. "To that funeral, of course. You ought to be paying your respects."

She didn't bother asking how Eli knew that she had been close to Mary at one time. Everyone in town knew everyone else's business. That's what had made staying here after her daughter was born so difficult. She doubted there was a single soul that didn't have their suspicions about the identity of Sharon Lynn's daddy, but as far as she knew only her own parents and Cody's brother Jordan and his wife knew the truth for certain.

She wouldn't have admitted it to Jordan and Kelly, but he had taken one look at the baby and guessed. She hadn't been able to deny it. Jordan had vowed to keep her secret and, as far as she knew, he'd been true to his word. She was ninety-eight percent certain that he'd never told Cody. Harlan had instilled a deep sense of honor in all of his sons. That included keeping promises, even when extracted under the most trying conditions.

She also had a hunch that if Jordan had told, Cody would have stormed back to Texas and raised a commotion that would have set the whole town on its ear. Or maybe that was just wishful thinking on her part.

"You'd better get a move on, if you're going to find a place in church," Eli prompted, clearly not intending to let the matter drop. "It's bound to be crowded. Folks around here think mighty highly of Harlan and his sons. They'll be there for them, even if most of them found Mary a little high-falutin' for their taste."

"I can't leave here now," Melissa hedged, taking another wipe at the already polished counter. "It's lunchtime."

"And who's going to be here?" he shot right back. "Everybody will be at the funeral. I don't expect we'll be doing much business. And you seem to forget that I was making milk shakes and sandwiches when you were still in diapers. I can handle things for the next couple of hours. If I make a mess of things, you can say you told me so when you get back."

He glanced over at Mabel and nodded in her direction. "Or she'll do it for you," he said with a sour note in his voice. "Now, go on. Do what you know is right."

Melissa didn't question the sense of relief she felt at being nudged determinedly out the door. If Eli didn't find it odd that she'd be going to the funeral, maybe no one else would, either. Maybe it would have been more noticeable if she'd stayed away.

Bracing herself against the brisk January wind, she rushed down Main Street, glad that she'd chosen to wear a dress to work rather than her usual jeans and T-shirt. Obviously some part of her had known even when she'd dressed that morning that she would change her mind about going to the service.

It was a dreary day for a funeral. Leaden clouds, practically bursting with rain—or, given the rapidly dropping temperature, more likely sleet—hung low in the sky. She tugged her coat more tightly around her, but gave up on keeping her long hair from tangling as the wind whipped it around her face.

All the way to the church she tried to keep her mind off Cody and on the service that was to come. Her best efforts, however, were a dismal failure. She kept envisioning Cody, wondering how he was holding up, worrying how he and all of his brothers were doing and regretting more than she could say that she couldn't take her place with them and offer the support she desperately wanted to give.

She was so late that she planned to slip into the back of the church and stand in the shadows. Cody would never know she was there. The last thing she wanted to do today was add to his misery.

She ran up the steps of the old church just as the bells were chiming in the tall white steeple. The sun peeked through the clouds for just an instant, creating a terrible glare. Going from that sudden bright sun outside into the church's dimly lit interior, she was momentarily blinded.

Apparently, whoever was hard on her heels was having the same problem because he slammed smack into her, his body rock solid as he hit her at full tilt. The contact almost sent her sprawling on the polished wood floor.

"Sorry," he said, gripping her elbows to keep her upright. "You okay, darlin'?"

Melissa's heart climbed straight into her throat. She would have recognized that voice, that automatic flirtatiousness, even if she hadn't heard it for a hundred years. The firm, steadying touch was equally familiar and just as devastating. If she'd brushed against a live wire, she couldn't have felt any more electrified.

"Cody?"

She spoke his name in no more than a whisper, but at the sound of her voice, he jerked his hands away as if he'd just touched a white-hot flame.

"Excuse me," he said, his voice instantly like ice.

As if she were a stranger, he shoved past her to make his way to the front of the church. No, she corrected, if she'd been a stranger, he would have been less rude, more solicitous.

Trembling from the unexpected face-to-face meeting, Melissa watched him stride up the aisle to join his father and his brothers in the first pew. In that single quick glimpse, she had seen new lines in his face. His sun-streaked, normally untamed hair had been trimmed neatly in the way his mother had always wanted it to be.

It was his eyes, though, that had stunned her. Once they'd been filled with so much laughter. Naturally she had expected to find sorrow today in the dark-as-coffee depths. What she hadn't anticipated was the cold antipathy when he recognized her, followed by an emptiness that was worse than hatred.

Well, she thought despondently, now she knew. Cody hadn't forgiven her. He'd looked straight through her as if he'd never known her, as if he'd never teased her or made love to her or shared his deepest, darkest secrets with her.

"Oh, God," she murmured in what could have been the beginning of a prayer, but instead simply died before completion. Their relationship was clearly beyond even divine intervention. She'd known it all along, of course, but she hadn't wanted to believe it. The last flicker of hope in her heart died like a candle flame in a chilly wind.

Though a part of her wanted to flee, she moved into the deepest shadows and stayed through the service, grieving not just for the woman lying in the flower-draped casket, but for the death of her own dreams.

"You went to the funeral, didn't you?" Velma Horton asked the minute Melissa walked through her mother's doorway to pick up her daughter after work.

"How did you know?" she asked, though it was easy enough to guess. The grapevine had probably been buzzing all afternoon and her mother was definitely tapped into that.

Her mother sniffed. "You think I didn't know why you wore that dress today. I know what you said, some nonsense about all your jeans being in the laundry, but I'm not a fool, girl. I knew you wouldn't miss a chance to catch sight of Cody. So, did you see him?''

''Briefly,'' Melissa admitted.

''And?''

''And what? We didn't talk.''

''Then you didn't tell him about Sharon Lynn.''

Melissa shook her head. ''He wouldn't care,'' she said with absolute certainty that was based on the way he'd looked straight through her for the second time in their lives.

To her surprise, her mother breathed a sigh of relief and some of the tension drained out of her expression. ''Good.''

There were times, like now, when Melissa didn't understand her mother at all. When Velma had learned her daughter was pregnant, she'd been all for chasing Cody to the ends of the earth and demanding he take responsibility for his actions.

''I thought you wanted him to know,'' Melissa said, regarding her mother with confusion. ''There was a time you threatened to go to Harlan and demand that he drag Cody back here. You thought he owed me his name and his money. The only thing that stopped you was Daddy's threat to divorce you if you did.''

Velma rolled her eyes. ''Your father's got more pride than sense. Anyway, that was before Sharon Lynn was born, back when I didn't know how you'd manage by yourself. Seems to me you've done just fine. There's no sense in trying to fix what's not broke.''

It was a reasonable explanation for the turnaround, but Melissa didn't entirely buy it. "There's something else, isn't there? Some other reason you don't want Cody to find out the truth?"

"There is," her mother admitted, an ominous note in her voice. "Harlan Adams is a powerful man."

"That's not news. What's your point? What does he have to do with this? It's between me and Cody."

"Not if Harlan gets it into his head to claim his granddaughter," her mother stated, a note of genuine fear in her voice. "There's no way we could fight a man like that."

Melissa was stunned by what her mother was suggesting. "Don't you think you're being a little paranoid? Jordan's known for almost a year now and he hasn't even spilled the beans. I suspect the rest of the family will react with just as much indifference."

Her mother didn't seem to be reassured. "Just watch your step. I'm warning you, Melissa, keep that baby as far away from Cody Adams as you can."

Though she didn't think the warning was necessary, Melissa nodded dutifully. "I don't think we have to worry about that. Cody will probably be gone before we know it."

Just then the sounds of her daughter's cheerful, nonsensical babbling echoed down the narrow hallway. Melissa smiled. Her heart suddenly felt lighter than it had all day. The baby had had that effect on her from the moment she'd been born.

"Did she just wake up?" she asked as she started toward her old bedroom.

"I doubt she's even been asleep. She didn't want to go down for her nap. I think she sensed the tension in both of us. You go on in. I'm going to fix your daddy's dinner."

Melissa went to pick up her daughter from the crib her mother had put up next to the twin bed Melissa had slept in for most of her life. Sharon Lynn was standing on shaky, pudgy little legs, hanging on to the crib rail. Her eyes lit up when she spotted her mother.

"Ma...ma...ma."

"That's right, darling girl," Melissa crooned, gathering her into her arms. "I'm your mama."

She inhaled the sweet talcum-powder scent of her baby and sighed as tiny little hands grabbed her hair and held on tight. "You've got quite a grip, little one. You must have gotten that from your daddy. I'm the original hundred-pound weakling."

"Da?" Sharon Lynn repeated, echoing a sound Melissa had taught her while showing her a snapshot of Cody. Her mother would have pitched a royal fit if she'd known.

"Oh, baby," she murmured, tightening her embrace. "Your daddy's right here in town. He has no idea what he's been missing all these months. He has no idea that he has a precious little girl."

Cody would have made a wonderful father, she thought with a sigh. He would have been too indulgent by far, too readily conned by sweet talk and a winning smile, but, oh, how he would have cherished and protected a child of his. Her foolish actions had cost him the chance to prove that. Worse, they had cost her daughter a chance to be loved by an incredible man. There were days when she almost made herself sick with regrets.

"We do okay by ourselves, though, don't we?" she asked, gazing into round, dark eyes that reminded her too much of Cody. The baby returned her gaze with the kind of serious, thoughtful look the question deserved. Melissa wondered how many years it would be before that innocent contemplation turned to something far more accusatory because her mother had robbed her of any contact with her father.

"Don't," her mother pleaded, coming up behind her.

"Don't what?"

"Don't tell him."

"Who said I was going to?" Melissa asked.

"I know that look. You're making up pipe dreams about what it will be like when Cody finds out he has a baby girl. You're expecting him to declare he's never stopped loving you and sweep you off to get married."

Her expression turned dire. "It won't be that way, I'm telling you. If he cares about the baby at all, he'll take her from you. That's how much he hates you for what you did to him. You made a fool of him in front of the whole town by going out with his best friend. A man never forgets a betrayal like that. I don't care if it was just a bunch of foolishness on your part. The results were the same as if you and Brian had had something going.''

''You don't know anything about Cody's feelings,'' Melissa argued, even though she had just seen with her own eyes that Cody did despise her. She didn't want to believe he could be cruel enough to try to take their daughter away from her.

''Are you willing to take that chance?'' her mother demanded.

The baby whimpered, either because she was picking up on the sudden tension or because Melissa was holding her too tightly. ''No,'' she whispered, fighting the sting of tears as she kissed her daughter's silky cheek. ''No, I'm not willing to take that chance.''

She had been weaving pipe dreams, just as her mother had guessed. The risk of trying to make them come true, though, was far too great. Rather than winning back Cody, she could very well lose her child. She would die before she let that happen. Sharon Lynn was the most important thing in her life.

All the way home she assured herself that she only needed a few days. If she kept the secret just a few more days, Cody would be gone and that would be the end of it.

Later that night she sank into the rocker beside Sharon Lynn's crib and set it into motion, hoping to lull the baby to sleep and to quiet all those clamoring shouts in her head that told her she just might be making the second worst mistake in her life by keeping silent. As much as she hated to admit it, her mother was right about one thing. If Cody did learn the truth from someone else, there was no telling what he might do to exact revenge.

Chapter Three

For the past two days Cody hadn't been able to stop thinking about his brief meeting with Melissa at the funeral. She looked exactly as he'd remembered her, her long hair a tangle of fiery lights, her body slender as a reed except for the lush, unexpected curve of her breasts.

Even before he'd heard her voice, in that instant when he'd caught her to prevent her from falling, he'd known it was her just from the way his body had reacted to touching her. He had hated that reaction, hated knowing that his desire for her hadn't waned at all despite the months of self-imposed exile. That seemed like the cruelest sort of punishment.

Late that night after the funeral he'd been pacing

downstairs when his father had come out of his office and caught him. Harlan had guessed right off that his agitation had to do with Melissa, though he'd been uncommonly cautious in broaching the subject.

"I thought I saw Melissa at the church today," Harlan had said casually after he'd pulled Cody into his office and they were both seated in comfortable leather chairs in front of a blazing fire, glasses of whiskey in hand. At the reference to Melissa, Cody had put his aside without tasting it. He'd feared if he got started, he'd never stop.

"She was there," he'd conceded, his voice tight.

"Did you get a chance to talk to her?"

"We have nothing to say to each other."

"I see," Harlan said. He'd let the silence build for a bit, taking a sip of his drink before adding nonchalantly, "I heard she's been working at Dolan's Drugstore, running the soda fountain for Eli. Doing a good job, too. Eli says business is up. The kids are hanging out there again instead of driving to the fast-food place out on the highway."

Cody hadn't even acknowledged the information. He'd just tucked it away for later consideration. Ever since, he'd been considering what to do about it.

He could drive into town, march into Dolan's and confront Melissa about what she'd done to him, something he probably should have done the very night he'd found her with Brian. He could raise the kind of ruckus that would be the talk of the town for the next year. It would go into the textbook of

Cody Adams lore that had begun when he was barely into puberty. If half the tales had been true, he would have worn himself out by the time he was twenty.

Sighing, he conceded he couldn't see much point to adding another wild exploit to his reputation. A scene would only rake up old news, embarrass Melissa—not that he cared much about that—and tell anyone with half a brain that Cody wasn't over her. Otherwise, why would he bother to stir up the cold ashes of their very dead relationship?

No, for the sake of his own pride if nothing else, it was better to stay the hell away from town. He repeated the advice to himself like a mantra, over and over, until he should have gotten it right.

Even as his old red pickup sped toward town late Tuesday morning, he was muttering it to himself, swearing that he'd have lunch with Luke and Jordan at Rosa's Mexican Café, then turn right around and go back to White Pines. A couple of beers and a plate of Rosa's spiciest food would wipe all thoughts of Melissa straight out of his head.

Unfortunately he hadn't counted on his brothers getting into the act. He'd been certain that they would leave the subject of his love life alone. He hadn't counted on the fact that both of them were now happily married and apparently intent on seeing that he took the plunge, too.

"Hey, Cody, why don't you drop by Dolan's as long as you're in town?" Jordan suggested after they'd eaten. He said it with all the innocence of Harlan at his matchmaking best.

"Any particular reason I should?" he inquired, refusing to fall into Jordan's trap.

He lifted the cold bottle of beer to his lips and took a long, slow drink just to show how unaffected he was by the prospect of seeing Melissa, whom Jordan clearly knew worked at Dolan's. This was probably the whole reason his brothers had suggested meeting in town in the first place rather than gathering at White Pines. They'd been plotting behind his back to try to force a reunion between Cody and his ex-lover.

"They still have the best milk shakes in the whole state of Texas," Luke chimed.

"We've just eaten enough food to stuff a horse," Cody stated flatly.

Luke and Jordan exchanged a look.

"Worried about your handsome figure?" Luke taunted.

Cody scowled at his oldest brother's nonsense. "No."

Luke went on as if he'd never spoken. "Because if that's it, I'm sure they have diet sodas in there, served up by the sweetest gal in all of Texas, or so I hear."

"I don't want a milk shake. I don't want a diet soda. There is nothing that drugstore has that I want," he said pointedly, scowling first at Luke and then at Jordan.

"Sounds to me like a man who's protesting too much," Jordan observed. "What does it sound like to you, Lucas?"

"Definitely a man who's scared out of his britches," Luke agreed.

Cody drew himself up indignantly. "Scared of what? A milk shake?"

"Maybe not that," Luke conceded. "How about Melissa Horton?"

Ah, a direct hit. Cody sighed. "I am not scared of Melissa," he said with extreme patience. "I feel absolutely nothing for Melissa."

"Cluck, cluck, cluck," Luke murmured, making a pitiful attempt to mimic a chicken.

The sound grated on Cody's nerves. He balled his hands into fists. He hadn't gotten into a rip-roaring fight with his big brothers in a very long time, but Luke was pushing every one of his buttons. And, from the teasing glint in his eyes, his big brother knew it, too. Even Jordan sensed that his patience was at an end. He eased his chair between them, a conciliatory expression on his face.

"Now, Luke, don't rile Cody," he said blandly. "If he says he doesn't want to talk to Melissa, then who are we to interfere?"

Cody didn't exactly trust Jordan's sudden taking of his side. Jordan had a knack for sneak attacks that could cripple a business adversary before he even knew he was under seige. Cody eyed him warily.

"That's true," Luke conceded, his turnaround just as suspicious. "Daddy meddled in our lives enough that we should be more sensitive to Cody's feelings. Besides, Melissa probably doesn't want to see him any more than he wants to see her."

"Why? Is she involved with someone?" Cody asked, regretting the words the instant they slipped out of his mouth. The triumphant expressions on Luke's and Jordan's faces were enough to set his teeth on edge.

Jordan stood as if he'd just recalled a business crisis that couldn't be put off. "Come on, Luke. We've obviously accomplished our mission here," he said blithely. "The man is on the hook. Let's leave him to decide whether to wiggle off or take the bait."

"A fascinating metaphor," Luke commented, joining Jordan. He glanced back at Cody. The teasing glint in his eyes faded. "Don't be a damned fool, little brother. Go see the woman. You know you want to. It's time you settled things with her once and for all. We want you back here for good."

Cody finished the beer after they'd gone. He thought about ordering another one, but decided against it. It would only be delaying the inevitable. Some sick, perverse part of him wanted to see Melissa, just as Luke had guessed. He needed to know if that reaction he'd felt at the church had been a fluke or the undeniable response of a man for the woman he'd belatedly realized that he'd always loved.

He paid the check—his damned brothers had stiffed him on the bill, on top of everything else— and then headed down Main Street. In the middle of the block he hesitated, staring across at the front of the drugstore that had been his favorite hangout as a teenager. His and Melissa's.

Little had changed. Dolan's Drugstore was still printed in neat black, gold-edged letters on the door. A display of toys sat on the shelf beneath the big plate-glass window, visible to any child passing by. A rack of comic books stood off to the side. Cody suspected they were the same faded editions that had been there a decade before. The toys looked suspiciously familiar, too. In fact, when he'd crossed the street for a closer look, he was almost certain that there was a ten-year layer of dust on the red, toy fire truck.

Telling himself he was fifty kinds of crazy for going inside, he found himself turning the knob on the door anyway. A bell tinkled overhead, alerting anyone working that a customer had entered.

The soda fountain was on his left, partially blocked by a section of shelves with first-aid supplies and a new display of condoms. Talk about times changing. He couldn't think of a better example. He recalled the first time he'd ever come into the store to buy condoms. They'd been behind the pharmacy counter then. He'd blushed brick red when he'd had to ask Mabel Hastings to give them to him. It was a wonder he'd ever gone back. His only consolation had been that she'd seemed even more embarrassed. After that he'd always made sure Eli was on duty when he'd returned for a new supply.

A half-dozen teenage girls were sitting on one side of the U-shaped soda fountain, probably discussing schoolwork, or, more likely, boys. An equal number of boys was on the opposite side, tongue-tied and uncertain. The sight of them brought back a slew of memories best forgotten.

There was no sign of Melissa, though clearly someone had served the kids their shakes and hamburgers. Cody fought a bitter feeling of disappointment. He hadn't wanted to come here, but now that he had gathered the courage, he wanted to get this encounter out of the way. He wanted to shove the past behind him once and for all. He doubted a meeting would be enough to keep him in Texas, but maybe it would buy him some peace of mind.

"Hey, Missy, customer!" one of the boys shouted as Cody slid onto a stool close to the cash register.

"I'll be right there," a voice capable of raising goose bumps on any man past puberty sang out from the back.

The door to the storeroom swung open. Melissa emerged, her arms loaded with two trays of glasses piled atop each other. Her gaze zeroed in on Cody with impeccable precision. Every bit of color washed from her face. The trays wobbled, then tilted. Glasses crashed to the floor. Her gaze never wavered from his, despite the sound of breaking glass.

Several of the teenagers sprang to their feet and rushed to clean up the mess. Cody couldn't have moved if his life had depended on it. Apparently Melissa couldn't, either. Not even the swirl of activity at her feet caught her attention. He felt as if he'd been punched in the gut.

This definitely wasn't the reaction he'd been

praying for. In fact, it was exactly the opposite. He'd wanted to look into those soft, sea green eyes of hers and feel eighteen months of hurt and anger boiling into a fine rage. Or, better yet, he'd wanted to feel nothing at all.

Instead it appeared his hormones were very glad to see her. Obviously they had a different sort of memory pattern than his brain.

"Missy, are you okay?" one of the boys asked worriedly. He scowled in Cody's direction.

"Fine," she murmured.

The youngster, who looked all of fourteen, clearly wasn't convinced. Just as clearly, he had a big-time crush on Melissa. "Is he a problem?" he inquired, nodding toward Cody.

Apparently the boy's itch to slay dragons for her got her attention as nothing else had. She jerked her gaze away from Cody and smiled at the teenager.

"It's okay, David. Cody and I have known each other a long time." She patted his shoulder. "Thanks for cleaning up the glass, you guys. Your sodas are on me."

"Nah, you don't have to do that," David said, pulling money out of his pocket and leaving it on the counter. "Right, guys?"

The other boys dutifully nodded and pulled out their own cash. Unless costs at Dolan's had risen dramatically, they were very generous tippers, Cody noted as all of the teens departed.

"See you tomorrow," David called back from the doorway. He lingered uncertainly for another minute, as if he couldn't make up his mind whether

Cody was to be trusted. When Melissa shot him another reassuring smile, he finally took off to catch up with his friends.

"Quite an admirer," Cody said. "I think he was ready to mop up the floor with me."

"David is just testing his flirting skills. I'm safer than those girls in his own class. He knows I won't laugh at him."

"Maybe you should. Better to hurt him now than later," he said with unmistakable bitterness.

Melissa looked as if he'd struck her. "I'm not going to hurt him at all. He's just a boy, Cody." She straightened her spine and glowered at him. "Look, if you came in here just to hassle me, you can turn right around and go back wherever you came from. I don't need the aggravation."

Cody grinned at the bright patches of color in her cheeks. Melissa had always had a quick temper. He suddenly realized he'd missed sparring with her almost as much as he'd missing making love with her.

"Actually, I came in for a milk shake," he said, coming to a sudden decision to play this scene all the way through. He propped his elbows on the counter. He waited until he'd caught her gaze, then lowered his voice to a seductive whisper. "A chocolate shake so thick, I'll barely be able to suck it very, very slowly through the straw."

The patches of color in Melissa's cheeks deepened. She twirled around so fast it was a wonder she didn't knock a few more pieces of glassware onto the floor with the breeze she stirred.

With her rigid back to him, Cody was able to observe her at his leisure. Her snug, faded jeans fit her cute little butt like a glove. That much hadn't changed, he noted with satisfaction. With every stretch, the cropped T-shirt she wore kept riding up to bare an intriguing inch or so of a midriff so perfect that it could make a man weep. Her long dark hair with its shimmering red highlights had been scooped up in a saucy ponytail that made her look a dozen years younger than the twenty-seven he knew she was.

And, to his very sincere regret, she made him every bit as hard now as she had as a teenager. He squirmed in a wasted effort to get more comfortable on the vinyl-covered stool.

When she finally turned back, she plunked his milk shake onto the counter with such force half of it sloshed out of the tall glass. Apparently she wasn't entirely immune to him, either, and she wasn't one bit happier about the discovery.

She grabbed up a dishrag and began scrubbing the opposite side of the counter, her back to him. Given the energy she devoted to the task, the surface was either very dirty or she was avoiding him.

"So, how've you been?" Cody inquired, managing the nonchalant tone with supreme effort.

"Fine," she said tersely, not even glancing around.

He frowned. Why the hell was she acting like the injured party here? She was the one who'd cheated on him. Getting her to meet him halfway became an irresistible challenge.

"How are you, Cody? It's been a long time," he coached.

She turned and glared. "Why are you here?" she demanded instead.

He could have shot back a glib retort, but he didn't. He actually gave the question some thought. He considered the teasing he'd gotten from Jordan and Luke. He considered his own undeniable curiosity. He even considered the size of his ego, which had found being cheated on damned hard to take. The bottom line was, he had no idea what had drawn him across the street and into the drugstore.

"I don't know," he finally admitted.

Apparently it was the right answer because her lush, kissable mouth curved into a smile for the first time since she'd spotted him at the counter.

"You mean to tell me that there's something that actually stymies the brilliant, confident Cody Adams?"

He nodded slowly. "It surprises the dickens out of me, too."

She leaned back against the counter, her elbows propped behind her. It was a stance that drew attention to her figure, though Cody doubted she was aware of it.

"You planning on sticking around?" she asked.

"A few more days, just till Daddy's got his feet back under him again." It was the same response he'd given everyone who'd asked. Now that he was right here with Melissa in front of him, though, he wondered if she might not be the one person who could change his mind.

At the mention of his father, her expression immediately filled with concern. "It must be horrible for him."

"It is."

"And the rest of you?"

"We're doing okay. Mostly we're worried about Daddy. He adored Mother. It's going to be lonely as hell for him with her gone."

"I'm surprised you're not staying, then."

He shook his head. "There's nothing for me here anymore," he said automatically, refusing to concede that he had evidence to the contrary in the tightening of his groin at the first sight of her.

She actually blanched at his harsh words. "I'm sorry," she whispered, looking shaken. "What about White Pines? You always loved it. You were building your whole future around running that ranch."

She was right about that. He'd fought tooth and nail to get Harlan to trust him with the running of the ranch. He'd spent his spare time building his own house on the property just to make the point that, unlike Luke or Jordan, he never intended to leave. Then in a matter of seconds after catching Melissa with Brian, he'd thrown it all away.

Now, rather than addressing his longing to be working that land again, he shoved those feelings aside and clung instead to the bitterness that had sent him away.

"There's no way I can stay here now," he said, unable to prevent the accusing note that had crept into his voice. "You ruined it for me."

Melissa swallowed hard, but she kept her gaze on him steady. Some part of him admired her for not backing down.

"Maybe we should talk about what happened, Cody. Maybe if we could put it behind us, you'd change your mind about staying. Your decision to stay or go shouldn't have anything to do with me."

Talk about finding her in the arms of his best friend? Analyze it and pick it apart, until his emotions were raw? Cody practically choked on the idea. Once he got started on that subject, he doubted the conversation would remain polite or quiet. Eli would be bolting out from behind the prescription counter and Mabel, whom he'd spotted lurking over toward the cosmetics, would get a blistering earful.

No, he absolutely did not want to talk about the past. Or the present. And most definitely not about the bleak, lonely future he'd carved out for himself.

He slid off the stool and backed up a step. "There's nothing to say," he said, hoping his tone and his demeanor were forbidding enough to keep Melissa silent. He slapped a five on the counter, then tipped his hat.

"It's been a pleasure," he said in a tone that declared just the opposite.

He had made it almost to the door when he heard a soft gasp of dismay behind him. He stepped aside just as Velma Horton opened the door and pushed a stroller inside. His gaze went from Velma's shocked expression to the chubby-cheeked little girl who promptly reached her arms up toward him, a thoroughly engaging smile on her face. He stared at the toddler in stunned silence, then pivoted slowly to stare at Melissa. Her face was ashen, removing any doubt at all that the baby was hers.

For the second time in a matter of minutes Cody felt as if he'd been hit below the belt. He could count backward as quickly as anyone in Texas. That darling little girl with the big eyes and innocent smile looked to be a year old, which meant she was Brian's.

His blood felt like ice water in his veins, but he forced himself to walk back toward the soda fountain. "I see congratulations are in order," he said so politely it made his teeth ache. "Your daughter is beautiful."

"Thank you," Melissa said so softly that he could barely hear her.

"I guess you and Brian were meant to be, after all," he said, then turned on his heel and bolted for the door before he made an absolute idiot of himself.

He brushed past Velma and the baby without giving them a second glance. Damn, Melissa! She'd turned him inside out again. For a fleeting moment he'd actually wondered if he could put the past behind him and move on, maybe get something going with her again since his body was as hot for her now as it had been eighteen months ago. He'd allowed old feelings to stir to life, indulged in a few quick and steamy fantasies.

One look at that baby had shattered any possibility of that. He should have known that Melissa and Brian were together. He should have guessed that the betrayal was more serious than the one-night stand he'd tried desperately to convince himself it was. He should have realized that neither of them would have cheated on him for anything less than powerful emotions they couldn't control. He should have given them credit for that much at least. He couldn't make up his mind, though, if that should make him feel better or worse.

It wasn't until he was back at White Pines, riding hell-bent for leather across the open land trying to work off his anger and his pain that he stopped to wonder why Jordan and Luke would have set him up for such a terrible sucker punch. Couldn't they just have told him and saved him the anguish of making a fool of himself over Melissa all over again?

Instead they had taunted him into going into Dolan's. They had poked and prodded at all of his old feelings for Melissa until he could no longer ignore them. Would they have done that if they'd known about Brian? If they'd known about the baby? Harlan had done his share of nudging, too. He'd been the first to plant the seed about finding Melissa at Dolan's.

It didn't make a lick of sense. How could they not have known? It was a small town. Harlan sure as hell knew everything that went on. And yet they had sent him like a lamb to slaughter, straight back to Melissa.

He reined in his horse and sat for a long time contemplating the possibilities. For once in his life he was oblivious to the raw beauty of the land surrounding him. Since he knew damned well his brothers weren't cruel, their actions had to mean something. At the very least, he'd bet that Melissa and Brian weren't married, after all. At the most...

He thought of that cute little girl who'd practically begged him to pick her up.

He didn't even want to consider the astonishing, incredible idea that had just popped into his head. What if she was his? What if he was actually a father?

He tried the idea on for size and realized that a silly grin had spread across his face. A father? Yes, indeed, the possibility fit as well as those tight little jeans had caressed Melissa's fanny.

Then his grin faded as he considered all the time he'd lost if it were true. If that little girl was his, he resolved there was going to be hell to pay.

Chapter Four

Melissa stood over Sharon Lynn's crib and stared down at her sleeping child. The baby's cheeks were flushed, her dark blond hair curling damply against her chubby neck. Her blue nightshirt was sprinkled with tiny yellow ducks. A larger, stuffed duck was cuddled next to her. It had been her favorite toy ever since she'd been to a duck pond a few months before. She refused to go to bed without it.

A smile curved Melissa's lips as she watched her baby and fought the desperate need to pick her up, to cling to her. She hadn't been able to let her daughter out of her sight since that terrible moment in the drugstore when Cody had come face-to-face with his child. In that instant her heart had ricocheted wildly and her breath had caught in her throat as she'd waited for him to recognize Sharon Lynn as his, just as Jordan had the very first time he'd spotted her. She'd almost been grateful that the decision to tell Cody or not to tell him had been taken out of her hands.

But instead of promptly recognizing the baby as his, Cody had clearly leapt to the conclusion that someone else was the father. Given the cold glint in his eyes when he'd stepped back to the counter to congratulate her in a voice devoid of emotion and his comment about her relationship with Brian having been meant to be, he must have assumed the father was Brian Kincaid. It was a further complication in an already complicated situation.

She sighed as she considered the terrible mess she had made of things. She should have told Cody everything straight off, right then and there, but her mother's terrified expression and her earlier dire warnings had kept Melissa silent, too fearful of the consequences of blurting out the truth.

She couldn't imagine what her life would be like without her baby. As difficult as things had gotten after she'd learned she was pregnant, there had never been a single instant when she'd regretted having Cody's child. Every time she looked into that precious face, she saw a miracle that she and Cody had created together. Beyond that biological tie, however, Cody had no right at all to claim his child. She was the only parent Sharon Lynn had ever known. If only she could keep it that way.

Unfortunately, though, there was no way the truth could be kept hidden forever. Cody had already seen his daughter. His brother knew that Sharon Lynn was Cody's. Sooner or later the pieces of the puzzle would come together, and when they did, she didn't have a doubt in her mind what Cody's reaction would be. If he'd been furious when he'd thought she was cheating on him with his best friend, he would destroy her when he found out about the baby she'd kept from him. Maybe he wouldn't fight her for custody as her mother feared, but he would make her life into the hell she deserved for deceiving him in the first place.

She rubbed her knuckles against Sharon Lynn's soft skin and sighed again. There was so much of Cody in her daughter. She had the same stubborn tilt to her chin, the same dark blond hair that streaked with gold in the summer sun. And, for the most part, she had the same sunny disposition and laughing eyes Cody had had before he thought Melissa had betrayed him.

It had hurt today to glimpse the old teasing Cody, only to see him vanish in the space of a heartbeat at the first mention of the past. When he'd walked out of Dolan's, her heart had been heavy with the burden of guilt and fear.

"I have to be the one to tell him," she whispered finally, her fingers caressing that precious cheek. "I have to tell your daddy all about you."

Maybe by revealing the truth herself, before he learned it from someone else, she would have some small chance of earning his forgiveness. They could work out a solution together.

Tomorrow, she vowed. First thing tomorrow afternoon when she got off work, she would drive out to White Pines and tell Cody everything. And then she would pray that it didn't cost her the only person on earth she held dear.

Too restless to stay in one place for long as he contemplated how to go about discovering whether Melissa's baby was his, Cody drove over to visit Jordan and Kelly. Six-year-old Dani was always a distraction and he just might get a chance to hold that nephew of his. He had a hunch it would be a bittersweet sensation given what he suspected about Melissa's child being his own.

"Uncle Cody!" Dani screamed when she caught sight of him. She ran and leapt into his arms, planting kisses all over his face. "I really, really missed you."

The weight of her in his arms, the peppermint-sticky kisses, filled him with nostalgia and accomplished exactly what he'd hoped for. "I really missed you, too, pumpkin. I'm sorry I didn't get to take those kittens you had for me awhile back."

She patted his cheek consolingly. "That's okay. Francie had more. Want to see? One is all black with a white nose. I think you'll really, really like him."

He grinned. "I bet I will," he agreed. "We'll go see him later."

"We'd better go now," Dani protested. "Later it will be my bedtime."

"Give me a few minutes inside to say hello to

your mom," he negotiated. "I'm sure it won't be your bedtime then."

Dani braced her hands against his chest, leaned back in his arms and studied him intently. "You promise you won't leave without going to see the kittens?"

"I promise," he said, solemnly crossing his heart as he put her down.

"Okay," she said cheerfully, and ran toward the house screaming, "Mommy, Uncle Cody's here and he says he's going to take one of Francie's kittens."

"Thank goodness," Kelly called back as she emerged from the house, a grin on her face. "Conned you again, huh?"

He chuckled. "If you're not careful, that child of yours is going to be the biggest scam artist in the entire United States."

"I prefer to think she'll have a career in diplomacy or maybe negotiating strike settlements," Kelly said. "Come on in. Jordan's still at the office, but he should be home soon."

His sister-in-law surveyed him closely. "How are you? You look lousy."

"Obviously Dani isn't the only one in the family with a silver tongue."

Kelly didn't bat an eye. "Did you see Melissa today?"

"I'm sure you know perfectly well that your husband and Luke badgered me into it."

"They said they were going to try. I wasn't sure if it had worked."

"I saw her," he admitted. "And her baby." He watched closely for Kelly's reaction. She remained expressionless.

"I see," she said blandly, keeping her attention focused on the vegetables she was chopping. "How did it go?"

Cody thought she was working awfully darned hard to feign disinterest. "Fine for the first few minutes, ugly after that."

"Oh, Cody," she protested softly. "Isn't it time you settled things with her and came home for good?"

Suddenly he didn't want to pursue the topic. He needed a break from it. They could get into it again when Jordan got home. Hopefully his brother would have answers that Kelly couldn't or wouldn't give him.

"I don't want to talk about Melissa right now. First I want to catch a glimpse of that brand new baby boy of yours," he declared just as Jordan came in and dropped a kiss on his wife's cheek.

"Hey, little brother, what brings you by?" Jordan asked, sneaking a carrot from the pile Kelly had just cut up.

"He's going to take a kitten," Dani chimed in. "Can we go see them now, Cody? It's later."

Since going to see the kittens would keep him from having to deal with the subject of Melissa and her baby a little longer, Cody stood and headed for the kitchen door. Dani tucked her hand in his.

"You should probably take two kittens," she said on the way out. "One might get lonely."

"Listen, young lady, I said one kitten," he protested over the sound of Kelly and Jordan's laughter.

"But you were going to take two last time." Apparently she caught his stern expression because she gave a little shrug of resignation. "I bet you'll change your mind when you see them."

A half hour later he was back in the kitchen with two kittens in a box. Dani had been giving him very precise instructions on caring for them ever since they'd left the barn. Kelly's expression turned smug when she saw him.

"You are pitiful," Jordan said, shaking his head. "Is there a female on the face of the earth you can resist?"

"Who are you kidding?" Cody shot back, gesturing to the big tomcat that was curled in Jordan's lap purring contentedly. "You always hated cats and now you're surrounded by them. I don't hear you complaining."

"You may not hear it," Kelly said, "but it is almost the last thing I hear every single night. He says 'Good night, I love you, no more cats,' all in one breath."

"I do not," Jordan said, dislodging the cat and pulling Kelly onto his lap.

Cody listened to their banter and watched their undisguised affection with envy. Until he'd lost Melissa he'd never thought he wanted marriage and kids. He'd been as commitment-phobic as any one of those jerks who made the rounds of the talk shows. Ironically, ever since their breakup, all he'd been able to think about was settling down and having kids. He'd deliberately isolated himself in Wyoming so he'd be far from the temptation to try something at which he knew he'd inevitably fail.

After all, he hadn't appreciated Melissa when he'd had her and she was as sexy and generous, as kind and intelligent, as any woman he'd ever known. He'd had a roving eye, just the same. He'd taken her for granted, which everyone in the family had accused him of doing at one time or another. He suspected he'd do the same with a wife. What was the point of ruining some woman's life for his own selfish longing to have just a taste of the kind of love Jordan and Luke had found?

"How long are you sticking around? Have you told your boss when you'll be back in Wyoming?" Jordan asked after Kelly insisted Cody stay for dinner.

Kelly dished up a serving of stew for him and lingered at his shoulder. "You are not going back until after J.J. is baptized," she said emphatically.

Cody glanced up at her. "When is that again?"

"Next weekend, which you know perfectly well. I sent you an invitation. We're going ahead with it. Harlan insisted."

Something in his expression must have given him away because she frowned. "You ripped it up, didn't you?"

Cody recalled the scattered pieces of the pretty blue invitation and felt a tide of red rising in his cheeks. Was the woman a damned witch?

"Of course not," he fibbed.

The response drew a disbelieving snort. "So you'll be here at least that long," she said.

Cody had a feeling once he learned the truth about Melissa's baby, he wouldn't be able to get away from Texas fast enough. He'd need to cool his temper for a good long while before confronting her with what he knew. He'd also need time to make up his mind exactly what he wanted to do about the baby she'd kept from him. He intended to learn that truth in the next twenty-four hours.

"Sorry," he said eventually. "I can't promise to stay that long."

Kelly glanced at Jordan, then back at him. "Your brothers said you were going to say no," she said.

"I had no idea I was so predictable."

"Lately you are," his sister-in-law said. "Lately, you've gotten downright boring."

He gave her a wry look. "More of that fatal charm, I see."

Kelly frowned at his teasing. "What if I told you that Jordan and I want you to be the baby's godfather?"

Something deep inside him shifted at the offer. He felt an unexpected warm glow. It was a feeling he told himself he didn't deserve, especially not if he had a real child of his own he'd never even acknowledged.

"I'd say you made a lousy choice," he responded.

"I told you he wouldn't even be gracious about it," Jordan chimed in. "Leave him be, Kelly. He's as stubborn as the rest of us when he digs in his heels. He'll change his mind, if we let the idea simmer long enough.''

''I won't change my mind,'' Cody said. ''Sorry.''

''You say that a lot these days,'' Jordan observed.

''Maybe I have a lot to be sorry for.''

''Well, this is one thing you can check off the list,'' Jordan said.

He spoke in that matter-of-fact way that indicated he'd reached a decision and wanted no further argument. It was a tactic that might have served him well in business, but it grated on Cody's nerves.

''I want you here, little brother,'' Jordan stated emphatically. ''And I want you to be the baby's godfather. It's settled.''

Despite his annoyance at Jordan's attempt to snatch the decision out of his hands, Cody could feel himself weakening, feel that odd, empty sensation in the pit of his stomach that always meant the loneliness was taking hold again.

''Did you check it out at the church?'' he inquired lightly. ''They'll probably be worried about lightning hitting the steeple if I show my hide in there.''

''There was some mention of that, but I believe there's a general consensus that your soul is still salvageable,'' Kelly said. ''Please, Cody. We've missed you. It's only for a few days more. How bad can that be?''

A few days, one hour, any time at all would be hell, especially if he discovered in the meantime that he had a baby of his own. Still, Cody had never been able to resist his sister-in-law. Kelly had been coaxing him into trouble since they were toddlers. Jordan had been too stuffy even at seven to fall in with some of her more outrageous mischief, though there had never been a doubt in anyone's mind that Jordan was the one she loved.

"I'll stick around," he said eventually. "Long enough to get that nephew of mine in good graces with the Lord. Then I'm heading right back out. Understood?"

"Understood," Kelly said meekly.

Kelly meek? Every alarm bell in him went off. Before he could get too caught up in trying to figure out her angle, she was gone. He was left alone with Jordan, while Kelly went upstairs to tuck Dani into bed. Suddenly the questions that had been tormenting him earlier in the day could no longer be ignored.

"Kelly mentioned that you saw Melissa and her little girl today, after you left Luke and me," Jordan said, his gaze fixed on Cody's face.

The comment gave him the perfect opening. "Why didn't you warn me?" Cody asked, trying to keep the anger out of his voice. "You knew about the baby, didn't you?"

Jordan sighed, then nodded. "I saw her once, about eight months ago. She was just a baby." He scanned Cody's face as if looking for answers. "What did you think when you saw her?"

"I figured Melissa and Brian had more going for them than I'd realized. I figured they were a happy little family now.'' Cody threw out the possibility to gauge his brother's reaction. If Jordan knew anything different, he'd find it out now.

The color washed out of Jordan's face. ''Did you say that to Melissa?''

''More or less,'' he admitted. ''Along with offering her my congratulations.''

''What did she say?''

''Nothing.''

''I see.''

Cody lost patience for the game. He knew darned well that Jordan knew more than he was saying. He could see it in his eyes. His brother was looking everywhere in the kitchen except directly at him.

''You might as well spit it out,'' he told him finally.

''What?''

''Whatever has you looking like you'd rather be in Kansas.''

A faint grin tugged at Jordan's mouth. ''Maybe Houston, not Kansas,'' he said. He sighed. ''How good a look did you get at the child?''

''Good enough,'' Cody said. He sensed that Jordan wanted him to reach a different conclusion than he'd just offered all on his own. He sucked in a deep breath. ''She's mine, isn't she?''

Once Cody had actually spoken the words out loud, Jordan nodded, confirming everything.

Cody's heart pounded. An uncommon mix of hope and dismay swirled through him. ''You know that for sure?''

''I saw it right off,'' Jordan admitted. ''She was

the spitting image of your baby pictures. I confronted Melissa about it straight out.''

Cody felt an icy chill settle over him as Jordan's earlier comment came back to him. He stood and leaned down to look his brother in the eye. ''And that was when? About eight months ago, you said?''

''Yes,'' Jordan replied softly.

''And Melissa confirmed your suspicions right then and there?'' he demanded, the hurt and anger of yet another betrayal slamming through him.

''Yes.''

''Damn you, Jordan,'' he snapped, backing up to prevent slamming a fist in his brother's face. ''How could you do that to me? How could you keep a secret like that? Didn't you think I had a right to know? Or was this another one of those big-brother-knows-best decisions?''

''She pleaded with me not to tell you,'' Jordan said simply.

Cody stared at him incredulously. ''And your loyalty was with her and not me?''

''Why the hell do you think I've done everything in my power to get you back here? I didn't want to lay this on you when you were in Wyoming. I wanted you here, so you could see for yourself. I didn't want you to accuse me or her of making it up just to get you back here.''

Cody wasn't buying it. ''No, you were more concerned with keeping your promise to a woman who betrayed me than you were with doing what was

right—giving me a chance to know my own child.''
He turned on his heel and headed for the door, the
box of kittens in tow. ''I can't believe you would
do something like this. Maybe family loyalty
doesn't mean anything once you're a big corporate
executive. Is that it, big brother?''

''Cody, you have it all wrong,'' Kelly protested
when she came back into the kitchen. Obviously
she had overheard the tail end of the argument.

''I don't think so,'' he snapped, shooting her a
look of regret. ''Don't expect me at the baptism,
after all. In fact, forget you even know me.''

Kelly called out after him. He heard the screen
door slam behind her, then Jordan murmuring
something he couldn't quite make out. Whatever it
was, though, it silenced her. When he looked back
as he drove away, he saw them standing on the
porch staring after him. He was sure it was only his
imagination, but he thought he saw his brother wip-
ing something that might have been tears from his
cheeks.

He slowed the car momentarily and closed his
eyes against the tide of anguish washing through
him. Melissa had done it again. She had come between him and his family. He vowed then and there
it would be the last time. This time he wouldn't
run. He wouldn't let her control his destiny as he
had before.

Forgetting all about his resolve to let his temper
cool, an hour later he was in town, pounding on the
Hortons' front door. Ken Horton, wearing a robe

and slippers, opened it a crack. At the sight of Cody, he swung it wider, a welcoming smile spreading across his weathered face. Cody could see Velma's panicky expression as she stared over her husband's shoulder.

"Cody, what on earth?" Horton grumbled. "You trying to wake the whole neighborhood?"

"Where's Melissa?"

"She's not here," he said as his wife tugged frantically on his arm. When he leaned down, she whispered something in his ear, something that wiped any lingering expression of welcome from his face. "Go on home, Cody."

"Not until you tell me where she is."

"Don't make me call the sheriff."

"Don't make me pound the information out of you," Cody shot back belligerently.

Ken Horton regarded him sympathetically. "Boy, go on home and get some sleep. If you've got things to talk over with Melissa, do it in the morning, when you're calmer."

Despite his earlier promise to himself to think things through clearly, Cody realized he didn't want to be calm when he talked to Melissa. He wanted this rage to keep him focused, to keep him immune to the sight of her. He wanted to have this out with her while he was hot with anger, not lust.

"If I have to knock on every door in town, I'm going to talk to her tonight," he swore.

"There's nothing you have to say, nothing you need to know, that won't be settled just as readily in the morning,'' Horton repeated, still calm, still intractable.

Cody considered it as much as an admission that he and Melissa had serious issues to resolve, such as his relationship to that baby. He gathered from the warning look Horton shot at his now tearful wife that they didn't entirely agree on whether Cody had the right to know the truth.

''Where can I find her in the morning?'' he asked finally, resigned to the delay. They all knew he wouldn't tear through town, creating yet another ruckus he'd never live down.

''She gets to work about nine,'' her father told him.

''I'm not talking to her at Dolan's,'' he said. ''I don't want the whole town knowing our business.''

Horton seemed about to offer an alternative when Velma piped up. ''That'll just have to do,'' she said. ''We're not telling you where she lives.''

He couldn't decide if Velma was worried about him throttling Melissa or if she was simply being protective of her daughter's secret. Because he wasn't sure, he backed down.

''If you talk to her, let her know I'll be by the minute the doors open. Tell her to arrange with Eli for someone to cover for her unless she wants her personal life broadcast to everyone in town.''

To his surprise, Ken Horton held out his hand. When Cody shook it, Melissa's father said, ''For whatever it's worth, Cody, I think it's about time you two got everything out in the open. The two of you had something special once. Melissa's been punished enough for making one foolish mistake.''

He gave his wife a defiant look. ''And a man has a right to claim his child.''

Velma Horton groaned and covered her face with her hands. Tears spilled down her cheeks. Cody wondered at the fear he'd seen in her eyes right before she placed her hands over them. She'd had the same terrified expression earlier in the day. He'd always thought Velma Horton liked him. Now she seemed to think he was some sort of a monster.

Was she blaming him for running out on her pregnant daughter? Or was it something more? He wondered what could possibly be behind the expression he'd read in her eyes.

Eventually, as he slowly walked back to his pickup, it came to him. She was actually afraid that he'd come home to take his baby away from Melissa.

Was that what he intended? He sat in his truck on the dark street in front of the Hortons' house, his head resting on the steering wheel. He honestly hadn't thought beyond discovering the truth and confronting Melissa with it.

Obviously, it was a good thing Ken Horton had prevented him from seeing Melissa tonight. He needed to get his thoughts in order. He needed to have a plan. For once in his life he couldn't act on impulse. Too many lives were at stake, his own, Melissa's, and that darling little girl's.

His heart ached every time he thought about his daughter. His arms felt empty, just as they did when

Dani climbed out of them or he had to turn Angela back over to Jessie or Luke. He wondered about that vacant place he'd thought would always be inside him and realized that there was someone who could fill it, a child of his own.

Tomorrow he would claim her. He realized he didn't even know her name or how old she was or whether she could walk or talk. So many precious details. He sighed. Tomorrow he would fill in the gaps.

Tomorrow he would finally experience what it was like to feel like a father. Right now it was all too abstract, but in the morning he would hold his child in his arms. Whatever else happened between him and Melissa, he vowed that nothing would ever rip his baby away from him again.

Chapter Five

Her mother had warned her. In fact, the first thing out of Velma's mouth when Melissa had dropped off her daughter for the day had been a detailed description of Cody's late-night visit. Based on Velma's panicked reaction, Melissa had been tempted to take Sharon Lynn and flee. She knew, though, that in his present mood Cody would only track her down.

Besides, hadn't she resolved just last night to tell him herself about Sharon Lynn? The decision on the timing had just been taken out of her hands. Of course, that also meant that his anger had had all night to simmer. She walked to work, dreading the confrontation that was clearly only minutes away.

She meant to ask Eli for an hour or so off to deal

with a personal matter. She meant to be outside, on the sidewalk, when Cody arrived. She meant to do everything possible to ensure their conversation took place in private, away from prying eyes and potential gossip. She meant to be calm, reasonable, even conciliatory.

Cody took any chance of that out of her hands.

Before the door to the drugstore fully closed behind her, Melissa heard the bell ring loudly as the door slammed open again. Without even turning around, she sensed it was Cody. The air practically crackled with tension. She pivoted reluctantly and found him so close she could almost feel his breath on her face. She surveyed him slowly from head to toe, trying to gauge exactly how furious he was.

He looked exhausted. His mouth was set in a grim line. His shoulders were stiff. His hands were balled into fists. He also looked as if he'd slept in his clothes, perhaps in his truck, right in front of the drugstore. That would explain why he'd appeared right on her heels.

Despite all that, her heart flipped over. Her pulse scrambled. She had the most absurd desire to fling herself straight into his arms.

But she couldn't. More precisely, she didn't dare. It would only complicate an already impossible situation. She sucked in a deep breath and waited. The first move was going to have to be his.

As she waited, she was suddenly aware of every sound, every movement. She could hear the hum of the electric clock, the rattle of plastic bottles and *ping, ping, ping* of pills being counted out as Eli filled a prescription in the back, the swish of a mop as Mabel dusted the floor. Mabel rounded the aisle of shelves, caught sight of the silent tableau at the front of the store and stopped and stared.

Melissa felt like screaming. Mabel's presence was anticipated, but unfortunate. Of all the people in town, she was the most likely to spread word of every last detail of any encounter between Melissa and Cody. Her pale eyes sparkled as she watched the two of them.

Cody tipped his hat to Mabel, but didn't extend even that much courtesy to Melissa before latching on to her arm and practically hauling her into the storage room, past the startled gaze of Eli Dolan. Cody kicked the door shut behind them, plunging them into darkness.

"Dammit, Cody, what do you think you're doing?" Melissa demanded, trying to wrench herself free and reach the light switch at the same time. She couldn't succeed at doing either one.

"We need to talk," he declared, seemingly oblivious to the lack of light.

"Fine. Then let's do it like two civilized adults. There's no need for your caveman routine."

He was close enough that she could see that his eyes sparked fire, but he released his grip on her. Melissa felt along the wall until she found the switch. She flipped it on, illuminating the room that was small under the best of conditions, but claustrophobic with Cody pacing in the cramped space.

Somehow he managed to neatly avoid the stacks of just-delivered boxes, metal shelves of inventory

and a disorderly array of cleaning supplies. Melissa
had the feeling that he was practically daring the
inanimate objects to give him an excuse to knock
them all to the floor. She couldn't recall ever seeing
him quite so angry or quite so speechless. Cody's
glib tongue was known far and wide, especially
among women.

She kept silent and waited. Finally he stopped in
front of her, his hands shoved in his pockets, legs
spread, a belligerent expression on his handsome
face.

"Whose baby is it?" he demanded in a tone that
made her hackles rise.

Melissa made up her mind then and there that
she wasn't giving in to his bullying or to any coaxing he might decide to try when that failed. Maybe
that had been the problem in the past. She'd been
too darned easy on him, too much in love to ever
say no. She hoisted her chin a challenging
notch. They were going to have a conversation on
her terms for a change.

"Good morning to you, too, Cody."

Cody's gaze narrowed at the sarcasm. "Dammit,
I asked you a straight question. The least you could
do is give me a straight answer."

She wasn't sure where she found the courage to
face him down, but she did. "Why should I, when
you're acting like a bully?"

"I think I have a right to act any damn way I
please."

"No," she said softly. "You don't. I told you
before that we can discuss this like two civilized

adults or I can go into the other room and go to work.''

He raked his hand through his hair in a gesture that was vintage Cody. She'd always been able to tell exactly how frustrated or annoyed he was by the disheveled state of his hair.

''If that baby's mine, I have a right to know,'' he retorted, his voice starting to climb.

''I was under the impression that you already know the answer to that. You certainly carried on as if you did when you dropped in on my parents last night.''

He didn't look even vaguely chagrined by the reminder of his outrageous behavior on her parents' doorstep. ''I want to hear it from you,'' he snapped. ''I want to hear why you kept it from me. If I am that child's father, I should have been told about her way back when you first discovered you were pregnant. I had a right to know. We should have been making decisions together.''

Melissa met his gaze unflinchingly. ''You gave up any rights the day you left town without so much as a goodbye. You never got in touch. I didn't know where you were. How was I supposed to let you know?''

''Jordan knew where I was, but you made damned sure he wouldn't tell me, didn't you?''

''Because your leaving town the way you did told me everything I needed to know about how you felt about me. What was the point of dragging you back so you could tell me to kiss off?''

She could almost see his patience visibly snap.

"Dammit, Melissa, you know that I had more than enough cause to go," he practically shouted, slamming his fist into a box and sending it crashing to the floor. Judging from the shattering noise it made, it was the glasses Eli had bought to replace the supply she'd broken only the day before.

Eli opened the door a crack and peered inside, his expression anxious. "Everything okay back here?"

"Fine," Cody and Melissa said in unison. The response wasn't very heartfelt from either of them.

Eli glanced at the box on the floor and shook his head wearily. He backed away without comment and shut the door.

Throughout the interruption, Cody had kept his gaze fastened on her face, sending color flooding into her cheeks. "You know I'm right," he said more quietly the instant they were alone again. "You cheated on me."

She had known from the beginning that that was what he believed. She had even wanted him to believe it…up to a point. Even so, it hurt to hear him say it. "Still jumping to conclusions, I see. That was always one of your worst habits, Cody."

He shoved his fingers through his thick hair again. "Jumping to conclusions," he repeated incredulously. "Did you or did you not sleep with my best friend?"

She was amazed at the speed with which the conversation had veered from the subject of their daughter to the real source of Cody's fury. He'd had well over a year to work up a good head of steam on the subject and clearly he intended to vent it now, unless she put a quick stop to it.

"I did not," she told him quietly.

"See—" he began triumphantly. His expression suddenly faltered as her reply finally penetrated his thick skull. "You didn't?"

"Never," she said emphatically, her gaze unflinching.

"But I saw…"

"You saw exactly what I wanted you to see." She shrugged. "Unfortunately, you leapt to the wrong conclusion."

He stared at her blankly. "I don't get it."

It was time—way past time—to spell it out for him. "Brian and I had one date. It wasn't even a date, really. It was a setup. Brian only went along with it because he knew I was crazy about you. You were supposed to get wildly jealous, realize you were madly in love with me, and propose. You were supposed to fight for me. You weren't supposed to haul your butt out of town without looking back."

"Jealous?" He stared at her in bemusement. "How the hell was I supposed to know that? You were in his arms. What was I supposed to think, that you were discussing the weather?" he asked in a tone loud enough to wake the dead.

"You're shouting again," she observed.

He scowled. "Well, so what if I am?"

Melissa chuckled despite herself. He was too darned stubborn to recognize even what was staring him straight in the face, much less the subtleties of the trap she had tried to spring on him. No wonder it had failed so miserably. She should have issued an ultimatum in plain English if she'd wanted him to marry her, not tried to trick him into recognizing his own feelings. As for right now, he obviously needed his present circumstances clarified for him.

"Mabel's probably taking notes," she stated patiently. "Eli may be calling the sheriff. Other than that, there's no reason to quiet down that I can think of."

Cody groaned and sank onto a stack of boxes. When he finally looked at her again, she thought she detected a hint of wonder in his eyes.

"Then the baby really is mine?" he asked quietly. "Jordan was right?"

"No doubt about it, at least in anyone's mind except yours."

His gaze honed in on hers and an expression of complete awe spread over his face. "I have a baby."

"Actually, you have a *toddler,*" she corrected. "She's thirteen months old."

"Whatever," he said, clearly unconcerned with the distinction. "Tell me everything. I want to know her name. How long you were in labor. What time she was born. I want to know what she likes to eat, whether she can talk, how many steps she's taken, if she has allergies, what her favorite toy is. I want to know every last detail."

The yearning behind his words struck her. He almost sounded as if he regretted missing out on so much. His eagerness was impossible to resist. Suddenly she couldn't wait to see him with his daughter. It was something she'd dreamed about since the first moment the doctor had confirmed her pregnancy.

"Wouldn't you rather just go and meet her?" Melissa inquired softly.

He nodded, apparently speechless again.

"I'll speak to Eli and be right with you," she promised.

"Don't try ducking out the back," he warned, but he was grinning when he said it.

"I'm not the one who runs," she reminded him.

His comment might have been half-teasing, but hers was not. She wanted him to know that she was stronger now than she had been when he'd abandoned her. She wanted him to know that she was tough enough and secure enough to fight him for her daughter, if she had to.

But she also wanted him to see that she was brave enough to allow him into his child's life, if he wanted a place there. This wasn't about her any longer. It wasn't about her feelings for Cody, though those clearly hadn't died. This was about her daughter and what was best for her. It was about giving her child a chance to know her father.

Even so, as they walked down Main Street toward the tree-lined street where her family had lived her whole life, Melissa couldn't help the vague stirring of hope deep inside her. The past year and a half of loneliness and regret had been wiped out of her heart in the blink of an eye. Left in its wake was anticipation, the eager-to-start-the-day anticipation of a woman in love. As dangerous an emotion as that was, she could no more have prevented it than she could have held back the wildness of a tornado's winds.

Cody was back and she might as well admit to herself one more truth. Time and distance hadn't dulled her feelings for him a bit. She wanted him every bit as fiercely as she ever had.

Cody was in a daze. He was only marginally aware of the woman walking beside him. Instead he kept seeing images of the child that he now knew without any doubt whatsoever was his. Melissa's confirmation kept echoing over and over in his head. He was a father.

The realization was both incredible and scary. What if he blew it? What if his daughter took one look at him and rejected him? Okay, the latter was unlikely. Just the day before she had reached for him as if she already knew who he was. He recalled the eager stretch of her arms in the air and the sensation of tenderness that had welled up inside him at her innocent smile.

On the walkway at the Hortons' he paused, his hand on Melissa's arm. "Wait."

She turned a quizzical look on him. "Second thoughts?"

"No." He swallowed hard. "What's her name?"

"Sharon Lynn."

He repeated it softly, just to hear how it sounded on his tongue. "I like it."

"I'm not sure she'll tolerate being called by both when she gets a little older, but for now that's what we call her. My father tends to call her Pookie. I'm trying to break him of the habit. I will not have my child go through life being nicknamed Pookie. Missy is bad enough."

He smiled at her and barely resisted the urge to reach over and brush a strand of auburn hair from her cheek. "I never called you Missy."

"For which I was exceedingly grateful. That's probably why I let you get away with so much."

"You never let me get away with a thing," he protested.

"That baby inside says otherwise."

"I'll have to remember that," he said, grinning. "If I just whisper your name in your ear, you'll do anything I ask, is that right?"

She frowned, probably at the sudden provocative note in his voice. He knew she didn't want him to guess how easily he got to her. She was going to fight him tooth and nail.

"That was then," she said staunchly, confirming his guess. "This is now and the tide has turned, cowboy."

He readily accepted the challenge in her tone. "Is that so, Me…liss…a?" He deliberately drew her name out. Before she could react to the teasing, he lowered his head and dropped a quick kiss on her parted lips. "See, it still works."

The startled, slightly dazed expression on her face almost tempted him to try again. That brief brush of his mouth over hers had been just enough to tantalize him. Memories of warm, moist kisses and stolen caresses slammed through him, turning teasing into something very, very serious.

How had he ever walked away from her? Why hadn't he stayed and fought, just as she'd demanded earlier? Had it been the gut-deep sense of betrayal that had driven him all the way to Wyoming? Or had it simply been the even more powerful fear of the commitment to which fighting for her would have led? He'd never thought of himself as a coward, but suddenly he was taking a long, hard look at his actions in a whole new light.

"Cody?"

He blinked and gazed down into her upturned face. Before he could question himself, he scooped his hand through her silky hair to circle the back of her neck. With his gaze fixed on her turbulent sea green eyes, he reclaimed her mouth, lingering this time, savoring, remembering.

He felt her hands on his chest, tentative at first, then more certain as she slid them up to his shoulders and clung. Her body fit itself neatly, automatically, into his, the movement as natural as breathing and far, far more exciting.

Cody couldn't believe he had ever walked away from this. He couldn't imagine how he had lived without the sweetness of her kisses or the heat of her body pressed against his. The swirl of sensations was overpowering, demanding...and totally inappropriate for a sidewalk in plain view, he realized as a passing car honked and the teenage driver shouted out encouragement.

Melissa backed away as if she'd been burned. Her face was flaming with embarrassment. A warning flashed in her eyes, turning them the shade of soft jade in sunlight.

"That can't happen again," she stated emphatically.

"It can and it will," Cody said with just as much certainty. "Count on it."

Alarm flared in her expression. "No, Cody, this isn't about you and me anymore."

"Sure it is, darlin'. It always was."

"No!" She practically shouted it, as if volume might make her edict clearer. "You and I are over. You saw to that."

Cody dropped his own voice to a seductive growl. "We'll see," he taunted.

"Dammit, Cody, do you or do you not want to see your daughter?"

"Of course I do," he said, amused that she seemed to think the two concepts were diametrically opposed. "Meeting Sharon Lynn has absolutely nothing to do with my intentions toward you."

"Yes, it does," she said stubbornly.

"You're not keeping me from my daughter," he responded emphatically. "And you're not going to put up much resistance, once I set my mind to winning you back."

A scowl darkened her face. "You are the most arrogant, most infuriating man on the face of the earth. It's too late, Cody. You couldn't win me back if you courted me from now till we're both tottering around in orthopedic shoes.''

A grin tugged at his lips. ''Is that a challenge?''

''That's a guarantee.''

Chuckling at her sincere conviction that she could win a test of wills with him, he took her hand and headed for the house.

''You don't have a chance, sweet pea,'' he told her solemnly as he ushered her inside, where Velma was waiting, her gaze wary. He lowered his voice to taunt one last time, ''You don't have a snowball's chance in hell.''

Melissa never responded because her mother spoke up just then.

''You brought him,'' Velma said, her tone accusing.

''You knew I would,'' Melissa told her mother. ''Where's Sharon Lynn?''

''Down for her nap,'' she said, a note of triumph in her voice. ''There's no need to wake her.''

Cody was aware of the undercurrents between mother and daughter. Clearly, Velma was angry about his presence. Once again he had the sense that she feared him having any contact at all with his child.

Melissa shot him a vaguely apologetic look. ''I'll get her,'' she said.

He fell into step beside her. ''Don't wake her. I'll come with you. Let me just look at her for now. Your mother's right. There's no need to wake her yet.''

If he had expected the suggestion to gain

Velma's approval, he failed. He should have saved his breath. An expression of doom on her face, she trailed along behind them. He had the feeling she would have thrown herself across the threshold to the bedroom if she'd thought it would keep him away from her granddaughter.

He couldn't waste time worrying about Velma, though. From the instant he stepped into the room his gaze was riveted to the child asleep in the crib. She was sleeping on her stomach, her legs drawn up under her, her butt sticking up in the air. He couldn't imagine the position being comfortable, but she was sleeping soundly.

Awestruck, he moved closer to the crib. Melissa stayed a few steps behind him. Her mother never budged from the doorway. He studied the tiny, balled-up fists. Her skin looked soft as down and her light curls feathered around her face like wispy strands of silk. Her mouth curved like a miniature bow of pink. She was perfect. Adorable.

An overwhelming surge of protectiveness spread through him. This was his daughter. *His!* He'd seen Luke with the newborn Angela. He had watched Jordan hold J.J., but he had never guessed the depth of emotions that his brothers must have been feeling. He'd never experienced anything like it before in his life.

"She's so beautiful," he whispered, his voice choked.

"She has your eyes, your hair," Melissa said quietly.

"And your mouth," he noted. "I had no idea."

"No idea about what?"

"That it was possible to create anything so perfect."

Melissa laughed softly. "You haven't seen her throw a tantrum yet."

He turned toward her and grinned. "Ah, so she has your temper, too?"

"Oh, no," Melissa protested. "You're not blaming me for that. Every ounce of stubbornness she possesses she got from you."

Gazing directly into her eyes, he slipped an arm around her waist and pulled her close. "Thank you."

"For?"

He wasn't certain how to explain all that he was grateful to her for. For having the baby, even without him in her life. For keeping her healthy and safe. For loving her. So many things.

"For our daughter," he said simply.

"Oh, Cody," she whispered, tears welling up in her eyes and spilling down her cheeks.

"Shh, darlin', don't cry," he said, pulling her close. "You're not alone anymore."

To his astonishment, he realized that after the loneliest year and a half of his life, he was no longer alone, either. He was just a visit to the preacher away from having a family of his own. And nothing or no one was going to stand in his way.

Chapter Six

Still awestruck, Cody was knee-deep in mental wedding plans before he and Melissa walked out the front door of her parents' house. He was so caught up in thinking ahead to the day when Melissa and Sharon Lynn would move into his old house out at White Pines, that he almost forgot to ask Melissa to have dinner with him that night so he could officially propose and go over the details.

"Both of you," he told her as they stood in front of the drugstore a few minutes later. "You and Sharon Lynn. We'll go to DiPasquali's. I'll pick you up at your folks' place after you get off work."

Her lips set in a stubborn expression he knew only too well.

"Was there an invitation in there somewhere or did you mean it to sound like an order?" she asked.

He supposed they could quibble all morning over the difference, but he didn't see much point to it. They had far bigger issues to worry about, like setting a wedding date in the next week or so. Now that he'd seen his daughter, nothing was going to keep him from her. The prospect of instant parenthood scared the daylights out of him, but he was eager to get started, anxious to make up for lost time. He considered Melissa part of the package, of course.

"An invitation, of course," he said, wise enough to pacify Melissa. He wanted her in a receptive frame of mind tonight. He didn't want her stubborn streak kicking in. "Would you like to have dinner with me tonight at DiPasquali's?"

"I think your daughter is a little young for pizza."

Based on the spark of amusement in her eyes, she might have been teasing, but Cody took her comment seriously. He hadn't thought of that. In fact, what he really knew about babies would fit on the head of a pin. That was easily corrected. He would buy a book on parenting at the first opportunity. He was going to be the best-prepared father on the face of the planet, even if he was getting a late start.

"There must be something on the menu there she can eat," he said. "Or is there someplace that would be better?"

"DiPasquali's is fine," Melissa soothed. "I'll feed her first. She can chew on a slice of bread while we eat. She'll be perfectly content. She loves to eat out. She gets a lot of attention.''

''Fine, whatever,'' he murmured distractedly, already thinking ahead to what he needed to accomplish between now and dinnertime.

He wanted to buy an engagement ring. And that book on parenting, of course. If he couldn't find one in town, maybe Luke or Jordan would have one he could borrow. He needed to call Lance Treethorn and tell him he wouldn't be returning to Wyoming. And he should sit down with his father and work out an arrangement for taking over his old duties at White Pines. Harlan would probably be relieved to be sharing the workload again.

''Cody?''

''Hmm?'' He glanced up and caught Melissa's serious expression. ''What's wrong?''

''Nothing. I'm just glad you want to be part of your daughter's life.''

He stared at her, uncertain what would have made her ever suspect he'd do otherwise. ''Well, of course, I do.''

Melissa shrugged. ''I wasn't sure how you were going to feel. And Mother, well, she had this crazy idea you were going to fight me for custody.''

Cody couldn't imagine why he would have to fight for custody. He was going to claim his daughter *and* Melissa. If he'd known about the baby eighteen months ago, he would never have left for Wyoming in the first place. The incident with Brian might never have happened. He and Melissa would have been married. Custody arrangements would never have become an issue. At least, he finally understood Velma's reaction to him.

"That explains why she's been looking at me as if I'm about to steal the silver," he said.

"Yes."

"Well, she can stop worrying. We'll settle everything tonight." He leaned down and dropped a kiss on Melissa's lips. "See you later."

"Settle everything?" she repeated, a note of anxiety in her voice. "Cody!"

He turned back.

"What does that mean, we're going to settle everything?"

He smiled. "Not to worry, darlin'. We'll talk about it tonight."

"Exactly what did he say?" Velma fretted as Melissa bathed her daughter and got her ready for their evening with Cody.

"He said we'd settle everything tonight." She grabbed Sharon Lynn's rubber duck in midair as her daughter hurled it from the tub.

"What does that mean?"

Melissa sighed. "I don't know what it means, Mother. I suppose I'll find out shortly."

"I don't like it. I think your father and I should be there to protect your interests."

"I doubt Cody intends to pluck Sharon Lynn out of her high chair at the restaurant and carry her off into the night," she said as she toweled her daughter dry. "Anything other than that, I can cope with just fine on my own."

"What if he does decide to take her?"

"He won't," Melissa repeated, not sure how she knew with such conviction that Cody wouldn't do something so outrageous. "Stop worrying. I can handle Cody."

"You couldn't handle him two years ago," her mother commented. "What makes you think things are so different now?"

Melissa thought carefully about that before she answered. She used the struggle to get Sharon Lynn into her red corduroy pants and a cute little flowered shirt to buy some time.

"I'm stronger than I was then," she said eventually. "I've had almost two years to see that I don't need Cody Adams in order to survive. Sharon Lynn and I are doing just fine on our own."

Her mother regarded her skeptically. "Are you saying you're immune to him now?"

The kiss they'd shared on the front walk burned its way into her awareness. "No," she admitted. "I can't say that."

Velma groaned. "I knew it. I knew it the minute I saw the two of you playing kissy-face on the front walk."

"We were not playing kissy-face," Melissa retorted, blushing just the same. "Maybe you and Mabel have the same vocabulary after all."

"Mabel saw you kissing, too?"

"No, she just accused me of making goo-goo eyes at him way back in junior high."

"If only you'd limited yourself to that," Velma said dryly.

Melissa frowned. "If I had, we wouldn't have Sharon Lynn," she reminded her mother quietly.

Velma retreated into silence after that. She was still looking anxious when Cody arrived to pick them up. Melissa had a feeling she had her father to thank for keeping her mother from racing down the driveway after them. He appeared to have a tight grip on her elbow and a glint of determination in his eyes as he waved them off.

The ride to DiPasquali's took only minutes. It was a wonder they didn't crash into a tree, though. Cody couldn't seem to take his eyes off his daughter. Sharon Lynn returned his overt inspection with shy, little peek-a-boo smiles. Apparently she'd inherited her father's flirtatious nature, too, Melissa thought with some amusement. Cody was clearly captivated. She should have been pleased, but the doubts her mother had planted kept her from fully relaxing and enjoying the way father and daughter were bonding.

At the small Italian restaurant where both she and Cody were well known, they were ushered to a back booth amid exclamations over Sharon Lynn's outfit and Cody's return. Melissa didn't miss the speculative looks sent their way by customers who knew their history only too well.

Though a high chair was set up at the end of the table for the baby, Cody insisted she was just fine beside him in the booth. Sharon Lynn stood on the vinyl seat next to him, bouncing on tiptoes and patting Cody on the top of his head.

He circled her waist with his hands and lifted her

into the air, earning giggles and a resounding kiss for his trouble. Melissa watched the pair of them with her heart in her throat. When Sharon Lynn climbed into Cody's lap, studied him seriously for a full minute, then cooed, ''Da,'' Melissa felt the salty sting of tears in her eyes.

Cody's mouth dropped open. ''Did she just call me Da?''

Apparently sensing approval, Sharon Lynn repeated the sound. ''Da, Da, Da.''

''She knows who I am,'' he whispered incredulously.

Melissa hated to disappoint him, but she knew that her daughter tended to call every man that. Besides, she refused to admit that she had tried to teach Sharon Lynn that very word while showing her a snapshot of Cody. She seriously doubted her daughter had actually made the connection between that blurry picture and the man holding her now.

She almost told him not to get too excited over it. Sharon Lynn might not even remember to connect that word with him tomorrow. The look in Cody's eyes kept her silent. He clearly wanted to believe that he and his child had made some sort of cosmic connection.

As she watched the pair of them, something shifted inside Melissa. Her earlier doubts fled. Maybe there really was some sort of instinctive bond between father and child. She wasn't sure what to make of this softer, gentler Cody. He had always been filled with laughter, but there was something incredibly sweet and tender in the way he teased his daughter and kept her giggling. Pride shone in his eyes at everything she did.

"She's brilliant," he declared every few minutes over the simplest accomplishments.

Sharon Lynn was clearly basking in the praise and the attention. Melissa held her breath, wondering just when exhaustion would overtake her daughter and turn that cheerful demeanor into far more familiar crankiness and tears. She couldn't help worrying about how Cody would respond to his child then. Would he turn tail and run again the instant the newness of this experience wore off, just as he had abandoned a long string of women once he'd tired of them? She was torn between anticipation and panic as she waited to see how the rest of the evening would play out.

They made it through their pizza without calamity striking. Sharon Lynn yawned a few times, grabbed a handful of the mushrooms Melissa had removed from her slice and squished them. When Cody tried to wipe her hands, she began sobbing as if she were being tortured.

Cody stared at Melissa helplessly as Sharon Lynn batted his hands away. "What did I do?"

"You didn't do anything. She's tired."

"Are you sure? Maybe she's hurt. Maybe there was a piece of glass and she cut herself." He unfolded her tightly clenched fingers and examined each one.

"Any sign of blood?" Melissa inquired, barely hiding her amusement.

He scowled at her. "How can you be so calm?"

"Because this is a nightly ritual."

He blanched. "Nightly?"

She nodded. "Just about. She gets so tired she can hardly keep her eyes open, but she doesn't want to miss anything, so she fights going to sleep."

Cody was regarding the sobbing child as if she were an alien creature. "Want me to take her?" she offered.

"No," he said insistently. "I have to learn how to deal with this."

He lifted Sharon Lynn up and sat her on the edge of the table facing him. Huge tears rolled down her blotchy cheeks. "Okay, kiddo, let's try to figure out a solution for this little problem you have with bedtime."

"Cody?"

He glanced up at her. "Hmm?"

"I don't think reason and logic are going to work."

"Sure they will," he argued. "Just watch."

He began talking in a low, soothing tone, explaining very patiently that sleep was very important. He added a lot of nonsense about fairy princesses and treasures that didn't come from any storybook Melissa had ever read.

Whether it was his tone or the actual words, Sharon Lynn's eyelids began to droop. The next thing Melissa knew, she was cradled in Cody's arms, sound asleep.

"Amazing," she admitted. "I should hire you to do that."

"No need to hire me," he said, his gaze suddenly

fixed on her in a way that had her pulse scrambling. "I intend to be available for bedtime duty every night from now on."

Melissa swallowed hard against the tide of panic that swept through her. Surely she hadn't heard him right. "Excuse me?" she whispered.

"Once we're married, I'll get her to bed," he said, making his intentions perfectly clear.

"Married?" she repeated as if it were an unfamiliar concept.

"Well, of course," he said. "What did you think was going to happen?" He reached into his pocket, scooped something out and set it on the table between them.

Melissa stared at the small velvet box incredulously. She looked from it to Cody's face and back again.

"Go ahead," he encouraged. "Open it. If you'd rather have something else, we can go together tomorrow."

She shook her head, fighting the urge to grab that tempting little box and claim not only the ring inside, but the future Cody had obviously mapped out for them. This reaction of his to discovering he was a father wasn't even remotely what she had expected. Obviously he wasn't thinking clearly. He hadn't wanted to marry her two years ago. She was faintly insulted that it had taken a baby to drag a proposal out of him.

Actually, it wasn't even a proposal. It was another of those orders she hated so much. Issuing edicts was something he had learned at Harlan Adams's knee. Considering how he'd rebelled against his father, she would have thought he'd be more sensitive to the crummy habit.

"No," she said flatly, meeting his gaze evenly. She was very proud of herself for getting the word out, for keeping her voice and her resolve steady.

He blinked and stared. "No what?"

She drew in a deep breath and, before she could change her mind, blurted, "I will not touch that box and I will not marry you."

A red flush climbed up his neck. "Of course you will," he said just as emphatically. "Don't be stubborn, Melissa. It's the sensible thing to do."

"Sensible," she repeated in a low, lethal tone. "I do not intend to get married because it is *sensible!*"

She stood and jerked on her coat, then moved to pick up Sharon Lynn. Cody held his daughter out of her reach.

"Sit back down and let's talk about this," he ordered. "You're causing a scene."

"I don't care," she said emphatically, though she didn't dare look around to see just how many people were fascinated by their argument. "There is absolutely nothing to discuss."

"Please," he said, sounding slightly more meek.

Since when had Cody cared about scenes? Melissa regarded him suspiciously, but she did sit on the edge of the seat. She did not remove her coat.

"How about another soft drink?" he coaxed.

"Cody!"

"Okay, okay." He leaned toward her intently. "Maybe I didn't go about this quite right."

"I'll say."

He reached awkwardly around his sleeping daughter and picked up the velvet box. He flipped it open to display an impressive emerald surrounded by diamonds. Melissa fought to pretend that the ring didn't just about take her breath away. The size of the ring and the sparkle of those stones were not important. A marriage based on obligation was the real point here. She wouldn't have it.

"It reminded me of your eyes," Cody said. He grinned. "The way they are right now, when they're shooting off sparks."

Melissa's resolve wavered. A little voice in her head gathered steam, repeating *no, no, no* so loudly she couldn't ignore it. Hadn't she told herself just a few hours earlier that she'd always been too easy on Cody? Hadn't she made a fool of herself over and over again by giving in if he so much as smiled at her?

And hadn't she learned that she could take care of herself? She no longer liked the idea of relying on anyone, either financially or, even more importantly, for her happiness.

"You're wasting your time," she told him emphatically before her resolve could falter. "The ring is beautiful. You're a fine man. I'm thrilled that you want to be a part of Sharon Lynn's life. But I will not marry you."

He looked absolutely dumbfounded. If the conversation hadn't been quite so difficult for her, too, she might have smiled at his flabbergasted reaction.

"Why?" he demanded, staring at her, indignation radiating from every pore.

"Because I will not get married for all the wrong reasons."

"What wrong reasons? We have a child. I intend to be a father to her."

"That's fine. It doesn't mean you have to be a husband to me. I'm doing just fine on my own. You were apparently doing so fine on your own that you saw no need to come back for almost two years."

"That's it, isn't it?" His gaze narrowed. "You're just doing this to get even because I left town and you had to face being pregnant all alone."

Melissa regarded him sadly. "No, Cody, I am not trying to get even. I'm just trying not to compound one mistake by making another."

He seemed thoroughly taken aback by the realization that anyone—and most especially the woman who'd always adored him—would consider marrying him to be a mistake. Obviously his ego hadn't suffered any during their separation. It was as solid as ever.

She reached across the table and patted his hand. "It's nothing personal."

He stared at her. "How can you say that? I think it's pretty damned personal."

"Once you've had time to think it over, you'll see that I'm right," she assured him. "Obligation is a terrible basis for a marriage."

This time when she stood and reached for Sharon

Lynn, he didn't resist. He pocketed the ring and stepped out of the booth. "I'll take you home," he said, his voice flat.

Melissa directed him to the small house she'd been renting for the past year, since about a month after Sharon Lynn's birth. Cody showed no inclination to get out of the pickup, so she let herself out. She hesitated for a moment with the door still open.

"I'm sorry, Cody. I really am."

He didn't look at her. "I'll call tomorrow and we'll work out a schedule for me to spend time with my daughter."

The chill in his voice cut straight through her. For the first time she wondered if she had made a terrible mistake in alienating him. Even though she knew in her heart that her decision was the right one, the only one to be made under the circumstances, perhaps she should have found a way to be more diplomatic about rejecting him.

"Fine," she said. "Whatever works for you will be okay."

She closed the door and started up the walk. An instant later she heard the engine shut off, then the slam of the driver's door behind Cody. He caught up with her before she could even make it to the front stoop.

Before she realized what he intended, he hauled her into his arms and kissed her so hard and so thoroughly that her head spun. Then, as if he suddenly became aware of the child she was holding or possibly because he figured he'd made his point, he released her.

"Give her to me," he said. "I'll carry her inside."

"Cody, she's fine," Melissa protested. She didn't want him inside, not when her knees were shaking and her pulse was racing.

"I said I'd carry her," he repeated, plucking her neatly out of Melissa's arms. "Open the door."

Following her directions, he made his way to the baby's small room. Angrily shrugging aside Melissa's offer of assistance, he fumbled with his daughter's clothes. He scanned the room, picked out a nightshirt from a small dresser, changed her, then laid her down gently.

Only then did a sigh shudder through him. His hand rested for a moment on the baby's backside.

"Good night, sweet pea," he murmured, his gaze riveted to his sleeping daughter as he backed toward the door.

The sight of Cody with their child, feeling his pain and his longing as he'd tucked her in for the night, had shaken Melissa. She was leaning against the wall outside the room, trying to gather her composure, when he finally emerged.

His gaze caught hers, burning into her. "It's not over," he said quietly. "Not by a long shot."

Trembling, Melissa stood rooted to the spot, staring after him long after she'd heard the truck's engine start, long after Cody had driven away.

Cody was right. It wasn't over. More than anything, she feared the struggle between them for their daughter was just beginning.

Chapter Seven

Cody didn't get a wink of sleep the entire night. When he wasn't overwhelmed by the amazing experience of holding his daughter, he was thinking about Melissa's astonishing transformation.

He had never noticed before how stubborn she was, nor how self-confident and independent. In fact, as he recalled, there had hardly ever been an occasion when she hadn't been thoroughly accommodating to his every whim. She'd picked a hell of a time to change, he thought, thoroughly disgruntled over having been shot down.

Sometime shortly after dawn, he finally forced himself to admit that he actually found the new Melissa ever so slightly more intriguing than he had the compliant woman he'd left behind.

Kelly, Jessie and the others had always warned him about taking Melissa for granted. It appeared he should have paid more attention to their advice. Melissa had used his time away to develop a very strong sense of who she was and what her priorities were. He was beginning to wonder if there really wasn't room for him in her life anymore.

Tired of his own company, he walked into the dining room at White Pines the minute he heard the rattle of breakfast dishes. Unfortunately, the housekeeper was very efficient. Maritza had already retreated to the kitchen, but she had left an array of cereals, a large pot of fresh coffee, a basket of warm rolls, and a bowl of berries, banana slices and melon. He noticed there were no eggs or bacon, no hash browns or grits. Obviously Harlan hadn't won his war to get what he considered to be a decent breakfast served during the week.

Cody was just pouring himself a cup of coffee when his father came in. He surreptitiously studied his father's face. Harlan looked tired and sad, but his complexion no longer had that unhealthy-looking pallor it had had when Cody had first arrived.

"You're up mighty early," Harlan observed, his expression sour as he surveyed the food the housekeeper had set out. "Dammit, I can't seem to get a decent piece of meat in the morning anymore." He shot a hopeful look at Cody. "Want to drive into town and get a real breakfast? Maybe a steak and some eggs?"

"And bring the wrath of Maritza down on my head? I don't think so. The fruit looks good."

"I don't see you eating any of it."

"I'm not hungry."

"Late night?"

"Something like that."

"I thought you were past carousing."

"Who was carousing? I had dinner with Melissa." He paused and drew in a deep breath. It was time to test the words on his lips, time to test his father's reaction. It would be a good barometer of what others would have to say.

"And my daughter," he added.

Harlan merely nodded, clearly not startled by the profound announcement.

"About time," he said succinctly.

Cody stared at him, his blood suddenly pumping furiously. "You knew, too? Dammit, Daddy, you're every bit as bad as Jordan," he accused. "You kept it from me, just like he did. What is wrong with everyone in this family? I thought we were supposed to stick together." He was just warming up to a really good tirade when his father cut in.

"Settle down, son. Nobody told me, if that's what you're thinking. Didn't take much to add up two and two, once I'd seen that child. She's the spitting image of you at that age. I've got a picture of you boys on my desk that would have reminded me, if I hadn't seen it for myself." He shrugged. "Besides, Melissa never had eyes for anyone but you."

Cody couldn't think of a thing to say. Apparently

his father had been willing to stand on the sidelines and wait for Cody to show up and discover he had a daughter. It didn't fit with his usual manipulative style. Either his father was mellowing or he had some other kind of devious scheme up his sleeve.

Harlan speared a chunk of cantaloupe, eyed it disparagingly, then ate it. "So," he began, his tone one of such studied indifference that Cody immediately went on alert. "Is that why you took off? Did Melissa tell you she was pregnant?"

Cody was horrified his father could think so little of him. Was that it? Had Harlan thought he'd already made his decision about marrying Melissa and being a father to his child?

"No, absolutely not," he declared indignantly. "Do you honestly think I have so little backbone that I'd run from a responsibility like that?"

His father shot a bland look in his direction. "I wouldn't like to think it, but the evidence was staring me in the face."

"What evidence?"

"You were gone. Your girl was pregnant. She quit college. She had to take that piddly job at Dolan's to make ends meet, which suggested that no one was paying a dime to support her or the baby. Didn't take a genius to add it all together and figure out that one."

"Well, your calculator malfunctioned this time," Cody snapped. "She never said a word, never even tried to track me down. The first I knew about that baby was when Velma Horton brought her into Dolan's when I was there the other day. Even then, I thought someone else had to be the father. It never crossed my mind that Melissa would hide something that important from me.''

''I see.'' Harlan scooped up a strawberry, eyed it with disgust, then put it back. ''Now that you know, what do you intend to do about it?''

''I proposed to her last night.''

Harlan's eyes lit up. His expression was suddenly more animated than it had been in days. ''Well, hell, son, why didn't you say so? Congratulations! When's the wedding?''

''No wedding,'' Cody admitted dully. ''She said no.''

Harlan's openmouthed expression of astonishment reflected Cody's feelings precisely.

''She flat-out turned you down?'' his father said incredulously.

''Without so much as a hesitation,'' he said. ''It was downright insulting.''

Harlan chuckled. ''Well, I'll be damned.''

''You don't have to sound so amused,'' Cody grumbled.

''Sure, I do, boy. Seems tame little Melissa has grown up into a spirited young woman. The next few months or so ought to be downright interesting.''

Cody glared at him. ''Months? Forget it. I'm giving her a day, maybe two, to get over this contrariness. Then I'm hauling her to a justice of the peace.''

His father started to laugh, then smothered the sound with a napkin. ''Sorry,'' he mumbled, then gave up the fight and chuckled. "Son, you're going to be able to sell tickets to that one."

Cody's frayed temper snapped. He stood and tossed his own napkin back on the table. "Well, get out your checkbook, Daddy. The best seats in the house are going to cost you. Melissa and I might as well start off our married life with a nice little nest egg."

Melissa wiped down the counter at Dolan's after the last of the lunch crowd had left and eyed Cody warily. He'd been skulking up and down the aisles of the drugstore since noon, but he hadn't come near the soda fountain. He seemed unaware that Eli and Mabel were watching him with overt fascination. Thankfully, he was also unaware of what his presence was doing to her pulse rate. Who knew what he would do to capitalize on that little hint of a fissure in her resolve.

"Mabel, why don't you take the rest of the afternoon off," Eli suggested, playing straight into Cody's hands.

"What's wrong with you, old man?" Mabel grumbled. "You planning on shutting down business?"

Eli gave her a pointed nod in Melissa's direction. "Go on, Mabel. You've been wanting to check out the new seeds over at the hardware store so you can get your garden in at the first sign of spring. Go do it."

Melissa almost chuckled as she watched Mabel struggle with herself. She'd been talking about those seeds for a week, ever since the hardware store owner had told her they'd arrived. She also hated to miss out on something with the kind of gossip potential that Melissa's next confrontation with Cody was likely to have.

"Go," Eli repeated, shooing her toward the door and taking the choice out of her hands. "I might not feel so generous again anytime soon."

"Don't doubt that," Mabel retorted sourly.

Mabel got her coat and left, reluctance written all over her narrow, tight-lipped face. Cody inched a little closer to the soda fountain, as if an invisible barrier had been removed from his path.

"Melissa," Eli called. "I'll be in the storeroom, checking this morning's delivery. Call me if you need me."

"Traitor," Melissa mumbled under her breath.

Cody had moved close enough by now to overhear. "Nice talk," he commented. "He's just doing you a favor."

"Me?" She stared at him incredulously. "Oh, no. You probably paid him to get rid of Mabel and to disappear himself. I noticed the other night that you'd inherited Harlan's knack for manipulation."

Cody clearly wasn't crazy about the comparison, but he let the charge roll off his back. "I'm not desperate enough to be paying anyone to give me time alone with you," Cody said, his grin widening. "I'm still relying on my charm."

"Take it somewhere else," she muttered.

"Tsk-tsk, Me…liss…a," he drawled, tipping his hat back on his head as he settled on a stool at the counter. "What does it take to get a little service around here?"

"More charm than you've got," she retorted. "Or cold, hard cash."

He plucked a twenty out of his wallet and set it on the counter. Then he winked. It appeared he was giving her a choice about which currency she wanted to accept. Melissa would have gladly taken the wink, if it meant she could shove that bill straight down his throat.

Since she couldn't, she snatched the twenty, tucked it into her pocket and withdrew her order pad and pen. "What'll it be?" she inquired in the same impersonal tone she used with other impossible customers.

Cody propped his elbows on the counter and leaned forward. "A kiss for starters."

"You wish." Her knees trembled despite the defiant retort. Why was it that temptation always entered a room right at Cody's side? Shouldn't she have been totally immune by now? Lord knows, she'd been lecturing herself on getting over him from the day he'd left town. Some of that advice should have taken by now. Apparently, though, it hadn't.

"Then I'll have a hamburger, fries and a shake," he said.

The mundane order was a disappointment. Melissa cursed her wayward hormones as she slapped the burger on the grill and lowered the fries into the hot grease. She sloshed milk into a metal container and out of habit added two scoops of chocolate ice cream, even though Cody hadn't specified the kind he wanted. Half of the mixture splashed out when she jammed the container into place on the automatic shaker.

"Nervous?" Cody inquired.

He spoke in a smug, lazy drawl that sent heat scampering down her spine. She scowled at him. "What on earth do I have to be nervous about? You're the one who doesn't belong here. You're the one making a pest of himself."

Sparks flared in his dark eyes. "Want me to ask Eli how he feels about you making a paying customer feel unwelcome?"

He didn't have to. She already knew that Eli would have heart failure if he heard her trying to run Cody off with her rudeness. He'd already taken Cody's side once today by slinking off to hide out in the storeroom to give them time alone. She'd never before noticed that Eli held Cody in particularly high esteem. His behavior must be part of some instinctive male support system that kicked in whenever one of them sensed that a woman might be getting the upper hand.

She turned her back on Cody, finished fixing his food, then set it down on the counter with a jarring thud.

He grinned at her. "Service with a smile," he commented. "I love it. You earn a lot of tips this way?"

Melissa closed her eyes and prayed for patience. When she opened them again, Cody hadn't vanished as she'd hoped. "Why are you in here?" she inquired testily. "Shouldn't you be out roping cattle or something?"

"We have plans to make, remember?"

"I told you just to tell me when you wanted to see Sharon Lynn. I'll make the arrangements so you can pick her up at my parents' anytime."

"Not those plans," he said complacently, picking a pickle off of his hamburger and tsk-tsking her, apparently for not remembering that he hated pickles.

"Sorry," she said without much sincerity. She should have dumped in the whole damned jar. "You could have eaten at Rosa's."

"I prefer the spice here," he retorted. "Now let's get back to those plans. I was thinking that a week from Saturday would be good."

Melissa was surprised he wanted to wait that long before seeing his daughter again. Maybe his fascination was already waning. At this rate he'd be moving back to Wyoming in a month. Surely she could wait him out that long. She'd probably be a tangled heap of frustrated hormones, but presumably her sanity would still be intact.

"Sure, if that's what you want," she said more agreeably now that she knew he was likely to be out of her hair in no time. "I'm off on Saturday, so you can pick Sharon Lynn up at my place."

"Not just Sharon Lynn," he corrected. "Can't have a wedding without the bride."

Melissa dropped the glass she'd been rinsing out. It shattered at her feet. Eli poked his head out of the storeroom, saw the glass and shook his head.

"I hope to hell you two settle this quick," the pharmacist said. "It's costing me a fortune in broken glasses."

"Don't worry, Eli," Cody consoled him. "I'll settle up with you." He fixed his unrelenting gaze on Melissa and added, "I always accept my responsibilities."

"Oh, stuff a rag in it," Melissa retorted, stripping off her apron and opening the cash register to shove in the twenty she'd pocketed. "Eli, I'm leaving. Mr. Adams has already paid his check. Keep the change."

She made it as far as the sidewalk, still shrugging into her coat, when Cody caught up with her. If her refusal to kowtow to his wishes for a second time had ruffled his feathers, he wasn't letting it show. He fell into step beside her, his expression perfectly innocent.

"Going to pick up the baby?"

Actually Melissa had no idea where she was going. She'd been so anxious to get away from Cody that she'd walked out of the drugstore without the kind of plan she should have had. It was an unfortunate sign of weakness, one she couldn't allow him to detect.

"No, actually, I have things to do."

"Like what? I'll help."

"No, thanks. I can handle it."

"Come on, Me…liss…a," he coaxed, planting himself on the sidewalk in front of her, legs spread. He rocked back on the heels of his cowboy boots and peered at her from beneath the brim of his hat.

It was a look that invited a woman to swoon. She ought to know. She'd done it often enough, flat-out making a fool of herself over him.

"Would spending a little time with me be so awful?" he inquired.

Awful? That wasn't the word she would have chosen. Dangerous, maybe. Stupid. Risky. There was a whole string of applicable words and none of them had anything to do with awful.

"I'd rather not," she said politely.

"Bet I can change your mind," he countered, grinning at her.

She scowled at him as he advanced on her step by step. "Don't try."

He shook his head. "I don't know. The temptation is pretty great. Your mouth is all pouty. Very kissable," he assessed, his gaze hot on her. He took yet another step closer, crowding her. "Your cheeks are pink. Just about the color of rose petals and twice as soft. It's all hard to resist."

As he spoke, her lips burned as if he'd kissed them. Her cheeks flamed, turning to what she was sure must be a deeper shade. Damn, it didn't seem to matter if he actually touched her or not. Her body reacted predictably just to the provocative suggestion.

"Go away," she ordered in a voice that was entirely too breathless.

His expression solemn, he shook his head. "I can't do that, Me...liss...a."

She sighed. "Why not?" she demanded far too plaintively.

He circled one arm around her waist and dragged her against him. She could feel the hard heat of his arousal.

"You know the answer to that," he whispered, his lips scant millimeters from hers. His breath fanned across her cheek.

"Cody." His name came out as a broken sigh, a protest that not even someone far less relentless than Cody would have heeded.

"It's okay," he consoled her. "Everything is going to turn out just fine."

He slanted his mouth over hers then, setting off fireworks in January. *Why, why, why?* her brain demanded. Why was her body so darned traitorous? Maybe it was like the tides. Maybe the way she responded to Cody was as immutable as the sun setting in the west.

She resisted the explanation. It meant she had no will at all to fight it. She put her hands on his chest and shoved with all her might. She might as well have been trying to topple a centuries' old oak. Cody didn't budge. He didn't stop that tender assault on her mouth.

For what seemed an eternity he coaxed and plundered, teased and tasted until she was shivering with urgent and almost-forgotten need. When she was weak with a desire she definitely didn't want to feel, Cody finally released her. She very nearly melted at his feet. In fact, she might have if he hadn't kept his hands resting possessively on her hips. Even through her coat, her skin burned at his touch.

"So, what are we going to do with the rest of the afternoon?" he inquired. The gleam in his eyes suggested he had an idea of his own. His lips quirked up in the beginnings of a smile.

"Not what you're thinking," she said curtly.

His grin spread. "Don't be so certain of that, sweet pea. It sounds an awful lot like a challenge and you know I never could resist a dare."

Desperate for space, she backed away from him. "Give it a rest," she said crankily.

He reached out and rubbed his thumb across her lower lip. The sensation sent fire dancing through her.

"I'm just getting started, darlin'," he murmured, his gaze locked with hers.

Melissa held back a sigh of resignation. "You're not going home, are you?"

"When I can be with you? No way."

"Come on, then."

His expression immediately brightened. Once more he fell dutifully into step beside her. "Where are we going?"

"To buy groceries," she said, plucking a boring chore out of thin air. "And after that, we're ironing." She slanted a look at him to judge his reaction. He didn't bat an eye.

"Sounds downright fascinating," he declared. He captured her gaze, then added slowly, "I've always been particularly fond of starch."

She ignored the provocative tone. "Oh, really?" she said skeptically.

"Yes, indeed," he swore. "In my shirts and in my women. And you, sweet pea, are full of it."

Melissa had a feeling it would take her weeks to puzzle out whether he meant that as a compliment. For the first time, though, she had this funny little feeling she was going to have the time of her life figuring it out.

Chapter Eight

Somewhere in the middle of the grocery store, Melissa lost track of Cody. She was aware of the precise instant when she no longer felt the heat of his stare or the sizzling tension of his nearness. She almost sagged with relief, even as she fought off a vague stirring of disappointment. Clearly his attention span was no better now than it had ever been.

Worse, he was getting to her. Despite her best intentions, she was responding to his teasing, to the allure of his body. She could not let that happen. Steering totally clear of him, however, seemed to be the only way she was likely to be able to avoid succumbing to that seductive appeal. Now seemed like a good time to make a break for it.

All she had to do was get through the checkout

line and race home before he caught up with her. She could barricade the door. Or maybe just hide out in a bedroom until he was convinced she wasn't home.

She tossed a six-pack of soft drinks she didn't need into the cart, just in case Cody wasn't as far away as she hoped. She had to leave the store with more than a quart of milk or he'd know that this trip had been nothing more than a ploy to avoid being alone with him.

She had rounded the last aisle and was heading for the cashier when she spotted him. He was positioned in front of the baby food, studying labels with the intensity of a scientist in his lab. Apparently, though, he wasn't so absorbed that her presence escaped his notice.

"Which of these does Sharon Lynn like?" he asked, holding up competing brands of strained peas.

"Neither one."

His brow knit worriedly. "Doesn't she have to eat vegetables?"

"Yes, but she's past the baby food. She has her first baby teeth. She can chew soft food." She regarded him oddly. "Do you really care about this?"

"Yes," he said succinctly, and replaced the peas. "Fill me in on everything."

Melissa shrugged. "Okay. She can eat the junior brands. Like these," she said, plucking a couple of jars off the shelf. "There are some foods that don't have to be specially prepared. She can eat the regular stuff. Peas, for example."

To her surprise, he seemed to be taking in every word as if she were delivering a fascinating treatise on something far more significant than baby food. In the past he'd reserved that kind of attention for very little besides ranching.

"What are her favorite foods?" he asked, studying the larger jars intently.

"Ice cream and French fries."

Cody stared at her. "That's her diet?"

"No," she said patiently. "Those are her favorites." She gestured to the junior baby food. "This is what she gets most of the time. When I have time, I even blend some myself from fresh fruits and vegetables. She's particularly fond of squishing bananas."

Cody eyed the jars of carrots and meats and fruits, seemed to struggle with his conscience, and then turned his back on them. "Let's go."

"Where?"

"To the ice cream section," he said as grimly as if he were going into battle and the enemy had pulled a last-minute tactical switch. "I'm not bringing home jars of that disgusting-looking liver or those limp little bits of carrot if she'd rather have ice cream."

"Cody, I do feed her. You don't need to stock my refrigerator, especially not with ice cream."

He stopped in his tracks and turned to face her. "Don't you see, this isn't about you. It's about me and my daughter. You've had her to yourself for thirteen months. Now I want a chance to be important in her life."

"By stuffing her with chocolate-fudge ice cream?"

Instead of taking her well-intended point, he seized on the tiny sliver of information she'd imparted about their daughter. "Is that her favorite? I'll buy a gallon of it."

He sounded relieved to know that he wouldn't have to resort to another round of guesswork and label-reading. In fact, he was loping off to the frozen food section before Melissa could gather her thoughts sufficiently to argue with him.

Okay, she told herself, it was only a gallon of ice cream. So what? It wasn't as if he could buy their daughter's affection or ruin her health with one extravagant gesture of chocolate fudge.

She had a feeling, though, that this was only the beginning. Cody was not a man to do anything by half measures. His retreat to Wyoming, abandoning not only her but his beloved home and family, was a perfect example of that. He could have straightened everything out between them with a few questions or even by hurling accusations and listening to explanations. Instead he had leapt to a conclusion and reacted by impetuously fleeing to another state.

He was doing much the same thing now that he had discovered he had a daughter. He wanted to be in her life—completely—right this instant. He wanted to marry Melissa…right this minute. The concepts of moderation or patience had obviously escaped him.

She sighed as he appropriated the shopping cart. The two half gallons of chocolate-fudge ice cream had turned into four. And she didn't like the gleam in his eyes one bit as he turned the cart on two wheels and headed straight for the shelves of diapers.

She'd been right. He was going to take over and she had a sinking feeling in the pit of her stomach that there would be very little she could do about it.

Cody realized he had almost lost it there for a minute at the supermarket. He'd wanted to sweep entire shelves of baby food into the shopping cart.

As it was, in addition to the ice cream, they had left the store with five, giant economy-size packages of disposable diapers, a new toy duck for Sharon Lynn's bath, five storybooks he could read to her at bedtime and an astonishing selection of her favorite juices. Melissa had just rolled her eyes at the startled checkout clerk.

"New father?" the girl had guessed.

"New enough," Melissa had replied.

Let them make fun, Cody thought. He didn't care. This was the first step in his campaign to make himself indispensable to Melissa and his daughter.

"Where to now?" he asked when they'd piled all those diapers and the rest of the shopping bags into the back of his pickup.

"I'm going home to iron," Melissa said, sticking to that absurd story she'd told him earlier in a blatant attempt to get rid of him. "Unless, of course, you'd like to do it for me?"

He frowned at her. "What about Sharon Lynn?"

"She's with Mother."

"I'll drop you off and go get her," he suggested eagerly.

"She's probably still taking her nap," Melissa said.

She said it in such a rush he had the feeling she thought he intended to kidnap the baby and take off with her. As much as he resented the implication, he kept his tone perfectly even. "She won't sleep forever," he countered reasonably. "I'll bring her straight home. I promise."

"You don't have a car seat," she noted pointedly.

Damn, but there was a lot to remember. "We'll stop now and get one."

"All of that ice cream will melt."

He frowned at the obstacles she kept throwing in his path. "Not in this weather. It's freezing out. And if it does, I'll buy more."

"Couldn't you just drop me off at home?"

"No, you need to come with me. You can show me the best kind of car seat."

Melissa sighed heavily. "Cody, what's the point? They're expensive and you probably won't..."

He guessed where she was going. "Won't what? Won't be here long enough to use it? You can get that idea right out of your head."

He tucked a finger under her chin and forced her to face him. "I've quit my job in Wyoming. I am home to stay, Melissa. Get used to it."

She held up her hands. "Sorry. I didn't mean

anything. I was just trying to keep you from wasting money.''

''If it's for my daughter, it is not a waste of money,'' he said curtly. ''Now, can I find the kind of car seat I need at the discount superstore out on the highway?''

She nodded.

He turned the truck around on a dime, spewing gravel. He drove ten miles before his temper had cooled enough to speak again. He'd set out today to woo Melissa into changing her mind about marrying him. His first overtures, however, appeared to have gone awry. He'd lost his sense of humor, right along with his temper. It was no way for the two of them to start over. He sucked in a deep breath and made up his mind to mend fences.

''Truce?'' he suggested, glancing over at her. She was huddled against the door, looking miserable. She shrugged.

''I'm not an ogre,'' he stated. ''I'm just trying to fit into Sharon Lynn's life.'' Her gaze lifted to meet his. ''And yours.''

She sighed. ''We don't need you,'' she repeated stubbornly. ''We were doing just fine before you came back.''

He ignored the tide of hurt that washed through him at the dismissive comment. ''Maybe I need you.''

Melissa frowned. ''Yeah, right,'' she said sarcastically. ''As if Cody Adams ever needed anybody. Didn't you pride yourself on staying footloose and fancy free?''

He saw no point in denying something she knew better than anyone. "I did," he agreed. He thought about the agonizing loneliness of that cabin he'd sentenced himself to in Wyoming. "Maybe being alone for the past eighteen months has changed me. Maybe I'm not the selfish, carefree, independent cuss who stormed away from Texas."

"And maybe pigs can fly," she countered.

He grinned at her. "Maybe they can," he said quietly. "If you believe in magic."

"I don't," she said succinctly.

Cody heard the terrible pain in her voice, even if her expression remained absolutely stoic. Dear heaven, what had he done to her by running off and leaving her to face being pregnant all alone? He saw now what he hadn't observed before. Not only was Melissa stronger and more self-sufficient, she also had an edge of cynicism and bitterness that hadn't been there before. The blame for that was his, no one else's.

At the discount store, when Melissa would have grabbed the first car seat they came across, Cody stopped her, deliberately taking the time to read the package for every last detail on safety. If nothing else, he intended to impress on Melissa that he took his parenting responsibilities seriously. Nothing was too trivial, too expensive, or too complicated to tackle if it had to do with his daughter.

Nearly an hour later they finally loaded the new car seat into the truck.

"I think that salesclerk despaired of ever getting

you to make a choice,'' Melissa said, the beginnings of a smile tugging at her lips.

"It wasn't for her kid,'' he retorted.

"Okay, forget the salesclerk. Should I point out that the one you ended up taking is exactly the same one I tried to get you to buy when we walked in?''

He scowled at her. "What's your point?''

"That I had already done the exact same research, reached the exact same conclusion. You insisted I come along because you claimed to want my advice. When it came right down to it, though, you didn't trust me.''

Cody carefully considered the accusation before turning to meet her gaze. "You're right. I should have listened to you. It's just that this is new to me. I'm trying to get it right. I don't want to mess up with something this important.''

Her expression softened. "Cody, I can understand that. Really, I can. I was just as obsessive when I first brought Sharon Lynn home from the hospital. Mother and Daddy thought I was a lunatic. I didn't trust a piece of advice they offered. I was convinced it was probably outdated. I had to do it all for myself. Talk about reinventing the wheel.'' She shook her head. "I wasted more time, only to find myself doing exactly what they'd suggested in the first place.''

He grinned. "You're just trying to save me traveling over the same learning curve, is that it?''

"Exactly,'' she said. She reached over and patted his hand. "I'm not trying to keep you out of Sharon

Lynn's life, or control your input, or anything like that. I promise.''

The impulsive touch didn't last nearly long enough. Cody grabbed her hand and pulled it to his lips. He brushed a kiss across her knuckles and saw the instantaneous spark of desire in her eyes. "I'll try to watch the defensiveness, if you'll do something for me."

She regarded him with conditioned wariness. "What?"

"Bring Sharon Lynn out to White Pines this weekend," he coaxed persuasively. At the flare of panic in her eyes, he pulled out his strongest ammunition—her fondness for Harlan. "I think seeing her would do Daddy a world of good. With Mother gone, he needs something positive in his life, something to cheer him up. You should have seen the look in his eyes this morning when I told him she was mine."

The hint of wariness in her eyes fled and was promptly replaced by astonishment. "You told him?"

"I did. But it wasn't news. He'd figured it out the first time he saw her, the same as Jordan had."

Her mouth gaped. "And he didn't do anything about it? I'm amazed he didn't haul your butt straight back here or offer to set up a trust fund for the baby or something."

"Frankly, so am I. Maybe he's learned his lesson about manipulating."

Melissa's expression was every bit as skeptical as his own had to be. "Okay," he said. "He probably has a scheme we don't know about yet. Even so, are you willing to take a chance? Will you bring her out? It's time she learned something about her father's side of the family.''

He was playing to her sense of fairness and it was clearly working. He could practically read her struggle with her conscience on her face.

''I'll bring her,'' Melissa finally agreed with obvious reluctance. ''On one condition—no tricks.''

Cody regarded her innocently. Now that he'd gotten her basic agreement, he could go along with almost anything she demanded. ''What kind of tricks?''

''No preachers lurking in the shadows. No wedding license all signed and ready to be filled in.''

He feigned astonishment, even though he thought she might actually have a very good idea, one that hadn't even occurred to him until just that minute. ''Would I do that?''

''In a heartbeat,'' she said. ''And even if you had an attack of conscience, Harlan wouldn't. No conspiracies, okay?''

''Cross my heart,'' Cody said, already wondering if there was some way to pull off such a wedding.

Melissa's gaze narrowed. ''Why doesn't that reassure me?''

''And you accused me of a lack of trust,'' he chided.

''I'm not the one whose brother threw a surprise wedding in place of a rehearsal,'' she said, reminding him of the sneaky trick Jordan and Kelly had pulled on his parents to avoid the out-of-control celebration his mother had planned for their wedding. The whole town had gossiped about that little stunt for weeks.

"I'm glad you mentioned that," Cody taunted. "It does give me some interesting ideas."

"Cody Adams, I am warning you…"

"No need, sweet pea. I'm not fool enough to take a chance on getting rejected in front of my family and the preacher. When you and I get married, it'll be because you're willing and eager."

"'When,' not 'if'?" she chided.

"That's right, darlin'. Only the timing is left to be decided," he declared with far more confidence than he felt. He unloaded the last of their packages under Melissa's irritated scrutiny. Apparently, though, his certainty about their future had left her speechless. He considered that a hopeful sign.

"See you on Saturday," he said, escaping before he had a chance to put his foot in his mouth. "Come on out about eight. You can have breakfast with us."

Besides, he thought, if Melissa was there by eight, that gave him most of the day to convince her to have a wedding at sunset.

Melissa debated bailing out on her day at White Pines. Handling Cody was tricky enough without having to worry about Harlan's sneaky tactics at the same time. Still, she couldn't very well deny Harlan the chance to get to know the granddaughter he'd just officially discovered he had.

That was what ultimately decided her, or so she

told herself as she dressed Sharon Lynn in bright blue corduroy pants, a blue and yellow shirt, and tiny sneakers. She brushed her hair into a halo of soft curls around her face.

"Ma? Bye-bye?"

Proud of Sharon Lynn's expanding vocabulary, she nodded. "That's right, my darling. We're going to see your daddy and your granddaddy."

Sharon Lynn's face lit up. She reached for the new toy duck that was never far from sight. "Da?"

Melissa shook her head at the instant reaction. Obviously Cody had had an incredible impact on his daughter in just one visit. Did he have that effect on all women or just those in her family? She tickled Sharon Lynn until she dissolved into a fit of giggles.

"Yes, Da," she told her approvingly. "We're going to see Da." And she, for one, was nervous as the dickens about it. Sharon Lynn clearly had no such qualms.

When Melissa pulled her car to a stop in front of the house at White Pines, she drew in a deep, reassuring breath, trying to calm her jitters. It was going to be just fine, she told herself, even as she fought the overwhelming sense of déjà vu that assailed her.

How many times had she driven out here, filled with hope, anxious to spend time with the man she loved, only to leave bitterly disappointed by his refusal to commit to anything more than a carefree relationship? Everything had always seemed more intense out here, the air crisper and cleaner, the terrain more rugged, the colors brighter. Similarly, her emotions had always seemed sharper, too—the bitter sorrow as well as the blinding joy.

Once she had dreamed of this being her home, the place where she and Cody would raise a family. Now with the snap of her fingers and a couple of "I do's," her dream could come true. But Cody's proposal, forced only by the existence of a child for whom he felt responsible, had tarnished the dream. She doubted it could ever recapture its original, innocent glow.

"Da, Da, Da!" Sharon Lynn screamed excitedly, bouncing in her car seat as Cody strode across the front lawn. He was wearing snug, faded jeans, a T-shirt that hugged his broad chest and worn cowboy boots. He looked sexier and more masculine than any male model ever had in *GQ*.

Before Melissa could fight her instinctive reaction just to the sight of him, he had thrown open the door and lifted his daughter high in the air, earning squeals of delight for his effort.

"Hey, pumpkin, I could hear you all the way inside the house," he teased the baby. "Your grandpa Harlan said you were loud enough to wake half the county. He's thinking of getting you geared up for the hog-calling contest at the state fair. What do you think?"

Melissa noted he reported his father's reaction with unmistakable pride. He glanced her way just then and the humor in his eyes darkened to something else, something she recognized from times past as powerful, compelling desire. Whatever was behind his proposal of marriage, the one thing she couldn't doubt was Cody's passion. He wanted her and he was doing nothing to hide that fact from her.

"Thank you for coming," he said, his expression solemn.

"I told you I would."

He shrugged. "You never know, though. Sometimes things come up."

Suddenly, for the first time Melissa was able to pinpoint the most devastating problem between them. Neither of them had so much as a shred of trust left for the other.

She didn't trust Cody not to leave again. She didn't trust him not to rip her daughter away from her.

And worse, to her way of thinking because she knew he had a right to feel as he did, he didn't trust her to keep her promises. She had kept the secret of his daughter from him. He had to wonder if he could trust her to be honest with him about anything.

All at once she was unbearably sad. Regrets for the open, honest relationship they had once shared tumbled through her, leaving her shaken.

Before she realized he'd even moved, Cody was beside her, Sharon Lynn in his arms.

"Are you okay?" he asked, his expression filled with concern.

"Of course. Why would you think I wasn't?"

"Maybe it has something to do with the tears."

She hadn't even realized she was crying. She brushed impatiently at the telltale traces. "Sorry."

"You don't have to apologize, for heaven's sake. Just tell me what's wrong."

"An attack of nostalgia," she said, knowing it was only partially true. "Nothing to worry about." She plastered a smile on her face. "Come on. Let's go inside before Harlan falls out of that window he's peeking through."

Almost as if he'd heard the comment, the curtains fell back into place and a shadow moved away from the downstairs window. Cody grinned at her.

"He can't wait to meet Sharon Lynn. If you think I'm bad, wait until you see the room he's fixed up for her visits."

The implications of the lighthearted remark sent panic racing through Melissa. If Harlan had fixed up a room, then he clearly intended for Sharon Lynn to be at White Pines a lot. Was this visit just a prelude to the custody battle her mother had warned her about? Cody might not be willing to fight her in court, but Harlan was another matter. With Mary dead and his life stretching out emptily in front of him, who could tell what kind of crazy notion he might get into his head.

Apparently her fears must have been written on her face, because Cody halted again. "Melissa, you don't have to worry," he reassured her. "It's just a room. You know Harlan. Everything drives him to excess."

"You're sure that's all it is?"

"Very sure. You don't have anything to worry

about from Harlan.'' That said, he winked at her. ''I, however, am another matter entirely. I've given up on winning you with diapers and juice and toys.''

''Oh?''

''I intend to win you with my sexy, wicked ways.''

He was up the front steps and in the house before she had a chance to react. When she could finally move again, her legs wobbled and her pulse was scampering crazily.

Suddenly any threat Harlan might pose dimmed in importance. Cody was the one she needed to worry about. Always had been. Always would be.

Chapter Nine

At the precise instant that Cody and Melissa entered the front door at White Pines, Harlan stepped into the foyer. His prompt presence indicated that he had indeed been watching for Melissa's arrival and was eager for an introduction to his granddaughter.

Cody studied his father's face closely as Harlan's gaze honed in immediately on Sharon Lynn. For the first time since the funeral, there was a spark of animation in his dark eyes. And when he glanced at Melissa that animation included her, only to be quickly replaced by questions, unanswerable questions Cody hoped he wouldn't get into right off.

To stave them off, Cody crossed the wide sweep of wood floor and woven Mexican rug to stand in front of his father, Sharon Lynn still perched in his arms.

"Daddy, meet your granddaughter, Sharon Lynn."

The baby responded to the cue as if she'd been coached. A dimpled smile spread across her face as she held out her arms to be transferred to her new grandfather's embrace. Harlan accepted her with alacrity.

"You are a mighty fine young lady," he told her, his expression sober, his eyes unmistakably welling up with rare tears. "I'm very glad to be welcoming you to the family." His gaze shifted then to encompass Melissa once more. "It's good to see you again, girl. We've missed you around here."

Cody saw the sheen of tears spring to Melissa's eyes and realized more than ever what he had cost them all by running off as he had. His parents had always accepted that Melissa would one day be his wife. They had approved of her spirit, her kindness and her unconditional love for him. Melissa had been present on most family occasions, welcomed as if their relationship had been sealed.

Though he'd never asked his parents if they had continued to see her, he had suspected Melissa wouldn't feel that same sense of belonging after he'd gone. He knew from his father's comment just now that she had indeed stayed away and that her absence had hurt them all, costing them a relationship they held dear. The severing of ties had been as complete as if he and Melissa had been married and then divorced in an incredibly acrimonious manner that had forced everyone to choose sides.

"Thank you, Harlan," she said, stepping closer to be enveloped in a fierce hug that included Sharon Lynn. "I've missed you, too. And I'm so terribly, terribly sorry about Mary."

"I know you are. Mary thought a lot of you, girl. She always hoped…" At a warning glance from Cody, he allowed his voice to trail off, the thought left unspoken.

It hardly mattered, though. The damage had already been done. Melissa's cheeks turned bright pink. Cody could feel the blood climbing up the back of his neck, as well. His father surveyed them both, then gave a brief nod of satisfaction as if he'd learned something he'd hoped for.

"Come on, then," Harlan said, his voice laced with a telltale trace of huskiness. "Let's go have some breakfast, before we all turn maudlin and start bawling."

To Cody's relief, his father left the subject of the past untouched beyond that single, oblique reference. Either he was far too fascinated by the child he held or he recognized that it was not a conversation to be held in the baby's presence.

There was no mistaking, though, that more questions lingered in his eyes. Cody guessed they would be as much about the future as the past. He also knew there were no answers his father would like hearing, not yet anyway. Harlan had the same impatience as his sons. He liked things settled to his satisfaction. Between Cody and Melissa nothing was settled at all.

Sharon Lynn patted her grandfather's face, then glanced to her mother for approval. "Da?" she questioned.

Cody scowled as he realized that he wasn't unique in his daughter's view. He caught Melissa's grin and realized how pitiful it was to be jealous of his own father.

Unaware, as Cody had been, that it was Sharon Lynn's universal name for any adult male, Harlan beamed at her. "Damn, but you're a smart one," he praised. "You and I need to have ourselves a little talk. What other words do you know?"

"Ma and bye-bye," Melissa offered. "It limits the conversations tremendously."

Cody noticed that his father didn't seem to mind. He seemed perfectly content to carry on a one-sided conversation with his granddaughter. It was probably the first time in years someone hadn't talked back to him.

The distraction also kept Harlan from touching the eggs and bacon he normally couldn't wait to eat on the weekends. Possibly that was the most telling indication of all of Sharon Lynn's power over this new male in her life.

"So, Sharon Lynn, have you ever seen a horse?" Harlan inquired.

Cody chuckled as his daughter tilted her head, a quizzical expression on her face as she appeared to give the question serious consideration.

"I'll take that for a no," Harlan said. "In that

case, I think it's about time to fix that. Can't have a rancher's baby who doesn't know about horses. Maybe we'll even go for a little ride.''

Cody glanced at Melissa to check her reaction to the instantaneous bonding between Sharon Lynn and his father. To his astonishment, the color had drained out of her face. Clearly the idea of Sharon Lynn going off with Harlan panicked her in some way. What he couldn't figure was why.

''Harlan, I really don't think—'' she began.

''Don't worry about a thing,'' Harlan reassured her, cutting off her words. ''I had every one of my boys up on horseback when they were no bigger than this. She'll fit right on the saddle in front of me. She'll be just fine. I guarantee I won't let her tumble off.''

Harlan and the baby were out the door before Melissa could offer the firmer protest that was clearly on the tip of her tongue. Cody knew better than to argue with Harlan. He also knew that Sharon Lynn would be perfectly safe with his father. However, he could see that Melissa wouldn't believe it unless she witnessed their adventure on horseback with her own eyes. He put down his fork.

''Come on,'' he said. ''You'll be worrying yourself sick, if you're not right alongside them.''

''She's too little to be riding a horse,'' Melissa complained, her complexion still pale as she followed him outside. ''She'll be terrified.''

''I doubt that,'' Cody said. ''You're projecting your feelings onto her. You never were much for horses. I guess you were more of a city girl than I realized.''

She shot him a wry look. "Hardly that."

He grinned at her. "I don't know. About the only time I could get you into the barn was when I wanted to tumble you into the haystack."

"Cody Adams, that is not true," she contradicted, patches of bright color flaring in her cheeks. "Besides, that has absolutely nothing to do with Sharon Lynn and this crazy idea Harlan has of getting onto a horse with her."

"Stop fussing. She's just the right age to be introduced to riding. Kids her age have no fear. It's not like Daddy's going to put her on the horse, hit its rump and send her galloping around the paddock. He's going to be in the saddle, holding her."

"I suppose," Melissa said, but her gaze immediately sought out some sign of Sharon Lynn the minute the barn came into view.

The little cutie was hard to miss. She was squealing with delight from her perch atop the fence around the paddock. Misty, the oldest, smallest and gentlest of their mares, had come to investigate. Sharon Lynn's eyes were wide with excitement as she patted the white blaze on Misty's head.

"This is Misty," Harlan was explaining quietly, his grip firm on the horse's bridle. "Can you say that? Misty."

"Mi'ty," Sharon Lynn dutifully repeated, surprising all of them.

The horse neighed softly at hearing her name.

Cody glanced at Melissa and saw that she'd finally begun to relax. Her gaze was riveted on her daughter, though. He sensed that if Misty so much as shied back a step, Melissa was poised to snatch Sharon Lynn out of harm's way.

Just when he thought the worst of her reaction was past, she turned and looked up at him, anxiety and dismay clearly written all over her face. "How can your father even think about getting on a horse ever again?" she asked in a low voice, not meant to carry.

As if he'd been struck by a bolt of lightning, Cody finally realized why Melissa had been so upset by Harlan introducing Sharon Lynn to riding. The accident that had cost his mother her life hadn't even crossed his mind when Harlan had suggested bringing Sharon Lynn out to see the horses. But obviously the way Mary Adams had died had left an indelible image on Melissa's mind, as it might on anyone who didn't have the sensitivity of a slug, Cody chided himself. She had been fearful of horses to begin with. His mother's death could only have exaggerated that fear.

"Damn, no wonder you turned white as a sheet a minute ago when Daddy suggested bringing Sharon Lynn out here," he apologized. "You were thinking about what happened to Mother, weren't you?"

"Aren't you?" she asked, staring at him incredulously.

"No," he said honestly. "There's no point in blaming the horse for what happened to Mother. It was an accident and not an uncommon one at that.

The horse was spooked by a snake. Even then, the fall might not have killed her. It was the way she landed.''

Melissa shuddered. ''Still, how can either one of you not think about it every single time you see a horse?''

''Because Daddy is a rancher, through and through. So am I,'' Cody said, trying to explain to Melissa what must seem inexplicable. ''There are some things over which a rancher has no control. Rattlers spooking a horse is one of them.''

He glanced at his father. ''If he blames anyone or anything for what happened to Mother, it's more than likely himself for suggesting that ride in the first place. He also knows that the only way to conquer the fear after what happened is to get right back on a horse. He's been out riding over that same stretch of land every single day since she died.''

Melissa clearly wasn't reassured. ''I don't care about conquering fear. All I see is that your mother's death should be a damn good reason for him not to bring his granddaughter anywhere near a horse,'' she argued. ''She's a baby, Cody.''

Cody was beginning to see there was no reasoning with her on this. It was too soon after his mother's tragic accident. ''If it's really upsetting you, I'll talk him out of it,'' he offered. ''But sooner or later, Sharon Lynn will ride. She can't have a cowboy for a daddy and not learn.''

Melissa rested her hand on his forearm. The expression on her face pleaded with him.

"Later, please," she said. "Just the thought of it after what happened to your mom makes me sick."

Cody could see that she wasn't exaggerating. Though he didn't agree with her, he could feel some compassion for the anxiety she was experiencing. He walked over and spoke to his father. Harlan shot a look over his shoulder at Melissa and gave an understanding nod.

"Of course," he apologized at once. "I didn't realize it would bother her so."

"Neither did I," Cody said. "But she's practically turning green."

"You take this little angel on inside, then. I'll be there in a bit."

Cody reached for his daughter, who let out a scream the instant she realized she was being taken away from the horse.

"Mi'ty!" she sobbed plaintively. "Mi'ty!"

"You'll see Misty another time," Cody promised. "Right now, I'm going to take you inside so you can see all of your new toys that Granddaddy bought you."

He wasn't sure if Sharon Lynn totally understood exactly what having Harlan Adams as a benefactor was all about until they reached the room he'd filled with everything from a set of white baby furniture with pink gingham sheets and comforter to every stuffed toy he'd been able to order straight from the biggest department store in Dallas. Even Cody had been bowled over by the assortment he'd assembled practically overnight. Melissa's mouth was agape as she surveyed the room.

"Did he buy out the store?" Melissa asked.

Before Cody could respond, Sharon Lynn was trying to scramble down, her gaze fixed on the rocking horse.

"Mi'ty, Mi'ty," she called joyously as she dropped from unsteady legs to her knees to crawl toward it. She pulled herself up beside it and tried to climb on. Cody lifted her up and settled her on the seat, keeping a firm grip on the waistband of her pants as she rocked enthusiastically.

He grinned at Melissa. "Told you she was going to be a natural on horseback."

"I think this one is a little more her size," Melissa retorted dryly. "The distance to the ground isn't quite so far."

Before he could comment on that, something else caught Sharon Lynn's eye and she twisted around and tried to clamber down. Cody lifted her off the rocking horse and set her back on her feet.

"How about you walk wherever you want to go this time?" he suggested.

Sharon Lynn clamped her fingers around his, wobbled precariously, then took an unsteady tiptoe step forward. With each step her confidence obviously mounted, though she kept that tight grip on his fingers.

"She's going to ruin your back," Melissa observed. "You're bent practically double."

Cody didn't give a hoot. This was the first time he'd witnessed his daughter's faltering, tentative footsteps. He'd bend over the rest of the afternoon and ache for a week, if she wanted to keep walking.

With every minute he spent with her, every experience they shared, the powerful sense of connection he felt with her intensified.

Just then she stumbled and fell. Her eyes promptly filled with tears. Certain that she must have broken something to be sobbing so pathetically, Cody knelt beside her and gently examined ankles, arms, knees and elbows. He even checked for a bump under her hair or on her forehead, though he knew perfectly well she hadn't hit her head. She'd landed squarely on her well-padded button.

Finally satisfied that she was more scared than hurt, he scooped her up, only to find Melissa grinning at him.

"And you thought I was overreacting. At this rate, you're going to be a wreck in a month," she chided, sounding smug. "Either that or you'll drive the emergency room staff at the hospital completely wild. They'll flee when they spot you coming."

He lifted his eyebrows. "Is this another chunk of that learning curve you're trying to help me skip?" he taunted.

To his amusement, she blushed furiously. "Stop teasing. I only took her in twice," she admitted defensively.

"Oh? When?"

"The first time I thought she'd swallowed the toy from a box of cereal."

Cody shuddered. He would have had her in for X rays himself. "Had she?"

"No, I found it later in the crack between the

refrigerator and the sink. I suppose she threw it across the room.''

''And the other time?''

''She fell and bumped her head,'' Melissa said, shivering visibly at the recollection. ''It terrified me. I'd never seen so much blood in my entire life. I was sure she was going to bleed to death before I got her to the hospital.''

Cody's heart skidded to a halt. He anxiously studied Sharon Lynn's face for some sign of such a traumatic injury. He smoothed back her hair to get a better look at her forehead.

''No stitches?'' he asked when he could find no evidence of them.

Melissa shrugged. ''Not a one,'' she confessed. ''They put a butterfly bandage on it and sent us home. Apparently head injuries just bleed profusely. There was no permanent damage done.''

Cody met her gaze and caught the faint signs of chagrin and laughter in her eyes. He also thought he detected something else, perhaps a hint of resentment that she'd been left to cope with such things on her own. Guilt sliced through him, even though part of the blame for his absence could be laid squarely at Melissa's feet.

''I'm sorry I wasn't here for you,'' he said, and meant it. He regretted every lost opportunity to share in the experiences—good or bad—of his daughter's first year.

The laughter in Melissa's eyes died at once. That hint of resentment burned brighter. ''I handled it,'' she said abruptly, and turned away.

He watched as she walked over and knelt down by their daughter, listening intently to Sharon Lynn's nonsensical jabbering. The hard expression on her face when she'd turned away from him softened perceptibly. A smile tugged at her lips as she cupped her hand possessively behind her daughter's head, caressing the soft curls. Sharon Lynn looked up at her, an expression of adoration on her face.

In that instant Cody saw what it meant to be a family... and he wasn't a part of it. Melissa couldn't have shut him out any more effectively, any more deliberately, if she'd tried.

He stood there, so close and yet very much apart from them. Longing welled up inside him, longing to know all of these little details of Sharon Lynn's first months that Melissa shared so grudgingly.

There was so much more he yearned for, as well. He yearned to share their closeness, to have Melissa look into his eyes with something more than distrust.

He sighed then, because it all seemed so unlikely, so impossible, thanks to his own foolish decision to accept what he'd seen that fateful night at face value. If only he'd stayed. If only...

Wasted regrets, he chided himself. This was his reality—a child who barely knew him, a woman who wanted no part of him, who was willing to allow him glimpses of his child out of a sense of obligation, not love.

He thought then of the flicker of passion he'd caught once or twice in Melissa's sea green eyes, of the heat that had flared when he'd touched her, and wondered whether her disdain ran as deep as she wanted him to believe.

Reality and circumstances could change, he reassured himself. Sometimes for the worse, of course. Harlan knew all about the dramatic, unexpected, tragic turns life could take. He'd lost a son and his beloved wife when he'd least expected it. Those losses had taught a lesson to all of them.

Harlan had also taught his sons that they could control most aspects of their lives if they set their minds to it and fought for what they wanted. In fact, he'd turned out a dynasty of control freaks, it seemed. Luke had built his own ranch from the ground up, rather than take the share in White Pines that Harlan had wanted him to have. Jordan had fought his father bitterly for a career in the oil industry. Cody had battled for a share of White Pines, and now, it seemed, he had an even more difficult war to wage.

Cody's gaze settled on Melissa and his daughter once again. They were worth fighting for. Harlan had given him years of practice at battling for everything from permission to go to a dance to the right to build his own house on White Pines' land. Apparently it had all been preparation for a moment like this.

His mouth curved into a slow smile. He'd just have to think of Melissa's rejection not as a setback but as a challenge. It was an opportunity to utilize all those lessons Harlan had not-so-subtly instilled in them. He would have to seize the initiative and keep Melissa thoroughly off kilter until she finally woke up and realized that this time he wasn't running.

This time he intended to be the steadying influence in her life and he meant to be there always.

Chapter Ten

The morning had been far too intense, Melissa thought as she finally escaped the house and settled gratefully into a chair on the patio with a tall glass of iced tea. The day had turned unseasonably warm and though she still needed her jacket, it was pleasant to sit outside in the fresh, clean air with the sun on her face while Sharon Lynn napped.

Her emotions were raw. Coming back to White Pines had been far more difficult than she'd anticipated. Part of that was because she felt Mary Adams's death here in a way it hadn't struck her even at the funeral. Some of it had to do with Harlan's warmhearted welcome and the obvious delight he was taking in getting to know his new granddaughter. Most of it, though, undeniably had to do with Cody.

At White Pines she was on his turf. Like Harlan, he reigned over the operation of this ranch as comfortably as she served burgers at Dolan's. His self-confidence radiated from him in this environment. It always had.

Cody might have been wickedly flirtatious and carefree in his social life, but when it had come to work he'd been mature and driven to prove himself to his father. His early success as a ranch manager had smoothed away any insecurities he might have had living in Harlan Adams's shadow.

Cody's command of this privileged world, combined with seeing how easily Sharon Lynn had been accepted into it as Cody's child, had caused her to rebel. Earlier, as Sharon Lynn had taken a few faltering steps with Cody's help, Melissa had had this awful, selfish feeling that Cody was benefiting from having a daughter without having done anything to deserve it beyond making her pregnant in the first place.

He hadn't coached her through labor. He hadn't walked the floor with Sharon Lynn in the middle of the night. He hadn't fretted and cried trying to figure out a way to calm her, all the while convinced he was a failure at parenting. He hadn't been there to panic over the sight of the blood from that cut she had described to him earlier.

No, he had simply waltzed back into their lives and expected to claim his parental rights by flashing his charming grin and dispensing toys like some cowboy Santa. Well, she wouldn't have it. She wouldn't let it be that easy. He was going to have to earn a right to be a part of his daughter's life... and of hers.

That decided, she was troubled only by the realization that her demands were vague, that even she might not recognize when Cody had paid the dues she expected. Should she have a checklist? A timetable? Or would she finally know somewhere deep inside when she was through punishing him for being absent when she'd needed him the most?

"You okay?" Harlan asked, coming out of the house and studying her worriedly.

"Fine," she said, fighting not to take her annoyance at Cody out on his father.

Harlan was innocent in all of this. She had seen for herself the toll his wife's death had taken on him and she was glad that bringing Sharon Lynn here had given him some pleasure. She was sorry that she had so stubbornly resisted the temptation to announce to all the world long ago that her child was Cody's, just so that Harlan and Mary might have had the chance to know their grandchild from day one. The irony, of course, was that everyone in town had known it anyway.

"If you're so fine, how come you're sitting out here in the cold all by yourself, looking as if you just lost your last friend in the world?" Harlan asked.

"I didn't lose him," she said dryly. "I'm thinking of killing him."

Harlan's blue eyes twinkled at her feisty tone. "Ah, I see. Cody can be a bit infuriating, I suppose."

"There's no supposing about it. He is the most exasperating, egotistical…"

"Talking about me?" the man in question inquired.

He spoke in a lazy drawl that sent goose bumps dancing down Melissa's spine despite her resolution to become totally immune to him. Obviously she still needed to work harder on her wayward hormones.

"Which part clued you in?" she inquired. "Exasperating or egotistical?"

Harlan chuckled at the exchange, then promptly clamped his mouth shut in response to a dire scowl from his son. "Sorry," he said insincerely. "You two want to be left alone, or should I stick around to referee?"

"Stay," Melissa encouraged just as Cody said, "Go."

"Thank you, Melissa," Harlan said, winking at her. "I think I'll stay. The show promises to be downright fascinating. This time of day, good entertainment's hard to come by. Nothing but cartoons on TV."

"Daddy!" Cody warned.

"Yes, son?"

"We don't need you here," Cody insisted rudely.

"Speak for yourself," Melissa shot back.

Cody strolled closer until he was standing practically knee-to-knee with her. He bent down, placed his hands on the arms of the chair and said very,

very quietly, "Do you really want him to hear our private, personal, *intimate* conversation?"

The gleam in his eyes was pure dare. Melissa swallowed hard. Surely Cody was just taunting her. She couldn't imagine him saying anything to her that Harlan shouldn't hear. And the truth of it was, she wanted Harlan here as a buffer just to make sure that the conversation stayed on a relatively impersonal track. She didn't trust those slippery hormones of hers. They were liable to kick in when she least expected it.

She shot a defiant look at the man who was scant inches from her face. "Yes," she said emphatically.

Cody appeared startled by the firm response. His lips twitched with apparent amusement.

"Suit yourself, Me…liss…a."

The breath fanning across her cheek was hot and mint-scented. The glint of passion in his eyes sent her pulse skyrocketing. She tried to avoid that penetrating look, but no matter how she averted her gaze she seemed to lock in on hard, lean muscle. Temptation stole her breath.

She saw the precise instant when Cody's expression registered smug satisfaction, and it infuriated her. It galled her that she responded to him, annoyed her even more that he clearly knew it.

She gathered every last ounce of hurt and resentment she'd ever felt toward him to slowly steady her pulse. With careful deliberation she lifted her glass of tea to her lips and took a long, deep swallow. She kept her gaze riveted to his as she drank, determined to show him that this latest tactic no longer had the power to rattle her. He would not win her over with his easy charm.

Yet even as she did, even as uncertainty and then a flash of irritation darkened Cody's eyes, she quaked inside and prayed he would back off before she lost the will for the battle. She was weakening already, her palms damp, her blood flowing like warm honey.

Just when she was sure she could no longer maintain the calm, impervious facade, Cody jerked upright, raked a hand through his hair and backed off.

"Score one for Melissa," Harlan said softly, his voice laced with laughter.

Cody whirled on him. "Daddy, I'm warning you…"

Harlan's dark brows rose. "Oh?"

Cody frowned. "Dammit, how come you two are in cahoots?"

"Not me," his father protested, his expression all innocence except for the sparkle in his eyes that was quintessential Harlan. "I'm just a bystander."

"An unwanted bystander," Cody reminded him.

"Speak for yourself," Melissa retorted once again.

Cody scowled down at the two of them for another minute, then muttered a harsh oath under his breath and stalked off. Only when he was out of sight did Melissa finally allow herself to relax.

"Whew! That was a close one," Harlan said, grinning at her. "Another couple of seconds and the heat out here would have melted steel. Scorched me clear over here. You sure have figured out how to tie that boy in knots.''

To her amazement, he sounded approving. ''Shouldn't you be on his side?'' Melissa inquired.

''I suspect Cody can take care of himself,'' he observed. ''I'm just relieved to see that you can, too.''

Melissa met his amused gaze and finally breathed a sigh of relief. She grinned at him. ''It's about time, don't you think?''

''Way past time, I'd say,'' he said, and reached over to pat her hand. ''You want some advice from a man who knows Cody just about as well as anyone on earth?''

''I suspect I could use it,'' she agreed, wondering at the turn of events that had truly put her and Harlan Adams in cahoots, just as Cody had accused. Maybe Harlan's wisdom would be more effective than his wife's advice had been.

''Despite all these centuries that have passed, the caveman instinct hasn't entirely been bred out of us men,'' Harlan began. ''Now I know that's not so politically correct, but it's the truth of it. A man needs to struggle to claim what he wants. It builds up his passion for it, makes him stronger. Call it perversity, but things that come too easily don't mean so much. Don't ever tell 'em I said so, but I made every one of my sons fight me to earn the right to become his own man. They resented me at the time, but in the end they were better for it.''

Sorrow flitted across his face as he added, ''Except maybe for Erik. He wanted to please too badly.

I made a serious miscalculation by forcing him to work in ranching, one I'll regret to my dying day.''

Listening to his philosophy about men, Melissa wondered if Mary Adams had put up much of a struggle. Her adoration of Harlan, her catering to his every whim, had been obvious to anyone who knew the two of them. Given Mary's advice to her about making Cody jealous, Melissa suspected she had given her husband fits at one time.

''Did Mary make you jump through hoops?'' she asked.

''She did, indeed,'' Harlan told her, chuckling even as his expression turned nostalgic. ''I knew the first minute I laid eyes on her that she was the woman I wanted to marry. She was smart as the dickens, beautiful and willful. She claimed later that she fell in love at first sight, too. She didn't let me know it for a good six months, though. In fact, for a while there I was convinced she couldn't stand to be in my presence. It was a hell of a blow to my ego.''

He shook his head. ''My goodness, the things I used to do just to earn a smile. That smile of hers was worth it, though. It was like sunshine, radiating warmth on everyone it touched. For thirty-six years, I was blessed with it.''

''You're missing her terribly, aren't you?'' Melissa said softly.

''It's as if I lost a part of myself,'' Harlan admitted, then seemed taken aback that he'd revealed so much. He drew himself up, clearly uncomfortable with the out-of-character confidences.

"Enough of that now. You didn't come all the way out here to listen to me go on and on."

"May I ask you a question?" Melissa asked impulsively.

"Of course you can. Ask me anything."

"Did you know Cody had asked me to marry him?"

"He told me."

"Did he also tell you I'd turned him down?"

Harlan nodded.

She looked over at this man who had always been so kind to her, who'd treated her as a daughter long before she had any ties to his family beyond her hope of a future with his son. Did she dare ask him what she really wanted to know, whether Cody loved her for herself or only as the mother of the daughter he was so clearly anxious to claim? She hedged her bets and asked a less direct question.

"Was I wrong to say no?"

Harlan regarded her perceptively. "Are you afraid he won't ask again?"

She drew in a deep breath, then finally nodded, acknowledging a truth that was far from comforting.

"What would you say if he does?"

"Right now?"

"Right now," he concurred.

She thought it over carefully. Given the unresolved nature of their feelings, she would have to give him the same answer. "I'd tell him no," she admitted.

"Then there's your answer," he reassured her.

"Look, I don't claim to know what happened between you and Cody that made him run off to Wyoming, but it's plain as day to me that it wasn't a simple misunderstanding. You keeping that baby a secret from him proves that. Feelings that complicated take time to sort out. Take as long as you want, just don't shut him out of your life in the meantime. Silence and distance aren't the way to patch things up."

Harlan's warning was still echoing in her head when she finally went in search of Cody. He was right, the lines of communication did need to remain open, for Sharon Lynn's sake, if not her own.

She suspected Cody was either in the barn or had taken off for his own place nearby. His father had promised to look in on Sharon Lynn and to entertain her if she awakened from her nap.

When she didn't find Cody in the barn, she set off across a field to the small house Cody had built for himself in defiance of his father's order that he should strike out on his own and work some other ranch, maybe even start his own as Luke had. Every board Cody had hammered into place, every shingle he had laid on the roof had been a declaration that he intended to stay and claim his share of White Pines.

Melissa had watched him night after night, at the end of long, backbreaking days running the ranch. She had helped when she could, bringing him picnic baskets filled with his favorite foods on the evenings when he'd skipped supper to keep on working until the last hint of daylight faded.

She had observed his progress with her heart in her throat, waiting for him to ask her opinion on the size, the style, the color of paint, anything at all to suggest he intended it to be their home and not just his own. Though he had seemed to welcome her presence and her support, those words had never come.

Even so, she had been there with him when the last detail was completed, when the last brushstroke of paint had covered the walls. Though she had only spent a few incredible, unforgettable nights under that roof, she had always felt as if this was home. It was the place Sharon Lynn had been conceived.

As she neared the low, rambling white structure with its neat, bright blue trim, she thought she heard the once-familiar sound of hammering. She circled the house until she spotted Cody in the back, erecting what appeared to be a huge extension off what she knew to be the single bedroom.

The sight of that addition didn't snag her attention, however, quite the way that Cody did. He had stripped off his shirt, despite the chill in the air. His shoulders were bare and turning golden brown in the sun. A sheen of perspiration made his muscles glisten as they were strained and tested by his exertion.

Sweet heaven, she thought, swallowing hard. He was gorgeous, even more spectacularly developed than he had been the last time she'd seen him half-naked.

"Cody," she whispered, her voice suddenly thready with longing.

She heard the loud *thwack* of the hammer against wood and something softer, followed by an oath that would have blistered a sailor's ears. The ladder he was on tilted precariously, but he managed to right it and climb down without further mishap.

His gaze riveted on her, he muttered, "Damn, Melissa, don't you know better than to sneak up on a man when he's halfway up a ladder?"

She knew his testiness had more to do with his injured thumb than her unexpected presence. She grinned at him. "I've been in plain view for the last half mile. You would have seen me if you were the least bit observant."

"I'm concentrating on what I'm doing, not scanning the horizon for visitors."

"Just what is it you're doing?"

"Adding on."

She gave him a wry look. "That much is plain. *What* are you adding on?"

"A room for my daughter."

Surprise rippled through her. "Isn't that room Harlan's prepared good enough?"

"I want her to have her own room in my home," he insisted, giving her a belligerent look that dared her to argue.

"Seems like a lot of work for an occasional visit."

He climbed down from the ladder and leaned back against it, his boot heel hooked over the bottom rung behind him. His chin jutted up belligerently. It should have warned her what was coming, but it didn't.

"We're not talking an occasional visit, Melissa," he declared bluntly. "I expect to have her here a lot. You've had her for more than a year. I'm expecting equal time."

A year, here with Cody? Away from her? A sudden weakness washed through her. "You can't be serious," she whispered, thinking of the warning her mother had given her at the outset. Had Velma been right, after all? Would Cody bring all of the Adams influence to bear to get custody of his child?

"Dead serious," he confirmed, his unblinking gaze leveled on her.

This was a new and dangerous twist to Cody's driven nature. Clearly he intended to go after his daughter with the same singleminded determination he'd devoted to securing his place at White Pines.

"Cody, she's not a possession," she said in a tone that barely concealed her sudden desperation. "She's a little girl."

"A little girl who ought to get to know her daddy."

"I've told you—I've *promised* you—that we can work that out. I don't want to prevent you from spending time with her, from getting to know her, but to bring her to a strange house, to expect her to live with a virtual stranger...I won't allow it, Cody. I can't."

"You may not have a choice," he said coldly. "I don't want to get lawyers involved in this, but I will if I have to."

Melissa had no trouble imagining who would win in a court fight. As good a mother as she'd been, Cody and his family had the power to beat her. "There has to be another way," she said.

He nodded. "There is."

"What? I'll do anything."

His mouth curved into a mockery of a smile. "You make it sound so dire. The alternative isn't that awful. You just have to marry me."

The conversation she'd just had with Harlan echoed in her head. She couldn't marry Cody, not under these circumstances, especially not with him trying to blackmail her into it. What kind of a chance would their marriage have if she did? None. None at all.

She forced herself not to react with the anger or counterthreats that were on the tip of her tongue. Reason and humor would be more successful against the absurdity of what he was suggesting.

"Cody, half of the women in Texas would marry you in a heartbeat if you're anxious to have a wife," she said, refusing to consider the terrible consequences to her emotions if he took her up on what she was suggesting. "Why try to blackmail me into it?"

"Because you're the one who's the mother of my child," he said simply.

"But that's all I am to you," she replied, fighting tears. "It's not enough to make a marriage. At the first sign of trouble, what's to prevent you from bolting again, just like you did when you saw me with Brian? You don't trust me. You don't want me.''

''Oh, I wouldn't say that,'' he said, straightening and walking slowly toward her with a look that flat-out contradicted her claim.

Melissa held her ground. If she backed down now, if she showed him any hint of weakness, he would win. The prize was more than her pride, more than her body. The prize they were warring over was her daughter.

Cody's advance was slow and deliberate. His eyes, dark as coal in the shadow of the house, seemed to sear her with their intensity. His lips formed a straight, tight line. Anger and frustration radiated from every masculine pore.

When he neared to within a few scant inches, the heat from his body enveloped her, tugging at her like a powerful magnet. And still she held her ground.

''I want you, Me…liss…a,'' he said quietly. ''Make no doubt about that.''

She shivered under his slow, leisurely, pointed inspection. Her skin sizzled under that hot gaze. The peaks of her breasts hardened. Moisture gathered between her thighs. Her entire body responded as if he'd stroked and caressed every inch of her. She ached to feel his fingers where his gaze had been. And still, unbelievably, she held her ground.

Her breath snagged, then raced. Her pulse skittered crazily. She longed for someplace to sit or lean, anything to keep her weak knees from giving away her shakiness.

"Tempted, Me...liss...a?"

"No," she squeaked, hating herself for not making the response firmer, more emphatic.

"Remember how it felt to have me inside you?" he taunted, hands jammed into his pockets, deliberately stretching faded denim over the unmistakable ridge of his arousal.

Her gaze locked on that evidence of his desire. A matching hunger rocketed through her. She swallowed hard, clenching her fists so tightly she was certain she must be drawing blood. But still she held her ground.

"In there, on that big, old, feather mattress," he reminded her silkily. "Our legs all tangled, our bodies slick with sweat. Remember, Me...liss...a?"

Oh, sweet heaven, she thought, desperately trying to replace his images with other, safer memories of her own. Memories of being alone and scared, when she realized she was pregnant. Memories of staring at a phone that never rang as day after day, then month after month ticked by. Thinking of that, she steadied herself and held her ground.

She leveled a look straight into eyes that blazed with passion and said, "It won't work, Cody. We can't resolve this in bed."

He reached out then, skimmed his knuckles lightly along her cheek and watched her shiver at the touch. "You sure about that, darlin'?"

She wasn't sure about anything anymore except

the tide of desire she was battling with every last shred of her resistance. Her breathlessness kept her silent, afraid that anything she said or the whispered huskiness of her voice would give her away.

His fingers traced a delicate, erotic path along her neck, circling her nape, pulling her closer and closer still until their lips were a scant hairsbreadth apart, their breath mingling along with their scents; hers, wildflower fresh, his, raw and purely masculine.

The touch of his mouth against hers, gentle as a breeze, commanding as the pull of the tides, sealed her fate. The ground she'd held so staunchly gave way as she swayed into the temptation of that kiss.

Cody gave a sigh that she interpreted as part relief, part satisfaction. He coaxed her lips apart, touched his tongue to hers in a provocative duet.

Melissa bowed to the inevitable then. She had no power or will to resist this lure. She gave herself up to the sweet, wild sensations that had always been her downfall with Cody. He knew every inch of her, knew how to persuade and cajole, how to tempt and tease until her body was his as it had always been.

Her heart, she prayed, she could protect a little longer.

Chapter Eleven

The dare was backfiring. Cody knew it the instant he saw Melissa sprawled across his bed, her long auburn hair tangled on his pillow, her skin like smoothest satin, her coral-tipped breasts beckoning to him.

Until this moment it had only been distant memories that tormented him, fueling steamy dreams and restless nights. Now she was here and this throbbing hunger he felt for her was real. Powerful sensations he'd been telling himself that absence—and abstinence—had exaggerated were reawakened now with passionate urgency.

There might still have been a split second when he could have reclaimed sanity and reason, but if there was, he let it pass. His need for her was too great. His conviction that making love to her once again would bind her to him forever was too compelling.

The soft, winter sunlight spilled through a skylight above the bed and bathed Melissa in a golden glow. An artist might spend a lifetime searching for anything so beautiful, he thought as he stood looking down at her. An artist might spend an entire career trying to capture that same sensual vision on canvas and fail in the end. Cody certainly had never seen anything to equal the sight. He couldn't tear his gaze away.

Pregnancy had changed her body, gently rounding it, where before it had been all sharp angles and far more delicate curves. He swallowed hard as he absorbed the changes, regretting with every fiber of his being that he'd never seen her belly swollen with his child or her breasts when they were tender and engorged with milk.

He was aware of the instant when embarrassment tinted her skin a seashell pink from head to toe. She grabbed for a corner of the sheet, but before she could cover herself, he caught the edge and tugged it gently from her grasp. He stripped away his own clothes and sank down beside her, his gaze never leaving hers.

His breath eased out of him on a ragged sigh. ''You are even more beautiful than I remembered,'' he said, touching his fingers to the pulse that hammered at the base of her neck, gauging her response. Her skin burned beneath his touch. Her pulse bucked like the most impatient bronco he'd ever ridden.

And her eyes, oh, how they pleaded with him. The delicate sea green shade had darkened with some inner turbulence. There wasn't a doubt in his mind that she wanted him with a desperation as fierce as his own.

He also knew with absolute certainty that she didn't want to desire him at all. Outside just now, she had fought her own passion valiantly, but nature and the inevitability of their mating were against her, just as they had been against him since his return to Texas.

He had always understood that internal war, perhaps even better than she did. Way back, when he'd waged his own battle to resist being hemmed in, when he'd struggled against commitment, his body had betrayed him, hungering for Melissa in a way he should have recognized as proof that they were meant to be. It had never been anywhere near as casual between them as he'd sworn to himself it was.

Now, with this second chance, his gaze intent, he skimmed his fingers over delicate skin, caressing new curves and exploring familiar planes. He scattered kisses in the wake of his touch, until her skin was on fire and her breath was coming in soft gasps and her eyes were the color of a stormy sea.

He wondered if he would ever understand the complex mix of raw, violent emotions she stirred in him. The primitive urge to claim and possess tangled with a more sensitive desire to awaken and give pleasure. He concentrated on the latter, judging the success of each stroke of his fingers, each dark and passionate kiss.

"Cody, please," she pleaded, her body arching upward, seeking his, seeking the very possession he held back.

"Not yet," he soothed, even as he intensified his touches, tormenting and teasing until he sensed that she was right on the edge of a shattering, consuming climax.

His own body was rigid with tension, his blood pounding hotly through his veins. He held his own satisfaction at bay with a will that was being tested beyond endurance. He had no idea if the torment was meant to incite Melissa or prove something to himself. Perhaps he was hoping for one last, tiny victory in his internal battle to demonstrate that she didn't have the power to captivate him so thoroughly, after all.

But of course, she did. And when her soft cries and his own demanding need could no longer be ignored, he slowly, *slowly* entered her, sinking into that moist, velvet sheath with a sigh of thrilled satisfaction. As the pace of his entry and retreat escalated, they rode each wave of pleasure together until willpower—his and hers—vanished in an explosion that made them one.

Afterward, still floating on the memories of that wild, incredible journey, Cody couldn't help thinking of the implication. Melissa was home at last, where she belonged...and so was he.

* * *

"I told you so," Cody murmured smugly sometime later, when the room was bathed in the last pink shimmer of a glorious sunset.

"Told me what?" Melissa asked, her eyes closed, her body tucked against his side.

"That being married to me wouldn't be so awful."

Her eyes blinked open and she rose up to lean on one elbow. "This isn't marriage, Cody," she reminded him with a scowl. "It's an interlude, one afternoon, nothing more."

He was stunned that she could be so cool, so dismissive, in the aftermath of such all-consuming heat and passion. "Are you saying that this meant nothing to you?"

"I'm saying it's not enough to make a marriage," she countered stubbornly. "Cody, if sex were all that mattered, you would never have left for Wyoming and we'd have been married long ago."

His temper snapped at that. "I would never have left for Wyoming if you hadn't deliberately tried to make me think you were becoming involved with my best friend," he shouted, flinging her responsibility for his leaving back in her face.

Even as he hurled the accusation, he climbed from the bed and yanked on his jeans. He stalked out of the bedroom, not sure where he was headed until he found himself outside on the deck, standing at the rail gazing over the land he loved. Not even such natural beauty had the power to soothe him now, though. Fury made his insides churn.

The quick escalation of the argument forced him to admit that Melissa was right about one thing: making love hadn't solved anything. If anything, it had complicated matters, because now they both knew that the explosive chemistry between them was as volatile as ever. It was going to be harder than ever to work things out with reason and logic, when the temptation was going to be to fall into bed.

He sensed Melissa's presence before he felt her slip up to the rail beside him. He glanced down and felt the sharp tug of desire flare to life all over again, proving the very point he'd just made to himself.

She had pulled on one of his shirts, which fell to midthigh, leaving her long, slender legs revealed. She'd cuffed the sleeves halfway up her arms. The sun turned her tousled hair to strands of fire. She looked part innocent waif, part sexy siren.

"It should never have happened," she said, meeting his gaze, her expression troubled.

"I don't—I *won't*—regret it." He studied her intently. "You do, though, don't you?"

"Only because it complicates everything," she said, echoing his own thoughts. "I want so badly to think clearly about all of this, to make the right choices this time. When you touch me, my brain goes on the blink. I'm all sensation and emotion and nostalgia."

"Stay here with me tonight," Cody blurted impulsively, suddenly wanting to seize the opportunity to force a resolution to their standoff. "Sharon

Lynn will be fine with Daddy. Maritza will be there to help him look after her.''

A wistful smile played around her mouth. ''Haven't you heard a word I was saying?''

''All of them. I was just thinking, though, that we're both stubborn, strong people. Surely we could sit down and discuss all of this rationally and reach a sensible conclusion.''

''Here?'' she said doubtfully. ''Within a few feet of that bed in there? Within a few feet of each other, for that matter?''

She was shaking her head before the last words were out of her mouth. ''Forget it, Cody. It would never work. Besides, this isn't something we can resolve in a few hours or even a few days.''

He sighed heavily. ''So what do we do?''

''We give it time.'' Her expression turned rueful. ''Preferably in very public places.''

Cody wasn't wild about her solution. Now that he'd made up his mind to make the commitment he should have made two years earlier, Melissa's insistence on a delay was exasperating. He also feared that a decision reached on cold logic alone might not work in his favor. He wanted the heat of their passion on his side.

Of course, he reminded himself, their chemistry didn't necessarily confine itself to suitable locations. It could flare up just about anywhere, anytime, with the right look, the right caress. And there was something to be said for deliberately, provocatively stirring it up, when fulfillment was absolutely out of the question.

Yes, indeed, he decided with a renewed sense of anticipation, he could make things between himself and Melissa hotter than a day in the sweltering Texas sun. He could make it his business to drive her wild.

The plan had only one drawback that he could think of—it was very likely to drive him to distraction at the same time.

"Okay, you win," he said eventually, pleased when he noted the faint hint of disappointment in her eyes. A less diplomatic man might have reminded her to be careful what she wished for. Getting her way obviously wasn't quite as satisfying as she'd expected.

"Let's get dressed and see what's happening up at the main house," he said, deliberately making it sound as if they'd just shared something no more personal than a handshake. "Sharon Lynn's probably awake by now. You shower first. I'll clean up the tools I left outside."

Melissa nodded at the bland suggestion and turned toward the house with unmistakable reluctance. Cody grinned at the dejected slope of her shoulders.

"Hey, Melissa," he called softly.

She glanced back at him over her shoulder, her expression uncertain.

"I'll be thinking about you in that shower," he taunted. "All wet and slippery and naked."

Color flared in her cheeks. The sparkle returned to her eyes. A pleased smile tugged at her lips as she turned and sashaycd into the house with a deliberate sway of her hips.

Oh, my, yes, he thought as he watched her go. This was going to get downright fascinating.

If there was a decidedly knowing gleam in Harlan's eyes when they eventually returned to the main house, Melissa pretended to ignore it. What worried her more was that he might be getting ideas after their long absence that she and Cody had spent the time wisely and worked things out. Harlan believed strongly in family. He clearly wanted them to resolve things in a way that kept them all together. Despite what he'd said earlier about taking all the time she needed, hearing that they had not settled a thing would surely disappoint him.

"I think we'd best be getting back into town," Melissa announced within minutes.

"What's your hurry?" Harlan asked at once. "There's plenty of room here, if you want to stay the night. I'm rattling around in this big old place all by myself. It would be a pleasure to have company."

Melissa couldn't help thinking of another very recent invitation to stay at White Pines, one she had firmly declined. Her gaze caught Cody's and picked up on the gleam of anticipation in his eyes as he awaited her answer to his father's plea. She felt the web of Adams charm being woven snugly around her.

"No," she said, breaking free for now. "Another time."

She scooped up her daughter. "Time to get home, pumpkin."

Sharon Lynn promptly tried to squirm free, holding her arms out plaintively toward her grandfather. "Da?"

"You can come to see Granddaddy again very soon," Melissa promised, forcing herself not to see the equally wistful expression in Harlan's eyes as she refused to relinquish her daughter.

Harlan leaned down and kissed them both. "You're welcome here anytime," he told her. "Both of you. Don't stand on ceremony. Come whenever you have some time."

"I'll walk you out," Cody offered, falling into step beside her. "Don't wait up for me, Daddy. I might spend some time in town tonight."

Melissa didn't have to glance back to know that the comment had stirred a speculative glint in Harlan's eyes.

"Why did you say that?" she demanded of Cody the instant they were out of earshot of the house.

He regarded her with his most innocent look, the one only a fool would trust. "Say what?"

"That you'd be staying in town for a while?"

"Because it's true."

"No, it's not," she said firmly. "We did not discuss anything about you coming into town."

"Who said I'd be with you?" he inquired, leveling a gaze straight into her eyes.

"But you said… W-who?" Melissa sputtered. "Dammit, Cody, you did that deliberately."

"Did what?"

"Let your father assume that you intended to spend the evening, maybe the whole night, with me."

"Is that what I said?"

"It's what you implied."

"You sure you're not projecting your own desires onto me?"

"No, I am not," she practically shouted, causing Sharon Lynn to begin to whimper. Melissa kissed her cheek. "Shh, baby. It's okay. Your daddy and I are just having a discussion."

Cody chuckled. "Is that what it is? You sure do get riled up over a little discussion."

"I am not riled up," she insisted, keeping a tight rein on her frayed temper.

"Could have fooled me."

"Oh, forget it," she snapped as she put Melissa into her car seat and buckled her in. As she walked around the car, she heard the driver's door open and assumed Cody was simply being polite. Instead she found that he'd climbed in behind the wheel.

"Now what?" she asked, regarding him suspiciously.

"I thought I'd hitch a ride."

"Why would you want to do that? It'll leave you stranded in town."

"Oh, I'm sure I can find someone willing to bring me home," he said, then winked. "Eventually."

He said it in a smug way that had her grinding her teeth. "Is that a new technique you've learned for luring ladies out to your place?'' she inquired testily. ''You claim to need a ride home?''

''Let's just say I'm trying it out tonight.''

''And what if no one responds to your plight?''

''Oh, I don't think there's much chance of that,'' he said confidently. He shrugged. ''If it does, I'm sure you'd be willing to take me in for the night.''

''When pigs learn to fly,'' she retorted, irritated beyond belief that mere hours after they'd made love he was going on the prowl again. ''Get out, Cody.''

''I don't think so.''

''Cody Adams, do not make me march back into that house so I can borrow a shotgun from Harlan.''

He chuckled. ''I'm not real worried about that, darlin'. You'd never shoot a man in plain view of his daughter.''

He was right, of course. But, lordy, how she was tempted. ''Oh, for heaven's sake,'' she muttered, flinging open the back door. ''If you want to behave like a horse's behind, go right ahead.''

''Thank you,'' he said, and turned the key in the ignition.

Cody was the kind of driver who liked to tempt fate. Melissa clung to the door handle, while Sharon Lynn squealed with excitement as they sped around curves. She knew they were perfectly safe. Cody never tried anything unless he was confident of his control of the road, the car, or the situation. In fact, she suspected that was exactly the point he was trying to make.

Even so, she was pale by the time he finally

pulled to a stop in front of Rosa's Mexican Café. She was faintly puzzled by his choice. It was hardly a singles hangout.

"This is where you intend to spend your night on the town?"

He shrugged. "I thought we could grab a bite to eat first."

"Uh-huh," she said, regarding him skeptically.

"Do you have a problem with that?"

"Not really, I suppose, but you could have asked."

"I just did."

"Funny, it didn't sound much like a question to me. Maybe I already have plans for the night."

His expression turned dark. "Do you?" he demanded, his voice tight.

She let him wonder for the space of a heartbeat, then shrugged. "No, but I could have."

"Melissa, I swear..."

"Tsk-tsk," she warned, enjoying turning the tables on him, albeit briefly. "Not in front of the baby."

He scowled at her, scooped Sharon Lynn out of her car seat and headed inside, leaving Melissa to make up her own mind about whether to join them or remain in the car and quibble over semantics. Sighing over this latest test of her patience, she reluctantly followed him inside.

On a Saturday night, Rosa's was crowded with families. Melissa spotted Jordan and Kelly with their kids right off. Cody apparently did not, because he was making a beeline for an empty table on the opposite side of the restaurant. He picked up a booster seat en route and was already putting Sharon Lynn into it by the time Melissa joined him.

"Didn't you see Jordan and Kelly?" she asked. "They were trying to wave us over. There's room at their table."

"I saw them," Cody said tersely.

Melissa studied the set of his jaw. "Okay, what's wrong?"

"I do not intend to spend the evening with my brother," he said. "If you can call him that."

"Cody," she protested. "Why would you even say something like that?"

He frowned at her. "Because he knew about Sharon Lynn and he didn't tell me."

Melissa flinched as if he'd struck her. "Because I swore him to secrecy," she reminded him. She didn't want this family split on her conscience.

"He should have told me," Cody repeated, his stubbornness kicking in with a vengeance.

Melissa regarded him with a mix of frustration and dismay. The last thing she had ever wanted was to cause a rift between the two brothers. Uncertain what she could do to mend it, she turned and walked away. Cody was on her heels in a flash.

"Where are you going?" he asked suspiciously, latching onto her elbow.

"To the ladies' room," she said.

"Oh." He released her at once. "Sorry."

Melissa rolled her eyes and continued on to the back, praying that Kelly would spot her and join her.

She was combing her hair when Jordan's wife came into the rest room. "What are we going to do about them?" Melissa asked at once.

"It's not Jordan," Kelly said. "He feels terrible about what happened. He doesn't blame Cody for being furious."

"Okay, then, how do I get through to Cody? It's my fault. I've told him that, but he says Jordan should have ignored my wishes."

"He probably should have," Kelly concurred. "I could have told Cody myself and I didn't. There's enough blame to go around. The point now is to make things right. I wanted it settled before the baptism tomorrow so that Cody could be J.J.'s godfather. But until this is resolved, Jordan and I have decided to postpone the ceremony. It was only going to be a small family gathering anyway."

"Maybe if Jordan made the first move," Melissa suggested.

Kelly shook her head. "It wouldn't work. This is Cody's call, I'm afraid. The trouble is, we're dealing with the stubborn Adams men here."

"Can you all stick around?" Melissa asked. "I'll think of something."

"Sure," Kelly agreed. "Our dinner's just now being served anyway. I can't imagine what you can do, but let me know if you think I can help." She paused on her way to the door. "By the way, it's good to see the two of you together again. How are things going?"

"Don't ask," Melissa said.

Kelly grinned. "That good, huh? Does that mean

you haven't signed up at the Neiman-Marcus bridal registry yet?''

"No, and I wouldn't be holding my breath for that if I were you. I am not inclined to marry a man who is as thoroughly, unrepentantly, exasperating as Cody is.''

"Interesting," Kelly murmured, a knowing twinkle in her eyes.

"Don't start with me. I've just been subjected to Harlan's knowing looks for the past few hours.''

"Not another word," Kelly promised readily. "Nobody understands the perverse streak that runs in this family any better than I do.''

After Kelly had gone, Melissa slowly put her comb into her purse and headed back to their table. She saw at once that Cody had been joined by Kelly's precocious six-year-old, Dani.

"I came to see the baby," Dani announced when Melissa had joined them. "She's cuter than my brother. I wanted a sister, but somebody got mixed up and gave me a brother instead.''

Melissa grinned at her. "I bet you'll be glad of that when you're older. I always wished I had a brother who'd look out for me." She shot a pointed look at Cody when she said it.

Cody rolled his eyes. Clearly, he didn't think Jordan had done such a terrific job of looking out for him when it counted.

Dani stood closer to the table and leaned her elbows on it, propping her chin in her hands as she regarded her uncle. "You know, Uncle Cody, I was thinking.''

He visibly contained a grin. "What were you thinking, you little con artist?"

"Maybe Sharon Lynn should have a kitten of her own."

"Maybe she should." He glanced at Melissa. "What do you think?"

"I think you two were plotting this," Melissa charged, trying not to chuckle at the guilty expressions. "Sharon Lynn does not need a kitten. More importantly, a kitten does not need Sharon Lynn. She'd probably scare it to death."

Dani's brow knit as she considered the argument. "She's probably right, Uncle Cody. Babies don't understand about kittens. Francie thinks that my brother is a pest."

"A valid point," Cody agreed. "Maybe after Sharon Lynn gets to know how to behave around those kittens you talked me into taking, she can have one of her own."

"Good idea," Dani said. "Francie will probably have more by then."

"Over my dead body," Jordan said, arriving to stand behind his stepdaughter. "Hello, Melissa." He looked straight at Cody, who avoided his gaze. "Cody."

After a visible internal struggle, Cody nodded curtly.

Jordan stood there, looking uncharacteristically indecisive for another minute before sighing and saying, "Come on, Dani. Your dinner's getting cold."

When the pair of them were gone, Melissa said,

"You were rude to him, Cody. He made an overture and you didn't even say hello."

Cody closed his eyes. When he opened them, his stubborn resolve seemed to be firmly back in place. "I had nothing to say to him."

"Cody, I'm the one who betrayed you, not Jordan. I'm the one you thought had cheated on you. I'm the one who kept it a secret that I'd had your baby. You're speaking to me. You've forgiven me."

She studied him intently. "Or have you? Are you taking all the anger you don't dare express against me because of Sharon Lynn and projecting it on to Jordan?"

She saw by the way his jaw worked and his gaze evaded hers that she'd hit the nail on the head. She sighed. "Don't do this, Cody. Don't let what happened between us come between you and Jordan. Please," she pleaded.

When he didn't respond, she gave up. "Just promise you'll think about what I said, okay?"

"Yeah," he said tersely. "I'll think about it."

With great reluctance, Melissa finally conceded it was the best she could hope for. For now, anyway.

Chapter Twelve

Sometime well after midnight, Melissa woke to the sound of Sharon Lynn whimpering. She tumbled out of bed, flipped on the hall light and raced into the baby's room.

Sharon Lynn was tossing restlessly. Her skin was dry and burning up.

"Oh, baby," Melissa soothed as she scooped her up. "Are you feeling bad? Come with Mommy. I'll get you some water and check your temperature."

She had barely made it into the kitchen and flipped that light on when the front door burst open, scaring her half to death. She grabbed the frying pan and peeked through the kitchen doorway, prepared to do battle with a lunatic. Instead it was Cody, his clothes rumpled, his hair tousled, who stood in the foyer.

"Cody, what on earth?" she demanded, trying to slow the pounding of her heart. She set the frying pan down, though she wasn't entirely convinced he couldn't do with a good whop upside the head for scaring her so badly.

"What's going on?" he asked, casting worried looks from her to the baby and back. "I saw the lights come on. Are you okay?"

She ignored the question and tried to figure out what he was doing at her house in the middle of the night. The last time she'd seen him he'd been sitting at the bar in Rosa's. He'd declared his intention of starting his night on the town right there, clearly implying he intended it to end in someone's arms. She'd choked back her fury and tried to exit with some dignity, when all she'd really wanted to do was have a knock-down, drag-'em-out brawl with him. She was still itching for a fight, as a matter of fact, but right now Sharon Lynn's condition took precedence.

"Where have you been?" she asked, pleased that she was able to sound so cool when she was seething inside.

"On the porch," he admitted, taking his feverish daughter from her arms. As soon as he touched her, alarm flared in his eyes. "Good heavens, she's burning up. Have you taken her temperature?"

"I was just about to." She tried to remain calm in the face of his obvious panic and her own. She'd experienced rapidly spiking temperatures before and learned that it was a matter of course for children. Still, she'd never felt Sharon Lynn's skin quite so hot.

The thermometer registered one hundred and three degrees. Cody's face blanched when she told him.

"We're going to the hospital," he said at once, starting out of the kitchen.

Melissa blocked his way. "Not yet," she said far more calmly than she was feeling. There was no point in both of them panicking. "Let me give her a Tylenol and try bathing her with cool water to see if we can't bring that temperature down. If there's no change, then we'll call the doctor."

Sharon Lynn patted Cody's stubbled cheek weakly and murmured, "Da." She sounded pitiful.

Cody looked thoroughly shaken. "Melissa, I don't think we should wait. Something's really wrong with her."

"It's probably nothing more than the start of a cold or a touch of flu," she said. "Stuff like that reaches epidemic proportions this time of the year."

"Her temperature's over a hundred," he reminded her. "That can't be good for her."

"Babies get high temperatures. It's nothing to get crazy about," she insisted, amending to herself, *yet.*

She gave Sharon Lynn Tylenol, then ran cool water into the kitchen sink. "Bring her over here and let's get her out of that nightgown. It's soaking wet anyway. Why don't you go back to her room and bring me a clean one, along with a fresh diaper. We'll need those after I've sponged her off a bit with cool water."

Cody looked as if he might refuse to budge, but eventually he did as she'd asked. By the time he'd returned, Sharon Lynn was no longer whimpering. In fact she seemed to be relaxing and enjoying the cool water Melissa was gently splashing over her.

"Are you sure that's good for her?" Cody asked, worry etched on his face.

"It's exactly what the doctor and all the child-care books recommend. If you don't believe me, there's a book in the living room. Go read it." Anything to get him out of the kitchen again before he wore a hole in the linoleum with his pacing. Worse, she was feeling crowded with all of his hovering.

"No, no, I'll take your word for it," he said, standing over her shoulder and watching every move she made. "Maybe we should take her temperature again."

Melissa sighed and stepped aside to allow him to put the fancy new thermometer in Sharon Lynn's ear for a few seconds.

"It's a hundred and two," he proclaimed. "That's it. We're going to the hospital."

"It's down a whole degree," Melissa observed, blocking him when he would have snatched Sharon Lynn out of the bathwater. "The Tylenol's working."

"Not fast enough."

"Let's give it another half hour," she compromised.

Cody hesitated, then finally conceded grudgingly, "A half hour. Not a minute more."

He sat down at the kitchen table and fixed his

gaze on the clock over the sink. Apparently he intended to watch each of those thirty minutes tick by.

"Da!" Sharon Lynn called out.

Cody was on his feet in an instant. "What's up, sweet pea? You feeling better?" he asked, caressing her cheek with fingers that shook visibly.

A smile spread across his daughter's face. "Da," she repeated enthusiastically.

A little color came back into Cody's ashen complexion. "She feels a little cooler."

Melissa agreed. "I'm betting when we check her temperature again, it'll be just about back to normal."

Twenty minutes later Sharon Lynn was no longer feverish. She was once again tucked into her crib. Cody, still looking shaken, stood over her.

"How do you stand this?" he murmured to Melissa. "I've never been so terrified in my life."

Melissa patted his hand. "It gets easier after you've been through it once or twice and know what to expect," she promised him, but he shook his head.

"I can't imagine it getting easier," he said. "What if her temperature hadn't gone down? What if you'd guessed wrong?"

"Then we would have called the doctor or gotten her to the hospital."

"It might have been too late."

"Cody, stop that," she ordered, not daring to admit that she'd been scared silly, too, that she always was, no matter what the books said. "It's over. She's going to be fine. It was just a little fever."

He closed his eyes and drew in a deep breath. "Okay, you're right. Just a little fever." He still sounded unconvinced. He definitely showed no inclination to budge from beside the crib.

Melissa grinned at him. "Cody, everything really is fine. You don't have to stand there and watch her all night."

"I am not leaving this house," he said, his jaw jutting out belligerently.

"Fine. You can sleep on the sofa." She yawned. "Good night, Cody."

"Where are you going?"

"Back to bed."

"How can you possibly sleep?"

"Because I'm exhausted. You must be, too." In fact, he looked as if he hadn't slept in days.

"I won't sleep a wink," he swore.

"Whatever," she murmured, and headed for her room. At the doorway she recalled that they'd never really talked about why he'd been on her front porch in the first place. "Cody, why were you here in the middle of the night?"

A sheepish expression spread across his face. "I figured if you found me on your doorstep in the morning, you'd give me a lift home."

She grinned. "Couldn't find another taker for that fabulous Adams charm, huh?"

"Never even tried," he admitted, then shrugged. "You've spoiled me for anyone else, Me...liss...a."

She studied his face intently, looking for signs that the comment was no more than a glib, charming lie. He appeared to be dead serious. A little flutter of excitement stirred deep inside her. Was it possible that Cody really did intend to stick around through thick and thin, through good times and bad?

For the first time since he'd come home from Wyoming, she dared to hope that he really had changed. If he had…

No, she cautioned herself at once. It was too soon to leap to any conclusions at all about the future.

"Good night, Cody," she whispered, her voice husky with a longing she would never have admitted.

"Good night, darlin'."

Cody felt as if he'd slept on an old washboard. Every muscle ached like the dickens. Every vertebra in his back had either been compressed, twisted or otherwise maimed by Melissa's sofa. He suspected she'd made him sleep there on purpose, knowing what it would do to him.

He also had the distinct impression that there was a tiny wanna-be drummer in his head flailing away without much sense of rhythm.

He groaned and opened his eyes, blinking at the sunlight streaming into the living room. That was when he realized that the loud clanging wasn't in his head. It was coming from Sharon Lynn's room. If that was the case, it just might be something he could stop before his head exploded.

Moving inch by careful inch, he eased to his feet and padded down the hall to the baby's room. When he opened the door a crack, he found her bouncing in her crib, banging a wooden block on the railing. The instant she spied him, a smile spread across her face.

"Da," she enthused, and held out her arms.

Cody wondered if he would ever get over the thrill that sweet, innocent gesture sent through him.

"Morning, pumpkin. I take it from all the commotion in here that you're feeling better."

"Ya…ya…ya."

"That must mean yes," he decided as he plucked her out of the crib and took the toy block from her as a precaution. His head was feeling marginally better, but another round of Sharon Lynn's musical skills would be a killer.

Her temperature seemed to be gone. He quickly changed her, then carried her into the kitchen. Once there, he was stymied. Was she old enough for regular cereal? Or was there some sort of baby food she was supposed to have? He didn't recall discussing breakfast when he and Melissa had shopped for groceries.

He settled Sharon Lynn into her high chair, found a soft toy bear to entertain her, and searched through the cabinets. Nothing conclusive there beyond an assortment of frosted cereals that seemed more likely to appeal to a one-year-old than her mother. Then again, he didn't know much about Melissa's breakfast habits, either. On the rare occasions when they'd slept in the same bed before he'd left for Wyoming, breakfast had been the last thing on their minds first thing in the morning.

A glance in the refrigerator suggested that juice might be a good place to start. He recalled buying an awful lot of apple juice at the store. He filled a bottle and handed it over. Sharon Lynn tossed her bear on the floor and accepted it eagerly.

Scrambled eggs struck him as a safe bet. Besides, he and Melissa could eat them, as well. Fixing one meal for all of them appealed to him. It struck him as cozy; a family tradition of sorts. Their very first.

He started the coffeemaker, popped four slices of bread into the toaster, put butter and jelly on the table, then broke half a dozen eggs into a bowl and whipped them with a fork until they were foamy. Suddenly he heard the faint sound of footsteps behind him. He pivoted around and discovered Melissa leaning against the doorjamb.

"My goodness, you've been busy," she murmured, yawning and bending over to pick up the bear Sharon Lynn had tossed aside in favor of her juice. "How long have you been awake?"

Goose bumps chased down his spine at the sleepy sound of her voice and the sight of that cute little fanny draped in a very short, very revealing, silk robe.

"Our daughter's better than any rooster I ever heard. She woke me at the crack of dawn."

"Obviously she's feeling better," Melissa said, going over to touch her hand to the baby's forehead. "No more temperature."

"Seemed that way to me, too."

"Did you take it?"

He shook his head, drawing a grin.

"Turning into an old hand already," she teased. "No more panicking."

"I wouldn't say that," he said, shuddering at the memory of that icy fear that had washed through him in the wee hours of the morning. "But I am going to borrow that book of yours and read it from cover to cover."

He reached for Melissa's hand and pulled her toward him. He was vaguely surprised that she didn't put up a struggle. Maybe he hadn't imagined the closeness between them the night before.

When she was standing toe-to-toe with him, he had to resist the temptation to tug the belt of her robe free. Instead he brushed a strand of hair back from her face and gazed into her tired eyes.

"You were wonderful last night," he said softly. "Not only were you good with Sharon Lynn, but you kept me from freaking out."

Her lips curved slightly. "Having you here helped me, too," she said, surprising him.

"Why?"

"Staying calm for your benefit kept me from freaking out myself," she admitted.

He stared at her in astonishment. "You were scared?"

"Terrified," she admitted. "But I knew I couldn't let you see it or you'd have insisted on borrowing your father's plane and flying us all to some critical care hospital in Dallas in the middle of the night."

"You've got that right." He grinned. "We're quite a pair, aren't we?"

"Just typical parents, Cody."

The simple words were no more than the truth, yet Cody felt as if he'd just heard something terribly profound spoken for the first time. He was a parent, a certified grown-up, with responsibilities he couldn't slough off. Responsibilities, in fact, that he actually yearned to accept.

He wanted more Sunday mornings just like this one, waking up to the sound of his daughter making some sort of commotion to get attention, fixing breakfast for all three of them, sitting at the kitchen table across from Melissa. He renewed his vow to himself to do everything within his power to convince Melissa they ought to be a family.

After they'd eaten and after he'd cleaned up most of the scrambled egg Sharon Lynn had managed to rub into her hair or fling halfway across the kitchen, he sat back with a sigh of pure contentment.

"Don't get too settled," Melissa warned, a teasing note in her voice. "Your daughter needs a bath. I think I'll let you do the honors since that egg she's smeared everywhere was your doing."

"You sound as if that's punishment," he said. "What's the big deal?"

"You'll see," Melissa retorted a little too cheerfully to suit him.

She ran the inch or so of bathwater into the tub, then left him to it. It didn't take long for Cody to figure out why she'd had that smug expression on her face when she'd exited the bathroom.

Sharon Lynn really loved water. She loved to splash it. She loved to scoop it up by the handful and dribble it all over him. She loved to throw her toys into it, sending yet more splashes into the air.

She wasn't quite so crazy about soap. She wriggled and squirmed, trying to get away from him. Slippery as an eel, she evaded capture until she'd managed to soak him from head to toe. In fact, he was fairly certain that he was wetter and soapier than she was.

Melissa chose that precise moment to reappear. He heard her chuckling as he tried to towel his daughter dry.

"You find this amusing?" he inquired softly.

"Mmm-hmm," she admitted. "I sure do."

He dipped his hand in the scant remaining water that was actually in the tub and splattered it straight in Melissa's smug face. A startled, incredulous expression spread across her face.

"You brat," she muttered, turning on the faucet in the sink and scooping up a handful of water to pour over his head.

Sharon Lynn squealed with glee as water splashed everywhere.

Cody nabbed a plastic cup from the counter behind him, dipped it into the bathwater and soaked Melissa's front. Only after the damp bathrobe clung to her body did he realize the mistake he'd made. His breath snagged in his throat at the sight of her nipples hardening beneath that suddenly transparent silk. He swallowed hard, aware of the tightening in his groin and the flood of color climbing into his cheeks—and equally aware of the impossibility of pursuing the desire rocketing through him.

Melissa's gaze locked with his for what seemed an eternity, then dropped to the unmistakable evidence of his arousal. A smile slowly tugged at the corners of her mouth.

"Serves you right," she taunted as she turned and padded off to her room.

Cody groaned and wished like crazy that he knew Melissa's neighbors so he could plead with them to baby-sit for the rest of the morning. He wanted to finish what she had started with that provocative taunt.

Instead he forced himself to concentrate on getting Sharon Lynn dried off and dressed. The task was somewhat complicated by the soaked condition of his own clothes. He was dripping everywhere.

As soon as he had his daughter settled in her playpen, he grabbed a towel, went into the laundry room, stripped, and tossed his clothes into the dryer. He wrapped the towel snugly around his waist and retreated to the kitchen to drink another cup of coffee while he waited for everything to dry.

When Melissa wandered in a few minutes later her mouth gaped. "Where are your clothes?" she demanded, her gaze riveted on his bare chest.

"In the dryer."

"Get them out."

"I can't wear damp clothes," he observed.

"Whose fault is it they're wet?"

"Yours, as a matter of fact," he said blithely.

"You're the one who insisted I bathe Sharon Lynn. You obviously know what she's like in water."

She fought a grin and lost. "Yeah, I do," she admitted. "But, Cody, you cannot sit around in nothing but a towel."

"You have any better ideas?" He didn't wait for any suggestions from her before adding, "We could go back to bed."

"In your dreams."

He deliberately caught her gaze. "Absolutely," he said softly. "You have no idea how vivid my dreams have become lately."

From the fiery blush in her cheeks, he had the feeling, though, that he'd been wrong about that. He got the distinct impression that Melissa's dreams had been just as erotic as his own lately. He vowed that one day soon they'd compare notes...and make them come true.

Chapter Thirteen

The rapport between them lasted all the way back to White Pines. In fact, Cody had high hopes that he was finally beginning to make progress with Melissa. He was convinced that his presence during the previous night's medical crisis had started the difficult process of convincing her that he wasn't going to bolt out of their lives at the first sign of trouble.

It had been such a small thing, being by her side during those tense moments, but he'd heard the gratitude in her voice this morning, seen the first faint flicker of renewed faith in her eyes. He couldn't allow anything to shake that trust again, not until he'd had time to strengthen it.

As they drove up the long, winding lane at White

Pines he was startled to see his father emerge from the house. It appeared Harlan had been watching for them and, from the too cheerful expression on his face and the contradictory worry in his eyes, Cody could only guess that there was bad news.

He stepped out of the car and faced his father warily. "Hey, Daddy, everything okay?"

"Fine, just fine," Harlan said too heartily. He darted a worried look at Melissa, then added, "You'll never guess who's here to see you, son."

Cody shot a desperate glance toward Melissa and saw that she was hanging on his father's every word. He couldn't imagine who might have turned up at White Pines uninvited, but experience with his father's demeanor suggested he was right to be concerned. He regretted more than he could say having Melissa here at this precise moment. He should have walked home, even if it was twenty miles. He would have if he'd had any idea that trouble was going to be waiting on the doorstep.

He drew in a deep breath and braced himself. "Who?" he asked just as the front door creaked open and a slight figure with cropped black hair and a pixie face emerged. Shock rendered him speechless.

"Janey? What the hell?" He looked to his father, but Harlan merely shrugged. Cody turned back to the teenager who'd apparently tracked him down and come after him all the way from Wyoming. "What are you doing here?"

Even as he sought answers for Janey's unexpected presence, he heard Melissa's sharp intake of breath behind him. Before he could turn around, the car door slammed with enough force to rock the sturdy vehicle on its tires. He knew what that meant. He forgot all about Janey as he tried to get to Melissa before she got the wrong impression and took off in a snit. Correction, she already had the wrong impression. He just had to stop her.

"Melissa," he protested just as the engine roared to life. "Dammit, we need to talk. Don't you dare drive away from here!"

He might as well have been talking to the wind. The order was wasted. She'd already thrown the car into gear, then backed up, spewing gravel in every direction. He slammed his fist on the fender as she turned the car, shifted again and headed away from the house at a pace that would have done an Indy 500 driver proud.

"Terrific," he muttered. "That's terrific. Not five seconds ago, I actually believed she was starting to trust me and now this!"

"Cody," his father warned, nodding toward the girl who had stopped halfway down the sidewalk.

Sure enough, Janey looked as if he'd slapped her. Cody raked his hand through his hair and tried to get a grip on his temper. It wasn't the teenager's fault that his personal life was a mess. He crossed to Janey Treethorn in three strides and looked into a face streaked with tears and eyes that were as wide as a doe's caught in the cross hairs of a hunter's gun. His anger dissipated in a heartbeat.

"Janey, don't cry," he said softly, pulling her into a hug. "Shh, baby, it's okay."

"I'm s-sorry," she stammered. "I didn't mean to mess up everything."

"I know," he soothed, awkwardly patting her back as he cast a helpless look at his father. Harlan shrugged, clearly as bemused by this turn of events as Cody was.

"It's not your fault," he told her, even though he very much wanted to blame her for ruining his fragile truce with Melissa. "Come on, let's go inside and you can tell me why you came all this way. Does your dad know you're here?"

"Ye-es-s," she said, sniffling. "Your father called him last night."

Cody's heart sank. Obviously, Janey had run away from home, if last night was the first Lance had heard of her whereabouts. His former boss was probably fit to be tied. Janey was the least rebellious of his daughters. If she had pulled a stunt as crazy as this, the other two were likely to drive him completely over the edge. Lance needed a mother for those girls and he needed her in a hurry.

Inside, Cody suggested that Harlan go and see if Maritza could rustle them up some hot chocolate. He knew it was Janey's favorite. There had been many cold winter nights when she'd fixed it for him and her father, then lingered in the shadows listening to them talk.

Before he sat down, he went into the closest bathroom and gathered up a handful of tissues and brought them back to her. He was careful to sit in a chair opposite her, since he had the terrible feeling that her crush on him was what had brought her all the way to Texas. He'd never done a thing to encourage it, except to be kind to her, but apparently that had been enough to cause this impulsive trip to Texas.

"Feeling better?" he asked after a while, when she appeared to have cried herself out and had finished the mug of hot chocolate Maritza had served with barely concealed curiosity.

Janey nodded, but wouldn't meet his gaze. Her cheeks were flushed with embarrassment. She tucked her jeans-clad legs up under her and huddled on the sofa like a small child expecting to be scolded. She looked so woebegone that Cody was having a difficult time maintaining what was left of his dying anger.

"Janey, tell me what this is all about."

"I c-can't," she whispered.

"There must be a reason you left Wyoming and came all the way to Texas. How did you know where to find me?"

"I found the address in Dad's papers."

"Did something happen at home?"

She shook her head, looking more and more miserable. Finally she lifted her chin and met his gaze for barely a second, then ducked it again. "You left," she said accusingly. "One day you just weren't there anymore and you never said goodbye."

Even though his reason for leaving had been an emergency, he could see how it might look from her perspective. He knew that in her reserved way, she counted on him.

"Didn't your dad tell you why I had to come home?" he asked.

"He said your mother died."

"That's right."

"But I thought you'd be coming back," she whispered. "But then you never did. And then Dad said you'd called and that y-you'd q-quit."

Her tears started all over again. Cody went for more tissues and brought back the whole box to buy himself the time he needed to figure out how to explain things to this shy, young girl who'd so badly needed someone that she'd chosen a miserable, cynical cowboy from Texas who already had a lousy track record for reliability.

"Janey, when I got here there were things that I realized I had to do. I couldn't come back. I explained all of that to your father."

"But...not...to me," she choked between sobs. "I thought you were my friend."

Cody sighed. "I am. I always want to be your friend."

"Then you'll come back as soon as things are settled here?" she inquired, hope written all over her tear-streaked face.

"No, sweetie, I can't come back."

"Why not?" she asked.

Not sure how she was likely to react, he drew in a deep breath before admitting, "Because I found out that I have a little girl and I have to be here for her."

Dismay darkened her eyes. "A baby?"

"Not so much a baby anymore," he confided. "She's over a year old."

"And you didn't know about her?"

"No."

Despite herself, she was apparently fascinated. For the first time since he'd arrived home, there was a sparkle in her dark eyes.

"How come?" she asked, her expression alive with curiosity.

"It's a long story."

"Was that her mom in the car just now?"

Cody nodded.

"Uh-oh," she murmured. Guilt and misery replaced the sparkle in her eyes. "I'm sorry if I messed things up for you, Cody. I really am."

He grinned ruefully. "Oh, the list of my sins is pretty long as it is. One more thing won't matter all that much."

"Want me to tell her you didn't know I was coming here?"

He had a feeling that the less Melissa saw of Janey, the better for all of them. Janey might be only fifteen, but she was a beautiful young girl who looked older than her years. It was the very fact that her body had blossomed so prematurely that had contributed to her shyness.

Ironically, he suspected she had been drawn to him for the very reason that he hadn't acted like the oversexed teens who attended school with her. She'd felt safe with him, free to talk about her dreams, and she had magnified that feeling into a giant-size crush.

"No, sweetie, I'll take care of Melissa. Now, let's think about getting you back home again. How'd you get here?"

"I used my savings for a bus ticket. Then when I got to town, I called the ranch. Your dad came and got me."

Cody shuddered when he thought of her traveling that distance alone by bus. He also suspected that Harlan had deliberately not tried to track him down when Janey turned up to give him more time with Melissa before throwing a monkey wrench into things.

"I'll talk to Daddy about having his pilot fly you back to Wyoming," he told her.

Her eyes lit up. "Really?"

Her instantaneous excitement told him that her heart was already well on its way to healing. Maybe all she'd really needed was closure, a chance to say goodbye and make sure that she hadn't lost a friend. If he'd been half so insistent on closure before he'd taken off from Texas, maybe he and Melissa would have been married by now, instead of trying to re-build their shattered trust.

Janey would be okay. He was sure of it. In the meantime, though, he had another heart to worry about. He had a feeling patching up the holes in Melissa's trust wasn't going to be nearly so easy to accomplish.

Melissa broke three glasses during the breakfast rush at Dolan's on Monday. As each one shattered, she heard a heavy sigh of resignation from Eli. She knew exactly how he felt. She'd had her fragile hopes shattered—again—the day before when she'd arrived at White Pines to find an adorable, sexy woman waiting on the doorstep for Cody.

As she swept up the debris from her latest round of clumsiness, she wished it were even half as easy to tidy up the aftermath of a broken heart.

When she finished sweeping, she glanced up and discovered Mabel sitting at the counter, curiosity written all over her face. To try to forestall the questions that were clearly on the older woman's mind, Melissa grabbed the coffeepot and poured her a cup.

"How about a Danish, Mabel?" she asked. "We have cheese and cherry left."

"No, thanks. So, did you and Cody have another fight?" Mabel inquired point-blank.

"No," Melissa replied honestly. They hadn't fought. She had taken off before her disillusionment could come pouring out in a wave of accusations.

"Now, why is it I don't believe that?" Mabel murmured. "You never broke a glass until that boy came back into town. Since then, you've been smashing them up so fast poor Eli's liable to go bankrupt."

"I'm going to reimburse Eli for the glasses," Melissa told her stiffly.

"No need for that," Eli called, proving that he'd heard every word of the discussion of her love life. "Maybe Mabel and I ought to sit that boy down and give him a stern talking to, though."

Mabel shot their boss a sour look. "What would

you know about straightening out a lovers' tiff, old man?''

''As much as you do about starting one,'' Eli shot back.

Melissa stared at them. For the first time she noticed that their bickering carried the unmistakable sting of two former lovers. *Eli and Mabel,* she thought incredulously. Surely not. Then again, why not? She knew of no one else in either of their lives. Maybe that was so because they'd spent years carrying the torch for each other, unable to heal some foolish rift.

''Maybe I'm not the one who needs an intermediary,'' Melissa suggested, observing their reactions intently.

''You don't know what you're talking about,'' Mabel snapped. She shot a venomous look at the pharmacist. ''Neither does he, for that matter.''

''I know what I know,'' Eli countered. ''Besides, we're not talking about you and me now. We're talking about Melissa and Cody.''

''I'd rather talk about the two of you,'' Melissa said hurriedly, dying to know the whole story of two people who'd worked together as far back as she could recall without giving away so much as a hint that there was anything personal between them.

''No,'' Mabel and Eli chorused.

Melissa winced. ''Okay, okay. We'll make a pact. You stay out of my personal life and I'll stay out of yours.''

Mabel gave an obviously reluctant nod. Melissa

waited for Eli to concur, but instead he muttered, "Too late. Yours just walked in the door."

Melissa's gaze shot to the front of the drugstore. Sure enough, Cody was striding in her direction, a glint of pure determination in his eyes.

"Go away," she said before he could settle himself on one of the stools.

"Is that any way to greet a paying customer?" he inquired.

He slapped a twenty on the counter. At the rate he was throwing them around, he was going to go broke.

"I'm not leaving until I've spent every last dime of that or you and I have talked," he announced. "You pick."

Melissa poured him a cup of coffee, snatched the twenty and tucked it in her pocket. "The coffee's on me. I'll consider the twenty a tip for services rendered."

Flags of angry color rose in Cody's cheeks. His grip on his coffee cup tightened, turning his knuckles white. "There's a name for taking money for that, darlin'."

Mabel sputtered and backed off her stool so fast it was still spinning a full minute after she'd gone. Melissa had a hunch she wasn't all that far, though, more than likely not even out of earshot.

"How dare you!" Melissa snapped.

"You started this round, not me," he said tightly. "Care to back up and start over?"

"We can't back up that many years," she retorted.

Cody visibly restrained his temper. Melissa watched as he drew in several calming breaths, even as his heated gaze remained locked on her. Her blood practically sizzled under that look. No matter how furious he made her, she still seemed to want him. It was damned provoking.

"Believe it or not, I came in here to apologize," he said eventually, his voice low.

"What's to apologize for? Just because you didn't mention that you were involved with another woman—a woman who apparently traveled quite some distance to be with you—that doesn't mean you owe me an apology."

To her annoyance, amusement sparkled in Cody's eyes. "I don't have a thing to hide, sweet pea. Want me to tell you about Janey?"

Melissa did not want to hear about the gorgeous creature with the exotic features, elfin haircut and sad, sad eyes. Cody had probably broken her heart, too.

"I can see that you do," Cody said, taking the decision out of her hands. "First of all, yes, Janey is from Wyoming. Second, I had no idea she was coming. Third, our relationship—then and now— most definitely is not what you think it was."

"Yeah, right," Melissa said sarcastically.

"Fourth," he went on as if she hadn't interrupted. "Her father was my boss, Lance Treethorn."

He leveled his gaze straight at her, until she felt color flooding into her cheeks. "Fifth, and most important, she is a fifteen-year-old kid."

Melissa stared at him. "Fifteen," she repeated in a choked voice. "Cody, that's—"

He cut her off before she could finish the ugly thought. "What that is, is a shy, lonely teenager with a crush on the first guy who didn't slobber all over her due to adolescent hormones," he insisted adamantly.

Melissa wanted to believe him. In fact, she did believe him. Cody was far too honorable a man to do anything so despicable. Harlan might have raised stubborn, willful, overly confident sons, but he'd instilled a set of values in them that was beyond reproach. She was the one who ought to be horsewhipped for even allowing such a thought to cross her mind.

She moaned and hid her face in her hands. "God, I'm sorry."

Cody shrugged. "Well, she does look older than she is. That's been her problem. The guys ahead of her in school think she's a lot more mature than she is and try to take advantage of her. She's coped by hiding out at the ranch."

"And you were kind to her, so she developed a crush on you," Melissa concluded, feeling like an idiot. "Why didn't you do something to put a stop to it?"

"For one thing, I had no idea it would go this far. The most overt thing she ever did before was leave food for me. She bakes a brownie that makes your mouth water."

Melissa grinned. "You always were a sucker for brownies."

"It was the first thing you learned to bake, remember? You were twelve, I think."

She remembered all right. Even back then she'd been trying to woo Cody by catering to his every whim. She wondered if it was ever possible to get beyond past history and truly have a new beginning. She'd been facetious when she'd snapped earlier that they couldn't go back far enough to start over, but maybe it was true. Maybe there was no way to ever get past all the mistakes and the distrust.

Despondency stole through her as she considered the possibility that they would never be able to move on.

"Melissa?" Cody said softly.

"What?"

"What's wrong?"

"Nothing."

"I don't believe that. You looked as if you were about ready to cry."

She tried to shrug off the observation. "Don't mind me. It's probably just Monday blues."

"I know how to cure that," he said. "Come out to White Pines tonight. We'll have a barbecue. It's warm enough today."

Melissa didn't think spending more time with Cody was such a good idea, not when parting suddenly seemed inevitable. Maybe Janey Treethorn's presence had been innocent enough, but sooner or later some other woman would catch his eye. They always did.

"The temperature's supposed to drop later," she

said by way of declining his invitation. "It might even snow overnight."

Cody's expression remained undaunted. "Then I'll wear a jacket to tend the grill and we can eat inside."

"You never give up, do you?"

"Never," he agreed softly, his gaze locked with hers. "Not when it's something this important."

"What is it that's important, Cody?" she asked, unable to keep a hint of desperation out of her voice. "What?"

"You, me, Sharon Lynn," he said. "I want us to be a family, Melissa. I won't settle for anything less this time."

She heard the determination in his voice. More important, she heard the commitment. He sounded so sincere, so convinced that a family was what he wanted.

"Will you come?" he asked again. "You and Sharon Lynn?"

Melissa sighed. She'd never been able to resist Cody when he got that winsome note in his voice, when that thoroughly engaging smile reached all the way to his dark and dangerous eyes.

"What time?"

"Five-thirty?"

"We'll be there."

"My house," he said. "Not the main house."

Thoughts of making love in that house flooded through her. Melissa shook her head. "No," she insisted. "Let's have dinner with Harlan, too."

"Scared, Me...liss...a?"

"You bet, cowboy. You should be, too." She lowered her voice. "The last time we were alone in that house, we made love and we didn't take precautions. I'm not risking that again."

Cody grinned. "Hey, darlin', that's something I can take care of right here and now," he offered. "I'm sure Eli can fix me right up."

Melissa's cheeks flamed at the prospect of having Eli and Mabel know any more of her business than they already did. "Cody, don't you dare. Besides, we decided that sleeping together only complicated things."

"Did we decide that?"

"You know we did. We have dinner at Harlan's or you can forget it."

"Okay, darlin', I'll let you win this round," he said, startling her with his lack of fussing. "See you at five-thirty."

It wasn't until she arrived at White Pines that she discovered the reason for Cody's calm acceptance of her edict.

"Where's Harlan?" she inquired suspiciously the minute she stepped into the too silent foyer of the main house.

Cody's expression was pure innocence as he gazed back at her. "Oh, didn't I mention it? Daddy's gone to spend a few days with Luke and Jessie."

With Sharon Lynn already happily ensconced in her father's arms, with a huge stack of ribs just waiting to be barbecued, Melissa bit back the urge to turn right around and flee. This round, it appeared, had gone to Cody.

Chapter Fourteen

For the next two months, Cody won more rounds than he lost, much to Melissa's chagrin. Though she'd turned down his proposals every time he made them, he took the rejections in stride. He just redoubled his efforts to change her mind. Her resistance was in tatters. Her senses were spinning just at the sight of him. She was clinging to the last shreds of pride and determination she had left.

There were moments, she was forced to admit, when she couldn't even remember why she was so staunch in her conviction that marrying Cody was positively the wrong thing to do. He had done absolutely nothing since his return to indicate that he wasn't thoroughly absorbed in his relationship with her and their child. He was sweetly attentive to her. He doted on Sharon Lynn.

And still, for reasons she was finding harder and harder to fathom, she kept waiting for some other woman to come between them, for some blowup that would send Cody racing away from Texas, away from them. It didn't seem to matter that his roots at White Pines ran deeper than ever. He'd left his home and her once before. She never forgot that, wouldn't let herself forget it.

She put more obstacles in their path to happiness than championship hurdlers had ever had to jump. Cody, just as determinedly, overcame each and every one, without criticism, without comment. He just did whatever was asked of him.

The truth of it was that his thoughtfulness and consideration were beginning to wear on her. She figured it was an indication of the depths of her perversity that she longed for a good, old, rip-roaring fight.

She was already working herself into a confrontational state when she reached her mother's after a particularly exhausting day at work, only to find that Sharon Lynn wasn't there.

"What do you mean, she's not here?" she demanded, staring at her father. Her mother was nowhere in sight, which should have been her first clue that her life was about to turn topsy-turvy.

"Cody came by," her father admitted. "I let him take her."

"You what?" Her voice climbed several octaves. Was everyone in town on Cody's side these days? She'd thought for sure at least her parents would stick up for her. Instead her father had joined the enemy camp.

"Why would you do that?" she asked plaintively.

Her father regarded her with amusement. "He's the child's father, for starters. He wanted to spend some time with her. He said he'd drop her off at your house and save you the trip. I guess he didn't tell you that, though."

"No, he did not," she snapped. "Which is a pretty good indication of why Cody Adams is not to be trusted."

"If you ask me, he's been jumping through hoops to prove he can be trusted. Why don't you give the guy a break?" He patted her cheek. "Come on, ladybug. You know you want to."

"I can't," she said simply.

"Why not?"

"Because he'll leave again at the first sign of trouble."

"He left before, because you provoked him into it. I can't say I blame him for being furious about finding you out with Brian. Going out with him was a danged fool idea to begin with."

Melissa's anger wilted. "I agree, but Cody should have stayed and talked to me. He shouldn't have run."

"Don't you think he knows that now?" her father inquired reasonably. "Don't you think if he had it to do all over again, he would make a different choice?"

"I suppose," she conceded reluctantly. "He says he would anyway."

"And aren't you the one who made things worse by refusing to tell him about the baby?"

She scowled at her father, the man who had stood by her even though he disagreed with her decision to keep Cody in the dark. "What's your point?"

"He forgave you, didn't he? Isn't it about time you did the same for him?"

Melissa was startled by the depth of her father's support for Cody. "How come you've never said any of this before?" she asked.

Her father's expression turned rueful. "Because your mother seemed to be saying more than enough without me jumping in and confusing you even more. Watching you getting more miserable day by day, I finally decided when Cody showed up today that enough was enough. I told her to butt out."

Melissa couldn't help grinning. "So there'd be room for you to butt in?"

"Something like that. Go on, cupcake. Meet Cody halfway, at least. For whatever it's worth, I think he's a fine man."

Melissa sighed. "So do I."

She made up her mind on the walk to her own house that she would try to overcome the last of her doubts and take the kind of risk her father was urging. There was a time when she would have risked anything at all to be with Cody. The pain of losing him once had made her far too cautious. It was probably long past time to rediscover the old

Melissa and take the dare he'd been issuing for months now.

She found him in a rocker on her front porch, a tuckered out Sharon Lynn asleep in his lap.

"Rough afternoon?" she queried, keeping her tone light and displaying none of the annoyance she'd felt when she'd discovered he'd absconded with her daughter. She sank into the rocker next to him and put it into a slow, soothing motion. She allowed her eyes to drift closed, then snapped them open before she fell completely, embarrassingly, asleep.

"Playing in the park is tough work," he said, grinning at her. "There are swings and scesaws to ride, to say nothing of squirrels to be chased." His gaze intensified. "You look frazzled. Bad day?"

"Bad day, bad week, bad everything," she admitted, giving in to the exhaustion and turmoil shc'd been fighting.

"I know just how to fix that," Cody said, standing. Hc shifted Sharon Lynn into one arm and held out a hand. "Give me the key."

Melissa plucked it from her purse and handed it over without argument. As soon as he'd gone, she closed her eyes again. The soothing motion of the rocker lulled her so that she was only vaguely aware of the screen door squeaking open and the sound of Cody's boots as he crossed the porch.

"Wake up, sleepyhead," he urged. "Here, take this."

She forced her eyes open and saw the tall glass

he was holding out. "Lemonade?" she asked with amazement. "Where'd you get it?"

"I made it."

Her eyes blinked wider. "From scratch?"

He grinned. "I didn't bake a chocolate soufflé, sweet pea. It's just lemonade."

They sat side by side, silently rocking, for what seemed an eternity after that. The spring breeze brought the fragrance of flowers wafting by. Hummingbirds hovered around the feeder at the end of the porch.

"This is nice, isn't it?" Cody said eventually.

"Not too tame for you?" Melissa asked.

"Don't start with me," he chided, but without much ferocity behind the words.

She thought of what her father had said and of her own resolution to start taking risks. "I'm sorry. I didn't mean to say that. I guess it's become automatic."

"Think you can break the cycle?" he inquired lightly.

Melissa met his gaze. "I'm going to try," she promised. "I do want what you want, Cody."

"But you're scared," he guessed. At her nod he added, "Can't say that I blame you. I spent a lot of years hiding from the responsibilities of a relationship. Once you make a commitment, there's a lot riding on getting it right. I never did much like the idea of failing."

"Can I ask you something?"

"Anything, you know that."

"What makes you so certain we can get it right now?"

He grinned at the question. "You know any two more stubborn people on the face of the earth?"

Her lips twitched at that. "No, can't say that I do."

"I pretty much figure if we finally make that commitment, neither one of us will bail out without giving it everything we've got." He slanted a look over at her that sent heat curling through her body. "Nobody can do more than that, sweet pea. Nobody."

He stood, then bent down to kiss her gently. "Think about it, darlin'."

"You're leaving?" she asked, unable to stop the disappointment that flooded through her.

"If I stay here another minute with you looking at me like that, I'm going to resort to seducing you into giving me the answer I want. I think it'll be better if I take my chances on letting you work this one out in your head."

He was striding off to his pickup before she could mount an argument. She actually stood to go after him, but a wave of dizziness washed over her that had her clutching at a post to keep from falling.

What on earth? she wondered as she steadied herself. Suddenly she recalled the occasional bouts of nausea she'd been feeling that she'd chalked off to waiting too long to grab breakfast in the mornings. She thought about the bone-deep weariness that had had her half-asleep in that rocker only a short time before. And now, dizziness.

Oh, dear heaven, she thought, sinking back into the rocker before she fainted. Unless she was very much mistaken, every one of those signs added up to being pregnant—again.

How could this have happened to them a second time? Melissa wondered as she left the doctor's office in a daze the following morning. How could she be pregnant from that one time they'd made love at Cody's? They'd been so darned careful not to repeat the same mistake. She'd held him at arm's length, refusing to make love again for that very reason, because neither one of them used a lick of common sense once they hopped into bed together. It was better not to let their hormones get out of hand in the first place.

She had no idea what was going to happen next, but she did know that this time she would tell Cody right away. There would be no more secrets to blow up in her face later.

Dammit, why couldn't everything have been more resolved between them? They were so close to working things out. She had sensed that last night in their companionable silence, in the way Cody had vowed to give her the time and space to reach her own conclusions about their relationship.

She knew exactly how Cody was going to react. Forget about time and space for thinking. He was going to demand they get married at once. She wanted that, wanted it more than anything, but not if he was only doing it because of the baby. Okay, both babies.

He was a fine father. He'd accepted his responsibility for Sharon Lynn wholeheartedly. That wasn't the issue. He'd been proving that over and over since the day he'd learned the truth about Sharon Lynn. She had seen the adoration in his eyes whenever he was with his daughter. She had watched his pride over every tiny accomplishment.

He had even behaved as though she were important to him, too. But never once, not in all these months, had he said he loved her. She would not marry a man who could not say those words. She would not marry at all just because she was pregnant.

It created an interesting dilemma, since there wasn't a darn thing she could do about being pregnant. There was nothing on earth that meant more to her than being a mother to Cody's children. And she knew from bitter experience that she could do it just fine on her own, if she had to.

Still, she had to tell him sometime....

She managed to hold off for a couple of weeks, but her symptoms were cropping up when she least expected it. She didn't want him guessing when he found her practically swooning in his arms.

After thinking it over, she chose the storeroom at Dolan's to tell him. Eli and Mabel were getting used to her dragging Cody into the back to talk. They'd probably heard enough muffled arguments and full-scale screaming matches to last them a lifetime.

At least, though, they would be there to intervene if Cody decided to try to drag her off by the hair to the preacher. At home she'd have no such protection. She doubted even her parents would stand up to him. Her father was already on Cody's side and her mother had maintained a stoic silence ever since her father's edict that she butt out of Melissa's and Cody's business.

She had one other reason for choosing the storeroom. She had noticed that Eli and Mabel were off by themselves whispering who-knew-what at the oddest times. Melissa had the feeling that the two of them were patching whatever differences had separated them years before. Maybe the very visible ups and downs of her relationship with Cody had set an example for them. They might as well be in on the denouement.

When Cody walked through the door as he'd gotten into the habit of doing around closing every day, Melissa's hands trembled. This time nothing on earth could have persuaded her to so much as touch a glass in Cody's presence.

Not even giving Cody time to get settled, she drew in a deep breath. "We need to talk."

"Okay," he said, giving her that crooked smile that made her heart flip over. "What's up?"

"In the back," she said.

Cody groaned. "Not again."

She glanced at Eli and Mabel, who were both suddenly extremely busy, their backs to the counter. "Will you just come on?" she muttered, holding the door open.

Cody trailed along behind her and propped a

booted foot onto an unopened shipment of new glasses. "What now?"

Melissa tried to gather her courage. Finally she blurted, "I'm pregnant."

Cody's eyes widened incredulously. "You're going to have a baby?"

She nodded, watching him carefully, not quite able to get a fix on his reaction.

"A baby?" Cody repeated.

"Yes."

"Oh, my God." He sank down on the box, which gave way just enough to shatter the two dozen glasses inside.

At the sound of all that cracking glassware, Melissa started to chuckle. Cody bounced to his feet, but there was no hope for the crushed shipment.

"You okay?" she inquired between giggles. "No glass in your backside?"

"Forget my backside. It's just fine. Tell me more about the baby. When is it due?"

"You should be able to figure that one out. We only slept together that once since you got back."

"I can't even add two and two right now. Just tell me."

"A little over six months."

He nodded. "Good. That's plenty of time."

Melissa regarded him suspiciously. "Plenty of time for what?" she asked, although she thought she had a pretty good idea of the answer.

"To get married," he said at once. "Finish fixing up my house at White Pines, decorate a new nursery."

Melissa held up her hands. "Whoa, cowboy. Who says we're getting married?"

A mutinous expression settled over his face. "I do. No baby of mine is going to be born without my name. It's bad enough that we haven't taken care of getting Sharon Lynn's name legally changed. I'm not doubling the problem."

"Okay, say I agree to get married—which I haven't," she added in a rush when she saw the instant gleam in his eyes. "Then what?"

He stared at her blankly. "What?"

"Are you planning for us to live happily ever after? Are you intending to get a divorce as soon as the ink's dry on the birth certificate? What?" *Please,* she thought to herself, *let him say he loves me. Please.*

"You know better than that," he said.

It was a wishy-washy answer if ever Melissa had heard one. "Do I?" she shot back. "How? Just because you've been here a few months now and haven't taken off?"

He raked his fingers through his hair. "Yes."

"Not good enough, cowboy," she said, exiting the storeroom and emphatically closing the door behind her.

Mabel and Eli were suspiciously close to the door, though their attention seemed to be thoroughly engaged in their work. Of course, Mabel was sweeping the exact same spot she'd swept not fifteen minutes earlier and Eli was dusting off a shelf, a task that usually fell to Mabel.

"I'm leaving," she announced, grabbing her purse and heading for the door.

Mabel trailed her outside. "Don't be a fool, girl. Marry that man and put him out of his misery."

"I can't," Melissa said, sounding pretty miserable herself.

"Why the devil not?"

"He's only thinking about the babies. He's not thinking about us at all."

"If that's all he cared about, he could file for joint custody, pick them up on Friday afternoons and send you a support check," Mabel countered. "I don't hear him talking about doing any of that. He's talking about marriage, has been ever since he got back into town."

"Because it's the right thing to do," Melissa insisted stubbornly. "The Adams men are nothing if not honorable."

Mabel shot her a look of pure disgust. "Maybe you ought to be thinking about doing the right thing, too, if that's the case. Those babies deserve a chance at a real home. Cody's willing to give them that. Why can't you?"

Mabel's words lingered in her head as she walked over to pick up Sharon Lynn. They echoed there again and again as she fought every single attempt Cody made to persuade her to change her mind.

She told herself she wasn't the one making things difficult. All it would take to make her change her mind was three little words—I love you. They were about the only words in the whole English language that Cody never, ever tried.

Chapter Fifteen

From the instant he discovered that Melissa was pregnant again, Cody tried to persuade her to marry him. He coaxed. He wooed. He pitched a royal fit on occasion and threatened to hog-tie her and carry her off to the justice of the peace.

For six solid months he did everything but stand on his damned head, but Melissa seemed to have clothed her heart in an impenetrable sheet of armor. He surely didn't remember the woman being this stubborn. The whole town was watching the two of them as if they were better than any soap opera on TV. He found it mortifying to be chasing after a woman who acted as if he didn't even exist.

He also discovered that this new side of Melissa was every bit as intriguing as it was vexing. He realized that he'd always taken for granted that sooner or later she would admit she loved him and accept his oft-repeated proposal. That she was still turning him down with another baby on the way shook him as nothing else in his life ever had. Maybe this was one time when his charm wasn't going to be enough.

And the truth of it was, she seemed to be getting along just fine. He'd seen that for himself ever since he'd gotten back from Wyoming. She had made a nice life for herself and Sharon Lynn. She would fit a new baby into that life without batting an eye.

She was strong and self-sufficient, downright competent as a single parent. She had her job at the drugstore. She had friends who were there for her. She had parents who supported her in whatever decisions she made, though he sensed that her father was not quite as thrilled with this independent streak as her mother was.

In short, Melissa had a life, while Cody was lonelier than he'd ever imagined possible even in the dead of a rough Wyoming winter.

The thought of Melissa going into that delivery room with anyone other than him as her labor coach grated. The prospect of his baby—a second baby, in fact—being born without his name made him see red. He wanted to be a part of that baby's life so badly it stunned him.

What flat-out rocked him back on his heels, though, was the fact that he wanted to be with Melissa just as badly. Maybe he'd started out just saying the words, asking her to marry him because of

Sharon Lynn and more recently this new, unborn baby. But sometime, when he hadn't been paying attention, he'd gone and fallen in love with the woman. Mature, adult love this time, not adolescent hormones and fantasy.

How the hell was he going to get her to believe that, though? Nothing he had done in the past eight and a half months since he'd come home to Texas had done a bit of good.

He'd been steady. He'd been reliable. He'd even managed to seduce her, which was what had gotten them into this latest fix. Melissa, however, had kept a stubborn grip on her emotions. She had refused to concede feeling so much as affection for him, much less love.

Cody was at his wit's end. He'd decided, though, that it was tonight or never. He was going to make one last, impressive, irresistible attempt to convince Melissa to be his wife. If it failed, he would just have to resign himself to this shadow role in the life of his children. Up until now he'd turned his back on his pride, but it was kicking up a storm for him to stop behaving like a besotted fool and give up.

He took hat quite literally in hand and went to visit Velma. He needed her help if his plan was to work. Responding to his knock on her door in midafternoon, she regarded him with her usual suspicion.

"What do you want?" she inquired ungraciously.

Cody lost patience. "I am not the bad guy here,"

he informed her as he stalked past her and stood in the middle of the foyer.

He could hear Sharon Lynn chattering away in the guest room. It sounded as if she were having a tea party. He longed to go down that corridor and spend some time with her. She was changing in one way or another every day and he hated to miss a single one. Today, though, he was on a mission here and he couldn't afford to be distracted.

"I came by to see if you could keep Sharon Lynn here tonight," he said.

"Why?" Velma asked bluntly.

"So that Melissa and I can have an evening together alone."

"Seems to me you two have found enough time to be alone without my help in the past. She's about to have a baby again, isn't she? She didn't get that way in public, I suspect."

Her sarcasm grated. Cody held back the sharp retort that came to mind. If this was going to work out, it was way past time he made peace with Melissa's mother. "Exactly what has she told you about our relationship?"

Velma didn't give an inch. "She doesn't have to say a word. I can see plenty for myself."

"What do you think you see, then?"

"That you think your money and your power give you the right to be irresponsible. You've used my daughter, left her, then come back here and used her again without ever giving a thought to the consequences."

"Are you aware that I have been trying to persuade your mule-headed daughter to marry me since the very first instant I got back into town?"

Velma blinked, but she didn't back down. Talk about stubborn pride. Velma had it in spades, which probably explained Melissa's streak of it.

"Too little, too late, if you ask me," she retorted.

Cody started to tell her he hadn't asked her, but of course he had. "Look, I don't blame you for resenting me, but the fact of the matter is that I love your daughter, stubborn as she is, and I want to marry her and be a father to our children. I think she loves me, too, but she thinks she's a fool for doing it."

He saw from the set expression on her face that Velma had probably reinforced that belief. Maybe if he could win over the mother, she'd change her tune with Melissa and give him a fighting chance.

"You want her to be happy, don't you?"

"Of course I do," she said indignantly. "What makes you think I don't?"

"Because I think she's taking her cue from you. I think if she and I had just a little time alone, we could work this out, preferably before another one of our children is born without my name. Will you give us that chance?"

Velma spent the next minute or two in an obvious struggle with her conscience. "What is it you want, exactly?"

"Keep Sharon Lynn here tonight. Don't interfere with my plans. That's all."

"You think you can convince her in one night,

when you haven't made any progress at all in the past nine months?'' Velma inquired with a shake of her head. ''You don't know Melissa half as well as you think you do.''

She sighed heavily. ''Okay, I'll keep Sharon Lynn for you,'' she relented to Cody's relief. ''But it'll have to be for the whole weekend. If you ask me, it's going to take you that long, maybe even longer, to turn that girl around. She's scared spitless she'll admit she loves you and you'll turn around and leave again.''

''I won't,'' he swore. He circled Velma's waist and spun her around. ''Thank you. You're an angel.''

She kept her lips in a tight line, resisting him to the bitter end, but Cody thought he detected a spark of amusement in her eyes. ''See that you do right by her, young man, or I'll have your hide.''

He kissed her cheek. ''Not to worry, Velma. This is going to be a weekend to remember.''

He was already making plans to sweep Melissa away to a quiet, secluded cabin for a romantic weekend by the time he hit the driveway.

His first stop was her house, where he managed to sneak in without being caught by the sheriff or a neighbor. He rummaged through her drawers and closets to find lingerie and the prettiest, sexiest maternity clothes she owned. He packed them, along with perfume and cosmetics, praying that he got the right ones. He didn't want her dissolving into tears because she couldn't find her blush or her mascara. Her hormones had her reacting in the most bizarre ways these days. He figured he ought to get a whole lot of points for just managing to stick by her anyway.

He'd considered taking her off to someplace fancy, maybe the most expensive suite in Dallas, but then he'd decided that would put her too close to taxis or planes or other means of escape. He wanted her all to himself.

He fought all of his old past resentments—most of them, as it had turned out, unwarranted—and tracked Brian down in San Antonio, where he was practicing law. He pointed out that his former best friend owed him one for the scam he and Melissa had tried to pull on Cody years before.

"I'm just grateful that you didn't come after me with a shotgun," Brian said. "Anything you want is yours."

"Does your family still have that cabin by the lake?"

"You bet."

"Can Melissa and I borrow it for the weekend?"

"It's all yours," Brian said at once.

He told Cody where to find the key, offered some unsolicited advice on taming the reluctant Melissa, then added seriously, "I'm glad you called, buddy. I've missed you."

"Same here," Cody said. "Next time you're down this way, we'll have to get together. You do have your own woman now, don't you?"

Brian chuckled. "Do I ever. Good luck. You and Melissa should have worked this out long ago. I'd have told you the truth myself, but Melissa swore me to secrecy.''

''Secrets are her specialty, it appears,'' Cody said. ''Anyway, thanks again for the cabin.''

Those arrangements made, Cody loaded groceries, flowers and nonalcoholic champagne into the back of the truck, then swung by Dolan's. He marched straight to the soda fountain, ignoring the startled gazes of the teens gathered there.

''Cody? Is everything okay?'' Melissa asked as he rounded the corner of the counter and headed toward her.

''Just dandy,'' he confirmed, tucking one arm under her legs and the other behind her waist. He scooped her up, amid a flurry of outraged protests from her and that same pimply faced kid who'd defended her honor once before.

''It's okay, son,'' Cody assured him. ''She wants to go with me.''

''I do not!'' Melissa protested.

''Eli, call the cops or something,'' the boy shouted, his face turning red as he bolted after Cody.

''Not on your life,'' Eli said, and kept right on filling prescriptions. Mabel held the door open, grinning widely.

Melissa huffed and puffed a little longer, but by the time Cody had driven to the outskirts of town, she'd retreated into a sullen silence.

''Was that caveman approach entirely necessary?'' she inquired eventually.

''I thought so.''

"I would have come with you, if you'd asked politely."

He shot a skeptical look in her direction.

"At least, I would have thought about it," she amended.

"That's why I didn't ask. You've been thinking entirely too much."

"Are we going to White Pines?"

"Nope."

"Luke and Jessie's?" she asked hopefully, the first little sign of alarm sparking in her eyes.

"Nope."

"Cody, where the hell are you taking me?"

"Someplace where we can be alone."

"Where?" she repeated.

"Brian's cabin."

Her eyes widened. "You talked to Brian?"

"I figured drastic measures were called for, and he promised the best and quickest solution." He glanced over at her. "I was willing to do anything it took to make this happen, sweet pea."

"Oh," she said softly, and settled back to mull that over.

It wasn't more than half an hour later when he noticed she seemed to be getting a little restless.

"You okay?" he asked.

She turned toward him, her lower lip caught between her teeth as she shook her head. Instantly, Cody's muscles tensed.

"Melissa, what's wrong?" he demanded. "Tell me."

"It's not a problem," she said. "Not yet, anyway. It's just that…'' Her eyes widened and turned the color of a turbulent sea. She swallowed visibly. ''Don't panic.''

Cody panicked. ''Melissa!''

''It's okay, really it is. It's just that it's entirely possible that I'm in labor.'' She sucked in a ragged breath, then announced, ''Cody, I think we're about to have a baby.''

Chapter Sixteen

Cody found his father already pacing the waiting room when he got Melissa to the hospital. He'd called him on his cellular phone, right after he'd spoken to the doctor. He'd asked Harlan to alert the rest of the family.

"Even Jordan?" his father had asked cautiously, aware of the friction between them.

Cody decided then and there it was time to get over the rift between him and his brother. This was a time for healing.

"Even Jordan," he'd confirmed.

He turned now to his father. "Did you reach everyone?"

"They'll be here in a bit. How is she?" Harlan demanded at once as the nurse wheeled Melissa away to prep her for delivery. "Is everything okay?"

Cody wiped a stream of sweat from his brow. "She says it is, but I don't know. You had four sons. Is labor supposed to be so painful?"

"How should I know? Your mama wouldn't let me anywhere near the delivery room. She said having babies was women's work." He glanced at Cody with an unmistakable look of envy. "Wish I'd had a chance to be there just once, though. Seems to me like it must be a flat-out miracle. You going in there with Melissa?"

"If she'll let me," Cody said. "She's still making up her mind whether to be furious at me for kidnapping her this afternoon." He moaned. "I must have been out of my mind. I didn't even think about the fact that she might go into labor."

"Cody, you weren't at the other end of the world," Harlan reassured him. "You'd barely made it out of town. You got her here in plenty of time. The only way you could have gotten here much faster would have been to park her in a room upstairs for the last month of her pregnancy. Now, settle down."

"It's easy for you. It's not your baby she's having."

Just then the nurse came out. "Mr. Adams, would you like to step in for a minute? We're getting ready to take Melissa to the delivery room."

Cody shot a helpless look at his father. "It sounds like she's not going to want me in there."

"Maybe it's time to stop bullying the girl and

tell her how much you want to be there,'' Harlan advised.

Cody doubted it would be as simple as that. Indeed, Melissa shot him a look of pure hatred when he walked into her room. Of course, that might have had something to do with the whopper of a contraction she appeared to be in the middle of.

He accepted a damp cloth from the nurse and instinctively wiped Melissa's forehead with it.

''You're doing great,'' he said.

''How would you know?'' she retorted.

He grinned at the fiery display of temper. ''Okay, you got me. I have no idea. No one's running around the halls panicking, though. That must mean something.''

''They're used to this,'' she retorted. ''I'm not. Besides, they're just observers. I'm doing all the work.''

''If you'd let me take those natural childbirth classes with you, I'd be more help about now.''

She latched onto his hand just then and squeezed. It was either one hell of a contraction or she was trying to punish him by breaking all of his knuckles. As soon as the pain eased, she glared at him again.

''Go away.''

''I don't think so,'' he countered just as stubbornly. ''I want to share this with you.''

''You want to see me writhing around in agony,'' she snapped.

''No,'' he insisted. ''Having a baby is a miracle.

I missed out on Sharon Lynn's birth. I'm going to be with you for this one.''

''Why?''

He regarded her blankly. ''Don't you know?''

''Cody, I don't know anything except that you've been making a pest of yourself ever since you got back into town. What I don't know is why.''

Before he could answer, the orderlies came to wheel her down the hall to the delivery room. He could tell by the set of her jaw that she was going into that room without him unless he could find the courage to tell her what was in his heart.

''Dammit, Melissa, I love you!'' he shouted after her, just as they were about to roll her out of sight.

''Stop!'' Melissa bellowed at the orderlies between contractions.

Cody reached her side in an instant. Even with her face bathed in sweat, her lower lip bitten raw, she looked beautiful to him. She always had, always would.

''What did you say?'' she demanded, then grabbed onto his hand with a grip so fierce he could have sworn that more bones broke.

He grinned through the pain—hers and his. ''I said I love you.''

A slow, satisfied smile spread across her face. ''It's about time, cowboy.''

''Haven't I been saying that for months now?'' he asked, vaguely bemused that she hadn't heard it before.

''Not the words,'' she told him. ''How was I supposed to believe it without the words?''

"Someone once told me that actions speak louder than words. I guess I was putting it to the test. I thought you needed to see that I wasn't going anywhere."

"I also needed to hear why that was so," she told him, wincing as another pain started and then rolled through her. "I didn't want you with me out of a sense of obligation."

Relief swept through him as he realized he'd risked everything and finally gotten through to her. "Does that mean you'll marry me?"

"Whenever you say."

Cody turned and motioned to the preacher he'd had Harlan call for him. He'd also had Harlan make a call to a judge to cut through the legal red tape. "Get to it, Reverend. I don't think this baby's going to wait much longer."

The minister had never talked so fast in his life, quite possibly because he was conducting the ceremony in the doorway of a delivery room. Cody figured as long as they didn't cross that threshold, the baby would have sense enough not to come until his or her parents were properly married.

The "I do's" were punctuated by moans and a couple of screams. And not five minutes later, Harlan Patrick Adams came into the world with an impeccable sense of timing, just as the minister pronounced his mama and daddy man and wife.

Melissa was beginning to wonder if she was ever going to be able to hold her own baby. Between Cody and his father, she'd barely gotten a look at him. Cody had finally disappeared a half hour before, but Harlan was still holding the baby with a look of such pride and sadness in his eyes.

"I wish Mary could have seen him," he said softly as a tear spilled down his cheek.

"Wherever she is, I think she knows," Melissa told him. "And I'll bet Erik is right beside her, watching out for all of us."

Her father-in-law gave her a watery smile. "I can't tell you how proud it makes me to have you in this family finally."

"I'm glad to be a part of it finally," she told him. "Though given the way my brand new husband scooted out of here after the ceremony, I'm not so sure I made the right decision. Any idea where he went?"

There was no mistaking the spark of pure mischief in Harlan's eyes. "Can't say that I know for sure," he said.

Melissa didn't believe him for a second. The old scoundrel and Cody were clearly up to their ornery chins in some scheme or another. Before she could try to pry their secret out of him, the door to the room slid open a crack.

"Everyone awake?" Cody inquired lightly.

"Come on in, son," Harlan enthused. "We were just wondering where you'd gone off to."

Cody stepped into the room and winked at her. "Should I take that to mean that you suspected I'd run off on you already?"

"It did cross my mind," she admitted. "You turned awful pale there in the delivery room. I figured you might be having second thoughts about marriage and fatherhood.''

''Not me,'' Cody retorted indignantly. ''I just figured the occasion deserved a celebration. You know how this family likes to party. You up for it?''

She stared at him as he watched her uneasily. ''What if I say no?''

''Then that's it. I send everyone away.''

''Everyone? Who is out there?''

''Sharon Lynn, first of all. She wants to meet her new baby brother.''

Melissa grinned. ''Bring her in. Of course I want her to see the baby.''

Cody opened the door and Sharon Lynn barreled in and ran toward the bed. Over the past few months she'd grown increasingly steady on her feet. In the final weeks of her pregnancy Melissa had had a heck of a time waddling after her.

''Mama! Mama!'' Sharon Lynn shouted.

Cody lifted Sharon Lynn onto the bed beside her. ''Harlan, bring the baby over so Sharon Lynn can get a look,'' Melissa said.

As Harlan approached with the baby, her daughter's eyes grew wide. ''Baby?''

''That's right, pumpkin. That's Harlan Patrick, your baby brother.''

As if she knew that newborns were fragile, Sharon Lynn reached over and gently touched a finger to her brother's cheek. ''I hold,'' she announced.

"Not yet," Melissa told her just as there was a soft knock on the door.

Cody reached for the handle, but his gaze was on her. "You ready for more visitors?"

"Who else is out there?"

"Your parents," he said.

"Luke and Jessie," Sharon Lynn chimed in, clearly proud that she'd learned two new names. "And Jordie and Kelly."

Melissa chuckled as she imagined straight-laced Jordan if he ever heard himself referred to as "Jordie." She gave her husband a warm smile, silently congratulating him for ending the feud that never should have happened.

"Let them in," she instructed Cody. "If I'd known you were inviting half the town, I'd have insisted on that private VIP suite they have upstairs."

As the family crowded in, a nurse came along, wheeling in a three-tiered wedding cake. Melissa stared at it in amazement. "When did you have time to order that?"

"Right after you said 'I do' and delivered our son," he said. "I told the bakery it was an emergency."

Kelly leaned down to kiss her cheek. "You should have seen the look on their faces when I stopped to pick it up. Obviously, they'd never heard of an emergency wedding before."

Melissa swung her legs over the side of the bed and prepared to go over for a closer look.

"Stay right where you are," Cody ordered, looking panicked.

"I'm not an invalid," she informed him.

"It's not that," he admitted, casting a worried look at the cake. "Actually, it was a little late to come up with an emergency cake. Fortunately, they had a cancellation."

Melissa stared at him, torn between laughing and crying. "That is someone else's cake?"

"They got the other names off," Kelly reassured her. "Almost, anyway."

Sure enough, when Melissa managed to get near enough for a closer look, she could spot the traces of blue food dye across the white icing on the top layer. Love Always had been left in place, but below it were the shadowy letters unmistakably spelling out Tom And Cecily.

Melissa grinned. "Get on over here, Tom," she said pointedly. "Give old Cecily a kiss."

Cody didn't hesitate. He gathered her close and slanted his lips across hers in a kiss that spoke of love and commitment and all the joy that was to come.

"Okay, that's enough, baby brother," Luke said. "Give the rest of us a chance to kiss the bride."

Cody relinquished his hold on her with obvious reluctance. He stood patiently by as she was kissed and congratulated by all the others. Harlan grabbed a paper cup and filled it with lukewarm water from the tap.

"A toast, everyone," he announced.

When they all had their own cups of water, he

lifted his cup. "To Cody and Melissa. This marriage was a long time coming. There were times I despaired of the two of you ever realizing that you belong together. Now that you have, we wish you every happiness for all the years to come."

"Hear, hear," Jordan and Luke echoed. "Much happiness, baby brother."

"Now it's my turn to kiss the bride," Harlan declared, giving her a resounding smack on the cheek.

Cody stole between them. "Get your own bride, old man. This one is mine."

"Maybe I will," Harlan said, startling them all.

Cody, Jordan and Luke stared at him in openmouthed astonishment while their wives all chuckled with delight.

"Do it," Melissa whispered in his ear, standing on tiptoe to give him a kiss. "Find a bride and live happily ever after. No one deserves it more. Mary would want that for you."

She had a feeling that when Harlan Adams set his mind to finding a woman to share his life, he was going to set all of Texas on its ear. And his sons were going to have the time of their lives getting even for all the grief he'd given them over their own love lives. Melissa was thrilled that she was going to be right in the thick of it all, where she'd always dreamed of being.

Her mother and father came over to her then. "You happy, ladybug?" her father asked.

She clung tightly to Cody's hand and never took

her gaze from his as she whispered, "Happier than I thought possible."

"About time," her mother huffed.

Cody leaned down and kissed her soundly. "Stop fussing, Velma." He grinned unrepentantly at her mother's expression of shock. "One of these days you're going to admit it," he taunted.

"Admit what?"

"That you're crazy about me."

Her mother scowled. "You're too sure of yourself, Cody Adams. Somebody's got to keep you in line."

He turned his gaze on Melissa then. "And I know just the woman to do it," he said softly.

"What if I don't want to keep you in line?" Melissa asked. "I kind of like your roguish ways."

"Told you she didn't have a lick of sense where that boy was concerned," Velma announced loudly.

Melissa glanced at her mother just then and winked. After a startled instant, her mother chuckled despite herself and winked right back. She tucked her arm through her husband's and added, "Married one just like him myself."

"Then I guess Cody and I are going to be okay, aren't we, Mother?"

Her mother glanced pointedly at Sharon Lynn and the new baby. "Looks to me like you've got quite a head start on it."

Cody brushed a kiss across her cheek. "Indeed, we do."

Everyone began leaving after that. Finally Melissa was alone with her husband. "I love you," she told him.

"I love you," he echoed. His expression turned serious. "Do you really think Daddy's going to start courting?"

"Sounded to me as if he meant what he said. How would you feel about that?"

Cody hesitated for a minute, then grinned. "Seems like a damned fine opportunity to get even with him, if you ask me."

"That's what I love about you Adams men," Melissa taunted. "You are so supportive of each other."

"You don't think he deserves to be taken on a merry chase?"

"By some woman," she admonished. "Not by you, Luke and Jordan."

He sighed and folded his arms around her middle from behind. His breath fanned across her cheek. "I suppose standing on the sidelines and watching him fall will have its moments," he agreed. "He sure seemed to get a kick out of watching that happen to the rest of us."

"Then I suggest you prepare yourself for the ride," she told him. "Knowing Harlan, it's going to be a bumpy one."

"As for you and me," Cody proclaimed, "from here on out it's going to be smooth sailing."

* * * * *

If you enjoyed what you just read,
then we've got an offer you can't resist!

Take 2 bestselling love stories FREE!

Plus get a FREE surprise gift!

Clip this page and mail it to Silhouette Reader Service™

IN U.S.A.	IN CANADA
3010 Walden Ave.	P.O. Box 609
P.O. Box 1867	Fort Erie, Ontario
Buffalo, N.Y. 14240-1867	L2A 5X3

YES! Please send me 2 free Silhouette Special Edition® novels and my free surprise gift. Then send me 6 brand-new novels every month, which I will receive months before they're available in stores. In the U.S.A., bill me at the bargain price of $3.57 plus 25¢ delivery per book and applicable sales tax, if any*. In Canada, bill me at the bargain price of $3.96 plus 25¢ delivery per book and applicable taxes**. That's the complete price and a savings of over 10% off the cover prices—what a great deal! I understand that accepting the 2 free books and gift places me under no obligation ever to buy any books. I can always return a shipment and cancel at any time. Even if I never buy another book from Silhouette, the 2 free books and gift are mine to keep forever. So why not take us up on our invitation. You'll be glad you did!

235 SEN CNFD
335 SEN CNFE

Name _____ (PLEASE PRINT) _____

Address _____ Apt.# _____

City _____ State/Prov. _____ Zip/Postal Code _____

* Terms and prices subject to change without notice. Sales tax applicable in N.Y.
** Canadian residents will be charged applicable provincial taxes and GST.
   All orders subject to approval. Offer limited to one per household.
   ® are registered trademarks of Harlequin Enterprises Limited.

SPED99   ©1998 Harlequin Enterprises Limited

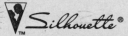

Coming in May 1999

BABY *Fever*

by

New York Times Bestselling Author

KASEY MICHAELS

When three sisters hear their biological
clocks ticking, they know it's
time for action.

But who will they get to father their babies?

**Find out how the road to motherhood
leads to love in this brand-new collection.**

Available at your favorite retail outlet.

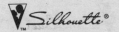

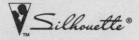